This book is dedicated to my ancestors and other American pioneers.

Also by Paul Varnes
Confederate Money

Black Creek

The Taking of Florida

Paul Varnes

Pineapple Press, Inc.
Palm Beach, Florida

Inquiries should be addressed to:
Pineapple Press, Inc.
4501 Forbes Boulevard, Suite 200
Lanham, Maryland 20706

www.pineapplepress.com

Library of Congress Cataloging-in-Publication Data

Varnes, Paul, 1934–
    Black Creek : the taking of Florida / Paul Varnes. — 1st ed.
        p.   cm.
ISBN 978-1-56164-686-9 (pbk. : alk. paper)
1. Seminole War, 1st, 1817–1818—Fiction. 2. Seminole War, 2nd,
1835–1842—Fiction. 3. Florida—Fiction. I. Title.

    PS3622.A75B56 2007
    813'.6—dc22

                            2007010725

Design by Shé Hicks

PART I

The First
Seminole War

June 27, 1817

It was a hot afternoon and we were crossing the St. Marys River from Camden County, Georgia, into Spanish Florida. The Spanish forces then trying to control Florida would not cordially welcome us. It was they and the English who had armed the Seminoles we were chasing.

The English and Spanish governments were not in collusion. The English had armed the Seminoles and encouraged them to raid and kill white Americans during the War of 1812. Spain, weakened militarily over the years, in 1817 was allowing, even

1

encouraging, the Seminoles to raid from Florida into the United States. Unable to defend Florida and the rest of their vast empire, the Spanish were using the Indians in Florida to help protect Spain's rights to those lands. The Indians thought they were only defending their own rights.

It was no secret that Congress, in 1811, had authorized James Madison to begin the takeover of Florida. This resulted in an invasion, which seized Fernandina. When the initial force of about eighty men got into trouble, Colonel Daniel Newman went to the rescue with 120 Georgia Militiamen. Newman planned to attack Chief King Payne at Payne's Town, destroy all he could not carry, and return with cattle, horses, and runaway slaves. Payne, the Indian leader, was said to have over a thousand cattle, four hundred horses, and a score of black slaves of his own. As a way of encouraging the Seminoles to fight, the Spanish told them the invaders planned to take the Seminoles' land and keep it.

Even though the attack on Payne's Town caught the Seminoles by surprise, it soon became a failure. Outnumbered by more than two to one by the Indians and blacks that Payne gathered, Newman was forced to withdraw. While he lost twenty-five percent of his force, they were lucky they were not all killed. Having used up most of their ammunition and with King Payne wounded, the Seminole and black forces did not continue the counterattack. When the word got out about the defeat of Newman, other units were raised and the fighting and raiding only escalated from there. It had been going on ever since.

My Pa, Isaac Senior, was an official member of the hundred-strong company that was in pursuit of the Seminoles. Pa was recruited to scout for Major Bailey. I was only there because Pa let me go. My name is Isaac, too, though Pa just called me Boy most of the time. Ma called me I. J. or just I., depending on the kind of message she wished to convey. Being sixteen years old at the time, I was big enough. Also, I could track and shoot with the best of them.

Though Ma didn't like it any that I went, she didn't put up a fuss. We had been having so much trouble from raiding Indians that she would be glad to be rid of them even if it meant that I went with Pa on the campaign.

Less than half of the unit was mounted. Pa and I were mounted on two Spanish-bred mares that he bought in St. Augustine a couple of years earlier. Having been through the area before on the trip to trade with the Spanish, Pa knew the area well. That, and the fact that we were better mounted and armed than most, caused Major Bailey to have Pa and me out front to prevent an ambush.

This was my first time at attacking an enemy. I had been in plenty of fights with the Indians, but it was always them raiding us and us fighting them off. It seemed a little scary at first, us being exposed and subject to an ambush. Before, we had been fighting from inside the cabin or from behind a wagon.

At thirty-seven years old, Pa was a veteran of a number of military operations. He and several hundred other Georgia men fought with Major General Andrew Jackson's Tennessee Volunteers when Jackson defeated the Red Stick Creeks at the Battle of Horseshoe Bend in 1814. That battle was fought on the Tallapoosey River in Alabama. The way Pa told it, the Tallapoosey had a bend that resembled a horseshoe. Protected on each flank by the river, the Indian's breastwork stretched three hundred yards and closed off the three hundred acres inside the horseshoe. General Jackson's army stormed the Indian's breastwork and broke through it.

General Coffe's army had formed a line at the bend of the horseshoe across the river from the Indians so the Indians couldn't cross the river and escape. Over a thousand Indians were killed in that battle. The Upper Creek Nation then asked for unconditional peace. Interestingly, the Lower Creek Indians fought on Jackson's side in the Creek Indian War. One group of Indians or another fought on our side in every war the United States fought.

That holds true even when we were fighting some of their relatives. If they had agreed to band together to fight, things might have turned out better for the Indians. Pa said the treaty the Upper Creeks were forced to sign was so merciless that they soon broke it. Following the battle of Horseshoe Bend and the Indians' breaking of the treaty, lots of the Upper Creeks started moving to Florida. After the Creek War was over, Pa then helped General Jackson whip the British. Me being only thirteen years old at the end of that war, Pa hadn't let me go on those trips.

Pa, Ma, my younger brothers, and me had fought off the Indian raids before, Pa and I had never followed them with a large force into East Florida. While we hadn't, others had. The Indians had been raiding north of Florida for years. Likewise, white Americans had been raiding Indian towns in Florida, taking their horses and cattle, trying to capture runaway slaves, and taking the Indians' own slaves. Pa had been involved in some of that. Not having any slaves, we hadn't lost any, however. The Indians had stolen some of our cattle, though. Some of our cattle were in the herd the Seminoles were driving ahead of us. We were hoping to get our animals back and to hit the Indians with such a blow that they would be discouraged from returning to Georgia on a raid.

We didn't expect any trouble from the Spaniards. They had enough trouble without bothering with us. As we were crossing the St. Marys River a Scot named Gregor MacGregor was solidifying his hold on Fernandina, Florida, which he had just captured from the Spanish. Pirates, smugglers, other riffraff, and the taking of land by white Americans were other problems the Spaniards had to deal with. They had not been able to deal effectively with any of those problems.

The tracks we were following were fresh. There were still damp spots where they came out of the river when they crossed ahead of us. There was just Pa and me on the south side of the river. Our people were still on the north side waiting for us to signal that the Indians had moved on. Pa soon waved for them to

4

cross and we moved ahead to scout.

There were no houses, no people, and no sign of anyone ever having lived in the area through which we passed. It was a true wilderness. Once we got out of the river swamp we were in an area where the vegetation consisted of huge pine trees, five to ten to the acre, and low bush palmettos. There was also lots of swamp and pond areas but the Indians avoided those. We did also in following their trail.

With dark approaching, Major Bailey called a halt so we could set up camp before dark. He ordered that there be no campfires so as not to alert the Indians that we were following them. As soon as the camp was settled in, Pa and I went forward as scouts again. Our task was to locate the Seminole camp and guide Bailey's outfit forward to attack them in camp if possible. We traveled on foot because our horses had worked hard that day and needed the rest.

Traveling on foot at night without a light bothered me some. Having lived most of my life in south Georgia, I was well aware of all the various things one might step on—rattlers, cottonmouth moccasins, copperheads, gators, and various kinds of varmints. One might even blunder into a panther or a mother bear ready to defend her cubs. We usually had a torch, lamp, or candle when we were hunting at night. Or we just sat around a campfire and listened to the dogs run. We couldn't possibly have a light that night, though.

In little more than an hour we located the Indians' camp. Indians don't make a very big campfire and theirs had burned down to red coals when we found them. The fire wasn't giving off enough light to give their location away until someone got in close, but the smell of wood smoke was strong from a mile away. We didn't try to get in too close at first because they would almost certainly have outriders holding the cattle. The herd was too big to build a temporary pen for. They wouldn't have any guards out other than those holding the cattle, though. At that time the

Indians had never been known to initiate an attack at night. They also didn't post guards at their own encampments at night. They were just as aware as I was of the dangers lurking in the night. Thinking that only a fool would wander around at night without a torch, the Indians, I guess, considered the dangerous animals to be their guards.

As we squatted downwind, a hundred yards from the nearest Indians, Pa whispered, "We best circle their camp and check out the terrain. The major will be asking about that."

His speaking made me realize we hadn't spoken in the last hour. Not having any reason to speak, I stood and followed Pa.

A sliver of moon caused every bush to look like a Seminole as we circled the camp and herd. Riding slowly, four mounted Indians circled the herd to keep it in place. The constant hum of crickets chirping and frogs croaking drowned out the sound of their horses' hooves on the ground as the riders circled the herd. Those noises also covered any slight sound we made. Once we crouched behind a bush and another time we lay behind a log as a rider went by. We both had rubbed dirt on our faces and hands to dull the glow from them.

I'm sure Pa was seeing everything and making mental notes to report back to the colonel. I was just trying to stay invisible and cover Pa's back. Our reconnaissance complete, we then headed for our camp. Traveling was easier going back to camp. On the return trip, we knew the hostiles were behind us and we moved with less caution.

It was after ten P.M. when we got back to camp and Pa whistled us in. I sure was glad Pa hadn't sent me back alone. In spite of the moonlight, when he stopped to whistle us in, I didn't even know we were near the camp. I had been lost for the last hour. The moon was up during our return, which was good for giving us direction, but it sure made things look different.

At the distance our camp was from the hostiles, it was safe to light a candle. Pa then gave his report and drew the positions of the Indian camp in the sand by candlelight.

Pa said, "There's over thirty of them, four miles south of here. They have four riders circling the cattle and have some horses in a rope-and-brush corral. From past experience, I would guess that each warrior also has a horse staked out near where he's sleeping. The horse pen and cattle herd is on the south side of their camp so the Indians are between the animals and us. There's a thick, deep pond to the east of them. It's so thick they can't go that way on horseback. We also can't approach from that way without them knowing. To the south, west, and north of them is open woods."

Major Bailey said, "You were there and saw the lay of the land. How would you suggest we handle this?"

Pa said, "It's tough. Except for posting guards, whoever's in charge there knows what he's doing. It's a good thing we've got a hundred men. Our best bet might be to get there before light and get in close with most of our men on foot. We should also have a dozen mounted men work their way to the south of the herd. Their job will be to stampede the horses and cattle. The boy," he pointed at me, "can lead that bunch. He knows the layout of the place. We can also work six men in close on foot and try to take out the herd riders at the first shooting. Those six can then help tear down the stick-and-rope corral holding the horses. If we start shooting and stampede the horses and cattle to the west, I think the Indians will try to follow the herd and turn them. Or, when they see we have them out-gunned, they might make a break to the south. With that in mind, we could send thirty men on foot with the twelve riders. They could set up behind trees and take the Seminoles on if some of them go that way. We would also set up with thirty-five men on the west side. That would leave a dozen to approach from the north on horseback and start the thing. I don't think the Indians would go north and overrun those twelve, especially if those twelve open up as soon as the herd riders are fired on."

I was so proud of Pa that my heart was all up in my throat.

He didn't usually say many words but he always said lots when he talked. I was also proud he would name me to lead the charge at the herd.

The major said, "That's how we'll do it." Looking at me he said, "Boy, when you get the herd away from the camp, turn it north and keep it running. Don't slow down until you hit the river. And don't stop until you're on the other side of the river. Stop the herd there and defend the river bank if necessary."

Turning to Sergeant Hunter, the major continued, "You and your men all have mounts. You go with the boy."

Major Bailey then made the other assignments. He didn't have to explain much, all of the corporals, sergeants, and lieutenants were gathered around watching Pa all the time and listening.

Pa and I then threw our blanket over us to keep the mosquitoes off and slept for four hours. We were under way by three A.M. As we traveled, I realized I could have gone alone without getting lost that time. It must have been the trip there and back with Pa, and traveling at night with a sliver of moon, that made the difference in my being able to orient myself. We did some night hunting at home, of course, but it was always in an area I knew. This was different. Still, I knew I would never be lost in these woods again. Learning to use the moon and stars, I might never be lost again, anywhere. Getting over the snakes, gators, and other creatures of the night was another thing entirely. It felt a lot safer at night while riding a horse.

As we traveled, the realization came to me that nothing had been said about the slaves the Indians had stolen. There were at least a dozen. If the Seminoles had guns for them, we could be facing forty or forty-five guns. Seminoles were known to pamper their slaves, so they might have guns. Usually not concerned with commerce, the Indians only required their slaves to plant and gather enough to eat. After a period of time, the Indians' slaves would then build their own houses and plant their own farms near the Indians. When the slaves gathered their crop, or killed some food, they would carry a portion to their Indian master. Thus, the slaves actually became sharecroppers. The Indians also armed their slaves and sent them hunting. The slaves then fought on the Seminoles' side when there was a conflict. Some Seminoles also took slaves as a mate. Theirs was a relaxed, even leisurely, life. Not many slaves ever tried to escape from the Indians.

It was about that time that Pa spoke to me. "Are you thinking about the fight, Boy?"

"No, sir. I was thinking about the slaves with the Indians."

"You keep your mind on the fight. You can get yourself or someone else killed by letting your mind wander."

"Yes, sir."

It wasn't something Pa had to tell me again, ever.

By a quarter past four, Pa and the men on the west and north sides of the Indian camp were sneaking up on it. The eleven riders and thirty men on foot with me were making a big circle to the west in order to come up on the south side of the herd. Under the protection of four men, the balance of the horses were left a half-mile north of the Indian camp.

By five, we twelve riders were in position two hundred yards south of the horse herd. The thirty men on foot with us slipped to within sixty yards of the Indian's cattle herd. We held the horses a couple of hundred yards away from their horse pen so ours wouldn't whinny at the Indian's horses. I circulated among the men and explained exactly where the Indian's cattle and horse herd was, and assigned six men to start the cattle running. The other six of us were to get the horses out of their temporary corral and get them to running after the cattle.

When it was light enough to see individual pine straws against the clear sky, we mounted and walked our horses toward where the Indian's horses and cattle were. It was still too dark to see the cattle, horses, or their Indian guards at that distance. We could see some movement around the campfire where some cooking was being done. I was hoping those assigned to take out the herd guards would do most of that job. If they didn't, it would fall to us to finish.

We were still a hundred yards from the herds when the first shooting started. I later learned it was the Indian nightriders being shot at and returning fire. In a line of twelve abreast, we kicked our horses into a run and within seconds passed through our line of thirty men who had taken positions behind trees and brush and were firing at targets of opportunity. Within ten more seconds, the designated six men had the cattle herd stampeding northwest. The other six of us were tearing down the temporary corral and getting the horses to running, and getting shot at some.

It seemed that mounted Indians were everywhere. Each Indian must have been sleeping with a pony by his side. The Indians' musket fire was mostly ineffective. Some of them were not even shooting. They probably hadn't had enough time to check the priming in the flash-pan of their weapons. With gunfire all around us we finally got the horses out of the pen and running. After the rope and stick fence was down, my mare was almost at a full run as I swung aboard. In a hail of gunfire we passed through the positions of our force on the west side of the Indians' camp. We soon got the horse herd turned north behind the cattle.

Within four minutes we were a mile from the Indian camp. The sound of gunfire was thinning some and growing dim. It was a wild ride but we were at the river in fifteen minutes. There, the herd slowed as they crossed. We stopped them a quarter of a mile past the river.

Riding up to Sergeant Hunter, I said, "Sergeant, the major didn't say, but you best take seven men and defend the river crossing against pursuit. I'll take the other three men and hold the herd here. It'll be easy. They're about tuckered out."

Without responding, the sergeant called out the names of the men to stay with me. He then left for the river. That's how we were situated when Pa and the main force arrived just before noon and set up camp there. They had already buried one of ours and we had a couple of wounded to care for.

Though everyone was talking about it, when things had settled some and we were alone, I said to Pa, "Tell me about the fight."

He said, "Not much to tell. You boys swooped in on your horses yelling and like to have scared all the Indians to death. There wasn't much for the rest of us to do."

Then he smiled and said, "They came after you and the horses and ran straight into thirty-five guns. They then turned south and ran into the thirty there. We got hurt some but not near as bad as them. Eight or ten of them got through on their horses. Some abandoned their horses and went in the swamp to the east on foot. We got the horses that they left when they went into the swamp, and those from the dead and seriously wounded. You did a fine job, Boy. I'm proud of you."

I didn't ask about the slaves because I could see they had brought eight with them. They were all women and children.

Pa asked, "Did you shoot either of your guns?"

We both carried a rifle and a short-barreled musket.

Hanging my head, I said, "No, sir. I was pretty busy."

He said, "Yes, I could see you were. I just asked in order to make sure you cleaned them if you had shot them."

We had been in camp for a couple of hours caring for our wounded when Major Bailey called a meeting.

He said, "Men, we all know the raiding party we just whipped was some of those from south of Payne's Town. Old Chief King Payne died not long after he was wounded in General Newman's attack six years back. Still, these Indians were some of his. We've done our job in getting the animals and most of the slaves, but I think we should do more. Knowing where these were from, I think we should follow them and hit their settlement while we've got them thinned down and disorganized. What I'm proposing is a raid with fifty mounted men. We'll hit and run, taking what food, horses, cattle, and runaways we can. The rest of you will take our wounded and the livestock home and give a report to each family."

Speaking to Pa, he said, "Isaac, I hope you'll go. You know the country better than most."

Pa said, "I'll go. And the boy will. Someone will need to drive our livestock home and tell our family. How long should we plan for?"

Major Bailey said, "Six days at the most. We won't stay around long enough for them to gather a force against us."

There was lots of talk after that. The major had to pick and choose because more than fifty wanted to go. I noticed that Sergeant Hunter was chosen. I liked him. He had treated me like an adult since we took back the livestock. He even called me by my name.

We left the next morning, riding south. Looking for tracks and other sign, Pa and I were out front about a hundred yards. The major also had outriders to his flanks to prevent a possible ambush.

South of where we fought the battle, we picked up the trail of the reassembled raiding party. They had returned to the battle site and cared for their dead and were then traveling south. They seemed to be returning to their village. There were about twenty of them. Some were riding double and five or six were walking. They were short on horses. In addition to recovering the horses they had stolen from us, we also had taken eighteen of their horses. The tracks were most of a day old so we moved along quickly. Pa and I were soon almost a mile in front of the major's party. We didn't figure the Indians would stop, but in case they did, we didn't want the whole force to blunder into them.

Shortly before midday we turned back to meet Major Bailey. When we met him, Pa said, "We've scouted most of a mile ahead,

I would suggest we stop here and cook enough for noon and night. That way we can run a cold camp tonight. We'll then have no fire or wood smoke to give us away."

The major gave the orders. He then sent two men out a hundred yards in each of four directions to act as pickets.

Thirty minutes before the others broke noon camp, Pa and I left. We had switched to fresh horses. Because we had lots of horses from those recaptured and the Indian horses we had taken, and because we would be riding more than the others would, we each had brought a spare. Covering lots more ground, and quicker than the others, Pa and I needed extra horses. Pa and I were soon ranging up to a mile in front of the major's party. The Indians we were following obviously knew the country well and were taking a route that avoided contact with anyone. That also kept us out of contact with anyone, which was fine with us.

It really wasn't hard to avoid contact with other people. There were not many people in Florida. The few that were there were located mostly on rivers or the coast. The territory was so thinly populated that, unless you knew where they were, you might have ridden for weeks without seeing anyone. Pa had been through this country before but over closer to the coast. From conversations he had, and from drawings in the sand during those conversations, Pa had a pretty good idea about where we were going. In addition to farming, Pa pulled a chain on a survey crew, did blacksmith work, and was a wheelwright. Due to his interest and inquisitive nature, Pa was always gathering information about places that could be of use in the future. He would squat and talk, and draw maps in the sand by the hour when he met someone who had been places he had not been. I'll bet he knew more about Florida than anyone else except the Indians.

Having scouted over a mile ahead, we turned back thirty minutes before dark to meet the major.

Though we were running a cold camp that night, the men sat around and talked in small groups. Most of them didn't go to sleep until eight or nine that night. Mostly they talked about being raided by the Indians or of raids on the Indians. Like Pa, lots of the men had fought the Red Sticks, the Upper Creek Indians. That war was brought on when the Red Sticks attacked Fort Mims in Alabama. The Red Sticks killed over five hundred white people there in 1813. The Creek Indian War then lasted until 1814 when Andrew Jackson, with a large white army and a couple hundred Lower Creek Indians, killed over a thousand of the Upper Creeks at Horseshoe Bend in Alabama. I moved from group to group and heard various versions of the battles that occurred during the Creek Indian War. There were lots of tales about battles against Billy Bowlegs, Josiah Frances, King Payne, and other Creek and Miccosukee chiefs.

A couple of men were giving different versions of an attack by Colonel Clinch on the Negro fort on the Apalachicola River. As Colonel Clinch was moving in to attack the fort, which was holding up shipments of supplies along the river, a round from a gunboat hit the powder supply in the fort. Almost all the three hundred people in the fort were killed in the explosion that followed. Thus, there was no real battle there.

I stayed up and listened to stories until the last of the men turned in.

Pa and I were mounted and rode out at first light the next morning. The Indian tracks were still evident as we rode. The worst part about riding alone, or with only a couple of riders, during the summer was the number of yellow flies, deer flies, and horse flies that gathered to us and the horses as we rode through the woods. It wasn't so bad when riding with a large group because there were lots of people and horses for the flies to bite other than my horse or me. We saw no hostiles, however. By mid-morning we came to the forks of a wide and deep creek.

Pa said, "This has to be the forks of Black Creek. I've heard it described. It's deeper than the St. Johns River into which it flows. Oceangoing ships could come up this creek to this point."

Driving a stake in the ground, he added, "I'm going to move our family here someday. Spain can't hang on to Florida much longer, even with the Seminoles' help. I'll bet there aren't more than eight hundred Spaniards in the Florida Territory anyway. If all of it's like St. Augustine, there are as many Italians and French here as there are Spaniards. The only requirement the Spanish have for anyone to live in Florida is that they have to be Catholic. Also, the Indians don't own it. They just moved in from Georgia and Alabama over the last few years. I'm betting Andy Jackson takes all of Florida sooner or later. We'll just go ahead and take us a piece of it before he takes the whole place. This is some of the best soil I've ever seen. We'll build docks on the creek and warehouses next to the docks. And we'll plant orchards and farm."

I figured that if Pa said it, he would do it.

From there, the tracks we were following swung slightly west, and we were traveling just a little south of southwest. Figuring we were getting close to the Indian village, we slowed some and traveled with caution. At full dark we still hadn't closed on the hostiles or found their village.

In a cold camp that night, the major said to Pa, "Isaac, I think we're close. Since we've been traveling in a straight line for some time, how about you and the boy going straight ahead and see if you can find them in the next few hours. If you haven't found the village within three hours, come on back. Or, if you find them, come back and get us. I'll have the men in their bedrolls by seven to get some rest. If you find them, we'll hit them at daybreak."

Pa said, "Okay. I'll need to take a third man. He and the boy can come back while I watch the village. Sergeant Hunter is a good man."

I had spoken to Pa about Hunter and was proud that Pa agreed with my judgment, though he probably already knew more about Hunter than I did. They didn't live far from us.

The sliver of moon was bigger than it was two nights before and gave enough light for easy traveling in the open woods. Since the moon was pretty high, the moonlight wouldn't last but a few hours so I studied the stars as we rode. I would need to know where I was going if Pa sent me back. After riding at a fast walk for an hour and a half, we heard a dog bark in the distance.

Pa said, "That's a yard dog barking. It's probably the village we're looking for."

If you've heard it enough, it's easy to tell the difference between the bark of a dog that's chasing an animal and a dog that's sounding an alarm around the house. They're two completely different kinds of bark. We then turned toward the sound. At two hundred yards from where the barking dog was, we dismounted and tethered our horses. We were downwind and the smell of wood smoke was strong. The dog soon quit barking and we began to work our way forward on foot. As we advanced it became apparent that this was a permanent Indian town. The town and cleared fields covered several acres.

After creeping around for some time and looking, Pa tapped Sergeant Hunter and me on the shoulder and pointed toward our horses.

Arriving at the horses, Pa said, "You two go back and bring the major. I'm going to ease around some and get a better feel for the layout of the place. One can move more quietly than two or three. Can you find the place we were when we first heard the dog bark?"

Both of us said we could.

"I'll meet you there an hour before daylight."

Sergeant Hunter and I then mounted and left.

I said to the sergeant, "Let's ride back to where we first heard the dog so we can identify some landmarks."

He said, "That's a good idea."

It took slightly more than an hour to make the return trip to our main camp. Having been through the area previously, we knew it was clear of hostiles so we made better time.

It was almost eleven P.M. when we finished making our report and answering questions for the major. We then pulled our blankets over the exposed parts of our bodies and slept until three A.M. It seemed like only ten minutes had passed when I felt Sergeant Hunter's hand on my shoulder.

He said, "It wasn't a very long night was it, Isaac?"

I said, "No, sir, it wasn't."

The other men had already been up for thirty minutes and were about ready to pull out. In ten minutes I had a fresh horse saddled and was ready.

The major said, "Jacob"—that's Sergeant Hunter's first name—"I want you to lead off. Travel at a walk and stop every so often to give everyone a chance to close up."

Turning to me, the major said, "Isaac, I want you to be the last person in line. If the line gets separated, you can get the stragglers to the right place."

It was the first time he had called me anything but Boy and I couldn't help but feel a flush of pride at that, and at being given the responsibility, though I don't know who else could have done it.

The moon having already set, we were then guided by the stars and by the landmarks Sergeant Hunter and I had picked out. Even with the lack of light, it was an uneventful trip. There were no stragglers and no one got lost. We arrived at the designated place at five in the morning. I was too far back to hear what he said as Pa spoke to the major from the darkness. The major then passed the word back for all the corporals, sergeants, and lieutenants to come forward. I went forward with them. There in the dark, Pa gave his report to the eight of us.

Pa said, "The best I can make out, there are twenty dwellings. Counting men, women, and children, there's close to a hundred people. There's not much in the way of guards. I didn't see any. There are some dogs though. As soon as they hear us, they'll raise a racket. Counting those from the raiding party, we know there could be more than twenty braves here. There are some boys and old men who were not on the raid. They'll also try to put up a fight. There's not much of a horse herd—twenty-five or so—and some staked out, or stabled, close to various dwellings."

Major Bailey said, "How do you think we ought to do it?"

Pa said, "Depends on what you want to get done. If you just want the horses and cattle, we can make a sweep from two sides on horseback and get most of them. If you want to do damage to their fighting ability, and their ability to pursue us or raid in the future, we probably need some people on foot and on horseback."

The major said, "We want to do both of those. We also need to scavenge for food for us and our horses."

Pa said, "That means taking the village and holding it for an hour or so. I would suggest a sweep through the village with twenty-five men on horseback, followed by twenty-one men on foot. That leaves four men to hold and protect the spare horses. Once through the village, the men on horseback, minus four to move the horses and cattle they gather a little further, would reload and sweep back through to the men on foot."

The major said, "We'll do it. We'll play it by ear from there. I want you people to make it clear to everyone that they are only to shoot fighting people—no women or small kids. Though they kill ours sometimes, I don't think it's right. Also, there's a better reason. If you shoot a noncombatant, you'll be standing there with an empty gun for someone with a gun to shoot you. We want to make every shot count."

Pa and I were with the mounted group. It was breaking daylight and we were on the move, seventy-five yards from the first dwelling, when their dogs started barking. We kicked our horses into a run and our men on foot broke into a run toward the village. As we rode into the village, heads started popping out of doors. Further across the village people started running toward the woods. Some tried to mount their horses and ride off. Very few succeeded. We shot some, and took their horses; and took the horses that were staked out or penned. We were almost through the village and my horse was at a full run when an Indian boy, who was younger than I was, stepped out from behind a house and let fly at me with an arrow that missed. I was past him before I could get my horse stopped and pulled around. He was standing there with another arrow almost nocked. Having fired my rifle at a man who had run out of a house, I leveled my short-barreled musket to shoot the boy. Without reason, I held my fire. Dropping his hands to his sides, an arrow in one and his bow in the other, he straightened himself up tall and stared at me. He knew he was going to die. Seconds passed as we each held our pose. Then I pointed at him with my left hand, while still holding my musket on him with my right hand, and pointed to the woods. After only a second's hesitation he ran for the woods, bow and arrow still in hand. I then heeled my horse and joined the others at the end of the village.

As we were reloading our guns for the return trip through the village, Pa said, "What was that about, Boy?"

I said, "I don't know, Pa. I just didn't want to shoot him standing tall like that. He was younger than I am."

At the time, I could not know this boy, two years my junior, was Osceola. Nor did I know we would meet again and recognize each other. Osceola, a Creek Indian boy, had moved to Florida from Georgia with Peter McQueen when Andrew Jackson and Pa had given the Creeks such a beating in 1814. His family members, like other Indians and many black people who moved to Florida, were to become Seminoles. Seminole means "wild one" or "runaway."

With our guns reloaded, we raced back through the village shooting at targets of opportunity. We took the village with little damage to our party and held it for most of two hours while we took almost everything of value. Though there was an occasional musket fired at us from the forest, it was ineffective because of the distance. We took horses, cattle, a large number of deerskins and cowhides, eight runaway slaves, and food. Releasing the captive Indian women and children, we then left. I had expected we would burn their houses and destroy everything we didn't take, but we didn't. No one even said anything about it. That was fine with me so I held my tongue. We had already done enough damage to those families.

Switching horses periodically, we pushed hard toward the St. Marys River. Sergeant Hunter, with ten men, acted as a rear guard. With no incident and no pursuit in sight, we crossed the St. Marys back into Camden County fifty-four hours later.

July 6, 1817

When Ma saw it was Pa and me returning from the raid, she leaned the musket she was holding against the cabin and stood in the yard while we got the horses and cattle we had brought into pens. Asa, age thirteen, and George, age ten, ran to open and close the pole gates to the pens. Samuel, age six, was with Ma. He was jumping up and down and clapping.

As soon as I swung down from my mare, Ma grabbed and hugged me. The kids also gathered around.

I said, "You all best go take on about Pa. He's the one who always carries the heavy load around here."

Using Ma's name for me, Pa said, "I. J. more than carried his end of the load on this trip. He'll have lots of tales for you kids."

Ma said, "That talk can wait. I'll have the food on the table in a few minutes. You two wash up."

But the tales couldn't wait. The kids were dying to know everything. They were asking new questions even before I could start to answer the previous ones. After twenty minutes Ma called us in to eat. When the evening chores were done, the questions and tales started again. We were up that night until almost ten.

Pa then said, "Boys, there's work to do tomorrow and we're behind schedule. Everyone get to bed."

Still, Asa and I whispered in the bed until we went to sleep.

The next two months were quiet compared to our trip to Florida. There's always enough work to keep everyone busy on a farm, but it being July and August, the farm work slowed some. We then took some time for fishing. Additionally, Pa did some survey work and some property trading. He had some kind of deal going about property all the time.

Pa couldn't read much English and was only fair with German. There wasn't much call for reading German in Camden County, Georgia, then. Actually, there wasn't much call for reading English either. Ma did most of the paperwork for Pa, or he hired it done. Pa was mighty sharp with numbers though, in English and German. I don't recall anyone ever getting the best of Pa where numbers were concerned.

There was no school to go to and we didn't have much time for it. Ma taught us about reading English from the Bible, and taught us to write some, too. There wasn't much to read but the Bible and property-related records. Ma did have a couple of books of her own; one of which only had poetry in it. She let us kids read those books as long as we were careful with them. Ma also encouraged us to read anything else she got her hands on. Due to Pa's efforts, we also learned to do numbers, using German and English. Since 1776, English was the official language in the United States. Before 1776 almost as many people in the United States spoke German as spoke English. Many of the people in South Carolina, where Pa moved to Georgia from, spoke mostly German.

Pa also taught us lots of other things. He seemed to know everything there was about living in the woods and using the things nature provided. There wasn't an animal that Pa didn't know everything about: what it ate, where it slept, its mating habits, the kinds of tracks it left, the kinds of calls it made, and any other peculiarity. An example of the kinds of things Pa knew happened when I was ten years old. It was a dry night, so we had been sleeping without a shelter while away from the house on a hunt. I awoke that morning to Pa's gentle, but firm, voice.

Pa was saying, "Boy, I want you to remain perfectly still when you wake up. Don't move a muscle."

Opening my eyes, I looked at him without otherwise moving. He was sitting in his sleeping roll, a musket in his hands, and was staring just inches over me.

Seeing I was awake, Pa said, "Don't move a muscle until I say, 'now.' Then, roll toward me as quick as you can."

I said, "What is it, Pa.?"

"A snake. Get yourself ready to move quickly. Are you ready?"

"Yes, sir."

Pa then tossed his hat over me toward the snake and said, "Now."

When I had rolled clear, Pa shot the head off the rattler.

Later, when things had settled down a little, I said, "Pa, why did you throw your hat at the snake? Why didn't you just shoot it?"

He said, "I didn't throw it at the snake. I threw it beyond the snake. The rattler was coiled, had his head up, and was staring at you. When I threw the hat past the snake, he turned to stare at the hat. That's just an old trick to freeze a snake in place. He would probably have stayed still, staring at that hat, for a half-hour if you hadn't moved and I hadn't shot him. If you had moved while he was staring at you, he might have struck. I didn't shoot before you rolled over because I would have been shooting only an inch or so above you."

Even as we were having a peaceful summer, trouble was still brewing between the white Americans and the blacks and

Indians. There were continuing small raids by the Indians and free blacks and return raids by the whites. Also, many of the raids by whites were not return raids; they were raids to steal something. Food, slaves, and animals were stolen and carried off by both sides. Adding to the distrust of the Indians, General Gaines had decided that the Indians in Florida were holding a large number of runaway slaves. He sent a message to the Indians seeking permission to enter their lands and kill or capture the slaves. Gaines also charged the Indians with several murders and demanded they deliver the guilty parties to him for justice.

The Indians blamed the whites for the troubles, saying the whites sold them slaves and then claimed them back as runaways. Indian leaders Peter McCloud and Chief Kinuche sent the general a message that the Indians would kill, or drive out with force, anyone trespassing on their lands. Those particular Indians had been neutral up to that point so their announcement presented a new problem. Since those Indian tribes were thought to have almost three thousand fighters, counting runaway and free blacks, it was a serious threat. Though many blacks were then slaves to the Indians, the blacks fought on the Indians' side to keep from having to return to their white masters.

General Gaines then announced that he would enter Spanish territory to gather all the slaves and return them to Georgia. Major D. E. Twiggs, the commander of Fort Scott, said about that time that he had been ordered by Neamathla not to cross the Flint River or his men would all be killed.

While this was going on, we were busy with our fall planting. Duties with these activities carried us on into the winter. Once the first cold spell hit, we set our trap lines and began tending them. Raccoon and fox hides, bringing ten to fifteen cents each, were valuable once the animals had acquired their winter coats.

While we were tending trap lines, General Gaines ordered Major Twiggs to attack Fowltown, the Indian village of which Neamathla was chief. Fowltown was located on American treaty land, about fifteen miles south of Fort Scott and the same distance north of Tallahassee, Florida. The Indians living there were trespassing. Twiggs carried out the attack in November with over 250 men. They only killed five Indians. The others escaped. Though the fighting had been going on for several years, that battle is considered by some to be the initial battle of the First Seminole War.

The Indians immediately set out to get revenge in any way they could. Some small parties raided farms and plantations in Georgia. Their most effective strategy in getting revenge was to line the banks of the Apalachicola River with warriors and shoot at passing boats. In addition to killing a number of Americans, this also caused the boat traffic to stop. Because its inhabitants depended on the boats for provisions, it was feared that Fort Scott would have to be abandoned.

The War Department then ordered General Andrew Jackson to raise an army and go to the relief of Fort Scott. Jackson gathered a few hundred volunteers and regular soldiers from Tennessee and Kentucky and marched his force toward Georgia.

On February 26, 1818, Jacob Hunter brought word that Andrew Jackson, with several hundred men, was en route from Tennessee to Fort Scott. Jacob was the same Sergeant Hunter who had served with Major Bailey.

Later, Pa called the family together and said, "Tomorrow, I. J. and I are leaving to help General Jackson in an attack on the Indians in west Florida. We might be gone for some time. I know you'll be all right. Asa is fourteen now and George is eleven. Just like you," he was looking at Ma, "they can shoot as good as most. Samuel knows how to load for you if necessary. If we put pressure on the hostiles there, it should be safe here."

Turning to the boys, he said, "Asa, George, your ma's going to have another baby in a few months. I don't want her to have to do any heavy lifting. You boys know what to do without being told. I want you to start the plowing tomorrow, and start planting on March fifteenth. God willing, we'll be back to help with the harvest before the end of May."

There wasn't any further discussion about it and Ma started gathering up some food for us to carry. Our guns and other things were always ready for instant use so we didn't have anything to do but put some things on a packhorse and go. Riding northwest on our Spanish mares the next morning, and leading a packhorse, we planned to stop off at Jacob Hunter's place and get him. Riding northwest would also take us around the Georgia side of the Okefenokee Swamp. That was the shortest way around it going west. Also, going south around the swamp would have taken us through Florida and we probably would have encountered Indians.

As we traveled, three other volunteers soon joined us. Further west we joined with another group of five, thus making eleven of us. Covering the 240 miles to Fort Scott in nine days, we arrived one day ahead of General Jackson and the thousand men he had gathered.

Jacob Hunter, having been a sergeant, and Pa, being a natural scout, organized us. It's a good thing they did because as we approached the fort, they decided to hold everyone up in a small covered area and do some scouting. We soon found sign of Indians. Shortly thereafter we discovered a party of thirty Indians. Had we stumbled into them, some of us would have been goners. We were on the east side of the Flint River, as were the Indians. The fort was on the west side.

After watching them for a short time, Pa said, "They're waiting for something. It might be for dark or it might be for others to join them."

Arriving back where our fellow volunteers waited, Pa said, "We best go upriver for a mile or so and cross. There's thirty Indians laying up on this side of the river and waiting for something."

One mile upstream, we were almost all the way across the

river when we came under fire from the riverbank behind us. There wasn't much damage, the Indians were doing their shooting with short barrel muskets. They were almost out of range with those weapons. As soon as we were on the west side of the river, and under the cover of trees, we returned fire with our long rifles. It looked like we hit a couple of the hostiles and they withdrew. We then turned downriver and soon arrived at the fort. We had to have one animal and one man treated for superficial pellet wounds. The pellets were removed. The distance had been so great that the pellets from the muskets hardly penetrated.

The people at the fort were extremely short on food. Leading three pack animals laden with considerable corn and dry beans and most of a deer we had killed that day, we were warmly greeted by Major Twigg.

When Sergeant Hunter explained the cause of the shooting, which had been heard at the fort, Major Twigg said, "This is the first time I've ever seen men fight their way into a fort. We certainly are proud you're here, though. We were about out of food. We can also use the additional guns in case of an attack."

An attack was not to come that night, however. The next day General Jackson and his men arrived. While they had seen sign, they had not encountered any hostiles. The Red Sticks had fled into the swamps before such a large force as Jackson had. Along with his white American troops, Jackson had several hundred Lower Creek Indians with him to fight against the Upper Creeks, or Red Sticks. Within days, several hundred additional Georgia militia also arrived.

From Fort Scott we moved down the Apalachicola River to the site of Negro Fort, which had been destroyed. Pa and I were asked to accompany the Lower Creeks of Jackson's army. Sergeant Hunter and the other eight men were assigned to a unit with Jackson. Pa was one of the best trackers anywhere and was also able to speak some Muskogee—a language common to the Indians in the southeastern United States. I think the general wanted assurance that the Lower Creeks gave him correct information. The general need not have worried because the Lower and Upper Creeks were mortal enemies. On more than one occasion I witnessed the Lower Creeks with us flush two or three Upper Creeks from hiding and kill them.

Once at the site of the destroyed Negro Fort, General Jackson ordered his engineer to build a new fort. As more volunteers from Tennessee and Georgia and over a thousand more Lower Creek Indians arrived, Jackson's army grew to 3,500 men. Fifteen hundred of them were Lower Creek Indians. William McIntosh, half Scot and half Indian, was the leader of the 1,500 Lower Creeks. In addition to being a chief, he was made a brigadier general by the United States government.

While most of General Jackson's men worked on the fort, and waited at it for food to arrive by boat, McIntosh and our friendly Creeks crossed the Apalachicola and raided Red Stick camps and towns on the west side of the river. The Upper Creeks were called Red Sticks because they carried a red stick for religious purposes. That also made it easy to tell which tribe was which. Pa and I went with them on those raids. We killed or captured almost three hundred Red Sticks. The captives were mostly women and children. Our Creek friends kept most of the women and children. We also took a large supply of corn and other food from the Indian camps and towns. Corn was badly needed as food for man and horse.

Ever since Pa brought my Spanish mare home I had been teaching her tricks that I had seen other horses and riders do on occasion. She also did the normal things that most good saddle horses do. Using only foot and knee pressure, I could have her back up, go forward, turn, stop, or travel at any gait. I had also taught her to lift a hoof for me to look at without me holding it. She would bow on command while I was standing in front of her or while I was in the saddle. It was while I was in the saddle and having her bow that, by accident, I caused her to lie down the first time. While bowing, she would lower her head and lift her right front hoof and tuck it under her. It was while she was in that position one day that a wasp stung me on the left arm. A reflex jerk on the reins in my left hand caused her to tip over to the right and lie down on her right side. Kicking my right foot from the stirrup to keep it from being broken, I also slid forward on her neck and head to avoid possibly getting crushed by her body. There she was, lying on her side with me lying on her neck and head. I don't know which of us was most surprised or frightened. In a few seconds she quieted down. Even after I got off of her neck, she remained quietly on the ground until I pulled on her reins to get her up. After a few minutes, I got up enough nerve to try it again. Though her fall was more controlled, she responded in the same way. From then on, I would cause her to lie down a couple of times each time we were riding alone. She soon got to where she was under full control as she went down. The mare seemed to like this new trick.

Not knowing what he would say about it, I never showed Pa that trick. It was while we were on one of those raids west of the Apalachicola River that he first saw it. In fact, it was performed in front of thirty of our Lower Creek Indian friends. While scouting, I was three hundred yards in front of, but still in visual contact with, Pa and our band of thirty Indians. I had dismounted and was leading my mare to give her a breather. That's something we did for ten minutes of every hour to rest the horses. As I was going between two ponds thick with tall gallberry and palmetto bushes, I spotted a band of fifteen Red Stick Creek warriors. Because I was dismounted and because the gallberry and palmetto bushes were pretty tall, they hadn't spotted me or my horse. They did, however, have an angle on me such that I was cut off from my group. If I ran for it, they could cut me off from my group and might be able to get me. If I tried to go straight back to my group, they would surely kill or capture me. Lifting a hand to Pa, I made a circle with it and pointed toward the Red Sticks.

That was our signal we had seen something. I then raised a fist three times, letting Pa know there were fifteen of them. The Red Sticks and the members of our group were not visible to each other because of the thick vegetation around the ponds. Pa acknowledged my signal. My job done, I then moved to take care of myself. Stepping in front of my mare, I signaled her to bow. I then jerked lightly with her left rein across her face to signal her to lie down. Certain that I had not been seen, I dropped across her neck and stroked her head.

Having been warned, and having twice the number of warriors the Red Sticks had, Pa's group had the advantage. As the fight started, I could tell the location of both parties by the sounds of gunfire and running horses. Pa's group wasn't fifty yards from me when I slid off my mare's neck and pulled on her reins. I then stuck my right foot over her back and was in the saddle as she came to her feet. I was right in the thick of the fight when my mare gained her footing. With a loaded rifle and musket, I was a welcome addition. The surviving Red Sticks were soon at full flight.

After our party was reassembled, Pa said, "What happened? I thought your mare stepped in a hole or something. Her foot seems okay now."

I said, "She's fine, Pa. I found out some time back how to make her lie down. We just did it as a stunt when we were alone. I never thought it might have a use. The mare just saved my life by lying still."

Back at the fort I was asked to demonstrate to those Indians who were with me how I got my horse to lie down. As the word got around about the incident, there were others, Indian and white, who wanted me to show them how to make their horse lie down. There were varying degrees of success by the warriors in teaching their horses the trick. Very few horses learned to lie down on command as quickly as my mare had. My mare became so famous that it would have been impossible for anyone to steal her. She would have been recognized anywhere. I soon started working with Pa's mare to teach her to lie down.

Going to war isn't all about fighting. There were lots of boring times between battles when we were looking for something to do. Teaching stunts to horses and showing off on horseback became one of the chief pastimes around the camp. It was amazing how many stunts some of the Indian ponies could do. I soon had my mare and Pa's doing many of those stunts.

After the fort was completed and food arrived, Jackson ordered his ships to blockade St. Marks and kill or capture any Indians they came across. He then turned his army loose on the towns and villages to the east around Lake Miccosukee. It was estimated that 1,500 Indians—men, women, and children— lived in that area. Accompanied by Pa, a white regiment, and me, General McIntosh and his 1,500 warriors swept through the area. In addition to killing those warriors we could corner, we seized everything we could use. Everything else was destroyed. In village after village we encountered little resistance. Sometimes we would be shot at from heavy cover. The attackers would then run. The size of our force was overpowering. Frequently, only empty villages awaited us. After taking what was useful, we then burned the villages. In most cases the villagers left in such a hurry that they left behind most of their food and other belongings.

One of the villages destroyed was that of a Red Stick chief named Peter McQueen. In that attack, over a hundred prisoners were taken—mostly women and children. As Pa and I rode past one small group of prisoners, I had an uneasy feeling and glanced about. Seeing an Indian boy who was standing and staring at me, I stopped my horse. Pa stopped, too. I said, "Pa, it's the same boy I let go last June."

Pa said, "It sure is. He's over a hundred miles west of where we last saw him."

I said, "We are too, Pa."

The boy and I looked at each other for half a minute. Neither of us smiled. I then raised my hand to him and he raised his hand in return.

Turning to Pa, I said, "Pa, we need to let him go and I haven't learned enough Muskogee yet to explain it to our Indian friends."

Pa then spoke to a nearby friendly Indian who returned his conversation in Muskogee.

Pa then said to me, "All of this little group is to be let go. That's why they're separated from the others. There's no point in looking a gift horse in the mouth so I didn't ask why they're to be let go."

Still not knowing his name, I looked back at Osceola. I thought of speaking to him, but I didn't know what to say or enough of his language to do a good job of it. I didn't know at the time that his pa was a half-Scot who had taught him English. Pa then heeled his mare and moved on. Raising my hand to the boy, I also rode on. The Indian boy once again raised his hand. Otherwise he didn't move. I was then seventeen. I was later to learn that Osceola was fifteen at that time. I was also to learn he had come to Florida with Peter McQueen's band when they were driven out of Alabama and Georgia.

In the meantime Jackson's white soldiers were crushing the other Seminole towns. Outnumbered by almost ten to one in most cases, the Indians put up little resistance. Jackson's troops burned town after town, took thousands of cattle, and took the Indians' supplies of corn, rice, beans, pumpkins, and other food. The Indians mostly vanished into the swamps.

Jackson then turned his army toward St. Marks and took the fort without a fight. The Spanish commander of the fort only protested.

Bowlegs' town on the Suwannee River, the black community on the Suwannee, and Arbuthnot's ship were the next victims of Jackson's attacks. Arbuthnot sold guns, ammunition, and cloth to the Indians from his ship, which was anchored in the Suwannee. He had done so for some time.

In the meantime, the friendly Indian army Pa and I were with turned toward the Suwannee to meet General Jackson for the attack there. As we approached the Suwannee, survivors from the towns we had ransacked arrived there and told what had happened to their towns and property. These people convinced those along the Suwannee of the danger they were in. Not knowing they were alerted, Jackson marched his men as fast as possible hoping to find and engage the enemy before they were alerted. Jackson wanted to end the war with one major attack. We needed to engage the enemy well before dark in order to have adequate time to finish our work before they could use the cover of night to escape. With the Lower Creek warriors, we arrived in advance of Jackson's white force.

Recognizing the futility of the situation, Chief Bowlegs' tribe disappeared into the swamp east of the river. His village was on the east side of the river so it was just a matter of them pulling out and vanishing into the swamp. The blacks, whose houses lined the west side of the river—the same side we were approaching from—set up a blocking force to stop us. They also started moving their families across the river. We arrived at that time. About four hundred black fighters and some Indians who stayed behind to help them held us off for the hour or so until dark.

Since Jackson's white force had not yet arrived, our Lower Creek Indian friends did most of the fighting against the black force holding the riverbank. Being there, and participating, I can tell you the fighting was not very ferocious. The blacks were dug in and our Indians never made an open charge. If they had, they would have overpowered and killed most of the blacks. A couple of hundred Lower Creeks might have also been killed if we had made an open daylight charge.

The way it happened was that we set up behind trees and logs and shot at the blacks with our long rifles. Armed only with short-barreled muskets, that's what they shot at us with. We were almost out of range of their muskets but were plenty close enough to be effective with the few long rifles among our force. Still, the blacks mostly kept their heads down and we didn't hit very many.

I can't fault the Indians for the way they fought. It was just their style to lay up behind trees. Pa and I were both happy with that. Neither of us wanted to lead a charge into the muzzles of over four hundred guns behind breastworks.

As soon as it was dark enough not to be committing suicide, we advanced. The instant we got within range of their muskets, we made a charge. The blacks chose that same time to make a break for the river and try to cross it. Most of them escaped across the river or drowned in it. If we had arrived at the settlement a few hours earlier, we would have had time to cross the river at another place and box them in. As it was, the attack might have cost the defenders a third of their fighters. It couldn't be determined for sure because most of their fallen died in the river and were never seen again. Only a dozen of the blacks were found dead in their fixed positions. We had no dead among our fighters and only a few slight wounds.

Taking advantage of the deserted houses, we camped at the site for several days. While camped there we scavenged the surrounding area for food and searched for those who might not have yet gotten out of the area. Our Indian friends killed or captured a few of the blacks and Seminoles we found in the swamps during those days. Two white men were captured: the trader named Arbuthnot, who sold arms to the Indians, and a man named Ambrister, a British subject who had been training the black people for war. Jackson took them to St. Marks where they were court-martialed, sentenced to death, and executed.

Jackson then moved on to Pensacola where it was said the Spanish were outfitting several hundred Indians so they could raid into the United States. After taking over Pensacola, Jackson then put the fort under siege. Following a brief fight, the Spanish garrison at Pensacola surrendered; thus ended the First Seminole War. It did not end the raiding and fighting, however—raiding by all parties continued at a diminished rate.

Pa and I didn't go to Pensacola. The two of us, along with the several hundred volunteers from Georgia, headed for home. We were dismissed because we were no longer needed. At the same time Jackson also dismissed the Lower Creeks who were fighting with him.

Once their towns were destroyed, the Red Stick Creeks and Miccosukees, except for roving bands, were driven from west Florida. We were to find that our position in southeast Georgia was no safer than it had been. In fact it was less safe. Except for raiding, scavenging, and pillaging east of the Suwannee for a few miles, what is officially called the First Seminole War had taken place between the Suwannee River and Pensacola. Only three hundred or so of the Red Stick and Miccosukees warriors were killed. Most just migrated east. We then had to contend with them at home because more of them were situated closer to our house than before. Also, many of the captive Indian boys had been released. Like me, they would soon be full-grown.

May 10, 1818

We arrived home from the First Seminole War in early May. Though it had been only ten weeks, it seemed like two years. I felt two years older. Ma said I looked just like I did the day Pa and I rode off, except for my clothes being dirty. They were a little worn, too. I had just about worn the seat of my britches out from sitting in a saddle.

As we arrived home we could see that Asa and George had worked hard with the plowing and planting. Some of the things in the fields would need harvesting within two weeks. I had a strange feeling as we rode in. A sort of peaceful feeling settled over me. A sense of responsibility also returned. It seemed to develop as we rode from Sergeant Hunter's place to ours. All those things I was usually responsible for had been gone from my mind and as we approached our place, they descended like a weight on me.

Though Ma was seven months pregnant, she came, almost running, to meet us. Pa stepped down from his mare and they embraced. After she hugged me, they walked arm in arm toward the horse pen.

I took Pa's mare's bridle and said, "Asa, George, and I will put the horses up."

Asa and George were coming at a full run from the fields. Pa didn't say anything. He and Ma just walked on in the house with their arm around each other. It was the most public emotion I have ever seen them show for each other. Also, Pa usually insisted that each man tend his own horse. I was happy he didn't that time.

The other kids stayed out at the horse pen with me. After we put the horses up, I sat my brothers down by the barn and we talked for most of an hour. They were anxious to know everything and I was giving Ma and Pa time alone. I also had some Indian things for each of them: bows and arrows, hatchets, knives, and moccasins. Those, some guns, and some Indian ponies we took and brought home was the sum total of our remuneration for fighting in the war.

After spending the afternoon and part of the night talking, we were up early and back to farming the next morning shortly after daylight. Asa and George had done a good job but they just couldn't keep it all going. Pa lasted at that for three days. He then saw everything was getting in shape. He also had some other things to tend to and he communicated that at supper the third night.

Pa said, "There's some property I want to look at. I'll be leaving tomorrow for two or three days. I want you boys to tend to things while I'm gone."

It was obvious he had discussed this with Ma because she didn't have anything to say. Pa then told us all the things he wanted us to do. Things were back to normal.

Over the next couple of months we harvested and stored the corn, fodder, potatoes, beans, and peas. Those things were mostly preserved in their natural state. Other than those Ma was going to cook daily, the peas and beans were allowed to dry on the vine before they were picked for shelling and storing. They could then be stored in containers for extended periods of time. We also planted some late crops: collards, sweet potatoes, pumpkins, and beans.

At that time of year we hunted for any meat we needed instead of killing our own animals. Hog killing was usually done in November, about the same time syrup was made. Shoulders, hams, and sausages were then smoked and left hanging in the smokehouse throughout the winter. Bacon and some other parts of the hog were salted down to preserve them. Also, Ma made bags of hog's-head cheese and left them hanging in the house after each hog killing. Though the smoked meat lasted throughout the year, we also hunted for fresh meat periodically. Alligators, deer, raccoon, turtles, turkeys, wild hog, bear, and an occasional buffalo were the usual wild game fare. Even though she had at times in the past when food was in short supply, Ma didn't ordinarily cook opossum or buzzard.

After the crops were gathered, we began mending the fences and the roofs on the buildings. We also worked constantly at clearing new ground for planting, or at least getting the stumps and roots out of the fields we had been planting. It was an ongoing way of life. It seemed it would take a lifetime to get all the roots out of a field. Many times I've broken a plow point, and the mule has been jerked almost to her knees, when the plow point caught a root in a field I thought was cleared of them.

During the summer and fall, while we were doing these things, the Indians were on the move. Their homes in west

Florida had been destroyed and they had been driven out of that area, so they mostly lived a nomadic life as they sought farmland and home sites in north and east Florida. In relative terms, northeast Florida was becoming crowded as the Red Stick Creeks and Miccosukee, and the blacks living among the Indians, sought new homes there.

Indian raids into Georgia decreased during that time. Oh, there were raids by small bands of Indians, which resulted in some stolen livestock, but nothing on the scale there had been. On the other hand, raids by white Americans into Spanish Florida for the purpose of taking Indian livestock, and gathering up any blacks they found for use as slaves, continued, even increased. Also, the incidence of Americans moving into Florida to take land and establish small communities or individual farms increased.

In late July Ma had a baby girl and named her Nancy after one of our aunts.

In October of 1818, the Spanish Minister, Luis de Onis, and the United States Secretary of State, John Quincy Adams, started negotiations about Florida being taken over by the United States. These negotiations dragged on because both sides had several other things they wanted agreed to at the same time. Also, there was the matter of the land grants the king of Spain had given to his friends just prior to starting the negotiations. The United States didn't feel these grants should be honored.

Except for one occurrence, our farm was spared from the various small raids going on during that time. In early November, Asa came in from checking his trap line and reported some trouble.

He said, "Pa, some of our woods cows have been rounded up and driven off. From the tracks, it looked like twenty or so cows and three riders."

Woods cows are cows that are left to run loose in the woods and forage as best they can, as opposed to milk cows, which are kept on pasture, fodder, or hay, and some grain.

Pa asked, "Did you track them enough to determine a direction?"

Asa said, "Yes sir. I thought it was kind of strange because they're going northeast."

Pa said, "It's probably white men. They might be headed for a cattle boat. There are lots of places where they could have a boat waiting. How old were the tracks?"

Asa said, "They looked fresh to me, Pa."

Asa already had his rifle and he got his musket. Pa and I were busy arming ourselves as we talked.

Pa said, "We'll have to hurry. If they're headed for a waiting boat, we might not have more than twenty-four hours to catch them."

Ma, who had busied herself packing us some food and helping get our bed rolls ready, said, "Isaac, don't you get my boys hurt over a few woods cows. You take proper care. I'm not saying you shouldn't go. Lord knows we have to take care of ourselves. But you be careful."

Turning to George, Pa said, "Get on your pony and get over to the Hunter place, quick. Tell Jacob what's been said here and tell him we could use some help. Tell him we're going northeast and he can probably pick up our trail at the north end of Moccasin Swamp. If he hasn't checked, some of his cattle might be gone, too. You come straight back here to help your Ma."

We were in the saddle and gone in fifteen minutes—Pa, Asa, and me. We were each leading a second horse. It was the first time on this kind of trip for Asa. At fifteen years old, he was old enough. We had plenty of confidence in Asa.

When we picked up the trail, we put our horses into a trot. It was apparent the thieves were pushing along pretty fast. It was also apparent from the tracks that they had a two- or three-hour head start on us. Since it was almost noon, we had only a little more than six hours to catch them if we were going to do it before dark. We couldn't track them after dark but they could keep the cattle moving, even if they lost a few head.

As we were riding three abreast in an open stretch of woods, Pa said, "Boys, I don't have much of a plan in mind. If we spot them ahead of us, we'll kick our horses and make a run at them. When we get within fifty yards, I'll shout. Each of you pick a tree to swing down behind. Brace your rifle on the tree and make your shot count. We'll reload there. We'll have to play it by ear after that. If they make a fight of it, use your rifle until they're within musket range."

When expecting a fight, we always carried short-barrel muskets in a saddle scabbard and our rifles in our hand. At night we reversed that. The musket is more effective for the close work of night fighting. When loaded with pellets it doesn't have to be aimed as carefully.

It sounded like a good plan to me. All of us could hit a running deer at a hundred yards with our rifles. If we stopped at fifty yards, by the time we dismounted and fired they would still be within a hundred yards, even if they kept moving with the herd.

After twenty minutes we switched to our second horses and continued at a steady trot. We were traveling faster than the thieves were. We were sure they had started their drive sometime during the late morning because there had been no dew on the tracks when we first saw them.

After another twenty minutes passed, in order to give the horses a rest we dismounted and jogged along leading them for ten minutes. We then remounted our original horses and continued to follow the trail at a steady trot. I was thinking Sergeant Hunter wouldn't have much chance of catching us before we caught up with the cattle. We had at least a mile-and-a-half headstart on him. I was thinking it sure would be good to have him with us when we caught the thieves. Also he had a boy, John, who might be coming along. John was the same age as Asa and was as good a shot as any of us.

Other than stopping to water our horses and get a drink, we

followed the same routine for two more hours. It being overcast, I figured we had three more hours until dark started closing in. I didn't know how long the horses could keep up the pace.

At that point the cattle's tracks showed that a larger herd and some more riders joined the herd we were following. We didn't stop to sort out exactly how many there were. The herd size had more than doubled, though.

It was after four when we got within three hundred yards and sighted them.

Pa said, "Let's go."

Dropping the lead ropes to our spare horses, we kicked the horses we were riding into a run.

Our horses at a hard run, we were less than two hundred yards from them when one of them looked back and spotted us. It took them a few seconds to decide what to do. Four of them then turned toward us.

When Pa shouted "now," we were still at eighty yards. By the time we stopped and dismounted we were at sixty yards. The four of them fired at us without effect. It's mighty hard to hit anything from a moving horse, regardless of how close you are. They were still mounted.

When we propped on trees and fired, two of them went down. The other two wheeled their horses and rode toward where their friends were still driving the herd northeast. Since it takes nearly half a minute to reload, they were well out of range by the time we could use our rifles again.

When we finished reloading, Pa said, "Let's go."

As we remounted to continue the chase, I heard running horses behind me and wheeled my horse to face that danger. It was Mr. Hunter and John coming at a dead run. By the time I got my horse turned and regained speed, they had come on line beside me.

Pa slowed a little to let us catch up and then we continued the chase. As we closed on the herd that time, leaving the herd to us, the thieves peeled off to one side and the other and ran for it. I guess when the Hunters joined us, there were just too many of us for their liking. We didn't get close enough to shoot again.

After we had the herd under control and turned, Pa said to Mr. Hunter, "There's not any use in following them. We got the cattle back and they probably won't be back to our place."

Jacob Hunter said, "Nope. I don't expect they will."

Most of the cattle that had joined the ones we were following belonged to the Hunters.

Our horses were too spent to continue, so we gathered up the horses we had let go when the fight started, built a brush-and-pole pen, and held the herd there all night. The next morning we found one of the two men we had shot and buried him. Pa said words over him while we all had out hats off. Pa always said words over those we had to bury regardless of who they were. The other one we shot had managed to get up and leave. He had to be walking, or dead someplace, because we found and caught the two horses they were riding.

While the burying was being done, Pa said, "I. J., you take a couple of extra horses to switch off on and ride ahead to let your ma know we're okay. Tell her we might be after dark getting there. We need to take it easy on these horses. Also, send George to tell Mrs. Hunter."

Riding a lot slower than we had the day before, I still arrived home an hour before dark. Ma was momentarily upset because of me riding in alone. I could see the concern on her face when she asked and the relief on her face when I told her why I had been sent ahead. After sending George to tell Mrs. Hunter, I hurried to get the chores done before dark. Pa and Asa rode in later that night. They had turned the herd loose between our house and the Hunters.' Once back in their home territory, the cattle wouldn't wander far.

PART II

Moving to Florida

February 1, 1819

In February 1819, Spain ceded the Territory of Florida to the United States. The last real sticking point for the Spanish was that the treaty made null and void all of those late land grants the king of Spain gave his friends. Under the treaty, those lands became part of the public domain of Florida. There were also other provisions: the United States canceled a $5,000,000 debt of Spain's, the United States gave up claims to Texas, and Spain recognized the United States' rights to the Oregon country. The most important part, to Pa, was that the Spanish land grant to the land he wanted became invalid.

The treaty was quickly ratified by a unanimous vote of the United States Senate. The Spanish government, on the other hand, did not ratify the treaty and came up with some additional demands. Basically their new demands boiled down to the United States not recognizing any other than Spain's rule in South America. Our government wasn't about to go along with that. From Pa's standpoint, those things served only to delay our move to Florida.

In 1820, Pa decided we would not wait for the Spanish to ratify the treaty.

One night at the supper table, Pa said, "I'm going down to Florida and build a cabin on Black Creek. If Spain doesn't soon ratify the treaty on Florida, I'm betting Andy Jackson will raise an army and take the whole Florida Territory. We'll just go on ahead and take us a little piece of it."

It was apparent that Pa and Ma hadn't talked about him going at that time because she had some questions and comments.

Ma asked, "When would we go, and where would we live while you build a place?"

Pa replied, "I wasn't thinking about all of us going. I thought to take I. J. and hire some additional help. We could build a place in a few months. It wouldn't be much more than a cabin and a barn at first. Once we got everyone moved there, we could clear land for farming and add to the buildings."

Ma said, "That might be best. It wouldn't be good for the little kids to have to live in the open until you get a cabin built. When do you plan to go?"

Pa said, "Since we already have the fall planting in the ground, I was thinking to go in a couple of days, or as soon as I can get a couple of helpers. I'd like for us to be on the place by the time winter ends. I think I'll take the Hunter boy if he wants the job."

Pa rode out the next morning and was back at the end of the second day. A free black man named Joseph was with him. We then spent a full day getting things ready to go. The things we were taking included hatchets, axes, saws, drills, other tools, and some rods for making nails. Pa had previously made most of those things. We also packed some cloth, fishhooks, and other trade goods. We also took food for us and the animals. As for meat, we only took salt pork. We planned to kill our other meat. Pa also laid out fifty varmint traps to take with us.

When I asked Pa about the traps, he said, "We'll run two trap lines once it gets cold. We're going to have to patrol and be alert for Indians, anyway, so we might just as well trap while we're making our patrol circuits. We'll run a line in a half-circle to the north and another in a half-circle to the south of us. It'll take two people half a day each to run the trap lines and skin and stretch the hides, but it'll be worth it in terms of money. We would have to be out scouting for hostiles anyway."

John Hunter showed up at the house the next morning while it was still dark and we left shortly after daylight. Pa took the same route we had followed in 1817 while chasing the Indians who had raided several places in Camden County. That night we camped not far from the place we had recovered the livestock and slaves from the Indian raid. On the third day we arrived at where Pa had driven the stake in the ground near the junction of the north and south forks of Black Creek. There was no incident worth noting on the trip. The same proved true of the next few days.

After staking out the cabin and doing some calculations, Pa started marking the trees he wanted us to cut and peel. He also told us the length and number to cut of each size log. Pa then busied himself with shaping and drilling the logs for pegs. We were also to collect any rocks we found for use in building a fireplace. When we got far enough ahead of Pa with the log cutting, he showed me how and I helped him. Pa did all the metal- and rockwork—making nails, hinges, a fireplace, and such. Pa was a first-rate blacksmith and mason, and a wheelwright, in addition to being a surveyor.

Since it was then only the first of September, it wasn't cold enough for the varmints to have fur thick enough to make them worth trapping. While we were out scouting the area for hostiles we still established routes for future trap lines. Scouting was an everyday activity that required two hours from both Pa and me. I rode a circle to the south and Pa rode to the north. On our scouting trips, neither of us saw any fresh sign of Indians.

We didn't see any Indians either until the third week. There were then logs lying about that we had cut, dragged, and peeled; and we had already started assembling the lower part of the house. I had just dragged in a new log and was unhitching the trace-chains from it when one of the horses raised his head and looked toward the woods. It was a motion that clearly told me something was there that hadn't been there before, something that wasn't normal.

Reacting as if there were danger, I dove behind the log I had been dragging. I was then between it and the house and couldn't be seen from the direction the horse was looking. We were living in a dangerous time and a dangerous place. Pa always told us to be safe first, even if it looked foolish later on.

As I dove, I shouted, "Take cover!"

I had barely hit the ground behind the log when a bullet plowed into it. The thud of the bullet striking the log was followed instantly by the unmistakable sound of a musket. After pausing five seconds, I then raised my head long enough to see where the puff of smoke from the black powder was hanging in the air. My head was only up for a split second and was behind the log again when two more musket balls struck the log. Pa and Joseph's rifles then responded to the hostile fire. We always worked with our weapons close at hand. I then retrieved my rifle, which was leaning against the log from which I had been preparing to unhitch the trace-chains.

Crawling to the other end of the log, I waited half a minute before playing turkey by raising my head again. That drew a shot from the woods and answering shots from Pa, Joseph, and John. They all were then inside the framework of the house and were shooting through prepared openings.

I lay still for so long that Pa finally said, "You okay, Boy?"

"I'm fine, Pa. I was just lying here trying to figure out what to do."

Pa said, "How many are out there?"

"I don't know, Pa. I haven't seen any. One of the horses raised his head and ears, which warned me."

He said, "I haven't seen any either, just puffs of smoke. If they didn't move immediately after they shot, we probably hurt one or two. If your horse hadn't alerted you, we could all be in big trouble."

I lay there for a full hour. There were a few shots from the palmettos, behind which the Indians were taking cover, and answering shots from the house. At least one of the Indians was hit hard. He could be heard letting everyone know he was in pain. A palmetto isn't much cover except visually. Assuming the shooter would drop to the ground, Pa and the boys were shooting low into any bush from which a puff of smoke appeared.

With the warm afternoon sun shining on me, for one stretch of time it got so quiet I dozed off. That was when I decided I should be in the house.

Loud enough for those in the house to hear but those in the brush not to hear, I said, "Pa, I'm going to give the three of you one minute to get ready to answer their fire, then I'm coming in there with you."

Lying there, I stretched my muscles and prepared them for sudden movement. Once my muscles felt loose, I sprang from behind the log and ran toward the corner of the house. After four steps I cut back toward the middle of the house so as not to let them draw too good of a bead on me. It wasn't but thirty yards to the house but I didn't make it all the way that time. Bullets were flying thick enough that while still fifteen yards from the house I dropped behind another log. Figuring they would get tired of staying ready for an instant shot, I remained where I was for ten minutes, then made it into the cabin.

Pa said, "Based on the number of shots while you were running, there are at least ten of them. We got lucky this time. If they had caught us out in the open and split us up, they might have got most of us. We'll have to change our scouting pattern. They might have just stumbled on us. Or, they might know we're patrolling in the early morning."

I said, "From out there in the open, it sounds more like there are a hundred of them."

We settled down in the house for the rest of the day. There was an occasional shot from the palmettos, which we answered. We took turns on guard duty and resting. Two of us would relax while two others aimed a rifle through an opening, waiting to answer a shot. We left four rifles pointed through shooting slits so they wouldn't know some of us were resting. Black Creek was to our back and they couldn't easily come from that way. We occasionally looked to be sure, but they were not about to expose themselves on the open water in a canoe. They probably didn't have one, anyway.

At one point I said, "Pa, who do you think they are?"

He answered, "No telling. They could be Miccosukee, Creek, or Black Seminoles. Or there could be a mixture. I'm sure it's not the Spanish troops. They don't fight like this."

All that time the two horses I was dragging the log with were just standing there, still partially hitched to the log. Our other animals were in the pen.

As dark approached, Pa said, "When it's dark, I'm going out and take it to them. If we stay here in the house, they'll take all our animals but those two hitched to the log."

I said, "I'll go, too."

"Okay," he said, "But with only me in the woods, I can shoot anything that moves. I think that when they know what's happening, they'll pull out. I want you to take two muskets filled with pellets and crawl out by the south side of the horse pen. You stay there and cover the stock. You can shoot anything that moves. If I approach that area, I'll speak first. I'll also take two muskets."

As dark settled in we crawled out the back of the house and toward the horse pen. There, Pa left me and vanished into the night.

Not five minutes had passed when I saw three shadows moving toward the horse pen. Aiming the best I could in the dark, I fired a musket at the lead shadow. As bullets plowed into the ground where I had been, I rolled over three times to the right and fired the second musket at a billow of smoke from one of their shots. Someone fell. There was some thrashing around in the brush and some moaning. There was then movement away from me. It sounded like something was being dragged. Reloading a musket as fast as I could, I stood crouched behind the corner of the horse pen. While was I reloading, there were three close-spaced musket shots seventy-five yards south of me. It then became quiet for some time.

Most of an hour passed before Pa whispered to me from the dark, "It's me, Boy."

I whispered back, "I'm at the southeast corner of the pen."

As Pa approached, he said, "I think they've pulled out. They took their dead and wounded. When I went back by where I left one, he was gone. What did you hit?"

I said, "I'm not for sure, Pa. I hit at least one and probably two. I'm not sure how hard."

Daylight revealed that they had indeed pulled out. Blood at various spots showed we had done serious damage to four of them. We tracked them for the better part of two hours to be sure they had left the area. They were riding south on a dozen ponies.

A month later I was on my daily patrol to the south when I next spotted some Indians. There were five of them, all men.

Mounted, they were also leading spare horses. They spotted me at the same time I saw them. Being seventy-five yards apart at the time, we all sat our horses for a full minute watching each other. They were talking to each other and I was trying to decide whether to talk, walk my horse slowly away, run, or shoot at them. Heeling their horses, they walked them toward me. That made the decision for me. I kneed my horse to the right, bringing my rifle barrel, which was lying across my saddle, to bear on them. I also removed the strap holding my musket in its scabbard and checked its priming. Though my movements were clearly observed by the Indians, they made no move to bring a weapon to bear on me. Since there was only one of me, they probably expected me to prepare to defend myself and overlooked my preparation.

At eighteen yards, their leader spoke and they all reined in their horses. He then spoke to me in what was obviously broken Spanish.

Only knowing a few words of Spanish, I said in English, "I don't speak much Spanish. Do you speak English?"

They then talked among themselves in Muskogee. Since the time we had spent fighting with the Lower Creeks against the Red Sticks, Pa and I had practiced speaking Muskogee some, so I understood most of what they were saying. It was clear they didn't speak English.

I then spoke to them in Muskogee. "I know a little of your language."

They were a little startled and obviously impressed. After I got them to slow down their words some and repeat their statements often, I found that they were on their way to a plantation on the St. Johns River to try to trade for some powder, shot, and cloth, and some other things they wanted. I knew Pa had brought some trade goods with us but, except for a horse one of the Indians was riding, I didn't see much they had that I might want. That Indian was riding a beautiful roan gelding. They did have some things wrapped in bundles, though. I couldn't know what was in those bundles.

Still in Muskogee, I said, "We're building a house where Black Creek forks. My pa has some goods he'll trade. It's lots closer than the St. Johns. Come eat with us and talk. Later in the year when the air is cold, you'll know where we are and we might trade for thick furs."

Their leader, Running Dog, then introduced his group and said they would go with me.

Confident of their intentions and goodwill, I introduced myself and led them to where we were building the cabin. We always had a pot of beans and salt pork hanging over the fire, and some cornbread and meat cooked. Pa always said an Indian has as much honor as a white man does and he wouldn't harm someone he has eaten with, at least not then. He might kill you later but, for that moment, eating together was as sacred as a white flag or wearing a silver headband and white feathers. The silver headband and white feathers was the southern Indians' form of a white flag. Still, Pa was a little startled when I came riding into camp with five Indians.

I said, "Pa, they want to trade. I don't know if they have much we might want, but they might bring pelts that are valuable after it turns cold. Also, I would love to have that roan gelding. I'm not sure he's to be traded though."

Pa said, "Anything can be traded for, Boy. It's just a matter of timing and price."

I explained to Pa that they only spoke Muskogee and some Spanish. That left us the opportunity to say anything we wanted to in English without them understanding. Pa spoke better Muskogee than I did. He soon understood what they were after.

Pa then served everyone some food. Dragging some logs, John and Joseph arrived and joined us. I filled them in on what was going on while Pa served up some food and talked to our guests.

As he always did when he had the chance, Pa was busy questioning our guests about the geography of the area to our south. They also talked about the major battles of 1812 through 1818. Them being Red Stick Creeks, and being at some of the same battles, it was apparent that Pa and I had fought against some of Running Dog's people at one time or another. I filled John and Joseph in on what the Indians and Pa were talking about as the talking and trading continued.

Pa didn't eat much so he finished eating first. He then got his trade goods—cloth, knives, hatchets, fishhooks, powder, lead, and such—and laid them out on a blanket. The Indians observed his actions but acted nonchalant about the whole thing. Running Dog then got a pack off of a horse and laid out their things—dry beans, buckskin shirts, moccasins, shell beads, some deerskins, and a buffalo skin. We had seen buffalo tracks but had not seen any buffalo in the area yet. The buffalo in north Florida, at that time, had been reduced to small groups and individuals because of the hunting pressure they were under.

Pa then started examining the Indians' goods and they started examining ours. I walked over to the roan gelding and looked at his teeth, hoofs, and legs. He was no crow-bait. I speculated that he had probably been stolen from somewhere.

While I was examining the roan, I kept an eye on Running Dog. In addition to trading for other things, he picked up a hatchet and examined it several times. It was a metal-headed hatchet that Pa had made in his blacksmith shop. He also kept an eye on me as I examined his horse.

After most of an hour passed, Pa had traded for several things he would later sell for a higher price in Fernandina, Cow Town, or St. Augustine. Cow Town got its name because it was situated at the narrowest point of the lower St. Johns River, a place used as a ford for cattle. Drovers would force a couple of bell cows into the river and swim their horses next to them, guiding them across the river. The other cattle would then follow.

Cow Town was called Cow Ford at first. Some people still called it Cow Ford. Three years later, Cow Town would be renamed Jacksonville, after General Andrew Jackson, even though he had never been east of the Suwannee River in Florida.

In spite of Pa's best efforts, Running Dog was not going to trade the horse. Running Dog also had not come up with an offer for which Pa would trade the hatchet. The hatchet wasn't all that valuable but Running Dog really seemed to want it. In the end, the Indians mounted to go and the hatchet was still lying on the blanket.

As Running Dog turned his horse, Pa said, "Running Dog." He then picked up the hatchet and walked over to the Indian's horse. Handing him the hatchet, Pa said, "A gift for a worthy opponent in battle. May we live in peace."

I think Pa intended all along to give Running Dog the hatchet. That's why Pa hadn't traded it to him. There always seemed to be a point to everything Pa did.

That Indian sat his horse for the best part of a minute looking at Pa, then at the hatchet, and then back at Pa. He then extended his hand for a white man's handshake, took the hatchet, wheeled his horse and rode away.

November 15, 1820

Things were quiet and work had progressed quickly since Running Dog's visit. We hadn't seen a soul, had finished cutting the logs for the cabin, were cutting logs for a barn, and splitting shingles for both. While I helped Pa work the ends of the logs to fit, John and Joseph also got busy cutting and splitting the materials for fence rails, and cutting materials for a smokehouse. As they cut those things, they also worked toward clearing a few acres for spring planting. They didn't dig the stumps except those from small trees. The big stumps were left to rot out. We planned to plant between them for a few years while they rotted.

The middle of November was the time Pa had chosen to set our trap lines. There had been an overnight freeze a week earlier and the animals should have their winter coats. Pa and I had set out on our different routes, the same ones we patrolled daily to inspect for signs of hostiles, to set our traps. We had already chosen the places to set our traps. Even with that, it was into the afternoon and I hadn't finished setting my traps. I had just set a trap in a coon's trail, sprinkled grass and leaves over it, and stuck small crossed sticks for the coon to step over from either side of the trap. That last part would make a coon step square on the treadle regardless of which direction the coon came down the trail. As I straightened up I saw Running Dog sitting a horse not fifty yards from me. The skin crawled all over my body. I had gotten careless and let him ride up on me.

As I walked to my horses—I was riding my Spanish mare and using a pony we had taken from the Indians some time back as a pack animal for my traps—Running Dog heeled his horse into a walk toward me. He was riding a big black stud horse and leading the roan gelding he had previously been riding.

Stopping ten yards from me, he pointed at the roan and at my packhorse and said, "I have a new horse. I'll trade the roan for your horse."

That roan was worth lots more than the pony I was using as a packhorse and I wasn't sure what to say. Finally I came to my senses and nodded my head. Running Dog then slid from his horse, stripped the pack from my pony, placed the pack on the roan, and handed me the lead rope to the roan. I was still standing there with my mouth open.

Still speaking slowly in Muskogee, and pointing at the black horse, Running Dog said, "I have a good horse."

I said, also in Muskogee, "Yes, he is a beautiful horse. You've also given me a beautiful horse."

Running Dog said, "He's a good horse. Don't ride him to Alabama because there could be trouble. We'll return before the spring to trade at your house. Your father is an honest trader and we plan to be friends."

Lifting his hand, he departed.

I then knew where the roan came from and how he was acquired. I also had a better idea about Pa's skill as a trader. In effect, Pa had traded the hatchet for a hundred-dollar horse and made a firm friend besides.

When Pa saw the roan, he said, "Did you kill Running Dog?"

I said, "No, Pa. He swapped the roan even for the pony I had with me." Feeling a little guilty, I added, "It was his idea. I think it was because you gave him the hatchet."

Pa just stood there grinning.

Pa had several things to trade that he had gotten from Running Dog, as well as some pelts from animals we had trapped, and we needed trade materials for the pelts Running Dog's band would bring, so in December of 1820 Pa and I went to St. Augustine. The only good crossing on St. Johns River, one a horse can swim, other than up toward where it begins, is at Cow Town. Though we had to go through Cow Town, we didn't trade there because there was no adequate trading post. That community was home to only seventy people at the time. St. Augustine was only thirty-five miles, straight-line, but it was a complicated trip. It took a good-sized boat to ferry man and horse across the St. Johns River where we would have to cross if we went straight there, and there was no ferry at the time. The St. Johns River is more than two miles wide at that point. Also, you might camp on the river-bank for a month and not have a big enough boat come along to carry you and your horses across. We went the long way through Cow Town. Pa took me along because I hadn't been before, and because he needed the extra eyes and gun to look after our goods.

As we traveled, Pa said, "As soon as we get back to Black Creek, I'm going to Georgia, settle our business there, and bring the family. I want you to stay at the place and keep clearing land and building fences. We'll ask John and Joseph to stay until I get the family here, and beyond that if they will. We need to put in docks and warehouses. There's no point in us trading at St. Augustine when we can sell and buy from our own docks to oceangoing ships."

I said, "I'll be glad to stay, Pa. With all the work we need to do, you should hire some more help to come back with you."

Pa said, "I'll do that. We'll need lots of help."

In St. Augustine we learned that Spain had ratified the treaty ceding Florida to the United States. The king had signed it in late October of 1820. Because almost two years had passed since the United States had ratified the document, and some changes had been made, the Senate would need to ratify it again. It being almost four months since we left home, and since we had been in the wilderness during that time, this was the first news we had about Spain's action on the treaty. Pa was excited over the news. That the Senate would ratify the treaty was a given. We had a head start on others who would then move to Florida.

I learned some other things in St. Augustine, too. In December of 1820, I was just two months short of nineteen years old. In all those years I had never seen over half a dozen white girls who were close to my age. Since most girls married older men, men who had a home and goods, I hadn't had much contact with those few girls. It soon became apparent to me that there were more girls age fifteen to eighteen years old in and around St. Augustine than I had ever seen before in my life. Between the Spanish, French, and Italian enclaves, there must have been seven hundred people in and around St. Augustine at the time. There was close to an equal number of each nationality, each group living in its own enclave. Being shy and self-conscious, I tried to pretend that each and every one of those girls didn't mesmerize me. Pa saw through my pretense.

Pa said, "You best go ahead and talk to one of these girls, Boy. You might not see another who's your age for a year or so."

I said, "I wouldn't know what to say, Pa. I'm not sure any words would come out if I tried. Also, other than English and Muskogee, I only speak a few words of German and Spanish. Though most of them speak Spanish, some of these people speak mostly French or Italian. They would be mighty hard to talk to."

Pa said, "You won't have to talk much if one's interested. Tell her what a nice bonnet or frock she's wearing and ask who made it. Or, comment on her hair or eyes. If she's interested, she'll take it from there."

Talking to myself, I practiced saying in Spanish what Pa had said but it sounded kind of stupid. I couldn't bring myself to just walk up to a girl and say something that didn't sound good to me. I finally got to talk to a girl, though, one who spoke English. She was helping her pa, who was doing the trading with my pa.

Without thought, I commented in English, "You've got more things in this warehouse than I've ever seen in one place, maybe all together in my whole life."

Smiling, she replied in English, "Where do you live?"

"'Round about," I said. "Right now we're building over on Black Creek. Ma and the children are still in Georgia. Pa's going to get them soon. I guess we'll be at Black Creek permanent after that. The way we came, our place is four days' hard ride from here. Pa and I have talked about rigging a sail on a big canoe. It would only take one day to get here then. How long have you lived here?"

The talk just rolled on then. I got so tied up in talking to her that I didn't know Pa was ready to go until he put his hand on my shoulder.

When we were out of hearing, Pa said, "It didn't sound like you were having trouble talking."

I said, "She was really nice, Pa."

He said, "Yeah, she sure is, Boy."

I promised myself I would go back to St. Augustine at the first chance. Whether I was asleep or awake, for weeks after that I could see and smell her.

An interesting thing happened on the way to Black Creek. We met a ship's captain who Pa made a deal with to take us home. The captain had a ship docked at a plantation on the St. Johns River. After talking to him for some time, for a small sum Captain Lewis offered to take us up Black Creek to its fork, if the water was deep enough for his ship. Pa assured him it was. He was excited about Pa's talk about building docks and warehouses. If it all worked out, it would be lots more convenient for the captain to load on timber and other cargo for Europe without having to go up the St. Johns River a considerable distance. Also, the virgin timber along Black Creek hadn't been touched. He could shorten his trip and increase his profit. It was for that reason he agreed to take us for a small fee.

Before the sun set that day the captain put us ashore less than a hundred yards from our cabin. The captain and Pa struck a deal for Pa to have him a load of timber, furs, and farm goods by April 1, 1821. Also, Pa gave him a list of goods to deliver to us.

February 1, 1821

Having hired three men to come with him, by the end of January Pa was back from Georgia with the family. While we had traveled with packhorses on our original trip down, Pa rigged a sail canoe for his trip home and brought the family by boat and raft. It was lots easier traveling with the family that way. The new men drove the livestock down. They were to stay on and clear land, build a dock and warehouse, plant a crop and an orchard, and various other things. John and Joseph had stayed with me and we had done a good amount of land clearing and fencing while Pa was gone. At least the trees were cut and burned and the brush was grubbed out and burned. Pa got back before Running Dog came to trade, which was good. I still had lots to learn about trading.

After hugging me, the first thing Ma said was, "Have you been back to St. Augustine? Your pa said you were sweet on a girl over there."

Blushing, I said, "I haven't had time, Ma. I'm not really sweet on her. We just talked a few minutes. She might not even remember me. Also, I won't be nineteen for a few more days. She can't be more than sixteen. She is real nice, though."

Ma said, "I. J., you just don't know girls. She'll remember you, right enough. In a couple of days you take some pelts over there and trade for powder, shot, and salt. It'll give you a chance to talk."

Pa said, "I found out that lots of people are leaving Georgia and moving into Florida. There's a family close to the creek north of us."

I said, "I know, Pa. I've seen one family of white people since you left, too."

I was sure glad to see Ma. In addition to thinking a great deal of her, I was tired of eating men's cooking. Ma was a great cook. Also, she brought the chickens with her and the hired hands drove the milk cow down. I sure had a taste for some fried eggs, sausage, and grits, along with a glass of milk for breakfast. Ma also cooked the best crackling cornbread and greens I ever tasted. We men cooked up lots of food but it was quite common for us to have beans cooked with salt pork for breakfast, dinner, and supper on some days when we were working real hard.

Before the week was up I loaded some pelts on a packhorse and, taking the direct route, headed for St. Augustine. I figured to hunt some along the way. I also figured to borrow a canoe from a planter on the river and, leaving my horse there, cross the river and walk the rest of the way to the trading post. At the river I ran into our friend Lewis, the ship's captain, who had anchored his ship and was visiting with his family. It turned out that Lewis owned a large piece of property on our side of the river that he was having farmed.

He said, "How's the work on your dock and buildings coming?"

I said, "Fine. Pa hired three more people. We'll be ready to ship out a load by April first."

The captain then asked me to eat with his family and I got a chance to meet them. He and his wife had six boys, ages five through eleven. They spent a couple of hours asking me about Indians and Indian fighting. I tried to make it sound like Indian fighting isn't very exciting, which it isn't. They also had three little girls, ages six, four, and three. The six-year-old, Louisa, would be seven years old in three weeks. She climbed on my lap while I was telling the boys stories.

When a suitable time had passed after eating, I excused myself to go on to St. Augustine and do some trading. They invited me to stop off with them and spend the night as I was coming and going to St. Augustine. Since there were nine children in the house under twelve years of age, I didn't think that was going to happen. After thanking them, I left.

Arriving at the trading post, I was greeted by the owner. "It's been a couple of months since we saw you, son. What can we do for you?"

"I've brought some pelts to trade for powder, shot, and salt," I said.

After looking at the pelts, he gave me the powder, shot, and salt I wanted and an extra dollar, and said, "That should fix you up. We'll trade for pelts of that quality every time. What else can I do for you?"

I was boxed in. His daughter, Susan, was nowhere to be seen.

I was traveling most of three days, round-trip, to see her and I wasn't planning to leave without doing so.

I said, "Sir, we did need the supplies, but that wasn't the main purpose of the trip. I hoped I might get to talk with Susan."

He stared at me for a moment, then grinned and said, "How far is it to your house, son?"

I said, "It's only thirty-five miles, one way, when you come the short way."

Still grinning, he said, "I see. Well, she's over at the house helping her mother. You're welcome to drop by and see if she would like to talk."

I said, "I sure will, sir. And much obliged."

In my embarrassment, I would have walked off without knowing where to go but he stopped me and, still grinning, told me.

Arriving at the house I found Susan and her mother washing and hanging clothes to dry. I was a stranger to her mother but Susan recognized me instantly.

Before her mother could say anything, Susan said, "Why it's been months since you were at the trading post. It's nice to see you again."

Within a few seconds I was in control of my voice and wits again, and said, "Your pa said you were here. I came by to see if you might like to talk."

Susan then introduced me to her mother and asked me to help hang a basket of clothes. That got us out of hearing distance of her mother. I not only helped hang clothes; I also stayed around and helped them finish their work. For my good work, or for whatever reason, I got an invitation to stay for supper. Before supper, Susan and I walked off by the water. We held hands some while we walked. Mostly I just let Susan talk. It sure was nice listening to her. Just as dusk was settling into dark, Susan rose from the rocks we had been sitting on to return to the house. After I stood, she placed her left hand on the right side of my face and reached up and kissed me lightly on the lips. My head was still floating as we ate supper. I had to concentrate or I wouldn't have heard her parents when they asked questions.

I was still walking on air while returning to Black Creek. As I traveled, I promised myself it wouldn't be two months before I went back to St. Augustine.

In February of 1821 I turned nineteen years old. In the same month Andrew Jackson accepted the appointment to be governor of the Territory of Florida. In late February, the United States Senate again ratified the treaty giving Florida to the United States. Because of Spanish bureaucratic delays, it was to be July 1821 before Jackson received some of the property records of Florida from the Spanish. He never did get all of the Spanish records. Getting the records would have taken longer if Jackson hadn't threatened to march into Pensacola and take over by force. As all this was happening, we continued to work hard and establish our place in Florida.

On March 1, 1821, Running Dog returned to trade his pelts and hides. He had numerous varmint pelts and over a hundred deer hides. He brought all of his people with him. There must have been forty, counting the women and children. Those people also brought durable farm goods such as potatoes, rice, and Indian corn to trade. They also brought various leather and shell goods they had made. Indians don't get in a hurry trading, so they were camped about a quarter of a mile from the house for three days.

It was toward the end of the trading that Pa asked Running Dog, "Who was it that attacked us here a few months back?"

Running Dog said, "I don't know. You never said you were attacked before."

Pa said, "I would be indebted if you could find out."

Running Dog said, "I'll ask among the people I see. I don't think it was anyone I regularly see or I would know"

Not knowing if Running Dog was being totally truthful about it, Pa let it go at that.

On March 30, Captain Lewis tied his ship up at our dock and started loading the timber, animal skins, and other things we had. He had brought the things Pa ordered. It was a profitable arrangement for both of them.

After we had the ship loaded, I set out to see Susan. Having rigged a canoe with a sail, I sailed down Black Creek and back up the St. Johns. Concealing my canoe and leaving it on shore, I then walked the twelve miles to Susan's house. By taking the canoe, I didn't have to take the long route through Cow Town or to get someone to ferry me across the river. Also, the trip took only one day.

Susan's Pa started grinning the instant he saw me. He said, "Thirty-five miles is a lot of walking just to hold hands with a girl."

I said, "Yes sir, it sure is. To cut down on the time and energy required, I rigged up a sailing canoe. By sailing down Black Creek and up the St. Johns, I can get within twelve walking miles of your place. The whole trip takes less than a day when there's a good wind."

Wrinkling his brow, he nodded. His voice then took on a friendlier note. Our talk was friendly and polite enough before, but our talk was more like man to man after that, as opposed to man to boy.

I spent two nights and a day there. Not being one to remain idle, I helped Susan's pa in his warehouse all day. Impressed with my work and mathematical ability, he offered me a full-time job. He also asked me to stay over at his house for the night, which I did. The job and being close to Susan was tempting but I politely declined. I had it in mind to take my own piece of Florida and to do some farming, which I was good at.

As I proceeded down the St. Johns River toward the mouth of Black Creek on the return trip, two canoes, containing three Indians each, were launched ahead of me. Setting a course to intercept me, the Indians were paddling as hard as they could. At that point, the St. Johns River is two miles wide and the current barely moves. I was a quarter of a mile from the east bank, the bank they launched from. As I observed their progress and mine, it was clear they had launched far enough in front of me to cut me off. It looked like they planned to try to capture me. Had they shot me, my canoe would have capsized, thus dumping everything I owned in the river. There wouldn't have been much profit in that. Of course they could have been just trying to kill me. War between some Indians and whites was an ongoing thing.

I was sailing north by northeast, straight down the river. Pa said the St. Johns is the only river he ever heard of that flows north. The wind was out of the west. While I was traveling at a much greater speed than they were, they definitely had the angle on me. With no other choice, I tacked and moved to the south. I then tacked a couple of more times and got myself to the middle of the river. The Indians, then two hundred yards straight downriver from me, were almost within range.

At that point I turned to run before the wind toward the east bank. They, too, turned to cut me off. There being a good breeze, it was too late for them to close on me. Even as they turned straight toward the east bank, it was clear that I would beat them to shore by a good bit. Once there, and safe behind a tree, they would be at my mercy if they came within rifle range of the east bank.

They also apparently assessed the situation in the same way. Laying down their paddles, they picked up their muskets and fired at me. I was then well out of musket range of them. Other than for a ball hitting the water near my canoe, their shooting was totally ineffective.

When they stopped paddling, even for the one shot, I stretched the gap between us some. At that point, I turned northeast. Holding that course until I was fifty yards from the river's bank, I then turned downriver and passed by them four hundred yards away while going north-northeast. I thought about sending one rifle ball in their direction but it almost certainly would have been a vain effort. Instead, I raised my hand and waved as a parting gesture.

It was a couple of minutes later before I realized how drained I felt as a result of the encounter. The encounter also caused me to be concerned about sailing up Black Creek. It being much narrower, a hostile would only have to lie on the bank and shoot me from concealment as I passed. Fortunately, I was not to be shot that day.

Ma seemed to be anxious for grandchildren. She wanted to know everything when I got home. She was more interested in the social things than in the Indians. I wasn't saying much because there wasn't really much to tell. I don't know why Ma was anxious to have grandchildren. She had a baby girl, Mary, who was less than a year old. Since her older kids were boys, Ma might have just been hoping I would bring someone home to help with the work. Susan and I were not close to doing that. Also, I felt like I had to have my own place before considering marriage.

It was in the spring of 1821 that I got Ma started with turkeys. As I did sometimes when I was in the woods, I was sitting behind some palmettos and leaning back against a tree. Sitting without the slightest motion other than my eyelids and eyeballs moving, I saw lots of interesting things and learned a lot about nature. I also managed to kill lots of game. This one time, my eyes caught the slightest motion. Within seconds, the form of a turkey hen took shape in the brush. She disappeared as I sat watching her. Since turkeys have a way of getting an object such as a bush or tree between them and a person and running straight away until they're safe, I assumed for a few minutes that was what happened. Still, I couldn't figure out what she had got behind or how she knew I was there. The more I studied on it, the surer I became that the turkey was still near me. I wasn't planning to shoot her. We almost never shot turkey hens and never in the spring when they might be laying or sitting on eggs. Then it struck me that she might have just sat down on her nest.

I sat there without moving for several more minutes, concentrating on the area where the turkey had vanished. Then, as if by magic, the turkey reappeared. She then walked off and vanished into the underbrush. After giving her time to clear the area, I stood and walked directly to the spot where she had vanished and reappeared. Standing near the spot, it was a couple of minutes before I spotted her nest. Using a stick to remove the leaves she had used to cover them, I exposed eleven eggs. Being careful not to touch anything with my fingers and leave my scent, I removed six of those turkey eggs. Turkeys cannot count so she would not know that eggs were missing. After using the stick to cover the remaining eggs just like they had been, I carried the six eggs to Ma. The turkey hadn't finished laying all of her eggs and was not yet sitting on them, so they were fresh and could be eaten. Ma had another plan. She had a hen that had been trying to set and Ma was trying to break up the hen's nests so as to keep the hen producing eggs. Instead of breaking the hen from setting, Ma then put those turkey eggs in the hen's nest. The old hen hatched those eggs and raised six turkeys—four hens and two gobblers.

July 15, 1821

General Jackson took over Florida by marching into Pensacola in mid-July. The date made little difference to us. We were busy clearing land and preparing for planting in the fall and the next spring, as well as building fences, docks, and buildings. A few new people were moving into the territory during that time and establishing their new homes but none were close enough for us to know about except for a few who showed up to trade with Pa. We had seen nothing of any hostile Indians since that one raid, either. The only Indians we saw were friendly Indians who came to trade occasionally. Pa was doing a fair business trading with them and with the new arrivals.

While we saw some Indians, it was rare that we saw any black Seminoles. Since they were mostly former slaves to white Americans, black Seminoles chose to remain away from locations that housed whites. Whether bought or stolen, most of the blacks living with the Indians were the Indians' slaves. The Indians sometimes had a white slave, or an Indian slave from one of their enemy tribes, but mostly their slaves were black people. The term slave, in describing the relationship between Indians and their black slaves, is used loosely. The black slave's Indian master was usually very lenient. Unless they were taken as mates or became trusted, Indians were less lenient with their Indian or white slaves than with their black ones. Indians only occasionally had a white slave they were lenient with. A white slave was less likely to gain their trust. Actually, the Indians had few white slaves. The whites they captured were more likely to be killed sooner or later.

Also, we were learning that the blacks, being intelligent and in most cases speaking another language in addition to Muskogee, yielded considerable influence over their masters. Speaking either Spanish or English, the blacks interpreted for their Indian masters. Because I spoke Muskogee and understood a little Spanish, I observed on some occasions that the blacks intentionally interpreted incorrectly. Fearing they might be captured and become the property of white owners, these slaves not only avoided whites, they took every opportunity to create a state of animosity and fear between the Indians and white people.

At the time, there was thought to be over five thousand Indians in Florida. Counting former white people's slaves, the Indians' slaves, and free black people, there were probably also five thousand black people living with or around the Indians, or in their own small villages. These two populations, combined, outnumbered the white people in Florida by more than two to one. During 1821 and 1822, Jackson considered using force to remove the black population living in Florida from the territory. There was a feeling that the Indians would have taken the black people's side in a fight, so no such effort was made at the time. Also, General Jackson said the Upper Creek Indians living in Florida should be removed to Alabama where most of the other Upper Creeks were. He said the other Indians should be rounded up and sent west of the Mississippi River—out of the United States. Jackson's contention was that neither the Creeks nor the Miccosukees had any right to land in Florida. As recent arrivals, they had just squatted on the land. Jackson had no political support from the United States government regarding moving the Indians so it didn't happen then. Most white people in Florida felt much the same way as Governor Jackson but we had just squatted on the land, too.

The Indians who lived nearest us changed their lifestyle to a great extent during the early eighteen twenties. While the men still trapped, hunted, and fished, the women soon began planting things in their gardens they could trade or sell to us. They also started making extra trinkets, moccasins, and leather goods for the same purpose. Pa's business provided a ready outlet for their manufactured goods and for their nonperishable products such as sweet potatoes, corn, citrus, rice, and dry beans that he could ship out.

We developed a good relationship with the local Indians. Still, there was cause for us to stay alert for trouble. In addition to all the different bands of Indians in Florida, there were smugglers, thieves, runaways who had jumped ship, and every other type of undesirable individual who had taken refuge in the 34,721,000-plus land acres of Florida.

When President Monroe would not allow Governor Jackson to remove the Indians from Florida, Jackson began to work to improve their life. He introduced a policy that, since many whites had been taking unfair advantage of the Indians, no whites would be allowed to trade with them without a license from the Indian agent. Since he hadn't heard about the policy, Pa didn't get a license for some time. Nothing was said about us not having a license. That must have been because Pa never cheated anyone.

Governor Jackson resigned at the end of 1821. In June of 1822 the new governor, William P. Duval, arrived to take over. Duval was from Kentucky. Territorial governors were then appointed by the president of the United States and didn't have to be from the territory for which they were appointed governor.

I continued visiting Susan every month or six weeks. We soon decided we would marry, but I was determined to have a place of my own before we married. Since Susan was of like mind, I continued working for Pa to save money, buy land, and build our place.

While people were moving into Florida then, it was only sparsely populated. Pensacola, the capital, had less than seven hundred inhabitants. Only half of those were white. There were said to be less than three hundred people of any color living in the southern half of Florida. The Indians lived in north Florida and used central Florida only for winter hunting. Almost no one ever went to south Florida, other than by boat to Key West. In spite of the migration of white Americans to Florida, an outbreak of yellow fever in 1822 served to hold the total population down. Living on the frontier and not coming in contact with many people, our family was spared the ravages of the fever. Most of the frontier families were spared. It was those people in communities who fared the worst from fever.

During 1822 and 1823, the United States moved to consolidate and demonstrate its power and authority over Florida. The most visible way was through the building of forts in various locations across the northern end of the territory.

Of particular interest to us during that time was the creation of a Board of Commissioners for East and West Florida. Also of interest, Congress passed a law under which the president appointed a surveyor general of Florida. The surveyor general was charged with mapping all of Florida's land. Over the next twelve or fifteen years, Florida was to be surveyed into sections measuring one square mile each. One square mile is equal to 640 acres. Survey contractors were paid four dollars a mile for the work. Of course, they had to pay for all of their help and expenses. It took some time before the surveying got under way but as soon as it did Pa started doing some surveying again. He also took me along some and taught me the trade. Ma, the boys, and the hired help were left to run the farm and businesses Pa had under way while he worked as a surveyor. Being a good shot, a great scout, a competent hunter, and knowing mathematics, Pa was a natural as a surveyor.

Traveling in small groups to remote areas, the survey teams were sometimes easy pickings for a band of thieves or Indians that might want their animals and guns. Several such groups found Pa's team was not easy pickings. In most cases Pa had discovered the culprits before they moved into action. There was one incident where four men were lying in wait with the obvious intention of shooting and robbing the survey team. Pa, who was scouting to prevent just such an occurrence, slipped up on them and captured three of them. The fourth, alerted by the noise of Pa capturing the others, chose to shoot at Pa. Pa was quicker and better with his rifle.

After dispatching that one, Pa used his short-barrel musket to cover the three he had captured. He held them until the other members of the survey team arrived. Some of the survey team members wanted to hang the rest of them. After some discussion, it was decided they would be turned loose without horses, weapons, clothes, or supplies. They were also posted out of Florida. Posting meant that anytime or anyplace in the future that they were seen in Florida, any member of the party could then shoot them. We later heard about a nude man who was found wandering through the wilderness. Covered with insect bites and racked with fever, he soon died. Assuming he was one of the three, the same fate probably befell the others.

The East Florida Board of Commissioners did not begin their work until the middle of 1823. The work of the commission was to examine land claims. Each person who claimed land had to provide the specifics about their land: number of acres, location, survey boundaries, and method of acquisition. Proof also had to be provided, in the form of written or verbal testimony, that the owner was living on the claimed land at the time of the cession of Florida to the United States.

Pa, being a surveyor, surveyed and properly claimed our land. He then had to provide proof to one of the commissioners. Interestingly, another person claimed part of our land. There were many such fraudulent claims. Though it took a long time and was lots of work, sufficient documentation and testimony was provided to sustain Pa's claim. Because Pa's claim was placed early, it was approved within a few years. We were fortunate—many of the claims were not settled by 1827, when the Board of Commissioners was abolished. Some of those that had not been settled were hung up in the courts and Congress for many years.

In 1823 the United States government began to encourage settlers to move to Florida. The population of north Florida increased slowly over the next few years. Since the land grant situation had not been settled, which of the lands were privately owned by a grantee and which were public lands was not then known. So the government had no price or policy for selling land at the time. These new settlers just squatted on land as we had. It wasn't until 1825 that a price and policy was made that allowed the United States to sell land. Any white adult who had built a cabin on a piece of land and farmed it in Florida prior to that time was allowed to keep it if their claim could be documented.

Hindsight is always better than foresight. Had I built my own cabin and worked some land around it before Florida became a

United States territory, I could have claimed up to 640 acres. As it turned out, I had to buy my land at the government established price of $1.25 an acre. That's how I got my first land. Choosing a site near Pa's property on Black Creek, I built a cabin and cleared a few acres. Of course Asa and George helped. My sisters were all too young to help. They were still at home making mud pies.

October 15, 1823

Running Dog showed up with two of his warriors on October 15. Their arrival and the fact they had left their families at home didn't seem out of the ordinary as we sat around going through the customary courtesies shown by host and guest. I did notice they were not carrying any trade goods.

At the proper time, Running Dog said, "The people who attacked you live four days from here, south of Paynes Prairie. Though raiding other whites in north Florida and Georgia since their failure here, they've avoided your place. You killed two of them and hurt three others when they raided here. Their leader, Spotted Horse, now knows about your prosperity and is hoping to get valuables and revenge by raiding here again soon."

Though Running Dog was speaking Muskogee, Pa and I both spoke pretty good Muskogee by then and we understood it even better than we spoke it, so we could understand everything he was saying.

Since Running Dog had paused to get Pa's reaction, Pa said, "Why are you telling me this, Running Dog?"

Running Dog said, "You asked. And, there's bad blood between Spotted Horse's clan and my clan. That's why I hadn't heard about it before. There has already been some stealing and raiding between us at times. Also, trading with you has been good. In addition to that we shook hands on living in peace and I consider you and your family to be friends."

It wasn't unusual for Indians to be friends with whites, or for Indians to be enemies of other Indians. And an Indian's word is as good as a white or black man's word. It all depends on the individual. I was fast learning that considerations of honor, personal well-being, and wealth are often more important than your color or nationality to most people. Still, I always try to consider all the motives I can think of and I was listening carefully.

Pa said, "What else do you know about the raid?"

Running Dog said, "Spotted Horse plans to raid here again in less than two weeks. Then, having all the supplies he needs, he'll go south for the winter hunt. He feels that even if you find out who raided, you'll not be able to follow them to the middle of Florida."

Pa said, "I'll ask again, why are you telling me this? Are there other reasons?"

Running Dog replied, "I have twelve warriors, not enough for a decisive raid on Spotted Horse's village. I propose we join forces and raid Spotted Horse's camp together before he raids yours. If you'll supply us with ammunition, I'll lead you there and join in the raid. Each person of yours and mine will then get an equal share of what we take during the raid. I don't do this only because we're friends. I know Spotted Horse would raid my camp. I suspect one of his people might have pretended to be drunk and talked about the raid here as a diversion. His plan might be to raid my camp instead of, or in addition to, yours."

Pa said, "How many braves does he have?"

"Twenty-five, plus some older and younger men who might fight. That's why I haven't already made an attack on his village. He only brought twelve when he raided here. He didn't think he would need more. There were only four of you. He thought to kill you before you knew he was here."

Pa said, "If it hadn't been for I. J.'s horse raising his head, he might have."

Lots of us were gathered around then: Ma, Joseph, Asa, George, John Hunter, the other hired hands, and me.

Pa said, "Stake out your horses and eat with us, we'll talk some more."

After the Indians left to stake out their horses so they could graze, Pa turned to us and said, "What do you think of this?"

Ma asked, "Do you believe him? Do you trust him?"

Pa said, "I have no reason not to. We fought alongside Indians in 1814 and again in the Seminole Indian War."

Feeling pretty brave, I said, "I believe him, Pa. He's pretty smart and he knows we're not stupid. He knows that if they tried a double-cross, one of us would kill him for sure."

After we had talked it over for a while Pa said, "I think we should do it. At the same time, I don't think all of us should go. There's always the chance this is a ploy to get us away from the place". Looking at Ma, he said, "I'm going to take I. J., Asa, and George. You and Samuel can shoot as good as most. There's also Joseph, John, and the other hired hands. By staying alert and close to the building while we're gone, you should be all right."

Samuel was thirteen at the time. He had been shooting since he was eight years old.

John Hunter spoke up then. "I'd like to go."

"Okay," Pa said. "I also plan to visit what few neighbors we have within a one-day riding distance, alert them so they can be prepared for a raid here or at their place, and invite any who want to go. I really think that if a raid occurs here, it will probably be at our place because of all the supplies we have."

Pa sent us boys to the closest neighbors' farms to carry his message. He then went to talk to Running Dog. We didn't have any real close neighbors so we traveled a considerable distance to carry the message. By the time we returned it was the middle of the night and there wasn't much more discussion then. The next morning at breakfast Pa gathered those of us who were going on the raid for a meeting. After we boys gave our reports, it was evident we would have at least eight people joining us from among our neighbors. Counting Running Dog and his twelve braves, we would be twenty-five.

Pa said, "Four nights from now we're going to meet Running Dog thirty-five miles south of here. He left one brave to guide us to where we need to go. We'll travel at night and lay up during the day. Since we have about the same number of fighters as Spotted Horse has, the element of surprise is essential. We have to shoot first and most often. With that in mind, we'll all carry a rifle and a musket. For our neighbors who don't have two weapons, I'll supply them with a spare for the trip. Running Dog's braves will only have one gun. That's one little precaution I'm taking just in case. We'll need everyone gathered here by noon the day after tomorrow. Tomorrow morning each of you go back to see those people you recruited and tell them."

Pa, my brothers, and I had started sticking a dueling pistol in our belts most of the time. The pistol was so we wouldn't have to carry a rifle or musket all the time in order to be armed. When we were away from home, we usually carried either a rifle and pistol, or a musket and pistol. We would be carrying all three on this trip. With the pistol, rifle, and musket, we would have three shots each without reloading.

As we went about our duties over the next couple of days there was lots of talk about the upcoming raid. In addition to our regular duties, we checked and rechecked all the prepared defenses for our place. We filled the water barrels, checked the shooting ports, moved the spare weapons and ammunition from the warehouse to the house, moved any log or other obstruction that could shield Indians as they approached one of the buildings, and reinforced the horse and cow pens. Pa also told everyone who was staying behind which building they would sleep in. The buildings were located in such a way that shooters from various buildings could cover the approaches to the other buildings.

When everyone gathered at our house to leave, there were three extra men. Word had spread and they had volunteered without being asked. Also, three of the farmers had brought their families to our farm so they would be in a safer place. Those who were old enough to do so would help with the chores and with fighting if need be. Pa assigned them buildings in which to sleep so their weapons would be put to the best use. Also, others of our neighbors had clustered at other farms that could be easily defended. A few of the smaller farms were left undefended but the people would be fairly safe.

Counting the Indian guide, when we left at noon there were sixteen of us. Our four packhorses carried spare ammunition, food for a week, grain for the horses, and what medicine Pa thought we might need. Pa had ordered that, for the purpose of secrecy, no shot was to be fired at fish or animal so we carried everything we would eat. Each of us carried our weapons, sleeping roll, and ammunition allotment.

Taking the same route we had taken in 1817 while going to destroy the village of the Indians who had raided us, we continued traveling even after the sun set. Though stopping frequently to rest our horses, it was three in the morning when we finally stopped to camp.

The horses were fed grain that morning. They were only allowed to graze while hobbled during daylight. Guards were positioned on all four sides of the designated grazing area while they were grazing. More than just watching the horses, the guards were stationed in such a way that we would know if we had been discovered, even if no attempt was made to take the horses. Pa was determined that our attack would be a surprise.

We stayed in camp that day until first dark. After riding south until almost four in the morning, our guide raised his hand and stopped us. Each of us, in turn, raised our hand to stop the person behind us.

The guide said, "Running Dog camps ahead of us."

Pa said, "How far?"

The guide said, "You'll hear."

With that, he twice gave a whippoorwill call. The answering call came from a hundred yards ahead. I pulled the hammer back on my musket. The sound of the hammer cocking was loud in the still and quiet of the night.

Pa said, "What's that for?"

I said, "If this is a trap, I'm going to shoot our guide."

I didn't really think it was a trap but I always thought one should be cautious. We were whispering in English. The guide didn't understand the words but he probably got the message from the sound of the hammer being cocked.

Pa didn't cock his musket but I noticed that his, and each of the others close enough to be seen by me, was in a ready position. We mostly carried our short-barreled muskets in hand while riding at night and put our rifles in a scabbard. This was reversed while riding during daylight. Rifles have a much greater range.

Running Dog and eleven braves were in a cold camp. Pa had said there should be no campfires on the trip, except during the daytime. Those daytime fires were to be small and fueled with dry wood so there would be a minimum of smoke.

Two days later, while camped for the day, Running Dog said we would reach the village that night. Pa had him draw a picture of the camp in the dirt. Pa then asked questions about the camp and the surrounding terrain for most of an hour. We learned there was a creek along one side of the village shallow enough to walk across, the creek bank was cleared of brush on both sides of the creek, and that there were twenty houses in the village. The village was spread over six acres. The surrounding fifteen acres were mostly cleared and had been farmed. Since the village had been there for five years, Spotted Horse having settled there after the Seminole War, most of the nearby trees had been cut for building or for firewood. It soon became apparent we could approach the shelters, without detection, only at night. Because of their dogs, we would also have to approach from downwind.

Pa asked, "How many rifles do they have?"

Running Dog replied, "None of them have long rifles like yours. They have short-barreled English or Spanish muskets."

We had already observed that Running Dog's band had only English muskets. Though supplying them with powder and shot, Pa hadn't offered them any rifles.

Pa said, "I want to take advantage of the range of our rifles. I would suggest that my men dismount and creep up close before daylight. We'll position ourselves sixty yards from the closest houses. You and your men would remain on your horses two hundred yards from the houses. When it's light enough to see the sights on a musket, your riders would ride in with fire buckets filled with hot coals and torch a few houses to provide good shooting light and get them out into the open. You would also shoot at any fighters who appear. Once you've torched the houses and fired your weapons, you would continue riding until out of range. There, you would reload your weapons and keep their warriors from running in that direction. Because of the burning houses, we'll have them out in the open and visible. If they have storage sheds, don't burn those. We'll want what's inside."

Running Dog said, "That sounds like a good plan except for one thing. Some of Spotted Horse's warriors will soon be on their horses. How will you know to shoot them and not us?"

Without answering, Pa reached in his pack and took out a stack of yellow, triangular pieces of cloth.

He said, "Each of us will tie one of these around our neck."

I made a mental note that Pa had suggested how the battle was to occur. Pa was our leader but Running Dog was the chief of his people. Though they talked about plans for a couple of hours, Pa's battle plan was agreed on.

Once in position that morning, we waited impatiently for it to be almost light enough to shoot. It was still too dark to see

77

Running Dog's warriors who were 150 yards behind us when they started walking their horses toward the village. We could, however, see them when they got within fifty yards of us. Their fire buckets of hot coals in hand, they passed through our position at a run. We could then see some movement near the Indian houses and several shots rang out. Running Dog's warriors fired those shots. As Running Dog's warriors swept through the village and tossed their fireboxes onto thatched roofs, the dry roofs sprang to life with fire. The whole world lit up then.

One adult male, who emerged from the house I was assigned, dropped his musket and fell forward as my shot struck him in the side. For the next twenty seconds I was so busy loading my rifle and observing my assigned houses that I couldn't see what was happening to the others of our party. I could hear our people fire their rifles, though. It was then quiet, as we were all busy reloading. In the meantime there were a few shots fired from the village.

Because everyone was busy reloading and there had been no shots fired from our position for a full twenty seconds, it was so quiet the Seminoles didn't know where all of us were. Lots of them ran toward us. They knew where the riders had gone who set their houses on fire and were running in the other direction. I was finishing reloading my rifle when a young man about my age armed with a musket, a couple of adult women, and several children emerged from a house I was assigned and ran toward me. When the young man running toward the stump behind which I was kneeling was at thirty yards, I shot him in the chest with my rifle. Standing, I lifted my musket and, in Muskogee, ordered the women and children behind him to lie face down. They did as ordered. I then kneeled behind my tree stump and reloaded my rifle.

Though there was mass confusion and Indians running everywhere, the shooting had about died down by the time I finished reloading. Running Dog's braves, on horseback, were busy rounding Spotted Horse's clan up in the middle of the village. We had killed or mortally wounded most of the warriors. Those being rounded up were women and children, a few wounded warriors, and slaves.

I then stood, ordered my captives to their feet, and walked over near them. My captives included an Indian woman and three Indian children, and a black woman with her small daughter.

To the black woman, I said in English, "Do you speak English?"

"Yes, suh," she replied.

"How long have you lived here?"

"Six months, suh."

"Where did you come from?"

"I was taken during a raid in southwest Georgia and brought here."

"You were a slave there?"

"Yes, suh, but my massa was killed in the raid."

"Do you have a husband?"

"Yes, suh, someplace in north Georgia if he is still alive. I also have older children there. I was traded for and carried south before I was stolen."

Pa then walked up. Running Dog and two of his braves also rode up on their ponies. Using their ponies, the braves started herding my captives toward the large group they had gathered.

Shouting at the braves, I pointed at the black woman and said in Muskogee, "Leave her and her daughter here."

Confused, the Indians stopped their activity while the black woman and girl walked toward me. She obviously understood some Muskogee. At that moment the youth I had shot in the chest rolled over and lined his musket up on Running Dog. Since I was standing with my musket held in both hands across my body, it was pointed toward the Indian boy. Moving the barrel of my musket slightly without raising it to my shoulder, I shot him again. Other than that slight motion, there would not have been enough time for anyone to move. For a few seconds everything seemed to move in slow motion; I began to reload my weapon and Running Dog sat on his horse thinking about his near death.

He then said to his braves, "Leave anyone he wants," meaning me.

Pa said, "What's this about the woman, boy?"

I said, "I caught her, Pa. I've talked with her and know her story and I'm going to say what happens to her. She deserves better than what has happened to her."

Pa said, "You have a soft spot that's going to get you killed someday. Also, she might rather go with them."

I said, "I'll let her say."

Without answering, Pa went to get our horses.

As the black woman walked over by me, I pointed at the group of captives and said, "You can go with them if you want to."

"No, suh," she replied. "I don't want to."

"Then think about what you'd like to do," I said.

"There's not many things I can do," she replied. "If it's all right, I guess I'd best go with you."

I then got busy helping the others gather the plunder we would be taking from the village. For our part, Pa took mostly hides, corn, rice, and other things he could send out on a ship from our docks. Pa also took on consignment some of the goods the other people got that could be shipped from our dock. Running Dog's group seemed more interested in keeping the Indian women and children we had captured than anything else. Some of the white men were most interested in having the runaway slaves and the Indians' slaves we had taken. Besides the woman and child I captured, there were eight black slaves. Nothing was left behind but the few Indians who had escaped into the woods. With Spotted Horse among the dead and few of the Indians left, this clan would not be a threat to us anymore.

As we were preparing to leave the burned village, the black

woman said, "I can't go to Georgia. I don't have any papers. I don't want to stay here or go with Running Dog's people, either. Can I go with you?"

I had not responded to her earlier comment, so I said, "Yes. I'll turn you over to Ma and you can work with her until you decide what you want to do."

On the trip home, we traveled during the day. There was no need for, or possibility of, us using the stealth we had used on the way to attack the village. Our group was too large to move with stealth. The captive Indians and slaves and the additional horses and cattle we were driving greatly increased the size of our party.

I got kind of spoiled on the way home. The black woman, Norma, treated me as though she were my personal servant. Most of the other captives were not given the liberty she had to move about. Given our location in the wilderness and the fact that she had a three-year-old daughter, Norma wasn't about to run off. If it had been a good option for her, I wouldn't have cared if she had run off. Because of the herd of cattle, some people walking, and the horses being heavily laden, it took seven days for us to get home. Once there I explained Norma's situation to Ma and turned Norma over to her.

Norma's presence created a situation I had not anticipated. Joseph trimmed his beard and started washing his clothes and bathing more often. Not only were they obviously attracted to each other, they were the only two adult black people on our place. Though she continued to work for Ma during the day, not a month had passed before Norma and her daughter, Isabelle, moved into Joseph's cabin. Joseph had become a trusted member of the family so Norma instantly attained that same status.

The first meeting of Duval's council was in July of 1822 at Pensacola. In 1823, they moved the meeting place to St. Augustine. Since it had taken a month for the Pensacola delegation to travel through dangerous territory to reach St. Augustine, a midpoint was selected for future meetings. Tallahassee, a former

Indian town then being surveyed, was chosen as that site. The third and subsequent sessions of the Governor's Council also met in Tallahassee.

South of St. Augustine, at Moultrie Creek, in 1823, some of the Seminole chiefs signed a treaty giving up their claims to any land in Florida except for some reservation land that the treaty provided. Had the decline not already started, the Moultrie treaty would have started the decline of the Seminole Nation. The treaty later split the people, moving most to central Florida and leaving some on small reservations along the Apalachicola River. As a part of the treaty the Seminoles were also promised a small amount of money. Most of the money was never given because of various penalties that were assessed. The Indians were hesitant to leave their homes in north and east Florida for the reservations. Those who did leave soon found the reservation land in central Florida not suitable for the kind of things they normally planted.

Though they promised to turn in runaway slaves, the Seminoles did not keep their promise. Additionally, the Seminoles had close to a thousand black slaves of their own who were not runaways. While taking the runaways, white raiders also frequently took some of the Indians' slaves by force. This resulted in continuing trouble with the Seminoles.

Both the Florida and federal governments were concerned with the development of transportation routes in Florida. In 1824, the United States government allocated monies to repair the King's Road from Fernandina to St. Augustine and to reopen the Old Spanish Road from St. Augustine to Tallahassee. Those roads had long since grown over with trees and other vegetation. Such as they were, they were the only major government roads in Florida. All trees were to be cut so that the stumps were no more than twelve inches high. Thus, a wagon axle would clear them. However, work was not begun on the St. Augustine to Pensacola road until 1826, the same time that a road was constructed from Pa's docks on Black Creek to Micanopy. That road was mostly used to deliver cotton from the new farms around that area to Pa's docks for shipping.

Also in 1824 the Governor's Council of Florida acted to improve transportation. The council passed laws to establish ferries at various rivers and to build roads and canals. These actions were, in large part, motivated by the difficulty of traveling to Tallahassee from Pensacola and St. Augustine.

Continuing conflicts between the Indians and whites over land ownership led President Monroe to recommend in1824 that the Seminoles all be placed on a reservation or removed from Florida. Few of the Indians had moved to a reservation at that time. This recommendation led to a meeting in which the precise location of the reservation and conditions were negotiated. The meeting was held five miles south of St. Augustine.

Since Pa had a steady trade relationship with some local Indians and was concerned about the terms of any agreement, he decided to attend the meeting. Given that the meetings were held near St. Augustine, I went with Pa and took advantage of the opportunity to visit with Susan along the way.

The lead Indian negotiator, Neamathla, was an earlier adversary of ours in the first Seminole war of 1817. While we were with the Lower Creeks in Andrew Jackson's army, we had attacked and burned Neamathla's village. He was still bitter about that attack and proved to be a tough negotiator. Fortunately he didn't know about our contribution to burning his village.

Even though there were three times as many Indians at the meeting as there were white Americans, Neamathla was negotiating without a position of strength. In the end he gave up claims to 24,000,000 acres of fertile farmland in north Florida for a reservation consisting of only 4,000,000 acres in central Florida and a few thousand acres in west Florida. The Seminoles were also to receive other assistance, including $100,000 paid over the next twenty years. The Indians never saw much of the money. It was used mostly to pay claims against the Indians made by white landowners who said their slaves or livestock had been stolen. Looking out for himself, Neamathla arranged for his band and four other bands to stay on smaller reservations in west Florida. Without that concession the deal probably wouldn't have been made.

Pa and I mostly stayed in St. Augustine at night and rode out to the negotiation site each day. That was a situation I enjoyed. It put me in nightly contact with Susan. Finally seeing how things were shaping up, Pa and I returned to Black Creek. It was clear the concessions to Neamathla and his friends would not benefit Pa's trade. Their small reservations were over two hundred miles from our place. The northern boundary of the large reservation was a two-day ride from our place. Still, there were many local Indians who didn't leave their homes for the reservation. They continued to trade with us.

While it was mostly peaceful at our place, trouble with the Indians continued throughout most of Florida. Many of them, including Neamathla, never moved to their designated reservation. While the raiding of white-owned farms continued, our plantation and docks were left alone. That was probably because we were friendly with the Indians and treated them fairly. There were also a few other places that were not bothered.

Also in 1824, Ma delivered us a baby sister. Norma, whose job it was to act as nursemaid to the children and help with the housework, had a new charge. To keep people from asking questions about Norma, we let people think she was our slave. Since we had no papers on her as a slave or as a free person, that seemed the best for her and for us. Pa paid her the same as Joseph.

Late 1824 saw little done to move the Indians south to their new lands. Neamathla, then past his seventieth birthday, failed to live up to his treaty agreement. Arming his warriors, he acted as though there would be another war. It was only after Governor Duval, backed by several hundred white militia and some Lower

Creek Indians, confronted Neamathla that he backed down. Though several hundred Indians then left west Florida and went south, the situation remained tense. There were still a couple hundred Indians in west Florida and additional whites were moving there.

While there was some Indian trouble near us in early 1825, there wasn't too much done to us. Hearing a few shots in the woods one day, Asa and I went to check it out. We found two of our cows dead from gunshots. After following the moccasin tracks of the shooters for over two miles, we lost them as dark set in. We had been tracking too slow and careful to actually catch the culprits. There had been rumors that some Indians had shot horses or cattle and left them. They then set ambushes for those following. Rather than fall into something like that, we just went back home and butchered the cows.

January 15, 1826

In January of 1826, Susan and I were married. At Susan's mother's insistence, we had the wedding in St. Augustine. Due to the distance, time, and danger associated with the travel, only Asa attended from our family. On a previous trip I had made arrangements with a plantation owner, whose plantation was on the west side of the St. Johns River, to transport us across the river. We took the shorter, thirty-five-mile overland trip. Most of the land along the St. Johns that wasn't swamp belonged to one plantation owner or another by that time. Their ownership mostly originated from Spanish land grants.

Other than Asa and the preacher, only Susan's family members were in attendance. After spending the night at Susan's house we returned to Black Creek. Susan and I then moved into the cabin I had built.

All of northern Florida was soon booming. Land in this wild frontier to which men were moving to make their fortunes was there for the taking. Some men were bringing their families on oxcarts or wagons. Some whole families arrived walking. Those seeking land, gamblers, thieves, and adventurers of all kinds were among those arriving. The arrival of these people, most with dueling pistols in sashes hung from their neck and with a skinning knife in their belt, made for a dangerous situation. Dangers were equally as present from men fighting with knives and dueling pistols in the streets as they were from raiding Indians. I don't know why they were called dueling pistols; while there were a lot of fights using pistols, I never saw anyone duel with pistols. The only real duel I ever saw was with rifles at a hundred yards. One of those men was shot in the chest and killed. There was plenty of fighting, but not as duels. There were no rules in most of those fights.

The frontier was so wild that Governor Duval chose to have his family live in Pensacola, two hundred miles from the capital city of Tallahassee. Though it was chiefly a community of mud huts, Pensacola was fairly peaceful compared to the new settlements. In spite of the violence, by 1826 Tallahassee had grown to the point that there were a number of houses built with sawed lumber. Previously, there were only log or dirt cabins. There being no sawmills in most of the territory, log houses were still going up across most of the north end of Florida. Also, wood-burning stoves were not yet in use. Those of us who had enough money, or the skill to build them, had fireplaces. Less than one in five houses even had a fireplace at the time. Cooking was done outdoors over an open fire at most homes. There was no heat of any type in the houses without fireplaces. And there are many nights during the winter in north Florida that the temperature drops substantially below freezing.

Cotton was the largest crop, and while most of it was grown a considerable distance west of us, some was grown near us. Some was also grown in the Micanopy area. Much of what Pa shipped arrived on the new road that had been built from Fort Micanopy to Pa's docks. From Pa's place the road went to the Garys' ferry that had been recently put in place on Black Creek. In addition to tending my own place, I still worked for Pa some. Other than our family food plot, we mostly planted Indian corn, sweet potatoes, sugar cane, rye, and a few pumpkins. A small orchard was also soon to begin bearing fruit.

We didn't have any slaves so we did our own work, or hired it done. Pa could afford to buy slaves, he just had not bought any. New lands were then being opened to farming and slaves were in short supply. It had been illegal to import slaves for a long time, thus adding to the shortage. The smuggling of slaves from Cuba and other places became big business under those conditions. With Florida's extensive coastline it was a simple matter to unload a cargo of illegal slaves without being noticed.

Pa's dock would have been the perfect place to unload smuggled slaves, but he wouldn't have any part of it. Pa taught us to step up and take what we wanted if it didn't interfere with other people. He also believed most everyone, black and white, should be free to lead their life like they wanted. I guess that's why I had allowed Norma to choose what she wanted to do. Pa didn't follow the letter of the law, but he believed in doing to your neighbor as you would want him to do to you. His philosophy stood us in good stead most of the time. It also occasionally led to trouble.

An example of that trouble occurred in April of 1826. Susan and I had taken the sailing canoe and gone to St. Augustine to see her folks. On the return trip we ran into a dangerous situation. The wind was against us as we started down the St. Johns River. The St. Johns is a wide and lazy river, two or more miles wide in lots of places. Its sluggish movement is so slow that the slight wind would have blown us upstream and set us adrift had we been in a canoe without a sail. As a result of the wind we had to tack frequently to make headway downstream. It took us until almost dark to arrive at the mouth of Black Creek.

As we made the turn up the creek, Susan said, "Let's find a good spot to camp and spend the night on the creek bank. It's such a beautiful night that I would like for us to be alone. Other than turning the canoe on its side and propping it up to use the sail for a shelter, we won't even have to build a shelter."

I said, "Okay. There's a high, grassy spot a couple of miles ahead. With the wind behind us going up the creek, we could be there by good dark. Actually, with the moon up like it is, we could go all the way home."

She said, "We could, but we would be exhausted by the time we got there. I don't want to be tired out when we stop."

Having been married only a short time, I saw the wisdom in that.

Running before the wind, I had to roll the sail up some to slow our speed as dark set in and we proceeded up Black Creek. Slowed to about the speed of a walk, I watched the tops of the trees on each side of the creek to maintain our proper location in the creek. When the treetops vanished to my right, it signaled that we had arrived at the grass-covered bank. I rolled the sail in further and nosed the canoe silently into the bank.

It was then that we began to hear voices around the bend of the creek ahead of us. We could also see a flicker of light through the trees and brush covering the far bank of the creek. Due to the fact that the creek took a sharp bend to the left, we couldn't tell whether the light source was on the left or right bank of the creek. It could even have been from the surface of the creek.

Susan said, "What do you suppose is happening?"

"I don't know," I said. "There's no house for five miles and none that close to the creek."

Taking sensible precautions, we pulled the canoe from the creek and concealed it among some bushes. Our eyes were well adjusted to the dark and, with no overhead trees, we could see fairly well by the light from the half moon overhead.

Once the canoe was concealed, I said, "I'm going to check out the voices and lights. You stay here."

"I'm going with you," she said.

I said, "Okay, but let's check the priming of our weapons before we go."

I was armed with a rifle and a dueling pistol. Susan was armed with a musket, which was loaded with buck-and-ball. There was an extra musket in the canoe; I took it and left my rifle.

As we rounded the bend in the creek it soon became evident that the lights and sounds were coming from the same side of the creek we were on and two hundred yards upstream. The sound of voices increased and decreased but we could constantly hear the clink of iron on iron. It was a strange and confusing sound, such as I had heard before, though I couldn't place it.

We were only a hundred yards from the source of light when a chill ran up my spine as I recognized the sound. It was the sound of slaves walking in ankle chains.

A shiver went through my body as I turned to Susan and whispered, "Slave smugglers."

After a moment, she whispered, "Can we do something?"

I said, "I don't know what. We best stay clear of it. They would as soon kill us as look at us. This is a dangerous business."

Hearing the pop of a whip and the cry of a young voice, she said, "You could get closer and check it out. You could find out how many slavers there are. It's against the law to import slaves and has been for a long time. It just doesn't seem right."

I said, "What if we managed to take some or all of them, what would we do with them? They're from Cuba or some place like that. They don't have any papers so we couldn't turn them loose. If we managed to take the sloop they're on, and turned it over to them, they couldn't sail it. I can't think of anything we could do."

I could feel Susan flinch next to me as another whip cracked in the night and another voice cried out.

I said, "I'll go take a look. It looks like they're all unloaded."

"I'm coming," she said.

We were fifty yards from the sloop when the unloading was finished. Twelve wretched souls were huddled together near the water. The black men, six in number, had their ankles chained together with a little slack so they could walk. They were also chained together, in pairs, at the wrist. There were four women who had their ankles chained together with some slack so they could walk; they were not chained to each other. There were also two children, who were not chained.

It soon became apparent that two men would stay with the slaves. The others moved to get the sloop ready to depart. We heard some of their conversation.

An authoritative voice said, "I don't know where the hell they are. I'm certain this is the place and time we were to meet them. I'll take the sloop upstream for two or three miles and make sure. Since I'll be showing a lantern bow and stern, if this is the wrong place they'll hail us from the shore as we pass. In case something has gone wrong, I'm going to leave you two here with the cargo. They'll not be on the boat if there's trouble."

Another voice said, "What if the new owners show up to get them?"

The first voice said, "Make sure you get the other half of the money, then turn them over. When I come back, shout at me from shore. If I'm gone more than two or three hours, something's wrong."

With that they shoved off and, using only part of one jib, moved up the creek.

Susan whispered, "We could take them now."

I said, "Sure we could, but what would we do with them?"

She said, "Set them free. Or, they could work for your Pa and us, for a wage of course. We could figure that out later. We need to take them from those two men and get as far from here as possible before the sloop gets back. They can't track us in the dark."

"They can tomorrow."

"There's not enough of them. They'll have to stay with their boat."

I was also thinking that the people who were buying the slaves might show up. I didn't say anything about it, though.

While we were whispering, the two guards who were holding the slaves had them sit in two rows with their backs to the guards. The guards then started a small campfire. There was no reason for them not to start one. The closest house was more than five miles. Counting those in all directions, there were not more than fifty people within fifteen miles. If we had not had a head wind coming down the St. Johns we would have passed here long ago and it was impossible anyone else but us would see their fire.

I said, "Okay. I'll circle to the far side and get them between their fire and me. You sneak up behind that oak tree and wait for me to do something."

Looking at her, I said, "They might not give up without a fight. You have to be ready to shoot if they don't. Are you ready to use your gun?"

"Yes. I think so."

"You can't think so. You have to know so. Both of them are armed with a musket and pistol. They would kill us without a thought. Are you ready?"

"Yes."

That said, I eased around in the dark to get them between their fire and me.

Finally satisfied with my position behind them, which was thirty yards from the guards, I shouted, "Don't move or you'll die. One at a time, you on the left first, toss your weapons toward me."

Surprised and confused, one of them said, "Did you bring the money?"

I said, "You speak again and you're dead."

They tossed their muskets then, and their pistols and knives. I then had them blindfold each other.

The black Cuban slaves sat without a sound as this was being done. I couldn't know that they didn't understand a word that was being said.

I then said to the guards, "Lie on your bellies and spread your arms and legs."

After checking their blindfold to be sure they couldn't see, I hog-tied and gagged them.

As Susan came toward the fire, I said, "Don't say a word. There's no point in them hearing your voice."

To the slaves, I said, "Do you speak English?"

They obviously didn't, so I whispered to Susan, "Speak softly to them in Spanish so the guards can't hear you and see if they speak Spanish. Tell them to remain silent until we are out of hearing distance of the guards."

I didn't want the two men I had tied up to know my helper was a woman. Nor did I want them to remember her voice if they ever met her again.

After she whispered to them, they nodded vigorously that they spoke Spanish but they remained silent.

I then whispered to Susan, "Take two women with you and hide the canoe better, and bring my rifle and the other things. Hurry. We're leaving as soon as we can."

While they were hiding the canoe, I gathered the guards' weapons and waved for our new charges to come with me to a point where we were out of hearing of the smugglers. Susan and the black women then returned and I told Susan to tell them they were to keep silent and follow us. Back at the campfire, I got six fat-pine torches to burning and soaked the campfire in water to put it out. Without them being able to shout, and without the campfire, it would be awhile before the men on the sloop found their friends.

Our destination was our cabin. It would be twenty miles the way we would have to travel while avoiding swamps. Though a number of plans were flitting through my head, I didn't come up with much of a plan beyond getting to the cabin and getting the chains off those people. I rejected each plan I conjured up as the flaws in it became apparent. Actually, since we had taken the slaves in a raid and no one could legally claim them, we could have just kept them as slaves.

As we traveled, I was thinking about potential pursuit. My concern was not of pursuit by the boat's crew. They wouldn't know this territory and probably wouldn't want to leave their boat. If they did pursue us it would be with only two or three people; and it would be the next day when it was light. Susan and I could handle that. Also, we had the weapons we had taken from the two guards. After removing their priming, I had given them to the children to carry. Not being chained, they had no problem with their chore. I was thinking to arm some of the Cuban slaves with those guns if we needed help.

It was the people who would probably show up to claim the slaves that worried me. They would know the territory, would not be tied down to a boat, and could travel much faster than we could. Traveling through a trackless wilderness at night while their legs were chained together, and each two of the men chained together at a wrist, was slow. There were frequent falls. We couldn't have been making much more than one mile an hour. Worse still, the people who were to meet the boat had already partially paid for these slaves. They would be anxious to get the slaves back. And, worst of all, they would probably have access to dogs. While it might take several hours to locate and/or bring the dogs, dogs can track in the dark and at a high speed. The new owners would not be far behind unless something continued to keep them from the meeting place.

With no other choice, those Cuban slaves did whatever we said. In spite of the travel being punishing to them, they pushed ahead without a whimper or complaint. In addition to being handicapped by the irons and harassed by insects, they had not recently been fed. We learned they had not eaten during the previous day. Susan distributed what food we had. It would not have made a suitable meal for four people, much less twelve.

Since it was impossible that we could outrun any pursuit, we didn't try. After the first two hours we rested for fifteen minutes. Thereafter, we took a ten-minute break every hour. There was no point in hurrying. If pursuit came at night, the pursuing dogs would alert us. If they didn't have dogs, we would have a ten-hour head start before they could start tracking the next morning. I was considering a couple of plans in each case. Time and location would dictate which to use.

One consoling thought was that what the slavers were doing was illegal. It had long since been illegal to import slaves into the United States and its territories. Still, I wasn't exactly sure about the legality of what we were doing. I didn't see how it could be illegal, though. No one in the United States or the Territory of Florida legally owned those slaves.

When daylight came we had traveled only a dozen of the twenty miles to our cabin. Weakened from inadequate food, bleeding from raw places torn by leg irons, and swarmed by mosquitoes, our group followed us as best they could. With daylight came our first big break. As frequently happens during April in Florida, it rained. Flooded would be a better description. Nature gave us an opportunity to take some evasive action.

Turning ninety degrees to the right we traveled northwest. Expecting to pick up our trail at the point we were when the rain stopped, their owners would forge straight ahead on the route we had been following when they lost our trail. Morning rains usually lasted thirty minutes to an hour at that time of year. Turning at ninety degrees would take us out of the area they would search. Heavy rain would also wipe out our tracks and scent.

When the rain stopped, we stopped. We were one and a half

miles from where we were when the rain started. Our pursuers would lose our trail at the point they were when the rain started. If they didn't have dogs, and I suspect they did not because if so they probably would have caught us by that time, our pursuers would only have started on our trail at daylight and with our trail washed out would not have a clue as to where we were. If the rain covered a large enough area, they might not even get within five or ten miles of us. It seemed we had escaped. To be sure we had, I decided to remain in that place for the remainder of the day. That way we would not lay a new trail for the dogs to find. Our companions also needed the rest and needed food.

Once everyone was busy cutting palmetto fans and poles to use in building temporary shelters, I went in search of food. In less than an hour I shot a deer and returned. I could have shot one sooner but didn't want to shoot close to our camp even though logic would indicate that pursuit could be no closer than seven or eight miles and the shot would not be heard. We started a small fire, the smoke of which was hidden by the tall vegetation until it disbursed, and spent the rest of the day and that night eating and resting in camp.

It was after noon the next day when we arrived at our cabin. Asa was there. He had agreed to tend to the place until we returned.

Asa said, "Where in the world did you get them?"

As we walked to the tool shed I explained what happened. Though we had done a foolish thing, Asa didn't say that. Our family members always supported each other.

We freed the women first and sent them to the house with Susan to prepare some food.

As we worked to free them, Asa said, "What are you going to do with them?"

"I don't know," I said. "I was thinking they might go back to Cuba but they were slaves there. They would just be slaves there again. They can't go to Africa. They don't even know how to speak whatever they speak over there. They're mostly fourth- or fifth-generation Cubans so they only speak Spanish. I guess I'll put them to work until I figure out what to do with them. I only took them because Susan was with me and talked it up. Technically, they're mine now. Ships stop at Pa's docks. Some of them might even ship out, one or two at a time, as deckhands on ships going where they want to go."

Asa said, "There's a ship tied up there now. They're probably bound for Europe, though."

As we freed them from their chains, I gave them axle grease to put on the raw spots where the chains had rubbed and let them rest until after we had all eaten. Then I called them all together and had Susan translate.

I said, "For now, you're going to be working for me. You can't go traipsing around the territory without papers or you would certainly wind up in trouble. If anyone asks, you'll need to say you belong to me. Or just say you don't understand and refer them to me. I'm going to put you to work either here or on Pa's place. The pay is ten cents a day plus food and sleeping quarters. You'll sleep in the barn until you can get some cabins built. Also, there might be a chance for some of you to get a job when a ship docks here that's going to where you want to go. Others of you might save your money and buy passage to another country. Born as slaves in Cuba, and speaking only Spanish, you wouldn't do very well in Africa or Cuba. The best place for you might be South America. You're free to leave when you're ready to leave Florida and the United States. As long as you're here, you'll have to work for me."

After telling Asa, who was going to Pa's place for the night, to explain the situation to Pa, I left the Cuban slaves to talk together for the best part of an hour. They then asked to speak to me. Susan translated.

Their spokesman, Juan, said, "We have no place to go and wouldn't know how to get there if we did. We appreciate the opportunity to work here. We'll work hard."

I said, "Good." I then put everyone to work plowing, planting, clearing land, and building fences, except for one of the women who was assigned to cook, churn butter, and do other kinds of housework.

Within days Pa had a couple of them working over at his place. Within the month, one of them left on a ship working as a deckhand.

A number of towns across the Territory had developed and taken on important functions by 1826. In addition to Cow Town—which had been renamed Jacksonville—Key West, at the tip of Florida, had developed into a salvage town. Across the middle and western parts of north Florida, from the Suwannee River to Pensacola, the cotton business was booming. Tallahassee was growing into a real capital city, in spite of the fact that it was still one of the wildest of the frontier towns. There were still gunfights or knife fights there almost daily.

The Indians who had been moved south in Florida faced a desperate situation. While they had been assured that white people would not be allowed to trespass on their property, trespass was a common practice. Some plantation owners and other people intent on stealing slaves, horses, and cattle continually made raids into the new Indian lands.

Many of the chiefs and other Indian leaders owned slaves. Their slaves were being claimed and taken by those searching for runaways. While trespass on Indian land was a common practice of whites, it was strictly forbidden for the Indians to leave their reservation. Indians were subject to arrest, loss of their guns, and being whipped if found off the reservation. Even though they were subject to arrest by any white person who chose to do so, in reality many Indians lived in peace off the reservation. In the northeastern part of Florida there were not enough white people to cause the Indians much trouble even if they wanted to.

In spite of being confined to the reservation, all over north

Florida the Seminoles visited stores, trading posts, and plantations to trade for cloth and other goods they didn't have. The Indian-black relationship was such that there were sometimes amorous moments between the Indians and plantation slaves during these visits. Some Indians took spouses who had to remain as slaves on plantations. Such secret relationships sometimes turned into a situation where the Indian bought the spouse. With less wealthy Indians, sometimes the spouse ran away to be with their husband or wife.

The Cuban slaves we rescued had been living with us for four months when a member of Chief King Philip's band, Four Toes, approached me about one of them. Four Toes had five toes on each foot. He got the name Four Toes because the second and third of his toes were webbed together on each of his feet.

He said, "I've taken Maria for a wife. I want to buy her from you."

His request was a shock to me. Even though Four Toes had been spending at least one night each week with Maria, I was unaware of it.

I said, "What does Maria say to this?"

He said, "She wants to go with me."

I said, "I'll speak to Maria. If she wants to go, okay. What do you think she's worth?"

He said, "She's worth four hundred dollars but I don't have that much. I offer a good horse and some cattle worth two hundred. I'll bring more cattle worth two hundred within the next year."

I said, "I don't want stolen cattle."

He said, "Then how am I supposed to get them?"

Smiling, I said, "You wait here, I'll speak to Maria."

Inside the house—Maria was our house worker—I said, "Susan, tell Maria that Four Toes wants to buy her. What does she say?"

Susan said, "What do you mean, buy her? We don't own her."

I said, "Though I planned to let her go when she has a place to go and the means to get there, Four Toes recognizes our ownership. Such a gift would place him under a heavy debt and he could never again feel like a free man. So, I plan to let him have her for half or less of what he offered."

Though she didn't speak much English, Maria waited patiently until I looked back at her. She then said in broken English, "I want to go with Four Toes. I'm going to have his child."

Ignoring Susan, who was still talking to me, I went outside to speak with Four Toes.

Outside, I said, "Maria wants to go with you. Where are the horses and cattle you want to trade?"

He said, "I offer the horse on my lead rope and twenty-five cattle, which I'll deliver in three days. I'll bring fifty more cattle within one year."

The horse he offered was worth lots of money.

I said, "I don't want stolen cattle. You can keep the horse for Maria to ride to your village. When you return him, bring fifteen cattle. Because we're friends, and because Maria is with your child, I'll give her to you for the horse and fifteen cattle."

Turning to the cabin I shouted, "Maria."

She and Susan were already coming out the door.

I said, "Susan, write Four Toes a bill of sale in English and Spanish for Maria. He'll need it in case someone tries to steal her."

To Four Toes, I said, "If anyone tries to take Maria, come directly to get me."

Because of the many complaints by white people, in 1827 the Legislative Council of the Florida Territory passed a law setting a specific penalty for Seminoles who left the reservation. The penalty was thirty-nine lashes with a whip on the bare back and the loss of their gun. Any white person could legally take the gun from an Indian who was off the reservation and administer the lashes. Due to the fact that reservation boundaries were not marked, undeserved punishment was given to some Indians. Lots of us didn't like the law and ignored it completely.

As time passed, the incidence of plundering of Indian possessions and the taking of the Indians' slaves became more and more of a problem. Additionally there was considerable settling on, and the claiming of, Indian lands by whites. In spite of requests for relief by the Indian agents, chiefs, and those of us who respected the Indians' rights, the United States government ignored those problems. As the complaints became more frequent, the government decided the solution was to remove the Indians from Florida.

It wasn't necessary for the white settlers to take the Indians' land. There were plenty of opportunities to buy land at $1.25 an acre, the going government price. There was a public land sale scheduled at St. Augustine for the second day of May, 1828. It was the first of several planned for that city. The sale was announced in the Jacksonville newspaper. Periodic sales had previously been held in Tallahassee. Sales were supposed to continue in both towns.

Pa, Asa, and George showed up to buy land in the May 1828 sale. Upon their arrival in St. Augustine, they found the sale had been rescheduled for the next year. The 1829 sale, too, was ultimately to be cancelled. Sales were regularly scheduled and held in Tallahassee. It being two hundred miles away—ten days of hard travel for us to get to Tallahassee on horseback—and then the sale might be cancelled, we did not ever go to those sales. In spite of there being lots of cheap land, there were those people who didn't have the money or who just wanted land for free so they squatted on reservation land.

June 12, 1828

In June a third member of the twelve Cuban slaves left. Taking a job as a deckhand on Captain Lewis' ship, he sailed for Norway and points beyond. Three days later Susan announced we would be having our first child. It had been three years since we married and we were wondering if it was possible for us to have children.

While there was still considerable trouble with the Indians at the time, we hadn't had any trouble in a couple of years. Most of our troubles were with white thieves. The size of our combined properties and the number of loyal people we had under salary held even that problem to a minimum. We also didn't overreact to an occasional missing cow or sheep, some of which might have gone down in a bog. Others might have vanished as some hungry Indians or settlers passed through. Since land used for farming was fenced and livestock roamed free on private and public lands, the occasional loss of a cow, hog, or sheep sometimes went unnoticed. Sometimes, however, several cattle would go astray at once and their loss would be noticed.

On one such occasion we became aware of some missing cattle soon enough to do something about it. The cattle were taken soon after a heavy rain. The damp ground and deep hoof imprints made for easy tracking. Three days later we caught up with the cattle where they were in a pen in Camden County, Georgia. At the time we got there a sale appeared to be under way between the thieves and a buyer. While there was little evidence to support our assumption, we assumed this was a usual place stolen cattle were taken.

While observing the transaction from concealment in the woods, we checked the priming of our weapons. Pa also assigned each of us to shoot one of them if a fight started. Pa was to hold his fire in case one of us missed, and was to shoot that person. As Pa, Asa, John Hunter, Joseph, and I rode in, we leveled our cocked weapons at the four men standing by the cow pen. Though it was against the law for a black person to be in possession of a gun under any circumstance, in Joseph's case we always ignored that law. We trusted him more than we did most white men. Knowing they were in trouble, the suspected thieves glanced about at each other as if looking for someone to provide a way out of the situation.

Stopping twenty yards from them, Pa said, "Boys, I see most of the cattle in your pen are wearing I. J.'s or my brand and ear mark. All of you lay your weapons down and we'll figure out how this happened and what to do about it."

None of them answered immediately. Only one of them had a weapon in his hands. They all had either one or two pistols in their sash, however. Since they hadn't had time to check the priming of their weapons, there was the possibility their priming had been lost and some of their weapons wouldn't fire. Also, we were holding our weapons in such a way that they were covered. They didn't have a single weapon covering us. Still, some of them didn't think they could afford to abandon their weapons. One man summed it up pretty well but he was mistaken. Pa always gave everyone a chance to tell his story.

The suspected thief said, "Boys, they're going to hang us. We just as well go down trying."

That said, three of them went for their weapons and ducked for cover. The fourth man fell on the ground and covered his head with his hands. It was lucky for him because he was assigned to me and I held my fire. When the shooting was over he was the only one of them still alive. In fact, he wasn't even hurt. The other three fired only one shot between them and it went into the ground.

Dismounting, I said to the fourth man, "You can get up and tell your story."

I also took the pistol from his sash.

He said, "I'm not with these people. I was just passing through."

Pa said, "Sure, you were. We've been tracking three men who were driving our cattle. If those three are the thieves, that leaves you as the buyer."

The man said, "Honest. I didn't have anything to do with your cattle."

Pa said, "Then why did we see you hand them money?"

The man was really frightened but he managed to say, "I owed them some money."

Asa, who had searched the three dead men said, "Pa there's a hundred dollars on them. That's about the amount they would get for our stolen cattle."

Pa said, "The evidence is pretty strong. What should we do with him?"

It was common in those days to shoot or hang cattle thieves. Still, I wasn't sure.

I said, "Pa, you're still well known in Camden County. You could take him over to the county seat and let them hang him legal. It would spread the word and send a message. Asa could go with you. Joseph, John, and I could take any money or other goods we want from here for our trouble and start our cattle home."

Pa said, "We'll take him in. I'll take John and Asa along and we'll drive the cattle to town and sell them there. That way we won't have to drive the cattle all the way home. Also, the owners of the extra cattle that are in the pen might be found there. If not, I guess they're ours. You and Joseph take these men's outfits and anything else worth carrying from here, and head for home. We'll be there in a few days."

After burying the dead and reading over them, we all rested our animals until the next morning. We then went our separate ways.

Also in 1828, our friend and former leader in battle, Andrew Jackson, was elected president of the United States. Since Florida was only a territory, we had no vote in the election. Everyone knew Jackson had fought in Florida and that he had a strong feeling about the Indian situation. They assumed he would quickly solve the Indian problems in the territory, probably by moving them west.

Susan, who had been frisky and robust all her life, became sickly in the last couple of months before the baby was due. She attributed her illness to morning sickness. Since three of the Cuban women slaves were still staying with us, Susan had nothing to do but rest and she assured us she would be all right. In spite of her reassurance I brought Ma over to see her every couple of days. I would have had Susan see a doctor but the only one anyone knew about lived in Jacksonville. Jacksonville was a full day away on a good horse, one way. The trip to take Susan there in a cart would have taken twice as long. Also, the jolting would have done her more harm than any good she might have gotten from a doctor's visit.

It was February 1, 1829, that Susan told me I should go get Ma because the baby was coming. When I got back with Ma, I sat on a bench in front of the house while Ma and the Cuban women tended Susan. It wasn't more than thirty minutes before Ma came out and put her arms around me. I knew there was trouble before she spoke.

Ma said, "We've lost her and the baby, son."

I couldn't speak. I couldn't even bear to go in and see Susan and the baby. I just went off in the woods and sat by an oak tree until after dark. We buried them both the next morning.

Heartbroken, I signed everything over to Pa a few days later. I was planning to leave but didn't know where I was going. One of the Cuban men told me they would all go with me wherever I went. I told him to stay on and work for Pa. I didn't feel like I could try to build anything again just then.

As fate would have it, Captain Lewis' ship was tied up at Pa's dock at the time. He soon approached me and said, "Isaac, I understand your pain. Life aboard ship is about hard work and dull living. It still might be the best way to get some time behind you. I'm bound for Amsterdam in two days and could use a good man."

I accepted and left with him.

Life aboard ship was very different from what I had previously experienced. The only sailing I had ever done was in my canoe. Observing everything while working, within a week I had learned all the words, phrases, and activities necessary to become a useful member of the crew. Since I was good at arithmetic and could read and write, Captain Lewis started teaching me the skills necessary to navigate the ship. The hard work and a busy mind were helpful, but Susan's death still hung heavy over me.

Though everything was new to me, Captain Lewis said it was a routine crossing. We were in Amsterdam within two months. There, I learned that Holland's economy was in shambles from the earlier French occupation. They had only regained their independence from France a few years prior to my visit and the economy had not yet begun to recover.

The city of Amsterdam was what could be called a sailor's dream port. Money from any other country had a high exchange rate. Also ladies of the evening and drinks were readily available. I soon found that Susan was still too close a memory for me to participate with the other sailors. I busied myself with the unloading and loading of the ship during the days and stayed close to my bunk during the evenings.

We were docked in Amsterdam for two weeks before Captain Lewis acquired most of a load of goods bound for Spain. The captain had thought to take on cargo bound for the United States but was offered a premium price to go to Spain. Not wishing to go through the English Channel because of potential encounters with French or English warships, the captain would not ordinarily take cargo from that part of the world to Spain. At least the cargo was only going to La Coruna in northern Spain. Had it been destined for a city on the Mediterranean Sea, thus causing us to sail down the coast of Portugal, Captain Lewis would probably have turned the job down. Given the big potential profit and the fact the cargo was bound for northern Spain, he took the job. The cargo on board, we then rode the outgoing tide and set a course for the English Channel and Spain.

Although Captain Lewis' ship, the *Pracilla Ann,* was a merchant ship, she was not totally defenseless, having a twelve-pound cannon fore and aft. Additionally, there were enough weapons locked in the captain's cabin to repel any but the largest boarding party. Most of the crew members were unarmed except when the captain saw a need to arm them. Only Captain Lewis and three others, including me, carried a pistol in our sashes all the time. That was at the captain's direction. My long rifle and musket were locked in Lewis' cabin with the other arms. Not being able to depend on just arms for defense, Captain Lewis mostly used wit and sailing experience to keep his ship from falling to privateers. He always kept a man aloft during daylight hours. When a sail was sighted while on the open sea, he calculated a course that would allow us to avoid being cut off before dark, even if it meant changing course ninety degrees. We had used this tactic on a couple of occasions during the crossing from Jacksonville to Amsterdam. The problem with the English Channel was that there was not always adequate room for maneuvering. Without major incident, however, we did clear the channel.

Captain Lewis even took the precaution of flying the Spanish flag after we cleared the channel. In spite of his fears, we encountered no danger beyond some rough weather on the rest of that trip. At one point we had to string some ropes about the deck to hold on to as we went about our duties. We also took in all but enough sail to maintain control of the ship until the storm blew itself out. Almost another month passed before we were docked in La Coruna, Spain.

Since I had learned to speak some Spanish, I was more at ease in Spain than I had been in Amsterdam. There, I joined with some of the crew in enjoying some of the waterfront establishments.

Captain Lewis soon contracted for a cargo bound for Venezuela. After three hundred years of Spanish rule, Venezuela had declared its independence from Spain in 1811. For political or other reasons, the cargo's owner wanted us to list our destination as Cuba. I guess relations between Venezuela and its former rulers were a little rough at the time. What we were doing could be called smuggling but the price was right.

Leaving Spain, we sailed south to pick up the West Wind Drift, which would carry us to the Canary Islands. There, we planned to take on fresh water, fruit, and other supplies for the long run across the Atlantic to Venezuela.

We were four hundred miles west of Lisbon, Portugal, and had just picked up a good wind from the West Wind Drift when we ran into some trouble.

It was near noon when the lookout shouted, "Sail, ho!"

"Where away?" the captain shouted.

"Eighty degrees to starboard, sir."

"It's probably a ship bound from the Azores to Portugal," the captain said to no one in particular.

The Azores is a large group of islands, a hundred miles west of us and on line with Lisbon and us.

Fewer than fifteen minutes passed before the lookout shouted, "They've changed course, Captain. It's a course that'll cross our bow before dark if they're fast enough."

Without answering, the captain paced the deck, his hands folded behind his back.

After an additional thirty minutes passed, the sails of the other ship were visible to those of us standing on deck. Their change in course and angle of their new course showed they intended to intercept us. It was possible they would do so before dark. It soon became clear that their ship was less heavily loaded and faster than the *Pracilla Ann* was.

Turning to the helmsman, the captain said, "Bring her ten degrees to port."

This move required no sail adjustment. It also put us in a position to be running directly before the wind. And it placed us on a course parallel to the other ship. They would also have to come ten degrees to port to be on a course that could intercept us. Their new course would give us a small advantage because they would not be running the best line for their sails to catch the wind.

Within minutes they adjusted their course to intercept us. Had the captain turned twenty more degrees to port, we could have kept them out of gun range until dark for sure. I expected him to change course but he didn't.

Captain Lewis said, "Hold your course. I'm going to rest for a couple of hours. If there's any change in the next couple of hours, call me."

Mentally marking its position, I made it a point to not look at the other ship for thirty minutes. When I did look, it appeared from how little they had closed on us that it would be close to dark when they got within range, if they did.

This slow chase continued the rest of the day with little change. An hour before dark, with them still several hundred yards out of cannon range, Captain Lewis had the ship brought twenty more degrees to port. Before the other ship could adjust her course we had picked up an additional hundred yards. Captain Lewis then ordered us back twenty degrees to starboard as the other ship was turning to port. Still, theirs was the fastest ship and they continued to close.

It was fifteen minutes until dark when the captain said, "Load the stern gun with ball-and-bar. Use one and a half charge of powder and set the gun at maximum elevation. I want everyone to stand clear except the gunner in case the gun explodes. If they come within range before dark, we'll fire one round into their rigging. If we can spill a little of their air, we can slip away in the night."

A ball-and-bar load consists of two balls connected by a solid bar, which is one foot long. This is used to fire at the rigging of another ship. As it rotates going through the rigging, the ball-and-bar is intended to do considerable damage to the sails and ropes.

Turning to me he continued, "Isaac, run up the Stars and Stripes."

Neither ship had been showing a flag. Even after the flag of the United Sates was raised, the other ship showed no flag. They were still closing on us.

Dark comes quickly when the sun sets below the horizon of the ocean and it was almost dark when they fired at us from one of the twin twelve-pounders on their bow. The cannonball splashed in the water fifty yards behind us. The shot was obviously intended as a warning for us to heave to. Wanting her as a prize, they didn't want to hit our ship if they didn't have to.

Less than a minute had passed when the Captain Lewis shouted to our gunner, "The next time the stern raises on a wave, fire."

The thunder of the twelve-pound cannon was deafening with the extra half-charge of powder in the gun. It was too dark to see at the distance but the round must have torn through sails and cut several of their lines because sails flapped loose in the wind and their ship slowed. Their captain then ordered them to turn for a broadside, probably into our rigging. It was too late for that. By the time they fired it was too dark to line their big guns up properly on us. Captain Lewis had cut it pretty close, dark came just in time. Also, it's a good thing our one shot did the job Captain Lewis had planned for it. The gun would have been useless for a second shot. The gun broke its lines when it recoiled from the overload of powder, and its carriage was lying on its side on the deck.

With the other ship's rigging damaged and us in total darkness, Captain Lewis then returned on our original course for the Canaries. We were never to learn who had been chasing us.

Twelve days later we dropped anchor at Tenerife, the biggest of the Canary Islands, and took on the supplies we needed. We then set sail and rode the Canaries currents and the North Equatorial Current toward Venezuela, which was almost three thousand miles away.

While the Spanish authorities would have pitched a fit if they knew our cargo was going to Venezuela, the Venezuelan authorities were happy it was coming there. We didn't have any trouble unloading. The captain was then able to pick up some cargo for Puerto Rico and Cuba. From there, we would eventually work our way back to Florida.

Carrying cargo from Venezuela to Puerto Rico seemed strange since Puerto Rico was a Spanish possession and Venezuela had torn itself free from Spain. Puerto Rico had belonged to Spain since Columbus claimed it in 1493. Like Venezuela, Puerto Rico's language is primarily Spanish. Having been there since 1510 when they were first brought as slaves to dig for gold and work the plantations, the Africans' descendants in Puerto Rico spoke only Spanish by the time we went there. The native Indians, Arawaks, had long since died out from European-introduced diseases, or had intermarried with the Spanish just as the Arawaks in Florida had. They had vanished a century earlier. Thus, Spanish was the language spoken on the island. Because of my ability to speak some Spanish, the stopovers in those places were enjoyable for me.

Due to continued pirate raids along the coast, Cuba was slow to develop its economy, other than its plantations. In 1830 Cuba was a thriving island, producing an abundance of tobacco and sugar. Lots of these products were sold in the United States. Such was our cargo as we left Cuba for New York. Also, some Cubans were engaged in manufacturing goods. One thing that caught my interest was a small-caliber rifle they were making. Thinking the rifle would be economical in the use of powder and lead for practice and for shooting small game, I got Captain Lewis' permission to purchase ten rifles to carry to Florida. Those rifles could easily be traded for a profit and would make good presents for family and friends.

Having been gone for almost a year, and most of our crew being from the St. Johns River area, we were to stop there on our way to New York. Also, Captain Lewis' wife and nine children were there.

As we approached our destination on the St. Johns, I said to Captain Lewis, "I think I'll leave you here. I appreciate you giving me a job and helping me get over Susan. However, it's time for me to get back to farming and trying to claim part of Florida for my family. I still hope to have a family some day."

He said, "I would appreciate it if you stayed on for the trip to New York and back. If you'll get a list of what your Pa wants, I'll pick his things up there and we'll come directly back from New York to Black Creek. I'll then pick up a load of furs, produce, and so forth for the New York market, or a load of timber for Norway. Either would be satisfactory. It'll be dark by the time we get docked. Stay at my house for the night and go to Black Creek tomorrow. You can take one of my horses. I'll be here for four days."

I said, "I'll do it. However, if something happens and I don't get back, go without me. Given the time it will take you to go to New York and back, Pa can have you a load ready. He always needs metal of various kinds for the blacksmith shop and rods for nail making. You could also bring cloth and the various other things he always buys to use as trade goods."

Lots of things had changed since I spent the time at Captain Lewis' house telling his children about Indian fighting. Two of the boys were married. Louisa, the six-year-old who had climbed on my knee while I talked, was fourteen. She and her two younger sisters had turned into beautiful young ladies. I teased Louisa some about sitting on my knee, and about being almost old enough to marry.

Not embarrassed in the least, she retorted, "I'm waiting until I grow up so I can marry you, Isaac."

Though it was a fun evening and we were up late, I was up early and gone an hour before daylight. It was a long, hard trip but I traveled the twenty-plus miles to Pa's place by early afternoon. The dogs announced my arrival at home. When I spoke to them they hushed and wagged their tails around my feet. Before the dogs stopped barking, Pa and others appeared from various places with guns.

I had not shaved for some time and had lost some weight, so Pa said, "Is that you, Isaac?"

"Yes, sir," I said. "I'm home for a couple of days."

Ma rushed out to hug and welcome me. Soon all my brothers and sisters had gathered. Most of the boys in our family married late in life, so they were still home at that time. The girls were still young.

I told them about my adventures, and we stayed up until almost nine that night. I gave each of them one of the small-caliber rifles. The next day I hung around Pa and my various brothers, told them more about my adventures, and learned what had happened in Florida over the past year.

Because of Indian Agent Humphreys' insistence, by 1830 the Seminoles had turned in some of the slaves they had stolen and some of the runaways living near them. Humphreys and Governor Duval defended the rights of the Indians to keep their own slaves. In spite of the fact that they turned in some slaves, frequent complaints arrived at the governor's and the president's offices about the slow way the Seminoles were responding.

Larger problems existed with the Indians in the middle of the Territory of Florida than with those in west Florida. The sandy, unproductive nature of central Florida's land was causing a famine and starvation for the Indians. To further aggravate the situation, those Indians in the middle of the territory were strictly confined to their reservations. The Indians in west Florida were allowed to travel from their lands to the plantations and cities where they peddled, or traded their goods, fish, and freshly killed game for whatever they wanted.

President Jackson was using considerable pressure to bring about the removal of all Indians from the eastern United States and the Territory of Florida. The plan was to resettle them in the west. There was strong support throughout the government for the passage of an Indian Removal Act that would initiate their removal and make it legal. I was sure we would hear more about that act as time passed.

At that time Florida was still sparsely populated, especially northeast Florida. The best estimate by the government was that there were a total of only thirty-five thousand people in Florida. This estimate included people of all nationalities and colors. Of the total, only a tiny fraction lived in northeast Florida. A large majority lived west of the Suwannee River. In spite of their small number, Andrew Jackson wanted the Indians out of the way so white Americans could easily settle the territory, thus laying a solid and permanent claim to all of Florida by the United States.

Pa also caught me up on all the local news. One subject was of particular interest.

Pa said, "While on a visit shortly after you left, Running Dog asked about you. I told him about Susan and that you had left on a ship."

I said, "Was it a courtesy call or did he want something?"

"At first I assumed it was a courtesy call. After I told him what happened and where you were, he became concerned. I could see your situation really troubled him. Ever since he gave you the roan gelding, I've suspected he felt close to you. There's also the time you shot the Indian who would have killed him."

"He didn't say anything else?"

"Not at the time. The next day he said to tell you he wanted to see you when you got home."

"I don't have time to look him up now. I told the captain I'd go to New York with him three days from now."

"That's not all. Running Dog has been back twice since then. He inquired about you both times. Also, he came alone both times. I suspect he came solely for the purpose of seeing you. He did trade for a couple of small things, but I think the trading was just an excuse to be here and check on you."

"I probably won't be gone more than a month on this trip. If he comes back, tell him I'll find him shortly after I get back."

March 15, 1830

I arrived back at Captain Lewis' house before dark. We were to sail the next morning so the other crew members spent the hours until dark checking the ship to be sure it was ready. Captain Lewis had already stored provisions and fresh water for the ten-day run to New York.

Though the rest of the crew ate supper on the ship, the captain asked me to join him at his house for the evening meal. Happy for the chance to talk with his boys and tease the girls, I accepted.

Captain Lewis' house was a large, European-style house with a big front porch. We men sat on the porch, had a drink of rum, and talked while the captain's wife and daughters finished preparing the meal. As usual the talk drifted back and forth between Indian problems and shipping. Pracilla, Captain Lewis' wife, whom his ship was named after, soon told us to wash up for supper.

At the table I found myself sitting between Louisa and Eliza, one of Louisa's younger sisters.

Always one to tease his sisters, Joseph, the oldest boy, said, "Louisa placed the chairs, Isaac. It looks like she's set her bonnet for you."

Pracilla said, "Don't pester the girls, Joseph."

Louisa said, "It's all right, Ma. Isaac knows I plan to marry him when I grow up."

I said, "You'll make someone a fine wife in a few years. You and your sisters better tend to your reading and arithmetic, though. There'll come a time when everyone will need to be able to read and write. I'm not going to have a wife who can't read."

"That's what I keep telling them," their ma said. "Louisa does a good job of reading, too."

Since Louisa wasn't upset at being teased, Joseph stopped doing it. The talk around the table then turned to the ongoing work on the plantation and the next day's departure. Following an after-supper drink of rum with the boys, I thanked the ladies for the meal, excused myself, and turned in on my bunk on the *Pracilla Ann.*

We stopped at Pilots Point near Jacksonville at noon the next day. The captain stopped and paid the pilot fee without picking up a pilot. There was a two-dollar fee if you picked up a pilot. The fee was fifty cents less if no pilot was used. Captain Lewis knew the waters as well as anyone. Picking up a pilot and having to let him off would have been a waste of time. Also, it didn't hurt to save four bits here and there. After getting well seaward of the Hazard Lighthouse we set a north-northeast course.

We soon picked up the Gulf Stream and with a favorable wind were docked at New York City seven days later. Unless the wind changed, with the handicap of sailing against the Gulf Stream the return trip would take almost three times as long.

After settling on a price for his cargo, the captain said, "This is one of the roughest waterfronts you'll ever visit. Since we'll be taking a bag of money with us back to Florida, everyone needs to keep a sharp lookout at all times. I'll also need three men to go with me to the bank when I get the money."

Pointing at two others, and me, he continued, "Each of you three carry a pistol and a musket loaded with buck-and-ball."

Once our cargo was offloaded and we had picked up cargo for Charleston, Jacksonville, and Pa's warehouse on Black Creek, the four of us left for the bank. Without telling him what our mission was, the captain hired a rig and driver.

The captain said, "Isaac, sit up by the driver. Let him drive around aimlessly for ten minutes and then tell him where we're going. If anyone's following us, that'll give us time to figure it out."

I did as I was told. There was no sign of anyone following us and twenty minutes later we were at the bank. The captain and one man went in the bank for the money while another man and I stayed with the rig. They soon returned carrying a bag. Within seconds we were headed for the ship. We had been traveling less than five minutes when it was obvious that a rig had come off a side street and was following and closing on us.

Palming a pistol, I said to the driver, "Trot the horses, we need to get to the ship ahead of that rig."

He said, "I don't want to be in the middle of a gunfight."

I said, "If you don't beat that rig to the ship, you'll probably be in the middle of one."

He did what I might have done had I been in his shoes. Throwing me the reins, he jumped.

I soon had the horses at a run. Knowing generally where the ship was, but not being an expert on the exact streets to take, I did the best I could. Guessing as to which street to take, I turned right at such a speed as to make the rig slide sideways. Throwing sand and gravel and scattering pedestrians, we continued at a breakneck speed. Realizing we were on the wrong street, I then did the same on a left turn at the next street. This maneuver, followed by another left turn at the next street to get back to where we had been, caused us to lose our pursuers. It wasn't planned like that; the other rig just didn't get to the corner in time to see where we went.

I then got on the right street to make a straight run to the ship. We left the rig standing, boarded the ship, tossed our mooring lines, and were shoving off when the rig that was chasing us came racing up. Taking cover at various places on the ship, we had them covered as they emerged from the carriage. Fortunately they emerged without guns in hand, for I had a bead on the first one out.

He shouted, "Captain, the banker hired us to follow you to your ship. With you carrying all that money, he was concerned for your safety. I'll report to him that he need not have been concerned."

Tossing a coin across the opening water between our boat and the dock, the captain said, "This is for our driver. He bailed out when he thought there was trouble so I didn't get to pay him."

The man said, "I'll see he gets it. I've got a job for the man who took the reins when the driver jumped."

I said, "Thanks, anyway. I've got to get back to Florida. There's an Indian there who's looking for me about something that might be important."

Stopping at Charleston and Jacksonville to unload and pick up more cargo, it took us twenty-two days to get back to Black Creek. Since we went to Black Creek to unload Pa's supplies before Captain Lewis went up the St. Johns River to his house, I didn't get to visit with his family.

As they shoved off from the dock at Pa's place I said, "Tell the ladies I sent them greetings and that I enjoyed the visit when last there."

Captain Lewis said, "I'll do that. You're welcome at our place any time. Also, there's work for you on my ship or farm if and when you want it."

Lifting my hand to the captain in farewell, I turned to Pa and said, "Running Dog's visits have been on my mind. Has he been here again?"

"No. He hasn't been seen," Pa said.

Since it was approaching dark, I then went to my cabin. Many of the stumps had been removed from the field and instead of being planted between stumps as they were when we first started farming there, the crops were laid out in neat rows. The corn was standing over a foot high. It was a beautiful sight and time of year. At the same time I was thinking those thoughts, Susan's death still hung heavy over the place.

Before the night was over I decided I wasn't ready to be back on the farm. Everything I looked at still reminded me of Susan. Also, it soon became apparent that I wasn't needed there. Pa had worked out a sharecropping arrangement with the Cubans who were working my land. The Cubans' enthusiasm and quality of work were such that we made more money than if we were paying them a salary. They also made more money.

Moving in at Ma's house, I stayed and visited with the family for a few days. All that time I was thinking about Running Dog and what he wanted. Then, still feeling the need for some time alone, I told everyone at the supper table that I was going the next day to look for Running Dog.

My Spanish mare had died of old age, so I left riding the roan gelding and leading two packhorses. In addition to carrying more food than I could possibly eat in six months, I carried three of the smaller-caliber Spanish rifles, my usual rifle, and a brace of dueling pistols. I figured to give one of the Spanish rifles to Running Dog and possibly trade another. Having found the Spanish weapon to be very accurate, I also planned to use one for small game. As to the large amount of food, Pa had told me that times were hard on the reservation. Food would be in short supply.

Since Running Dog's band was among those who had moved to the reservation, I didn't know exactly where to find him. The main reservations consisted of over 4,000,000 acres in the heart of Florida. I knew generally where the boundaries of the reservations were. The boundaries were spelled out in the treaty drawn up at Camp Moultrie in September of 1828. Without survey markers it would be impossible for anyone to know for sure when he or she was on or off the reservation. At some places it would be possible to miss its boundary by twenty-five miles. While the treaty gave locations such as Salarky's settlement, Okahumkee, the Big Hammock, and a point twenty miles from the Atlantic Ocean, one would have to know where the former three were and only a survey could produce the latter point. The reservation was not yet completely surveyed. Walking or riding a horse through the wilderness, one would usually be lost until coming to a place that was recognized. Also, the military was barely into the process of building roads through the reservation to connect various forts. The right to build the roads was provided for in the Moultrie treaty.

While figuring it would take two days to reach the reservation, I did not expect it to be that long before I met some Indians. Thinking it best if I saw them before they saw me, I rode slowly and with all senses alert. Also, since most plantations were on waterways, I stuck close to those for the first couple of days. I then had safe places to camp at night, places where I would not have to sleep with one eye open.

Since I spoke pretty good Muskogee and was on a peaceful search for Running Dog's clan, I didn't expect trouble from most Indians. Some Indians, however, are just as mean as some white men are. There were Indians and whites that would kill to gain fewer possessions than I was carrying. I had one major disadvantage, too. Having to travel to find Running Dog, I was constantly on the move. Any Indian encountered in the woods would probably be stalking game. He would not be moving much. He might even be sitting in a tree by a game trail waiting for his dinner to walk under him. Movement catches the eye like no other thing in the woods and I was the one doing the most moving. My eyes scanned the trail for tracks, and the trees and brush for Indians while traveling.

On the second day, and near the Ocklawaha River, I spotted the tracks of six buffalo. Other than those buffalo tracks, which were becoming rare in Florida at the time, there were only the tracks of panther, bear, deer, and wild cattle, along with the tracks of smaller animals in the trails.

Later that day I found the tracks of five horses. Their tracks started at the point the game trail I was following joined another game trail. Less than six hours old, the tracks were going the same direction I was. I was certain about their age because it had rained earlier.

An hour before dark I turned off to the downwind side of the trail at ninety degrees and rode a couple hundred yards through the brush. I then paralleled the trail north for a hundred yards to a place where I made camp for the night. While it was still light, I started a cook-fire. The small fire was covered with dirt before dark so it could not be seen or smelled. Then I slept.

A few minutes after daylight the next morning I left the horses fifty yards from the trail I had been following and, on foot, inspected it. Only small, wild animals had been on the trail to leave tracks on my horse's tracks since I last rode there. Returning for my horses, I then proceeded south on the trail again.

It was near noon the third day when I encountered the first Indians of the trip. Still following the trail of the five horses, I was at the edge of a clearing with shelters in it almost before realizing it. The Indians' fields were west of their shelters, on the side away from the Ocklawaha, so I emerged from the brush close to the shelters. Several Indian children who were playing a game saw me. Having stopped momentarily, I touched my heels to the roan and walked him directly toward the center of the cluster of Indian dwellings. Having seen me, the children stopped their game and were staring at me, except for one who was running toward the village. Armed Indians began to appear everywhere. Raising my left hand, my right was holding my reins and was also near a pistol, I rode until stopped by three Indians who placed themselves in front of my horse.

Since they hadn't said anything, I spoke to them in Muskogee, "I seek my friend, Running Dog."

After looking at each other, one replied, "You come well-armed to our land."

I said, "I always travel well-armed. This time I also bring one rifle as a gift to my friend, Running Dog, and one to trade."

A large crowd had gathered by that time and seeing no point in having a hand near my pistol, I dropped my reins and placed a hand on each thigh.

An Indian in the crowd said, "He rides a horse that once belonged to Running Dog. I've seen that horse before."

Amazed that the horse was remembered, I said, "You haven't seen him for many years. Running Dog gave the horse to me more than ten years ago. I'd like to camp in or near your village tonight and ask about Running Dog's location."

It seemed that things were going pretty good. They hadn't shot me yet, or offered to. Also, I didn't think any of them would kill me in the village without a strong reason. What I didn't know was they thought they had a reason. I soon found that out.

The brave who had spoken first said, "I think you came about the hogs. I think others might follow you."

So as to be able to look them in the eyes on their level, I swung down from my horse and said, "I know of no hogs other than my own and my family's hogs near Black Creek. I seek my friend, Running Dog, because he was looking for me."

Trying to keep eye contact with those to whom I spoke, I failed to see a tall handsome fellow of about thirty who had come up on my right side.

He said, "If those were not your hogs, you're welcome here. If they were your hogs, I'll pay for them and you're welcome anyway. We've met before. I'm Osceola."

Walking forward, he extended his hand for a white man's shake. Although he could speak almost perfect English, since he had spoken in Muskogee every man, woman, and child knew what he said.

Shaking his hand, I said, "I'm Isaac. I know nothing about the hogs of which you speak. Thanks for your welcome. I only look for my friend, Running Dog."

Osceola said, "We know him. Tomorrow, I'll send someone to guide you. Today, you'll eat with me and we'll talk. Though we've met twice, we've never talked."

Turning to the forty or so Indians who had gathered, he said, "Though I didn't know this man's name, I owe him more than I can repay. Anyone who raises a hand against him will also be raising it against me."

Though he offered no other explanation, a path opened before us as we walked to his dwelling.

Later, when we were eating at Osceola's cook-fire, I said, "Tell me about the hogs your friends were talking about."

He replied, "Five horses came in a short while ahead of you."

When he paused and looked at me as if waiting for me to respond, I said, "Yes. Two riders were leading three packhorses. The horses were carrying a heavy load. They got in front of me off of a side trail late yesterday."

Smiling, and nodding approval at my tracking ability, he said, "I hope the owner of the hogs can't track as well as you can. I trust this information does not ruin the taste of the pork and sweet potatoes you're eating."

"The food's excellent," I replied. "Thanks for speaking up for me."

He said, "If every man treated his brother as you've treated me there would be little fighting. Running Dog is lucky to have a friend like you. How did you learn to speak Muskogee?"

I said, "Much as I helped you, I had the good fortune to be

able to help Running Dog one time. Though we were already friendly, we then became friends. We first met while trading. I got the roan from Running Dog about then. As for the Muskogee, Pa has been speaking it from before I can remember. He has been working to improve so he can talk easily with those with whom he trades. I soon picked it up and we often talk together in Muskogee."

Osceola said, "The roan's growing old and might stumble at a bad time. You need a younger horse."

I said, "That's true. I own younger horses but rode the roan to honor Running Dog from whom I got him. Both of my pack-horses are good horses. I'll ride one if the situation requires it."

We talked of many things: Osceola's and my life as children, our prior encounters, what we had been doing the past few years, the decline in the number of buffalo in Florida, Susan's death, and the future of the red and white men in Florida. Osceola was very knowledgeable. A man of pride and ambition, he was also a pragmatist. He told me, with what proved to be great insight, what was going to happen in Florida. Since he liked to practice speaking English, that was the language we used.

When he talked of the Indians' land, I said, "Pa says the key to success is to own land. The problem is that you own no land. You have title to nothing. You only live on the land by treaty agreement as one nation to another. The secret to holding your land is to have title to it as individuals and under the laws of the nation with the most power. A treaty is not long enduring. A treaty is only an agreement that'll be changed as the desire or need for change by the strongest nation occurs."

Osceola said, "The United States government won't give us title to the land. They don't want us to own it. Your people might wind up owning all the land, but it will cost."

I said, "The government cares little about the cost in money or lives. A few lives, even two or three thousand lives, mean nothing. I've been to New York, a village where there are more white people living in one village than all the Indians living in Florida, Georgia, Alabama, Tennessee, Kentucky, and the Carolinas."

The next morning Osceola provided a young man to guide me to Running Dog's camp. In parting, he wished me well and asked me to return and visit anytime. I told him I didn't know when I would be back at Black Creek, but he would be welcome at my place or Pa's. He then asked me to draw a map in the sand so he would know exactly where my place was.

We arrived at Running Dog's camp at noon the next day. Knowing many of Running Dog's braves, I spoke to them as we entered his village. Word of our arrival spread quickly in the small village and Running Dog soon approached.

As Running Dog approached, he stuck out his hand and said, "It's good to see you, Isaac. I was concerned for you when I heard your wife died and that you had gone to sea. Come sit by my cook-fire and talk."

After some small talk, which was required to welcome any visitor, Running Dog said, "Have you taken a wife?"

"No," I replied. "I've seen many women in my travels, but the cloud of Susan's death still hangs over my head."

Running Dog said, "A man should have a wife. I looked for you so I could ask you to come live with us while you get over your grief. I have a niece who could live with you and cook for you. Her parents are dead and she doesn't have a husband so she lives with me. Or you could live in my house until you decide to build your own or decide to go back to Black Creek."

Considering what to say, I sat silently as he looked at me expectantly. His suggestion was one that could not easily be declined without hurt feelings. In fact, living with Running Dog and spending my time hunting and fishing seemed like a good idea at the time. It would provide solitude when I needed it. His niece was another matter entirely. While I've never been opposed to a male-female relationship, I also had never met his niece.

I said, "Your offer is good. However, I don't believe I can live with another woman right now. I'll build a shelter and stay with you for a while, though. We can hunt and fish together and you can show me the lay of the land."

He said, "You'll stay in my house. My niece, Mourning Dove, can help cook for both of us."

I said, "Expecting that I would be traveling for some distance, I brought a large supply of food. I'll turn it over to your wife. Also, on the trip here I saw the tracks of six buffalo. They should still be close to where I saw their tracks. I thought that you and I, and some of your friends, could go kill some of them."

He asked, "How far are they?"

I replied, "More than a one-day ride."

He said, "It has been a long time since we ate buffalo. There aren't as many as there used to be. We should get started this afternoon."

I said, "Yes. But first, I brought you a gift."

Getting one of the smaller-caliber Spanish rifles from my pack, I gave it to him. Then, leaving the rest of my belongings in Running Dog's shelter, we soon left with a mixed group of fifteen men and women in search of the buffalo. The women were along to assist with the butchering and processing of the animals. We also took a good trail dog. Running Dog said his old trail dog would trail any animal track Running Dog snapped his fingers over. Had it been ten years earlier, Running Dog would have taken all of his tribe on the hunt. Since the buffalo might be off the reservation, we felt a smaller party was more appropriate. Because the Indians use every part of an animal they kill, we took enough spare horses to handle the load. After I described the location to Running Dog, he led the group. We camped that first night northwest of the village in which Osceola was living. Without encountering any people along the way, the next day before noon we arrived at the place I had seen the buffalo tracks.

After setting up a temporary camp, Running Dog made a circle on the ground and drew eight lines, equal distance apart, extending from the circle's center to its outer boundary. Each line, extended, was the line-of-search for one of the eight men in our party. While each of us followed the direction one of the lines pointed, we were to look for fresh buffalo tracks and report back shortly before dark. If we had found no fresh buffalo tracks after traveling along our line-of-search until half the remaining daylight hours were gone, we were to ride to our left until we had about split the difference between our line extended and the line to our left. Still looking for tracks, we were to then ride toward camp. In that way the group of us could cover an area of almost ten miles in diameter during the afternoon.

Returning to camp at first dark, I learned that one of the braves had located the small buffalo herd only a mile from our camp. Having come upon a single buffalo at another location, another of the braves had killed him. Returning for the women and some packhorses, they had butchered him.

Contrary to popular opinion, Indian men assist with much of the work around camp. The butchering of animals is not left entirely to the women. As in other cultures, there are some duties that are mostly the domain of one sex or the other. However, in time of need the boundaries of those domains are crossed without hesitation. Generally the men do the heavier work and the women do the lighter work. In this case, because of a sense of urgency to finish our work and to return to what we were sure was the reservation, everyone pitched in with all the chores. In times past, when the entire clan would have been there for several days, a more orderly and culturally traditional work arrangement would have been followed. But we wished to be gone from there as soon as possible. With most of the work related to the slain buffalo finished, we then sat around the cook-fire, ate, and talked.

After considerable conversation, Running Dog said, "We'll leave tomorrow just after daylight to hunt the other buffalo. Except for the fact that most of our people are still at the village, and the need for us to finish our work and get back on the reservation, this is almost like the old days."

I said, "This would be a good way to live. Unfortunately, those times are past. New settlers arrive frequently and the rate of arrival will only increase. The time will come when this area will have as many people as Georgia or South Carolina has. In fifteen or twenty years, Florida might even become a state."

Running Dog said, "I'm troubled about the future of my people. It's being said that President Jackson wants a treaty under which he can move us west of the boundary of the United Sates, beyond the Great River."

I said, "That's true. I've heard it from good sources."

Later, with the cook-fire still burning, I pulled my blanket over me to guard against the cool April night and the mosquitoes, and slept. As was the habit with most southern Indians, no night guard was posted. The lack of night guards always troubled me some when I was sleeping in an Indian encampment but not enough to keep me awake.

Soon after leaving camp the next morning we found fresh tracks of the small buffalo herd.

Running Dog said, "Four of you fan out to my left and three to my right, about forty yards apart. As the dog trails and barks, try to stay up with or ahead of the dog. When the shooting starts, ride toward the shooting so as to close on the buffalo. If you shoot one down, stay with that one until the women arrive. We don't want to lose an animal we've killed because we can't find it in a thicket. When they're all dead, or when some have escaped, if we can we'll drag the buffalo we've killed to a central location to butcher them."

In all probability the braves would only have one shot each. Since it requires half a minute to reload, and the horse has to be still in order to do it that quickly, only exceptional good fortune such as the buffalo changing direction would allow for a second shot. Leaving my smaller-caliber rifle behind with the women, I was armed with my sixty-nine-caliber American-made rifle and my two dueling pistols. Thus, I potentially would have three shots. It would he hard enough to ride at breakneck speed through heavy underbrush while maintaining control of my horse, one rifle, and myself, and impossible with two long guns.

After giving us a few minutes to position ourselves, Running Dog put the dog on the trail of the buffalo. I was on the outside of the left flank, 150 yards from the dog. Though the dog was a slow trail-dog, I received a beating from the heavy brush and limbs as I rode hard to keep abreast of the dog. In less than five minutes the tone of the dog's barking changed, indicating he had closed on the buffalo. In less than another minute a shot was fired a hundred yards to my right. Within seconds, a second shot was fired.

Changing direction, I raced toward a spot fifty yards in advance of the second gunshot. It was a good choice of directions; I soon found myself ahead of the dog and only twenty yards behind three buffalo that were running, single-file, down a trail through a thicket. It was impossible to do more than follow a few yards behind them. In less than a minute they came to a clearing. There, I kicked my horse for more speed and turned him slightly to the left. Thus getting a good angle for shooting, I shot the closest buffalo behind the left shoulder with my rifle.

Shoving my rifle in its boot, I then drew a pistol and continued the chase. Within twenty-five yards, the buffalo I had shot with my rifle fell. The grassy clearing being only two hundred yards across, we were then near the middle of it. My horse was closing on a big bull and, as we reached a point thirty yards from the woods, I placed the muzzle of a pistol almost against a spot behind his shoulder and fired.

At the moment my pistol fired, the roan stumbled and went down headfirst. I was thrown clear of, and in front of him. Momentarily dazed, I struggled to get to my feet. The buffalo I shot with my pistol had vanished into the thicket. As I gained my feet the bull charged back out of the thicket at my horse and me.

He had, perhaps, decided he had his adversaries helpless on the ground. Fortunately for me, the bull headed for the roan instead of me. I'm not sure how it came to be there but my second pistol was in my hand. I fired at the bull's head moments before he would have rammed the horse. Much practice and some good fortune produced a brain shot. The bull collapsed beside the roan as the horse was scrambling to get to his feet. Hearing the sound of running horses, I looked up to see Running Dog and two braves approaching.

Looking at Running Dog, I said, "I think the roan stepped in a hole."

The horse had managed to stand up, but a front leg was obviously broken. Mercifully for the roan and me, one of the braves took on the chore of killing the horse.

They dragged the other two buffalo that had been killed to the clearing. We then set up a temporary camp and started working on the dead animals. As soon as the animals were skinned, I loaded the skins and some fresh meat on a packhorse and left for the village. Being personal friends with the roan, I didn't feel like watching them work on him. I had been riding him for ten years. But, times were hard on the reservation and everything was needed. Running Dog and his people stayed behind to cure the meat. Otherwise much of it would have spoiled.

I spent the next two years with Running Dog. The buffalo and horsemeat wouldn't have fed Running Dog's fifty-person clan for more than three or four months. Coupled with what garden products they had, the supplies I brought, the fish we caught, other animals we killed or trapped, and the berries and such gathered by the women, we ate pretty well the first year I was there.

Running Dog and I made hunting trips and exploratory excursions to various parts of the reservation. One time we traveled south for many days beyond the reservation boundary until we saw a huge lake, Lake Okeechobee. Also during that time Mourning Dove and I became good friends. An attractive and pleasant young woman, she was easy to get to know. At their request, I began teaching Running Dog and Mourning Dove to speak some English. We switched back and fourth between languages as time passed and they mastered enough English words to communicate in English. Already having a pretty fair command of the language, I soon became very proficient at speaking Muskogee.

In midsummer of 1830, Running Dog received word through the tribal network that the Congress of the United States had passed an act providing for the creation of Indian lands in the west. The act also provided for the removal of all Indians from the eastern United States. The Government soon set about moving the Indians. Those from the northeastern United States were moved to Kansas. The southern Indians—the Miccosukees, Creeks, Choctaws, Cherokees, and so forth—were to be taken to a land south of Kansas. That area soon became known as the Indian Nations, later to be known as Oklahoma. The Florida Indians and about a fourth of the Choctaws, a few Creeks, and some Cherokees who lived in various southeastern states escaped the first relocation effort. I was still living with Running Dog's band when that effort began, but we heard nothing about it as it progressed.

After the first year passed, food became a problem for Running Dog's band and the other bands. Drought conditions reduced their crops by more than half. It would have been a simple matter to provide food for myself or for a few people. The problem of feeding fifty people, however, was much greater. We were then reduced to strictly hunting and fishing for food. After the hungry winter months of 1830 and 1831, the plight of the Seminoles only became worse. In the spring and summer of 1831 a drought destroyed all of the Seminoles' crops. Already hungry and malnourished, we were surviving on fresh-killed game, the few fish left after many lakes and ponds dried up, roots, and the heart of cabbage palm trees. With the heavy, year-around hunting, the supply of game was decreasing. Due to the drought and the drying up of their usual habitat, only an occasional alligator could be found. There seemed to be no more buffalo.

March 1, 1832

Thinking to learn the status of developing laws affecting the Florida Territory, and to perhaps influence future developments, after two years I left Running Dog's camp for Black Creek. Also, I thought I might be able to return at some time to help my Indian friends with food obtained at the farm. While I had left home almost two years before with three horses and a six-month supply of food, I returned with two horses and no food.

Upon arriving home, I received the prodigal son's welcome. Not having heard from me in two years, they thought I was dead. Ma, who always set a good table, overdid herself.

She kept saying, "You look like you've lost thirty pounds." I expect that was a good guess.

I replied, "Ma, the Indians are all in poor shape. I've been living with Running Dog for two years. With the government reneging on their promise to supply food, the drought last year, and too many people hunting year-round to supplement what they have, there's just not enough food for them."

Concerned about more than my weight loss, Ma said, "You haven't taken up with an Indian woman, have you?"

I said, "Not exactly, Ma. I have lots of Indian friends, some women among them."

Pressing on, she said, "No special one?"

I replied, "Nothing you would consider permanent, Ma. Most of the time I hunt or fish with Running Dog and his braves. Also, Running Dog and I have explored lots of the reservation and some points south of there. We've covered more than half of Florida in our travels."

Always interested in geography, Pa butted in and that kept Ma from pressing for a better answer. He said, "I want to hear about your travels—the lakes and rivers, the soil, the vegetation, everything."

The talk drifted off toward that direction then.

Financially, Pa and the boys were doing well. Asa, age twenty-eight, George, twenty-five, and Samuel, twenty-four, were still working with Pa. None of them had married. Jane, age twenty, and Mary, twenty-two, were the only girls who had married. There were not very many people available to marry at the time. There were fewer women than men. John Hunter had left to get his own place. Joseph, Norma, and Isabella were still on Pa's place. Also, nine of the twelve Cuban slaves we took from the smugglers were still working for us. Actually it was then eleven, counting two babies.

It was after dark the first night back home and I was lying under my blanket staring at the darkness when I first realized Susan's death no longer hung over my head. I guess it was the two years I spent with the Indians, observing their plight, which allowed me to place everything in perspective. It was not uncommon for an Indian woman and child to die during childbirth. The number of occurrences among the Indian women had only increased with their lack of proper nourishment since they moved to the reservation.

From an old Jacksonville newspaper I learned that James Gadsden had been chosen to negotiate with the Seminoles for their removal from the Florida Territory. President Jackson was pressing forward with the Indians' removal from all the eastern states and territory. Due to the plight of the Seminoles, it was thought by some that he would have an easy job in Florida. Gadsden was then in Florida working toward gathering enough chiefs for a meeting, without much success. Many of the chiefs were deep in the interior of Florida hunting for food.

With many of her children growing older without marrying, Ma's actions and words betrayed a concern she continued to have. At breakfast, she said, "I. J., you should visit Captain Lewis' family. They ask about you every time we see them. Louisa will turn eighteen next week and she's a beauty. Someone's going to grab her soon."

Asa said, "She's the main one to ask after you. I asked her to go for a walk but she said, 'I'm waiting for Isaac. He'll get over Susan soon. Also, Isaac thinks I'm not old enough yet. I'll wait.'"

I said, "I'll pay a courtesy call on the captain's family. I owe him for taking me on after Susan's death. I'll see if there's any way I can help them."

Pa said, "Lewis doesn't think you owe him, son. He said you're one of the best hands he ever hired. He said he would put you on anytime. And he said you would make a good captain if you would stick with it. Lewis tells about the rig chase in New York every time I see him."

I laughed out loud as the recollection of the chase came back. It was the first time I could remember laughing out loud in more than a year. While some of the moments had been pleasant, the past year had been hard.

After lying around for a few days and eating well, following breakfast one morning I left for Captain Lewis' house. Arriving there, I was given a warm welcome. Seeing how thin I was, Louisa's ma insisted on feeding me, even though the family had already eaten. Having only eaten some pork and a sweet potato as I rode, I didn't resist. After getting my stomach stretched back to its proper size with the first few meals after I got back home, I couldn't seem to eat enough. I made them proud of me before I got up from the table.

While eating, I watched the women work around the kitchen. In addition to Mrs. Lewis, there were Caroline, Eliza, and Louisa; ages fourteen, fifteen, and eighteen respectively. As much as I ate, I still had to keep my hands over my plate and keep saying "no, thank you" to keep them from putting more on it.

As I finished swallowing the last bite of pie, I said, "That's the best meal I ever ate."

Louisa's ma said, "It doesn't look like you've eaten very often the last couple of years."

I said, "Food's a little short for the Seminoles."

I had already told them a little about the past two years. I soon found that I was being tactfully questioned about the Indian women. As I had with Ma, I just as tactfully and politely put them off.

Finally, Louisa came straight out with it. "Isaac, you haven't taken an Indian wife, have you?"

I said, "That's a good question and to the point. And I'll answer to the point. No. No, I haven't."

Relief and embarrassment showed in her face, both at the same time. She blushed slightly. Around me, it was a first time for her.

Still looking at Louisa, I said, "I commented upon arriving about how good you all look. What I didn't say, and should have, is what a beautiful woman you've turned into."

Her blush deepened and, without comment, she turned to the cooking. That ended the talk about Indian women, which was what I intended to do.

I stayed the rest of the day and night. Some of the time was spent with Louisa's six brothers in talking and riding around the plantation. Captain Lewis was off to Norway on his ship again. The boys were all still single and working the place. Just as they had twelve years before, they wanted to hear everything about my experiences with the Indians. I also was with Louisa frequently: sitting on the porch steps, sitting in the swing on the porch, or walking around the yard and stables. I couldn't help but look at her. And, afraid I was too old for her, I couldn't help but wish she was a little older.

After thanking everyone for their courtesy, and after being cautioned about eating properly, I mounted my horse for the long ride to Black Creek.

As I sat on my horse, Louisa's ma said, "Isaac, you're welcome here anytime and everytime. If you need somewhere to stay that's away from home, all you have to do is make the ride over here."

It was clear she was saying I didn't need to go back to live with the Indians.

I said, "Thank you, ma'am. There's no place I feel more welcome or comfortable. I'll make it a point to get by this way more often."

Looking at Louisa, I smiled and lifted my hand. She seemed to smile all over as she raised her hand in return. She was such a beautiful young woman.

Everything was moving along real smooth at Black Creek. My place was still being sharecropped by some of the Cubans. There seemed to be little need for me. Still, there are always things that need doing around a farm—picking green horned-worms off of the tomato plants and stepping on them, digging cutworms from around plants, repairing fences, tending a sick animal, and such. I busied myself doing various things for a few weeks. Within that time, I gained ten pounds.

Though there wasn't much I could do to reduce the plight of Running Dog's band of Indians, all that time I was thinking about returning to his camp. While a couple of packhorses loaded with food would only last a few days when feeding more than fifty people, it would supplement what little they had. I felt that I needed to do something. Also, I was beginning to realize how nice it was to be around my Indian family—and Mourning Dove.

Thinking to influence what James Gadsden would do related to negotiating with the Seminoles about moving west, I finally went in search of him. Since the logical place to start my search would be in St. Augustine, I started for there first. Taking advantage of Captain Lewis' plantation being en route to St. Augustine,

I timed my departure so as to arrive there a little before dark. Naturally I received an invitation to supper and a place to sleep for the night. It was always fun to visit with Louisa and tease her a little.

Crossing the St. Johns River on the new ferry and arriving at Picolata, I found Gadsden there. After our introductions were over, I said, "Mr. Gadsden, I'm here to talk with you about the Seminoles' situation. Having friends among them, and having lived with them for two years, I have an understanding of their needs and desires."

He said, "Call me John, Isaac. You have to understand I'm here at President Jackson's request to move the Indians west. They should have gone two years ago when we moved the other tribes from the eastern states. Speaking very frankly, the president said I could, 'persuade or coerce them. Try persuasion at first.' He also said, 'If after a few months they haven't agreed to go, then use coercion. If they haven't moved after a couple of years, I'll send in five thousand regulars and move them.' "

I said, "I hope it doesn't come down to sending five thousand soldiers. That would only get lots of people killed on both sides. Five thousand men, fighting the way our regular army fights, wouldn't be enough. Persuasion or bribery has got to be the best way."

Looking perplexed, he said, "What do you mean, the way our army fights?"

"I mean the way they line up like the French army and march into battle, and haul around their heavy wagons and cannons. They wouldn't get through the first forest or across the first river without being cut to pieces. Their wagons would slow them to such an extent they would only see an Indian when the Indian chose the time and place. Then they might wish they hadn't seen the Indian."

"The army did pretty well back in 1818 in west Florida."

"Yes, sir, I know. Pa and I were there in those fights. At

General Jackson's request, we fought with his Lower Creek Indians. They did much of the damage in that war. There were fifteen hundred of the Lower Creeks with us. For all our running around and burning houses, there were not many more than three hundred Indian men killed in the whole war. The others just moved east. There are supposed to be five thousand Seminoles south of us now and they'll fight, but not the way our army will want to fight. There'll be an Indian behind every tree and bush. You won't see them very often but you will feel their bullets. Also, the black people living in Florida will fight with them."

"You seem to like the Indians, Isaac."

"Respect is more nearly the right term, at least as far as fighting goes. They work as hard at not getting killed as they do at killing people. They do as my favorite poem by Goldsmith that Ma always read says, 'He who fights and runs away, may live to fight another day, but he who is in the battle slain, can never rise and fight again.' "

That was something Ma read to us kid lots of times. It was one of the things she told us to pattern our life after.

He said, "I doubt seriously it would take more than five thousand regulars to move the Indians."

"It would take more than five thousand to even find most of them if they didn't want to be found. Moving them would then be another problem."

"What would be your answer to the problem?"

"If you want to move them, buy them out. It would cost lots less than a war with them would."

"Isaac, I haven't had much luck getting the Indians to negotiate. I can't even get most of them to come to a meeting."

"That's because their people are hungry. They're covering the whole territory hunting and fishing. You should be providing food as the government promised in the treaty."

"You seem to know the Indians: their ways, their trails, and their lands. You could help deliver a message for their chiefs to come to a meeting."

"You set up a meeting time and place, and I'll help get the word out. I can't promise they'll come, though."

"How about May fifth, at Payne's Landing on the Ocklawaha River?"

"I'll help spread the word. If I help get them in, I'll expect you to negotiate in good faith," I said, before shaking his hand and leaving.

The Indian agent, John Phagan, and others would also be spreading the word, but I knew exactly where several of the chiefs were and could go directly to them. Since it was then the fifth of April, all haste had to be made. I did take time to buy two bushels of shelled corn to put on my packhorse before leaving.

My conversation with Chief Alligator was much like my conversations with the other chiefs as I found and talked to each. The only difference was that Alligator was the only Seminole I knew—other than Osceola, Running Dog, and Mourning Dove—who spoke some English. We still conversed in Muskogee because his English was not very good.

I said, "James Gadsden sends word there'll be a meeting on May fifth, at Payne's Landing. He wants to negotiate a treaty to move your people out west. I came to encourage you to attend the meeting."

He said, "I've heard of this meeting. It's a meeting for James Gadsden. We don't need a new treaty. We signed a treaty at Moultrie Creek that was good for twenty years. It still has many years to go before it ends. When the twenty years end, we'll meet for a new treaty."

I said, "What you say is true. My pa and I were at that meeting and know of the treaty. However, President Jackson has decided it will be best if the Seminoles move to a new land so he wants a new treaty."

"My people don't want to leave this land."

I said, "How do you know? You've never seen the new land and haven't heard James Gadsden's offer. Are you happy here? Does your tribe eat well?" I knew the answer to those questions were no.

He said, "It's said this new land is barren and also cold in the winter. It's hot here in the summer but not so cold in the winter."

"Who said it's barren and cold? Do you trust this person? I've never seen this new land. I would want to see it before I decided."

"I know of you, Isaac, and your father, who is also called Isaac. While your word is said to be good, I have no trust for most whites. I know we now have a treaty that is good for many years. They want to break this treaty for a new treaty. Can you guarantee the new treaty will be a good one and will not be broken?"

"No. I have no official or unofficial position in the government. The government changes—new presidents are elected, new congressmen are elected, and new agents are appointed. Unfortunately, we can't even be sure those in power now can guarantee a new treaty for a definite period of time. I don't think anyone can even guarantee the treaty you have now."

"Then tell me as best you can why I should attend this meeting."

"Okay, I will. President Jackson has decided that all of you will be moved to the land in the west. He wants to negotiate a treaty to do so. If you do not negotiate, he will make life miserable for you until you decide to go. At that point you will have lost a negotiating opportunity and will move with less in your favor. If you still don't go, he'll send the military to move you. You now have an opportunity to gain something through bargaining."

"It'll cost them dearly for the army to try to move us. We would kill lots of them."

"Yes, you would. You would kill more than they think. However, in the end they would kill all of you or move you.

There are only five thousand of you in Florida. If you kill one of them every time they kill one of you, in the end there will be none of you and there will still be more whites than there are grains of sand at the lake's edge. The buzzard will eat you and the fox will chew your bones. There won't even be a burial place for your people. I say it's better to negotiate and gain something, perhaps even more than you have here. You lose nothing by listening to their offer and in making your offer."

After pausing for a full minute while he stared at the fire, Alligator said, "I'll talk with Jumper, Amatol, and Micanopy about this. We might go to the meeting and hear what's said."

Since most Seminoles knew nothing about the white man's calendar, I gave Alligator the correct number of grains of corn to count the days until May 5. Removing one from the pouch each morning, he would know when May 5 arrived because he would be out of corn. I then visited the village where Osceola lived and talked with the sub-chief there. Osceola was not yet a chief. Later, while spending the night with Osceola, I also talked with him.

After hearing me out, he said, "As you know, I'm not a chief. It's my wish someday to be a leader but the time has not arrived. But I'll go to the meeting and give my opinion when asked."

I said, "I've seen you speak to the people. They listen with respect. I think you're a leader now. You have influence."

He said, "We only want to live as people should live, without being humiliated and treated as animals."

"I know this," I said.

Later, arriving at Running Dog's camp, I spoke with him about the meeting and told him of meeting with the other chiefs.

He said, "I'm an unimportant chief of a small band. I would not be missed at the meeting but if you feel it's important, I'll go. I'll also go with you to visit other bands and encourage their chiefs to go. Micanopy and King Philip are the most powerful chiefs. It has to be they who conduct the council vote."

Mourning Dove was very attentive as she served me food

while Running Dog and I talked. Graceful and sure of foot and hand, she had a presence that could not be ignored. As I watched her and listened to Running Dog, my mind strayed to Captain Lewis' plantation and Louisa, comparing her to Mourning Dove. Chastising myself for not paying attention to my host, I soon returned my attention to Running Dog to find he was only talking about our buffalo hunt.

In order to persuade others that negotiating was better than the other alternatives, Running Dog and I left the next morning to travel to various villages and talk with the leaders. In each place we said the same thing and, at first, heard the same responses. Additionally, there were those hotheads at most locations who continued to argue that the meeting should be ignored. They wanted to buy more rifles and ammunition and prepare to fight.

As we were riding between two villages, Running Dog said, "If it comes to fighting, on which side would you fight?"

I said, "I'd fight on the side of my brothers. That said, I could not pull the trigger if I saw you or your family in front of me. I consider you to be an older brother."

Running Dog said, "I, too, would find it impossible to shoot you or any of your family." Then, smiling and laughing at me, he added, "Mourning Dove would shoot me when I got back to the village if I shot you."

On May 1, we returned to Running Dog's village and on May 3, departed for Payne's Landing. When we arrived, there was a large contingent of both Seminoles and white soldiers encamped at the landing. Of the more than two hundred chiefs in Florida, only thirty were among the three hundred–plus Seminoles in attendance. The two top chiefs, Micanopy and King Philip, were there. None of the chiefs from the separate small reservations along the Apalachicola River had come.

Seeing me, James Gadsden approached and said, "It looks like some people have been working hard to spread the word. There's a good turnout. It seems that many of the chiefs are here."

"Yes. Some important ones are here but many more are missing than are here. The ones here might have come because I told them the government was furnishing food for the meeting and that there would be a feast. Many of them brought their family and friends. They have little food," I said.

Taken aback, he said, "I made no such provision."

I said, "It should be a small thing for a government willing to spend great sums on moving these people to spend a token sum to feed them properly for a few days. You have army cooks here to cook for your soldiers. It would be easy for them to triple the size of what they cook. If you don't have enough, I'm sure there are plantations nearby where you could buy food. If it would be helpful, I could arrange those purchases."

Running Dog, understanding much of what was said, turned away to hide his smile as I talked to Gadsden.

When it became obvious to Gadsden that I spoke fluent Muskogee, assuming I might be representing the Seminoles interest, he asked, "Are you here to speak for the Indians and interpret for them?"

I said, "Neither. I have no voice, official or unofficial, in these proceedings. I thought only to help you provide a cordial situation in which meaningful negotiations could be held."

Running Dog and I then proceeded to set up our shelter. Later, as we mingled with others at the gathering, based on smiles and some little compliments I became aware that Running Dog had told of, and perhaps embellished on, my conversation with James Gadsden. Gadsden soon made an announcement that food would be provided for everyone in attendance.

The negotiations went on for five days. In his opening speech, James Gadsden told everyone what the government wanted. Basically, the government wanted a treaty agreement that would trade a place west of the Mississippi River for the Seminoles' current reservation. In spite of the fact the Upper Creeks and Miccosukees had been at war with the Lower Creeks for years, they would be sent to the same reservation the Lower Creeks were then on. This provision would place them all on the same five million acres. They would also receive a one-time sum of money as part of the deal. Some of their money was to be held back for various claims against the Seminoles, however.

It was rare to find an Indian who could speak more than a few words of English, so a free black man, Abram, interpreted for the Seminoles. Abram had been a slave to Micanopy, but had been set free for faithful service.

After listening to Gadsden make his speech and glancing at several of the chiefs, Abram said, "We already have a treaty that's good for many more years. When that treaty is near an end, we'll talk about a new treaty. What we need to talk about now is the United States keeping the white men off our land and delivering the food that was promised in the existing treaty."

Determined to have his way, and thinking Abram didn't understand, Gadsden repeated his speech and said, "Tell them what I said."

Turning to the chiefs, Abram translated to them most of what Gadsden had said. Two things you could say about Indians at a meeting are that they almost never interrupt unless they feel insulted and they never get in a hurry. I could see we were in for a long meeting. After Abram finished translating, the chiefs talked among themselves for several minutes. I didn't hear much said about the proposal. They all knew what the proposal was. They just talked among themselves to let Gadsden think they were discussing it.

Then, Chief Micanopy said to Abram, "Tell him we understand and have discussed his proposal. Tell him we have a treaty. We need the government of the United States to enforce the current treaty."

Toward the end of the day I began to wonder how many ways James Gadsden could say they needed a new treaty and Abram could tell him the Seminoles did not need a new treaty.

After numerous recesses during the day, an hour before dark Gadsden recessed the meeting until after breakfast the next day.

Later, while I was getting food from an army food line, Gadsden approached me and said, "You've been listening to this all day. We haven't accomplished a thing."

I said, "I don't know, you've made your position clear. So have they."

He said, "They haven't offered to negotiate anything."

I said, "No, and neither have you. You might try offering them something in trade for what you want. I thought that was how negotiating was done."

He said, "They'll come around in the end."

I said, "I wouldn't want to bet anything important on it."

The next day went the same way and the next. Just when James Gadsden thought he had things going his way, Abram would say, "We have a treaty. We won't need a new treaty for many more years."

By the middle of the third day, James Gadsden had changed his tactics and started threatening to withhold their monthly food allotments, as well as other similar threats. That did not serve as a very productive avenue of discussion. The government had already been delinquent in meeting that responsibility.

Abram's response was, "The Seminoles have a treaty with the United States and expect the United States to enforce that treaty. Part of the treaty is that you will provide food, which you are not doing except for this meeting."

It was the third night before James Gadsden spoke to me again. He said, "Isaac, I need a breakthrough. Can you speak to the chiefs, or do you have a suggestion?"

"I'm glad you asked, James. No, it would be a waste of time for me to speak to the Council of Chiefs. I'm not even sure they would let me speak. I do have a couple of suggestions, though. First you might actually offer them something, some money perhaps. Or ask them what they would want to be given in order to

move. You might also tell them more about the land you're offering. It might be wise to offer Abram a bonus payable on the day
most of the Seminoles arrive west of the Mississippi. A thousand
dollars would be a cheap price to pay. It would probably have to
be just between you and him or it wouldn't work. It might not
work anyway."

"Abram isn't their leader."

"He's the only one here who speaks English and Muskogee
well enough to translate, other than me and Osceola; and he has
the ear of the chiefs. Alligator speaks fair English but not enough
to serve as a translator. And Running Dog speaks a little and
understands most of what is said. None of them, not even Abram
or Osceola, can read or write. And Osceola usually won't speak
English except to practice, or among friends."

"I see your point. You said you had two suggestions."

"Yes. Late tomorrow you might offer to sign a temporary
treaty that would only be good after a delegation of chiefs had
been taken on a tour of this new land and a second treaty is
signed by the Council of Chiefs."

"That could take a year."

"Or longer. An Indian war would certainly last longer than
that. I have another suggestion, too. Watch Osceola without
looking straight at him. His body language often tells the others
what he thinks."

"Why Osceola? He's not a chief. I don't know much about
him."

"He will be a leader. His father's father was Scottish so he has
no birthright to be a chief. Even now, however, many look to him
for approval. If his manner is approving, then you're headed in
the right direction. If it isn't, you can talk forever and nothing will
happen."

Within minutes James Gadsden was having a private conversation with Abram.

The next day, talks started out just as they had before with

James Gadsden blustering about what would happen if the Seminoles didn't agree to a new treaty. As the day wore on Gadsden changed his attitude and the chiefs began to listen to him. Sitting on the sideline and watching Gadsden and Abram, and watching Osceola's impact on the session was interesting. Gadsden was observing Osceola to see how the meeting was going. Sensing that Gadsden was reacting to his body language, Osceola was almost running the meeting. Knowing there were few of us who spoke fluent English and Muskogee, Abram began putting some polish on Gadsden's words that had not been there. Frequently he would negotiate back and forth between Gadsden and the chiefs without saying exactly what the other said until he had reached an accord between them. Still, no treaty was signed that day.

Curious, I sought an audience with James Gadsden that night and asked, "What did you offer Abram?"

"Two hundred dollars."

"That's like stealing from a child, if he goes along. I would be cautious, though."

"I will be. Though he's extremely intelligent, he has no concept about money beyond a couple of dollars. Two hundred is more than he knows how to count."

"Ten is more than he knows how to count. See that he gets the two hundred. If he doesn't, I'll take it personally. I'm only helping with this because of what'll happen to the Seminoles if they don't go west."

"And what do you think will happen to them?"

"There'll be a long war in which most of them—men, women, and children—will die or finally be sent west."

"I think you overstate their ability to resist."

"I've fought with and against them for almost twenty years. I know what they can do."

The next day, May 9, 1832, the meeting progressed rapidly. Gadsden agreed to take seven chiefs to see the new land. Because of the colder climate, he also agreed to provide blankets and clothes to each person who moved west permanently. Additionally, the Seminoles were to receive money for various inconveniences. Out of those funds they were to pay for all fugitive slaves under their control whom they did not return.

It was made clear in writing, and verbally, that this was not a final agreement. The final treaty would only be signed if the seven chiefs and Abram returned and reported the land to be acceptable. Then the Council of Chiefs would vote and decide.

Only half of the chiefs who were present made their mark on this provisional agreement. Micanopy and King Phillip, the two head chiefs, did not.

Returning to Running Dog's village, we stayed there until I got the urge to visit Black Creek.

Leaving for the west, the seven chiefs and Abram were escorted by John Phagan. Phagan had only recently succeeded Humphreys as Indian agent. Leaving from the west coast of Florida, they were to sail to the mouth of the Mississippi River, then travel up the river on riverboats. Leaving the boats, they were then to travel overland to the reservation and look it over.

During the next year I lived alternately at Black Creek and in Running Dog's camp. Most of the late spring and summer I was at Black Creek. Most of the winter was spent with Running Dog's band as we hunted deep into south Florida.

Though their crops were better than the prior year, the Indian's situation was still miserable. As it had before, conflict continued between the Indians and whites. If anything, the situation grew worse as more whites arrived to buy cheap land from the government or to move in on Indian land. Running Dog's band was better off than most of the larger bands. It's easier to feed a smaller group. Also, I provided some assistance when I made occasional visits back and forth from Black Creek to Running Dog's village.

Unlike the Indians on the southern reservation, as long as

they adhered to the laws of the Florida Territory and the United States, the small bands of Indians in west Florida were given the choice of remaining there. They were also given a choice of emigrating to any other country they chose, at the government's expense. On October 11, 1832, a separate treaty of emigration was signed with some of those Indians. The treaty stipulated that those bands, consisting of approximately 250 people total, would move to a location of their choice west of the United States. The move was to be made no later than November of 1834. Sums of money ranging from $2,000 to $13,000 were to be paid to the various chiefs in west Florida who chose to move under the terms of the Payne's Landing treaty. Also, monthly payments of $500 would be paid until the government of the United States arranged for such a move.

PART III

War on the
Horizon

August 10, 1833

Over a year passed before we heard from the committee of seven chiefs who had gone to Arkansas. I was squatting in the shade talking to one of the Cubans when Running Dog came riding out of the woods with word of that trip.

Dismounting and squatting by us he said, "Trouble's coming. John Phagan tricked the committee of chiefs into signing a treaty while they were visiting the new land. Those chiefs didn't have the authority to sign a treaty. The authority to sign rests only with the Council of Chiefs."

I said, "What do you mean, Phagan tricked them?"

"It's said that he got them to drinking and then didn't clearly explain what they were signing. Everyone knows none of them can read."

"But Abram was there to interpret and explain."

"Somehow that didn't help clear things up. Perhaps because Abram can't read either. He only translated what the commissioner told him."

"What does the treaty say?"

"It says the committee of chiefs is satisfied with the new land. It says all Seminoles must leave Florida before three years have passed. It also says we must live between the Canadian and the North Fork Rivers with our enemies, the Lower Creeks."

Almost in disbelief, I stared at the ground and said nothing. I fully understood that the Council of Chiefs must make such an agreement or it was not valid. Phagan understood it, too.

Finally, I said, "This isn't turning out very well."

"No," Running Dog replied, "It's the worst possible thing that could happen. Even those like me who had decided we would have to move will change their minds. There will be fighting. Neither the committee of chiefs nor the government's commissioners who were with them has authority to ratify such a treaty. Ratification is the responsibility of the Council of Chiefs and the United States Congress. In fact, the United States Congress has not yet ratified the tentative treaty from the meeting last year. Still, the government now says this new treaty makes the treaty of Payne's Landing valid and we must prepare to leave. We can't possibly live as a smaller group among our enemies, the Lower Creeks."

"I don't know what I can do. If I can help, tell me."

"You can come with me to Micanopy's camp and read the paper. At least we should know what it says from someone we trust. The chiefs asked that a council meeting be called to discuss the treaty. John Phagan refused to attend such a meeting, saying the treaty was valid and final."

Micanopy was the top chief of the Seminole Nation at the time. At his plantation, I read the papers he had been provided. The wording was so vague that it could be interpreted in any way one wanted. Also, since the United States Senate had not ratified it or the treaty it was predicated on, it was not a valid document.

We all knew that Abram, the interpreter at the Paynes Landing meeting and for the land visitation committee, was formerly one of Chief Micanopy's slaves. As I talked with Micanopy and others at the plantation I soon learned that Abram was not only Micanopy's interpreter, he was also Micanopy's chief advisor about most things. Even before Micanopy set him free, Abram had great power over the other slaves. After being set free he still lived on Micanopy's plantation most of the time. He had lots of influence over the whole situation.

During the afternoon and night that we were at Micanopy's place, I observed several people, including Micanopy's slaves, who had smaller-bore Spanish rifles like the one I had given Running Dog. As I've said before, the Seminoles had a different relationship with their slaves than that of whites and their slaves. Though it was illegal under United States law for any black person to have a gun, it was not uncommon for an Indian's black slave to have one. What caught my attention, though, was the type of weapon. Indians and their slaves usually owned the larger-bore, but less accurate, English or Spanish musket.

When I was alone with Running Dog, I said, "You noticed the Spanish rifles?"

"Yes. The word is that Abram is responsible for those. He talked Micanopy into buying them. It seems that Abram only pretended to go along with Phagan in persuading the chiefs who were visiting out west to sign. He has been preparing for war all along. The last thing he and the other blacks want is to be under the white man's rule, even for a short time."

"Those rifles had to be smuggled in," I said. "They could not have been legally bought by Micanopy within the last year. Also, black people have never been able to legally buy or possess guns. The law has always prohibited the sale of weapons, powder, and lead to them."

"That's true. They got them from the people who fish the west coast of Florida in Cuban fishing boats. They were unloaded at Charlotte Harbor," Running Dog said. "Like I said, there's going to be fighting. While a few chiefs want to move to the new land, most don't. Such a move would be the worse possible thing for the black Seminoles. If they're rounded up, they might be claimed and put back to work on a plantation. It's also probable that most of those who are legally free would also be claimed. Most of them don't have any papers. They don't know how to read and wouldn't know what the papers said if they did have them."

It was soon discovered that Major John Phagan's government accounts had not been handled properly. He was discharged and replaced by Wiley Thompson in September of 1833. In December of 1833, Agent Wiley Thompson received instructions to begin preparing the Seminole chiefs on the Apalachicola reservations to be removed.

Meanwhile, back in our part of Florida, the ex-slave Abram was traveling the area and encouraging slaves to run away and join the Seminoles when the serious fighting began. Running Dog told me that John Caesar, one of the leaders among the black Seminoles and an associate of Abram, had approached our Cubans about joining the fight against the whites. The Cubans confirmed it. Caesar mistakenly thought, as everyone else did, that they were my slaves. There was also escalation in the conflict between the Indians and whites at that time. White slave owners and those pretending to be owners in order to steal slaves from the Indians were stepping up their efforts to take the Seminoles' slaves; probably because they thought the Indians would soon be moving. At the same time the Lower Creek Indians who were still in the area were trying to get their slaves back that the Seminoles had taken from them. Those two efforts were causing constant conflict.

While still spending some time at Running Dog's village, I was spending more and more time at the farm on Black Creek. I also still visited with Louisa and her family frequently, mostly with Louisa. I found that my thoughts were constantly about her when I was not with her.

Though the raiding was increasing from both sides, our place and Captain Lewis' place was pretty much left alone. This might have been because of my relationship with the Indians or because of Pa's trading with them. There were a few other plantations that were also not being raided. Some of those plantations, like the captain's and ours, also had a pretty powerful fighting force with just the family members and the hired help on the place. That might have also caused the small raiding bands to avoid us.

Even though the Indians were being held to the strict interpretation of the Payne's Landing Treaty, at least as the United States government interpreted it, the government failed to adhere to most of what the treaty required of the United States. One area in which the government was in severe violation was the time line for various events to occur. The treaty said the Indians would all be gone within three years of the ratification of the treaty. Once the treaty was ratified, a third of them were to leave in 1833 and another third in each of the next two years. Congress failed to ratify the treaty until April 12, 1834. Also, the government didn't have money allocated or have the logistics in place to move a third of the Indians in 1833. Once the United States ratified the treaty, the President then ordered that a third of the Indians were to be moved in 1835. The United States was clearly in violation so the treaty legally should have become null and void even if it were previously valid. The president ignored that and several other irregularities of the document.

There was considerable discussion and confusion on the part

of the Indians about the treaty. They considered it totally invalid. None of the major chiefs had approved it. Also, the Council of Chiefs hadn't voted on it. I heard lots about this while in Running Dog's village. I also heard about the political changes that were occurring in the Seminole Nation, and about the emerging of new leaders.

While not yet a chief, Osceola's reputation was growing. Osceola was also rapidly becoming the most militant of militants with respect to not moving from Florida. The blacks and the militant younger Miccosukees supported him.

As time passed, Abram and some of his followers increased their effort to recruit slaves to run away and join them. They also pressed Micanopy, and other chiefs, to purchase supplies of ammunition. It was, however, not until after the meeting between the chiefs and Agent Thompson in October of 1834 at Fort King that the Indians started seriously buying powder and lead from any source they could get it. The purpose of that meeting was to discuss the treaty and to organize the Indians so they could be removed from Florida. At the meeting, Osceola was openly defiant and shook his weapons in the air. He also shouted out on occasion against the meeting and encouraged others to protest.

If there is a single point in time that can be pointed out as to when crystallization occurred in the minds of the Indians that there would be war, that was the time. The inability of the United States to form a policy to deal with the Seminoles, and to follow through on the policy, finally became so evident that most of the Indians realized they could place no faith in the government. In spite of all this, as many as a half of the Indians would have voluntarily gone west except for the coercion of the militants among them.

At the time, almost two-thirds of the Seminole Nation was composed of Upper Creeks and about one-third were Miccosukees. The Miccosukees were strongly opposed to emigration. They and the blacks made up the strongest opposition. Most prominent and most militant among the Creeks who opposed being moved was Osceola.

As the situation in Florida became more dangerous the United States government made the situation worse by its actions. In November of 1834, Agent Wiley Thompson was ordered to withhold all supplies and payments from the Indians. Then, after issuing a proclamation that they must move, and in an effort to intimidate the Seminoles, Andrew Jackson placed seven hundred regulars under General Clinch and ordered him to remove the Indians from Florida by force. President Jackson should have known better. Seven thousand soldiers would have stood a better chance. Even with that many soldiers, the effort to remove the more hostile of the Seminoles would have failed over the short haul.

At a council meeting at Fort King in April of 1835, the more militant of the Seminoles declared they were not going to move. In the argument that followed, Osceola became verbally abusive and threatened to kill Thompson and some other whites. General Clinch then gave the Indians one day to make up their minds about signing up to leave Florida. If they did not sign, he told them they would be removed by force. The meeting then almost broke up. Only eight of the almost two hundred chiefs present stayed around to sign the agreement. None of those eight were important chiefs.

Thompson had Osceola arrested for his threats. Osceola soon figured out how to get out of jail. He apologized to Thompson and promised to leave Florida. He also promised to persuade others to leave. Thompson was so impressed and appreciative that he released Osceola and gave him a rifle as a present.

As this was going on we heard that Sam Houston was planning to gather volunteers to take Texas from Mexico. Texas, Arkansas, and the other areas outside the United States where various tribes might be sent were being contested by a number of groups, countries, and Indian tribes already there. Those were dangerous places.

While all this was all taking place, Louisa reached her twenty-first birthday. A beautiful young woman, she was being courted by every eligible man within twenty-five miles of her house who thought he had a chance. That still wasn't very many. Other than in St. Augustine, the population was pretty sparse. Though received in the home with courtesy, none of them were making any headway.

Since most of Louisa's suitors came calling on Sundays, I usually timed my visits for the middle of the week. Most of the suitors worked pretty steady during the week at farming. While working quite a bit when at Black Creek, I left most of the farming to the Cubans. Some of them drifted away one at a time as good opportunities presented themselves, and there were only seven adult Cubans and some children left. These few seemed to be very happy with their lives and it looked as though they had become permanently associated with our family.

Louisa being twenty-one and me being thirty-three at the time, it was no longer difficult to consider myself to be a suitor even though she was younger than I was. It seemed as though I was spending half my time riding back and fourth from Black Creek to her home. As time passed, I teased Louisa less about her other suitors. While welcomed graciously by all of her family, I also found that Louisa's mother and siblings found cause to leave us alone more often. Our relationship was then far more than just being friends. She could cause my heart to pound just by smiling.

Following the disastrous breakup of the 1835 meeting and the subsequent jailing and release of Osceola, violence increased significantly. Outlying farms were burned, there were several murders by Indians, and farm animals were stolen. In small parties, the Seminoles seemed to be everywhere. Some of the planters from the smaller farms gathered together for protection at a single farm. Others stayed home to defend their possessions.

Wiley Thompson was then ordered to prepare a complete plan for the removal of all Indians from Florida. In late August Thompson announced his plan. December 1, 1835, was selected as a date the emigrating Indians could bring their livestock to the agency and offer them for sale to the highest bidder. The Indians were then to gather at the Indian Agency at Fort King on January 1, 1836, to be transported to ships. They were to start their journey in ships from the west coast of Florida at Fort Brooke, near Tampa Bay. Thompson estimated it would take two weeks for the military to round up those Indians who didn't want to go. It was an almost laughable conclusion.

On a visit to the agency, while I was on my way to Running Dog's camp, Wiley Thompson engaged me in conversation.

He said, "Fewer Indians are visiting the agency this summer. That and the attitude of those who visit makes me think they might be preparing for war. You know the Indians, Isaac. What can you tell me about that? Are they preparing to fight?"

"They're ready now," I said. "They've been prepared for more than a year."

He asked, "What are they doing now?"

"They're storing their food supplies in safe places and are moving their families to islands in the swamps. Not all of them want to fight. Some are planning to go west. I fear for those. They might not be allowed to leave peacefully."

He said, "I've written the secretary of war and the president, telling them there might be fighting here. I'm afraid they don't think the situation here is serious."

"They better think it's serious," I said. "But I don't think even you know how serious it is. It would take years to move the Indians by force and then you might not get them all."

He said. "I know it's a serious situation. However, I'm sure the soldiers can remove them in short order."

I didn't even respond to that comment and left shortly thereafter.

By the end of September there had been several small skirmishes between some volunteer militia and small bands of Indians. In October, General Clinch, the commander of all regular troops in Florida, warned the secretary of war that war was almost at hand. Also in October, the Indian chiefs held a council meeting without the Indian agent present.

The day after the meeting I received word that Running Dog needed to see me but that he didn't feel he could come to Black Creek. Running Dog's messenger said he would meet me north of Fort King in two days. The meeting would be at the place where the main trail crossed the creek leaving Lochloosa Lake at the lake's south end. Since it was two days' ride to our meeting place, I left immediately.

Running Dog, Mourning Dove, and Running Dog's son, Spotted Buffalo, were waiting when I arrived at the designated spot.

Running Dog said, "These are troubled times, Isaac, but it's always good to see you."

I said, "It's always good to see you, my brother."

I also gave Mourning Dove a hug and embraced Spotted Buffalo.

Continuing, I said, "Why couldn't you come to Black Creek? You're always welcome there regardless of what others say or think."

"I know," he said. "It's all the things that have happened. At a recent council meeting of the chiefs, some chiefs said they would go to the new land. Others are violently opposed to moving. As the discussion proceeded, Osceola stood and said he would kill any chief who tried to take his clan west. Several chiefs agreed with him. Also, Abram and several others of the black leaders agreed with him. Furthermore, the militants have been importing more Cuban rifles and ammunition. The Cuban fishermen who work the west coast have been delivering the supplies. In spite of claims by the military, Charlotte Harbor still isn't being guarded. It's easy to unload there."

I said, "Does Osceola now have the right to address the council?"

He said, "No. But he does speak and many people listen, especially the black people. They are adamantly opposed to moving. I think he means what he says. Also, I think some of the black people of my own clan might betray me if I don't go along with the militants. That's why I asked you to meet here. We can talk without being overheard."

I asked, "Do you want to go west? Is that the problem?"

He replied, "Yes, though I haven't said as much to anyone other than my immediate family. I must do what's best for my people. I feel that you're right. In a long war, most of us would be killed and for little purpose. Osceola might murder some people as an example to others who want to move. Though intelligent and persuasive, he's also violent."

I said, "Why did you ask me to come here?"

He replied, "First, to warn you that Micanopy, Alligator, Jumper, and others among the most powerful chiefs said we'll fight. We will not move. The Indian agency could be the first place attacked. You should carry word to Thompson to be on guard because he might be targeted. Second, the plan Thompson has in place is too cumbersome and is known by everyone. It would be too easy for a person like Osceola to meet those who are moving and kill some of them. Also, the announced date to sell our livestock gives anyone who wants to cause trouble a target, location, and time to kill someone."

I said, "You could sell your livestock some other place. Though it's a three- or four-day drive to Black Creek, I could buy your livestock and drive them there."

He said, "There's still the problem of the black people in my clan. I don't trust all of them. Beyond you and my family, I don't really know whom I can trust. I also think that if we sell the livestock and have a large sum of money, we might be killed for the money."

Out loud I said to myself, "I probably should have killed him back in 1817."

Running Dog asked, "Who? What are you talking about?"

I replied, "Osceola. I was sixteen and he was thirteen or fourteen. He shot an arrow at me and missed. I then held a musket on him for several seconds. He was standing motionless, prepared to die, but I waved for him to get into the woods."

Running Dog said, "So that's why he treats you the way he does. It's a debt he could never repay."

I said, "He owes me nothing."

Running Dog said, "It's the ultimate debt. Neither he nor anyone in his band will ever do you any harm. I could sell you livestock and you could drive them through the middle of Florida. No one would interfere with you."

I said, "If that would be helpful, my friend, I would be glad to take them off your hands. I could also hold some of your money and pay you at a safe time and place, perhaps as you leave on a ship going west."

Mourning Dove interrupted then. She had been preparing food and it was late and time to eat. We spent the night there. After our talk of cattle, war, and emigration was over, Mourning Dove and I sat by the creek and talked of more pleasant times and places. Even sitting there with her in that romantic setting, my thoughts were mostly of Louisa.

After a quiet time, she said, "I'll go soon, either to hide in the swamp or to go to this new land. I might never see you again."

There was no good response, so I didn't say anything.

We left the next morning, Running Dog and his companions to his village and me to Fort King. We had made a deal on the livestock and I was to go from Fort King to Running Dog's village and, with some of his people's help, start a drive to Black Creek.

Arriving at the Indian Agency at Fort King, I advised Wiley Thompson of what I had heard.

He said, "I know there are some problems. There have been indications that there might be some fighting. I can't convince myself, however, that it's as serious as you think. Where did you get your information, Isaac?"

I said, "From a trusted friend who also wants my help. He wants to move his clan to the new land, not because he thinks it's a good place, but because moving is better than his people getting killed here. He's afraid to follow your plan because it will expose his people to harassment and even death from Osceola's group, or to being robbed of their goods and slaves by some white people."

He said, "You overstate the case about the danger from Osceola. It's foolish for any Seminoles to fear Osceola. The army will protect them."

I said, "Sir, you don't even have enough army in the Florida Territory to protect itself, much less protect a group of Indians. The army can't protect you, either. And my friend thinks you should be cautious, that your life is in danger. Stay in the fort for the next few weeks"

He replied, "I can't hide in the fort. I can't believe there is any danger to me. We have almost a thousand regulars in Florida. Also, the War Department is sending fourteen more companies—seven hundred men."

I said, "That's less than a tenth of what might be needed."

He said, "Really? Do you think so? What would you expect me to do?"

I replied, "Just be warned. They might target you. Also, I would like to make a request in confidence."

He replied, "Go ahead."

"The friend about whom I spoke is Running Dog. He would like to move his band suddenly and without notice so as to avoid those who would interfere. He feels very strongly that there will be opposition to any attempt to move."

Thompson replied, "I've met Running Dog, though I don't know him well. We can't make any exceptions. Everyone has to move at the same time. The boats are ordered for then."

We debated the subject for almost an hour but came to no resolution satisfactory to me. Asking him to think about it and see if the government would pay for a ship for another place and time if I arranged it, I left for Running Dog's village.

There we agreed on a price for Running Dog's livestock. I left two days later with most of his livestock and with eight braves to help drive the herd. Selling some at Fort King and a couple of plantations on the St. Johns River, I arrived at Black Creek seven days later with only twenty percent of the livestock remaining unsold and a good profit for Running Dog and me. After buying some supplies they needed from Pa, my helpers left for their village.

PART IV

The Second Seminole War

November 10, 1835

*D*ue to the murders being committed by the Indians, and due to the skirmishes between small groups of volunteers and the Indians, the government began raising a volunteer army. Among the first companies assembled was that of Captain J. E. Hutcherson. His company, formed on November 10, 1835, was in the 4th Regiment, Second Brigade of the Florida Militia. Pa and two of my brothers, George and Asa, joined the company. One of Louisa's brothers also joined. Since I was the oldest son and Samuel the youngest, Pa asked us not to join at that time. We were to stay home and look after things. I guess Pa thought it would take two of us because I was always subject to leave for a few days or weeks at almost any time.

Though Captain Hutcherson's company was an infantry company, those people who owned horses were mounted. Since we owned a number of horses, our family members were mounted. Because he was fifty-five years old, Pa might have had to strain a little at times to keep up if he hadn't been mounted. Being mounted, and having considerable experience, Pa was soon appointed as the company's chief scout. With a horse he had greater mobility than the younger men without horses.

After three days of training and organization, the battalion was ordered to scout the area south of Black Creek. Before they left, the colonel sent word by one of my brothers that he wanted to see me.

Upon my arrival at his camp, the colonel said, "I understand that you know the Indian lands like the back of your hand. Also, it's reported that you speak Muskogee better than any white person in the area."

I said, "I know the area pretty well and can speak Muskogee well enough. I don't know about better than anyone else. Pa speaks pretty good Muskogee."

He said, "I want you to sign on as the battalion's chief scout."

"You have adequate scouts, both white and Indian. Pa taught me lots of what I know. He can track a fish across a lake. You should use him."

Grinning, he said, "I don't have any as good as you're supposed to be. It's been said that you're better than the Indians are. Also, I think I can trust you. I'm not always sure about the Indians."

I said, "Running Dog's as good or better than I am. But yes, once committed to something my word is good. But I'm not ready to commit now. I'll tell you what I will do, though. I'm going south for a while to see to the welfare of some friends.

Once that's taken care of, I'll talk to you about scouting. In the meantime, Pa's as good as I am."

Smiling, he said, "The story's around that you once let Osceola go when you had him under a gun."

I said, "That's true. He was only thirteen or fourteen and I was sixteen then. It seemed like the right thing to do at the time. Now, I'm not so sure."

Several days later, with a packhorse and part of Running Dog's money, I left for Fort King. At the fort, I learned from Wiley Thompson that he had not received a reply to his inquiry about the government paying for a ship to move Running Dog's band. I then proceeded to Running Dog's village. At his village I caught him up on what was going on.

He asked, "How much does a ship cost?"

I said, "Five hundred to a thousand dollars, depending on the size ship I could get. There are also other costs. Once you get to New Orleans, you'll have to get a riverboat up the river. When you leave the river, you still have a long overland trip to the reservation. Wagons, food, animals, and other expenses will also have to be paid. It would be too much without the government's help."

After digesting this for most of a minute he said, "We have to do something. Micanopy opposes war but he also opposes emigration. He has asked us Creeks to remain neutral when the fighting starts."

I said, "I'm afraid that minor fighting has already started. Also, the United States Government is sending regular troops to Florida and is raising a volunteer army. Members of my family have joined. There will almost certainly be heavy fighting. I've been asked to help."

Running Dog said, "What do you think I should do?"

I said, "There are no Upper Creeks involved that I know of, but friendly Indians are being recruited to fight for the United States. That's one possibility. You could, of course, also fight with Osceola and his band. In order to stay neutral, you would have to

165

emigrate or move your family far to the south in Florida. It would be better to stay near the west coast of Florida if you move south. Because of the lack of population on the west coast and the rivers that serve as transportation routes in the east, most of the fighting will likely occur in north, central, and east Florida."

Touching his red stick, he said, "While there are some Indians I would fight against, I can't fight my own people, the Red Stick Creeks. The Miccosukees and blacks are the most avid about fighting. I'm afraid, however, the fighting will drag on until the Creeks are heavily involved. If I fought for the United States, I would have to fight against the Red Sticks. I can't."

I said, "The only option I see left is to move south with your entire clan."

Taking out a map of Florida, I pointed out a spot north of the Everglades, east of the Peace River, and west of Lake Okeechobee.

I said, "You and I have been there together. I think that's the most northerly location you could be in and still avoid the fighting. Fighting might even occur there if the war drags on. In the end, you might have to go to the new lands in the west anyway. Now is about the time you would ordinarily go south to hunt. Why don't you pack up everything you own and take your entire clan with you? In the spring, move further south. At some time in the future, when the need arises, I'll find you. Until then you could live without being molested. Being only a two-day ride from the west coast, and having some of the gold from your livestock, you could buy anything you need from the Cuban fishermen who visit there. For a price they'll bring anything. I'll bring the rest of your money before you need to leave for the west. Or I can give it all to you now."

He said, "You keep half of the money safe. I'm not sure I can insure its safety under the present conditions. We would need extra horses for a move south. Yes, that's the thing to do. I'll do it. Stay with us until we leave. I could use your help and thoughts."

I stayed until they left on December 3, 1835. The first few days were spent in finding and buying horses for Running Dog. We tried to operate in such a way that no one would be suspicious that the entire clan was leaving.

Before the clan left we received news from a rider that Osceola had murdered one of the chiefs who advocated emigration. Charlie Emathla, one of the more powerful chiefs, had sold his livestock at Fort King at the sale arranged by Wiley Thompson. Charlie planned to lead his people to Fort Brooke and take the government's ships from there to New Orleans. Confronting Charlie, Osceola shot him in the chest and he died. Wanting everyone to know the reason for the killing was not robbery, Osceola left Charlie's gold with his body. It was a warning to all those who favored emigration.

As Running Dog and his clan moved south, in spite of Emathla's murder several chiefs who favored emigration moved their people to Fort Brooke. They expected to be protected there by the soldiers until the ships sailed with them early in January 1836.

About that same time some other chiefs started moving their people to islands, deep in the swamps. Fearing the Indians were preparing for war, white settlers began moving their families to the safety of forts or larger settlements so they could be protected. Some farmers even moved their families to Georgia, then returned to protect their farms. Most of these settlers then enlisted in the various volunteer companies being formed.

I rode south with Running Dog's clan for a couple of days. Saying goodbye to Mourning Dove for what might be the last time, I then turned north expecting to find and join the colonel's battalion as a scout. I found the colonel on December 13, 1835. He had been ordered to sweep the area between Hog Town and Fort King in search of hostiles. He was then in an area south of Hog Town and the big prairie and north of the town of Micanopy. The big prairie south of Hog Town was created when

Alachua Lake dried up some years earlier and was named Paynes Prairie. The name Hog Town was later changed to Gainesville because of General Gaines, who fought throughout the area. Also, Fort King later became the city of Ocala. Lots of plantations had been raided, their livestock stolen or killed, and buildings burned. Those actions prompted the deployment of the battalion.

The colonel said, "You've come to join up?"

"No. I've come to scout if you still want me. I don't plan to enlist for a whole term at this time. If I decide to leave, I'll leave. If I leave, I'll tell you before going."

"That's fair enough. Do you have any compunction about shooting Indians?"

"None about these Indians. The only Indians I wouldn't shoot have gone south. They'll not be in any of the fighting."

"Good," he said, extending his hand for a shake. He then told me what his mission was.

I said, "Osceola and his band are someplace between the prairie and Fort King. He's never far from Fort King."

"How do you know?" he asked.

"I just rode through the area," I said. "Also, I hear things from lots of Indians. And there were tracks. He's there all right."

He asked, "Do you know how many men he has?"

"Yes, I do," I said. "He has a little over fifty warriors in the band directly under his control. Eight or ten are Miccosukees. The rest are black. From the sign I saw I would say three other bands of the same size are with him. There might be two hundred fighters all together."

He said, "I would like to get them into a fight."

I said, "You better understand that Osceola is not stupid. He won't take you on in a standup fight. An Indian figures to kill a few of his enemies while taking minimum casualties. He'll then withdraw and wait for another day. They aren't paid to fight and don't get medals for being heroes. They also don't have political ambition. They only think that they are defending their homes and families. Ambush and hit-and-run will be Osceola's tactics."

He asked, "Can you find Osceola?"

"Without a doubt. I'll start before daylight. I'd suggest you move toward an area south of Paynes Prairie. I'd also suggest you move slow, keep outriders out in all directions, and keep your entire unit together until I can tell you where Osceola is."

"Do you want any scouts to go with you?"

"Not this time. When I want someone, I'll want Pa or one of my brothers from Captain Hutcherson's company."

I found Pa and the boys and spent the night with them. I had sweet potatoes, beans, rice, and salt pork on my packhorse so we cooked a better meal than the cornbread and beans they had been eating. They spent most of the time questioning me so they would know the lay of the land ahead of us.

I left thirty minutes before daylight in order to avoid being seen by any Indians who were watching the battalion. I was sure there would be Indians watching. Riding south by southeast, I soon saw the sign left by a couple of different small groups of riders. These, however, were not the ones I was looking for. Osceola would be with a large party. Those were only scout groups.

Constantly seeking cover to avoid detection, it was the second day before I found the signs of a large party of hostiles. I could have ridden openly, counting on my relationship with Osceola to keep me out of trouble, but somehow that didn't seem right. If I was going to be an enemy, I was going to act like an enemy.

I found the main Seminole camp the night of December 15, and got close enough to see that there were close to two hundred warriors. Those, plus the other small groups and some I probably didn't know about, meant we would be facing more than two hundred braves. That is if we could get them into a fight. I didn't see Osceola in the camp but he could have been asleep. I didn't get in real close to look.

I found the colonel's battalion on the sixteenth and reported to him.

He said, "How long would it take us to get to their camp?"

I said, "It would take all day tomorrow if we moved fast, but he probably won't be there when you get there. You're being watched all the time. He would hear about you coming hours before you got there. Actually, the way a group of soldiers move, wagons and all, it might take you two days to get there."

He said, "We'll leave the wagons with a company to guard them and they can come on behind. We'll get there before dark, surround their camp, and take them all."

I said, "I don't think I'd do that, Colonel. I'd be concerned about the wagons. There are close to two hundred Seminoles. One company might not be enough to guard the wagons. Also, like I said, he won't be there when you get there."

The colonel just stared at me for a few moments, then started issuing traveling orders.

As we were riding, Pa rode up beside me and said, "What's the plan?"

I said, "I think it's us going for a long hard march and finding an empty camp."

Pa said, "You told the colonel the Indians would be gone?"

"Yes, sir," I said, "but he didn't want to hear it. I also told him I wouldn't leave the wagons behind but he didn't want to hear that either."

Pa just shook his head.

By first dark we were only one mile from where the Indians had been camping. An hour later I was back from scouting and reported the camp was abandoned.

The colonel said, "Do you know where they went, what direction?"

I said, "No, I don't. You can't tell much in the dark. I sure would feel better, though, if your wagons were with us. Toward the wagons would be a good bet on the direction they're headed. It might be good to send another company back to help them."

He said, "Everyone is too exhausted to make a forced march

back to the wagons. You can locate the Indians for us tomorrow."

The next morning the colonel sent Pa and me to locate the Indians and turned his command back toward the trailing wagons. Pa and I hadn't followed the tracks a mile before they turned north.

Pa said, "The wagons."

I said, "That's what it looks like. They'll hit those wagons before any of us can get there. I hope they're set up in a good defensive position."

While Pa rode back to tell the colonel, I put my horse into a trot following the Indians' tracks. I didn't expect to get there in time to be of any help, but you can't just give up without trying. Hopefully the company that was left behind would be deployed properly. They just might be able to hold off the hostiles until help arrived.

It was the middle of the afternoon when I arrived at the badly bruised company that had been left to guard the wagons and the captain told me his story.

He said, "About twenty of them attacked us from the rear. Taking most of the company, I routed them and gave chase. We had followed them less than a mile when I heard shooting from around the wagons. Their main force attacked the small guard I left with the wagons. A few of those at the wagons escaped and joined us. I then ordered a bayonet charge on the wagons but most of the men refused to follow me. We had to fall back. I'm afraid the Indians have all of our supplies."

I said, "I don't much blame your men for not attacking, Captain. What's left of your sixty-five-man company wouldn't stand much chance in an assault on a hundred or more Indians who were behind trees and wagons. They might have killed all of you."

Leaving them, I again took up Osceola's trail. The Indians abandoned the wagons and packed everything on their ponies and the mules and horses they had taken. Walking and leading their animals, they only traveled a few miles before it became dark and they made camp. After finding them I returned to where the colonel, having joined together with his guard company, was camped.

After I reported to the colonel, he said, "I really would like to get them into a fight, do you have any suggestions?"

I said, "I never was short on giving advice, Colonel. Lots of folks don't take it though. First, I'd send your wounded men home. With outriders to prevent an ambush, I'd then follow the Indians' trail. It's plain enough for anyone to follow. You should also send out two or three small groups with four or five men in each group. Their job would be to get ahead of, or at least even with, Osceola's main group. These groups could get in close and shoot and run. If they get a chance, they should repeat the same thing over and over. That'll slow the Indians. They won't know for sure where your main body of troops is. It might even get Osceola mad enough to fight for a while. If you say so, I'll take three men and get in front of them. Pa could take three or four and hit his left flank. George and another group could hit their right flank. I can tell them where Osceola is and where he's likely to be tomorrow morning after sunup. All of these men had better be well-mounted, though, because they'll have to ride hard to get there and might have to run for their lives."

It surprised me a little when the colonel said, "We'll do it."

I said, "I'll pick three men from Captain Hutcherson's company that I know and leave about midnight. The others should leave at the same time. I can get them close to where they're going by daylight. If we were all rested a little bit, we could get the whole battalion there by daylight, but we're not. After two days hard march, most of your men and horses aren't in shape to make it tonight."

With some hard riding on the best horses available, by sunup I was a half-mile west of where the Indians were camping. There, my group parted with George and his group, whom we had escorted to there. By that time I figured Pa should be located on the east side of the camp. I then pushed on in a line parallel to the Indian's line-of-march of the previous day. Fifteen minutes later we turned east in an effort to get in front of Osceola's band. Selecting our positions carefully we notched trees to brace our rifles on while standing behind the trees, cut palmetto fans to stake out in front of us for additional concealment, and waited. We took turns dozing off for a few minutes as we waited.

It was more than an hour later when the first member of Osceola's band came into view two hundred yards from us. Waiting for their front person to get within a hundred yards, I squeezed off a shot that hit him in the chest. That was the signal for my companions to shoot. Those Indians with ponies got their animals back under the cover of the trees they had just left. The others dropped to the ground behind whatever bush or other cover they could find. Actually there were only about twenty in the open. The rest of them were still in the trees.

Within twenty-five seconds I was reloaded and waiting for a target; seeing none I decided to shoot at a puff of smoke. Based on the smoke from our first shots, they were firing at where they thought we were. Having moved after we fired, we were not there.

They soon decided there were only a few of us and started to send people to flank us on both sides. I then heard some scattered shots to their left. Pa and his group were obviously getting in a few good shots at those trying to flank us. Within seconds there were shots from the Indians' right. It seemed George was also in the correct position. Firing my reloaded rifle, I whistled for my men to withdraw and we crawled away to our concealed horses. There were a few more scattered shots from the Indians' right and left flanks as we withdrew.

Our work done there, we set out to ambush the Indians at another place when they moved again. However, I expected them to spend some time searching and scouting to determine how many of us there were and where we had gone before confronting us. They were slow and meticulous about their scouting. It was two hours before they covered the two miles to where we deployed that time. We only saw two Indians then. Both dropped when we fired. Whether from injury or to take cover, I'm not sure. But we had definitely slowed the Seminoles and the battalion was coming on behind them. A few more scattered shots were heard before dark, which I assumed was Pa or George.

Our use of Indian tactics caused Osceola's band to slow. Being fired on from various locations, they couldn't know if a large force was coming in behind any of the three small groups that fired on them. Their confusion, and subsequent hesitation, allowed the colonel time for travel. With them not knowing where our main force was, it was possible the colonel might engage the Indians before they found out. I was under no illusion that Osceola would hold still in a standup fight for very long when he was outnumbered. Shortly after he was sure where our main force was, he would overpower one of our small groups and vanish into the forest and swamp.

As dark fell, the colonel still hadn't closed on the main band of Indians. After dark, I placed my three men in positions where they might get to shoot at some of Osceola's retreating warriors the next day, told them to fire no more than two shots before abandoning their position and saving themselves, and left to find Pa's camp. The men were to make a wide circle and try to rejoin the battalion once they fired their shots.

It was through a series of whippoorwill calls that I found Pa's camp over an hour later. We had done the same thing a hundred times over the years.

When I walked into camp, Pa said, "We've got them confused, Boy."

I said, "Yes, sir, it looks like we have. I'm going to find the colonel's camp and hurry him along in the morning. I told the men in front of the Indians to fire a couple of shots and then get out of the way tomorrow morning. You and your men should do the same. There's no point in getting run over by a large party. Hopefully, the colonel might get in a lick on them before they can escape."

He said, "I'll see you after the fight."

I then headed off into the darkness in search of the battalion. It wasn't too hard to find. Although the cook-fires had burned down to almost nothing, the smoke could be smelled for a mile. Knowing they would have pickets out, I stood off and gave the whippoorwill call until my brother, Asa, answered me. He then let me know with a whistle that he had alerted the pickets. It was only then that I stood and walked into camp.

When my report to the colonel was finished, he said, "What I'm hearing you say is that we should start out just before daylight and make a run at them."

I said, "Yes, sir. What I'd do is keep outriders out at a hundred and two hundred yards, front and sides. A full company could be behind the forward outriders. The rest of your command could follow fifty yards behind that company. You could then deploy them to the hostiles' flanks as needed, or make a bayonet charge depending on the situation."

Referring to Osceola, he said, "Do you think he'll stand and fight?"

I replied, "Not for very long. He'll want to know where your main force is before he withdraws, though. He's not stupid."

The colonel said, "I've learned that already."

In the darkness of the early dawn, we could barely see forty yards when the colonel ordered his outriders out the next morning. Moving at a rapid march, we had traveled for an hour when we heard scattered shots less than four hundred yards ahead of us and slightly to our right. The colonel started to move in that direction but I told him the firing was just Pa and his group probing. The main party was straight ahead of us. In less than five minutes, our forward outriders received and returned fire.

Colonel Warren then ordered the forward company to advance on the double. Within three minutes the major part of the fight was under way.

After thirty minutes of flanking by us and counter-flanking by them, Colonel Warren, thinking he had isolated a large group, ordered a bayonet charge. The Indians withdrew for two hundred yards and again established their defenses. Twenty minutes later the colonel ordered another bayonet charge. The Seminoles, taking their dead and wounded with them, then withdrew from the battle. There were only some scattered shots over the next few minutes.

When they withdrew, the Indians took all the food and ammunition they had captured from the supply wagons. They did abandon some other small items of equipment, which we recovered.

Pa showed up by my side while the last few shots were being fired.

He said, "That's about as good as it could be done. We'll face Osceola lots of times before we get him. Hindsight's always better than foresight, but it would be good if you had shot him fifteen years ago."

The colonel then asked me and Pa to locate the Seminoles and advise him where they were. Taking three men each from Colonel Warren's command, we both left taking separate routes. After traveling a couple of miles from the site of the battle, the Seminoles separated into smaller bands and left, traveling in different directions. A half-day of hard tracking showed they were not going to reassemble any time soon. By good dark that night, my group returned to Colonel Warren's camp and made a report.

Within an hour Pa reported in and confirmed what we had reported. The Indians had split up and returned to their swamp hideouts.

While there had been earlier encounters between small parties, murders, and raids on the white plantations, farms, and

Indian villages, the battles of December 17 through December 19 signaled the formal opening of the Second Seminole War. Not only did the Seminoles attack and take the supply wagons on December 17, there were also coordinated attacks on five plantations on that same day. The plantations were burned, some people were killed, slaves were taken, and livestock was killed or run off. In the three days of fighting between Osceola's group and the colonel's battalion there were several dead and thirty wounded on our side. We don't know how many casualties the Seminoles suffered; they took their wounded and dead with them.

Things only got worse after that. A number of slaves, perhaps hundreds, ran away and joined the Seminoles. The United States government then began raising more volunteer units. Militia units were being raised not only in the Florida Territory but also throughout most of the United States. Also a large number of companies were recruited from several friendly Indian tribes.

Because of concerns that the sugar plantations along the Mantanzas River, the St. Johns River, and in the Mosquito County areas would be attacked, militia units were raised and stationed in those areas. One of the biggest of them was the Anderson Plantation, formerly the Dun-Lawton Plantation. James and George Anderson had purchased it in 1832. It contained a steam-powered sugar mill and sawmill. Also concerned about the small size of the force stationed in and around Fort King, reinforcements were dispatched from Fort Brooke to assist there. Those troops left Fort Brooke on December 22, 1835, for the hundred-mile march to Fort King.

On December 25, 1835, the war escalated. There were a number of simultaneous, coordinated attacks on several more of the sugar plantations. Of the thirty or so large sugar plantations still in operation, six were destroyed and others were damaged. The St. Johns area Seminoles, led by King Phillip and John Caesar, were responsible for those attacks. Because of those successes, more slaves ran away to join the Seminoles.

Also on December 25, the relief column from Fort Brooke, led by Major Dade, was then three days on the road toward Fort King. Followed by Indians, but unaware of the escalation in the fighting, Major Dade felt that his column of 108 officers and men was safe traveling on the military road. After all, the road was authorized in the treaty. Also, Dade had no information on the escalation of the fighting.

Major Dade assigned no advance guard or outriders. Riding his horse, he led the column—an infantry and artillery unit combined. Dade's troops were not mounted. Massed in marching formation of four abreast as they were, his troops made easy and inviting targets. Still, the Indians waited until the sixth day of the march to attack.

As was their custom, the Seminoles had intended to attack the column at a river crossing. At a crossing, some of the troops would be at their mercy. In addition to being able to attack the command while it was divided on each side of the river, some of the soldiers would be in the water. But the Seminoles were waiting for Osceola and his band.

Chiefs Micanopy, Jumper, and Alligator, with the 180 warriors shadowing the Dade Command, finally decided to wait no longer. They placed their warriors on the west side of the military road at a point where a large, rain-filled pond prevented the soldiers from escaping to the east. Placing their warriors behind trees and palmetto bushes thirty yards from the trail, they had the warriors lie flat until the first shot was fired. The Indians remained hidden until almost midmorning when Major Dade's force arrived. Dade still had no outriders in any direction.

Major Dade, riding well out front, was shot by Micanopy, who fired the first shot. Micanopy's shot was the signal for the Indians to shoot. Firing a volley into Dade's massed troops at point-blank range, the 180 Indians killed over half of Dade's force with the first volley.

Trying to mount some defense, the remaining soldiers fired back as soon as they could get their weapons loaded. They were marching without loaded weapons, as it was a common practice to not load a weapon until combat was imminent. If weapons loaded with black powder are left loaded for as little as three days without unloading and cleaning the barrel, the black powder will corrode and pit the barrel. Pulling the ball from the barrel and cleaning the weapon is a major undertaking. Ammunition is also scarce and expensive and gunpowder is lost in the pulling and cleaning process.

Because the weather was cold the soldiers had their overcoats buttoned over their powder and shot. The Seminoles—not realizing the effect of their first volley, not aware the soldiers had empty weapons, and frightened the first time the six-pound cannon was fired—retreated. Observing that the soldiers remained in a fixed position and were building a triangular breastwork of logs, the Indians began to return to the attack. Had the soldiers immediately returned fire and charged, as was their normal practice, the Indians would have almost certainly split up and retreated to their swamp hideouts.

The cannon was fired several times, which only caused the Indians to dodge behind trees or drop to the ground when the motion was made to light the fuse. There were two other effects of firing the cannon. First, the soldiers had to be exposed to load the cannon; many were killed while trying to accomplish this. Second, the cannon's powder supply was soon exhausted. The Indians then moved in and killed and scalped the rest of them. Two privates survived the attack and escaped. One soon died of his wounds. The other, though wounded, walked and crawled the seventy miles to Fort Brooke and reported the ambush. Later, Alligator said the Indians only had eight casualties—three dead and five wounded.

Osceola did not arrive at the scene of the Dade massacre until two days later. During the entire time before and during the attack on Major Dade, Osceola was lying in wait to kill Wiley Thompson outside Fort King. With Osceola were his forty black and ten Miccosukee warriors. When the sun was still two hours high, Wiley Thompson and a lieutenant went for a walk outside the fort. When they were well clear of Fort King, the Seminoles shot them from ambush and took their scalps. They were hit with over a dozen rounds each. Osceola supposedly used the same rifle he had been given as a gift by Thompson. After they killed the trader and his assistants who supplied the army, they looted the store. The trader's slaves were spared and told they must join the Seminoles. Most of the command at Fort King was away on a mission at the time. Since his command was small, it was some time before the fort commander left the fort and recovered the dead. In killing Thompson, Osceola had taken revenge for what he felt were earlier insults by Thompson.

Since the Seminoles we were chasing had split up and gone back to the swamp, we headed to General Clinch's plantation, Auld Lang Syne, to secure supplies. Having lost our supplies to the Seminoles, we were in desperate need. General Clinch's plantation was soon named Fort Drane after a Major Drane who supervised its construction. South of Micanopy and about twenty miles northwest of Fort King, the plantation was barely out of the designated Indian reservation.

At Fort Drane we joined with several hundred other Florida militia under the command of Governor/General Richard Keith Call. Also at Fort Drane were six companies, 250 men total, of regular soldiers under the command of Lieutenant Colonel C. W. Fanning.

We hadn't been at the fort many days when some friendly Indian scouts brought word that a force of three hundred Seminoles was assembled across the Withlacoochee River from us. The Withlacoochee is close to forty miles south of Fort Drane. After building new villages there, most of the Seminoles had settled south of the river in a marshy area where the river makes a loop and partially encloses a hundred square miles. The news was just what General Clinch wanted to hear. It presented an opportunity to try to defeat the Seminoles and help his political career. Clinch had little respect for the Seminoles' fighting ability. Thinking to move quickly and catch the Seminoles by surprise, General Clinch ordered us to be ready to move out the next day.

We were under way early on December 29. There was considerable discussion by some of the west Florida militia about not going. While some of them had signed up at the same time as Pa and my brothers, others had signed up earlier and their tour of duty ended at midnight on December 31. They didn't see much point in marching to a battle they would immediately leave. We had not, at the time, heard about Dade's encounter of December 28. That knowledge might have convinced some of the short-timers not to go. It might also have given General Clinch reason to reevaluate his plans.

While no one asked me, I was impressed with General Clinch's order of march. Not only did he have outriders in advance of the column, he had mounted militia a hundred yards to the right and left. Our supply train, including a wagon and several one-horse carts, followed close behind the regulars. The balance of the militia followed the supplies. There would be no ambush of our column. Our total column numbered 950 men—250 regulars and 700 militia. The regulars were armed with the standard-issue musket and bayonet. We volunteers were armed with whatever kind of weapon we happened to own and like, or an army issue if we didn't own proper weapons.

The one thing causing me the most concern was the fact that a large pack of dogs accompanied us. From the start of the trip the dogs were running everywhere, shaking the woods with their barking. It would be impossible to surprise the Seminoles—not that I thought we could surprise them under any circumstance. I relayed my concern to Colonel Warren.

He said, "That's a concern I share. I'll speak with Clinch

about it when we camp tonight, though he's probably thought of it already. Hopefully he has. He has a good-sized ego and doesn't like to be prompted."

Slowed by having to clear the trail so it was wide enough for the wagon and carts, and by having to get them out of a bog occasionally, we didn't make it halfway to the river that first day. As we camped, I was again impressed by General Clinch's placement of picket.

The second day of travel was much like the first. On the positive side, we were not rained on during the second day. The ground, however, was wet from earlier rains and the wagons and carts frequently bogged down. The weather was cool and damp, so the hard work of clearing a trail for the supply train was at least bearable. In spite of the narrow trail and the extra work required to clear it, we covered most of the rest of the distance to the river that day.

My own knowledge of the area, from traveling there with Running Dog, placed us three miles from the Withlacoochee River as we camped for the second night. General Clinch's Indian and black scouts confirmed my estimate. Since Clinch had his own scouts, I rode close to Colonel Warren without being called on to scout. While being only three miles from the river, I knew we were five miles, as the crow flies, from the best ford, which was three miles upriver from where we would reach the river if we continued on our present course. I said as much to Colonel Warren.

He said, "Are you sure?"

I said, "Pretty sure. I've crossed there a dozen times with Running Dog. When the river's at its normal level, it's only about three feet deep at the ford. Since there has been lots of rain, it might be four or five feet deep. I could be a little off in my estimate of the distance. It's easy to misjudge in the woods."

He said, "Can we cross at the point ahead of us?"

I replied, "You can cross the river anywhere you want to, but

182

you might have some difficulty. It's deep, but only thirty-five or forty yards wide in many places. The horses, and those men who can swim, can swim it. There's no way to get the wagons and carts across without building a bridge. I would also like to point out one other thing—"

Without waiting for me to finish, he said, "What?"

"What with the dogs barking, horses whinnying, and the chopping of trees to clear the path for the supply train, I'm certain the Seminoles know we're here. You can bet your horse that their scouts know where we are."

Impatient, he interrupted and said, "What's your point?"

I replied, "The Indian's favorite place to fight is at a river crossing, while their enemy is trying to cross. If they know about us, which they most certainly do, they'll be waiting in ambush at the ford. They'll expect us to cross there."

Most of a minute passed before he said, "Maybe we should not have a conversation with General Clinch. He might want to cross at the shallow point."

I said, "I could take a couple of men and check it out. Or better still, I could go by myself."

"No. Clinch has his scouts out. If he had plans to cross at a ford, then his scouts might have had reason to bring us here."

"It might be that they're afraid to cross at the ford. Or it could be there's an ambush where they're taking us," I said.

He said, "Let's sleep on it. Thanks for the information."

Having several sick men who couldn't travel, and not wanting to drag the wagon train through the thickets and bogs to the river, the next morning we left the wagons at the campsite. Clinch left a full company, fifty men, to guard our supplies. I would have felt better if he had left 150 men. We didn't need all of the nine hundred who were still in our party. Also, that was the last day of their ninety-day enlistment for lots of the volunteers. They could have been left as guards. I couldn't see them trying to get killed in a bayonet charge on their last day. But then, I wasn't in charge.

General Clinch still planned on making a surprise attack. In order to keep them quiet, the general had all the hounds rounded up and penned before leaving. I left an hour before the others moved out. Colonel Warren asked me to go.

By the time they were moving, I was sliding off my horse and holding on to the pommel as he swam the river a half-mile downstream from the unit's probable crossing place. Turning upstream after crossing the river and riding as far as a hundred yards from the riverbank, I thoroughly scouted a distance of a mile and a half upstream. There were a number of moccasin and horse tracks, all headed upstream.

While the column was still two miles from the river, I heard the dogs join them. They had broken loose and followed the column. In the still, cold morning air, their barking was loud and clear as they chased animals of all types. Any thought of a surprise attack should have vanished then.

Crossing the river at the furthest point upstream I had scouted, I then rode toward the column. Riding in from the side of the column to join it, I reported to Colonel Warren.

"Colonel, I saw tracks on both sides of the river. They were all going upstream. Most of them were a day old or more. I saw no sign left by Clinch's Indian scouts. I don't know where they've been scouting but it's not on the other side where we'll reach the river. Still, there are no Indians on the other side where we're going to cross."

He said, "You're sure there's no ambush at the river?"

"Not where we'll hit it. I don't understand why our Indian scouts are leading us to this place. Also, the river's up about a foot."

He didn't respond or give me further instructions so I pulled my horse up and followed a few yards behind him.

Once at the river it became clear that General Clinch had no idea that there was no ford until he got there. He clearly had no plan as to how to cross the river. Clinch soon gave orders to build some rafts out of some logs that were lying about. He also gave orders to start building a bridge. Most of the logs were so wet they would hardly float so the rafts were a failure. I couldn't figure out why he didn't just order a hundred or so of us to swim our horses across. The river wasn't more than thirty-five yards across. Traveling alone, I wouldn't have done more than pause at the river to strip and get a firm grip on my things to hold them up and keep them dry. That's what I did earlier when scouting.

As the morning fog lifted from the river, someone spotted a canoe on the other bank. A couple of lieutenants volunteered to go across and see if it was useable, but General Clinch said it was too dangerous for his officers.

Standing nearby, I said, "There aren't any Indians on the other side right here."

Turning to me, Clinch said, "How do you know?"

I said, "I was over there an hour ago. All the Indian tracks go upstream. They're someplace up there. They could have heard all the barking and commotion and be on the way here by now, however. Also, I didn't see any sign that your scouts had scouted the other side of the river."

Two regular soldiers stripped and swam across. The general didn't try to stop them. I guess they were not all that valuable. After turning the canoe upside down to dump the water, and securing some limbs to serve as paddles and poles, they rowed it back across.

The canoe was large enough to hold eight men and their equipment. General Clinch then had Lieutenant Colonel Fanning start his regulars across. Ropes were tied together and tied to each end of the canoe and, after the first eight men crossed, it was pulled back and forth across the river with the ropes. Eight men could then be ferried each time and a space in the canoe was not wasted in rowing it back across. At the rate they were progressing it would have taken two days to get all the troops across. Some of the men then started stripping and swimming across. The canoe was then used to send their things across so the speed of the crossing was increased.

When the first men were across, they set up a defensive perimeter. As the morning passed without any trouble, they became a little casual about the situation and began lying around. The colonel then called on some of the Florida militia to swim their horses across. Some of the men who were to be discharged that night declined to cross the river. Almost a full company of the short-timers even started back down the trail toward the previous night's camp. About fifty of the militia members joined the colonel in crossing the river. Pa, my brothers, and I were among those.

As soon as we were across the river, the Indians opened fire. They had heard all the commotion and slipped into the area. We dismounted, tied our horses to some trees, and fought on foot with the regulars. We didn't fight like the regulars, though. They sometimes formed in ranks to fight. Seeing the folly in that, we volunteers fought from behind trees and bushes. We were holding the left flank of the regulars. After a number of casualties were taken, the regulars began using our tactics.

It soon became clear that the Indians were more than holding their own in the fight. Their small-caliber Cuban rifles were more accurate from a distance than were the regulars' muskets. Some of us volunteers, armed with larger-caliber rifles, were doing a little better than the regulars. Most of the volunteers were only armed with muskets, however. At the distance we were shooting, they were not having any more impact than the regulars were.

Unknown to us, the five hundred militia still on the other side of the river were receiving fire from the Indians on our flanks. Thinking they were being attacked from the rear and from their side of the river, or just using that as a pretext to keep from crossing the river, they set up in positions facing away from the river.

The Indians were using a tactic we always used. After firing their weapon and giving away their location in the brush with the puff of smoke, they moved quickly in one direction or the other to avoid those firing at their smoke. In spite of being wounded, many of the regulars held their position and continued to fire. The Indians' rifle balls were of such small caliber that they did not always put the wounded out of action.

As the fight progressed I spotted Osceola wearing a blue officer's coat. While we didn't know it then, Osceola got the coat from a Seminole who had taken it at the Dade massacre. Trying to atone for a mistake made years before, I tried to shoot Osceola. Because he moved after each time he fired his rifle, I waited for Osceola to fire and then fired two yards to his left. He moved to the right. Again I loaded my rifle and again searched among the potential targets for him. Finding him, I again fired to his left immediately after he fired. Again he ducked to the right.

General Clinch then ordered a bayonet charge. We moved forward, fired, reloaded, and fired again. As the regulars brandished their bayonets while they moved forward firing and reloading, the Indians fell back. When General Clinch halted the charge and regrouped, the Seminoles stopped retreating and reengaged us.

Since I had chosen him as my personal target, I again looked for Osceola. He had moved along the line of his warriors and was no longer at a place where I could get a good shot at him.

After fifteen more minutes General Clinch ordered another bayonet charge. It produced the same result as before. The Seminoles stopped retreating when the regulars stopped charging. Again we entered a period of exchanging gunfire with them. After another fifteen minutes, General Clinch called for a third bayonet charge. It occasioned no result except to cause the Seminoles to again temporarily withdraw.

As we again entered a period of being stationary and exchanging fire, I saw Osceola working his way back down his line of warriors to encourage them. Occasionally he would stop to fire. Concentrating on him, I soon noticed that every time he fired his rifle he then moved quickly to his right. Calling to Pa, who was some fifteen yards from me and behind a tree, I gave him the information about Osceola's habit.

I then said, "Pa, I'm going to shoot two yards to his right and low when I see the smoke from his rifle. You shoot one yard to his right and low. One of us might hit him."

Still shouting encouragement to his warriors, three minutes later Osceola was in front of us. Raising his rifle, Osceola aimed carefully at something and fired. As the smoke from his rifle billowed out in front of him, I fired at the spot I had picked out. Pa's rifle fired at near the same time as mine. When the smoke cleared, Osceola was down. When he got to his feet, one of his arms was hanging useless at his side. I'm not saying it was Pa's ball or mine that hit his arm as there were lots of people shooting at the time, but Osceola left the field and the fight ended. The battle had lasted for more than an hour. The Seminoles then withdrew. My brother, George, a corporal and a good scout, and I scouted the area to be sure they were gone.

Returning from the scouting mission, we found the log bridge had been completed across the river. Our return to the other side was much more orderly than the original crossing. That was the only benefit of having built the bridge.

Word released later by the Indians told of three dead and five wounded Indians at the river fight. It soon came to me that the Indians had reported the exact same number killed and wounded at the Dade massacre. I later heard from Four Toes that thirteen Seminoles died of their wounds and two dozen more were wounded at the river. I knew that Four Toes could count. Using his fingers, I taught him something of counting when I sold him his wife, and on a couple of other occasions. That's when I began to doubt the numbers given by the Indians at the Dade massacre. The Seminoles were known to give low counts in order to discourage the white fighters. I later learned there were only two hundred Seminoles in the fight at the river, twenty-five of whom were black Seminoles. By our best count, four of our regulars were killed and a combination of fifty-nine regulars and volunteers were wounded. Fortunately for us, the small-caliber Cuban rifles the Indians were using didn't make a gaping wound so almost all of the wounded survived.

Once back across the river, General Clinch ordered us to form in a column of twos for the march to Fort Drane. General Clinch blamed the militia for him having to leave the battlefield. He said the militia refused to fight beyond their enlistment date, which ended at midnight on December 31. In our opinion it was the general's doing. There were over three hundred militia members who would not be discharged until March. Also, Clinch had over two hundred regular soldiers still able to fight. Additionally, many of those who were to be discharged would have reenlisted if asked. They were never asked. Even without them we had the Seminoles outnumbered more than two to one. It appeared to me that Clinch had caused the situation.

One major problem caused by Clinch was that each man who left Fort Drane for the fight had only three days' rations in his pack. Even without counting the time needed to fight and build bridges, it was four days' march to the river and back. Also, there was little food other than corn for the horses in the supply train. We were down to eating a few handfuls of corn each day before we reached Fort Drane—corn intended for the horses. It might be that the general secretly envisioned us plundering the Indian villages in the cove of the Withlacoochee River. Had we pressed on, we probably could have plundered a village or two but as it turned out we never reached a village. The friendly Indian scouts did not seem to be much help but Pa, George, Asa, and I could certainly have found a village or two.

I couldn't help but think it was the blunders of some of the officers that led to the embarrassment at the river. It was a mind-set of most white commanders that they were not going to take any risks in a fight that might make them have to break off and retreat. That would hurt their reputation. They wanted to have overpowering numbers and position before they fought. The Seminoles had no compunction about fighting for a few minutes and then running. It's the intelligent thing to do. Had I been in charge, I would have ordered the five hundred mounted volunteers to swim their horses across the river first. Covered by that powerful force, we could have built a bridge and marched the other four hundred across. Within hours we could have flanked and routed, killed, or captured the two hundred Indians led by Osceola and Alligator. We then could have plundered and destroyed their villages at will. But hindsight is usually better than foresight.

Back at Fort Drane the volunteers from the Tallahassee and middle Florida area who were discharged left for their homes. After speaking to Colonel Warren and saying goodbye to my pa and brothers, I left for Black Creek.

As I traveled home, I viewed some of the damage done to the plantations along the upper St. Johns River. A number of plantations were burned. Others were fortified for defensive purposes. The people at some plantations had packed up and abandoned their property. Scores, perhaps hundreds, of slaves had run away, some to join the Seminoles.

Violence had broken out all over the Florida Territory. Word was just arriving at St. Augustine and Black Creek about Indian attacks as far south as Key Biscayne and as far west as the Apalachicola River. Back while we were chasing Osceola near Paynes Prairie, some of the Alachua area Seminoles had attacked north into Duval County. A number of people near Black Creek and in Mandarin were killed. Also, several homes and plantations were plundered and burned, and slaves were stolen or had run away. Many of the farmers along the bank of the St. Johns and along Black Creek were moving their family and what goods they could carry to Mandarin or Jacksonville.

I stopped at Captain Lewis' farm before going home. His five sons who were still at home had fortified his place. Though they had been attacked once, they had repelled the attackers. The Indians then proceeded to less well-defended farms. One of the boys was wounded, but his wound was slight. I would have inquired about Louisa, but she came running from the house to meet me, eliminating the need for me to inquire.

Openly throwing her arms around me, she said, "Oh, Isaac, you're safe. I've been so worried."

Returning her hug, I said, "You worried without need. There have been long marches and little enough fighting where I've been."

Her mother and a couple of the boys arrived as I was speaking.

Henry, one of the brothers, said, "There has been enough excitement around here. We fought off one attack. They'll think twice before attacking us again." With admiration and for an obvious purpose, he added, "Louisa loaded and fired a dozen times during the attack."

Taking her by the shoulders and holding her at arm's length, I said, "I want to look at this great Indian fighter who was only a beautiful young woman when I left."

Pracilla hugged me then and led me inside. She then set in to pampering me with hot coffee and food, just as she did on all my visits. The boys gathered round the table and we told of our adventures. I learned that, in addition to Louisa and her mother, the younger two girls—Eliza and Caroline—had repeatedly fired a musket during the attack on their farm. While they had lost some livestock and a barn, they had also inflicted some pain on the Indians.

Osceola's name was a hot brand that was burning in the ears of everyone at the time. I drew stares of admiration while telling about Pa or me, probably, putting a ball in his arm. Since I had everyone's attention and they had just been in a fight with the Indians, I took advantage of the opportunity to give some advice.

"It's been said that the Seminoles have taken women as captives and the women then vanish never to be seen again. I hope that never happens to any of you. If it does, I have a suggestion. It seems the Seminoles are inclined toward fighting in large groups and then splitting into small groups to hide in the swamps and avoid those who're following. If you ever find yourself in such a situation, keep your wits about you. When the large group splits up, do something to mark the trail of the group you're with. Mark it as soon as possible after they split up, hopefully within a hundred yards or so. Tear off some pieces of cloth as soon as you're captured and have them ready to hang on bushes soon after your group splits off. If you don't have an opportunity to do that, just drop some along on the trail. This should be done at a time you are not being watched, of course. You could also use sticks to form your initials or name on the ground. Few of the Indians speak even a few words of English. None of them can read or write. The Muskogee language doesn't even have a written form. They would think nothing of two sticks arranged to form the letter L for Louisa, for example. Those following would then know which small group to follow."

I would have left immediately for Black Creek but Henry told me he had just been there the day before to check on the family. Except for one visitor, the Seminoles had bypassed our farm. Four Toes had gone by there to call out from the darkness and tell the Cubans they would be passing our place by. So I stayed the night at the captain's place.

After a short time on the porch talking that night, Louisa's brothers and sisters left us alone.

Slipping an arm around her shoulders, I baited her a little by saying, "You'll be having a birthday in a couple of months. You'll be twenty-one then."

Exasperated, she replied, "Isaac! I'll be twenty-two years old on March the seventh."

Turning her head slightly toward me with my left hand, I

kissed her lightly on the lips and said, "Well then, it's about time I asked you to marry me. It's a poor time, though, with the Indians going wild like they are."

Throwing both arms around me, she said, "It's never a poor time, Isaac. You know I've waited for you since I was six years old."

"One of the things I was waiting for was to ask your Pa for you, but he left for Norway over three years ago."

"He has been gone so long that we have about given up on him returning. His ship must have gone down or been taken by pirates." She turned her head and wiped her eyes. "But since you've finally asked I'll set the date for the middle of May whether Pa gets back by then or not. I know most of your family is off with the militia. We'll want them to be here so we'll wait till then."

I said, "It doesn't matter to me whether they're here or not."

She replied, "It matters to me. I've waited sixteen years. Four more months won't hurt."

January 8, 1836

I was still at the captain's house when a sergeant came by trying to gather volunteers. He said, "We're trying to place some people at the Anderson sugar plantation and a couple of other places. The Indians have burned several plantations and we hope to keep them from burning the other large plantations."

Henry replied, "Our farm isn't as big as some of the others but we think it's worth defending. We'll stay here."

The sergeant said, "My lieutenant could come with a squad of men and force you to help."

Henry looked him straight in the eye. "If he comes trying to force us to abandon our place, he'll have one less squad left to defend the other places. You'll also wind up with one less lieutenant."

Saying he was getting the same response from lots of places, the sergeant left. When he left, I left for Black Creek.

The normal January activities were ongoing at Black Creek. Cane was being ground and the juice turned into molasses and sugar. The byproducts of this procedure, skimmings, were being processed into rum. Also, a couple of people had a line of varmint traps set. Others had set lines out for catfish and had some fish traps in the water. In spite of all this activity, expecting an attack at any time, they were ever vigilant. Naturally I had to tell everything I knew about Pa, George, and Asa, and about our adventures.

When I finished with the stories, up to my arriving at Captain Lewis' farm, Ma said, "And how is Pracilla?"

I said, "She, and everyone else, was fine, Ma."

She said, "And Louisa, she hasn't married has she?"

I said, "You know full well she hasn't, Ma. Henry was over here a few days ago. I know you wouldn't pass up the chance to ask him."

Undaunted, she said, "I was hoping you might say you had asked her."

"I did, Ma, but she wouldn't have me."

There for a couple of seconds I had her going. Her face took on a troubled, even desperate look. Then she broke out into an unsure half-smile and said, "You're just funning me, aren't you?"

"Yes, ma'am. We're to be married in May. Hopefully, her pa and mine will be back by then. She thinks some of the Indian trouble might be settled by then, though I don't think there's a chance of that."

Ma's eyes were dancing. I thought she would come around the table and hug me, but she didn't.

She just said, "I'd like to be at the wedding. You know that civilization has caught up with us and you'll need to get a license to marry this time."

I said, "Yes, I've heard something about that. I've also heard that a license can be obtained in Jacksonville and St. Augustine."

Concerned that because of the Indian troubles something might happen to my family and me, I also was concerned with the subsequent fate of the Cubans. In spite of their being in the Florida Territory illegally and there being no papers of any kind on them except what we had written, they were thought to be our slaves by everyone. If something were to happen to us, they would be dealt with as slaves. Though they were like trusted members of the family, they had no more rights than my pack of hounds. In fact, they had fewer rights than the hounds. Since the start of the Second Seminole War, the governor of Florida had issued an order that any black, free or slave, not in the presence of his or her owner or employer would be apprehended and detained. The hounds, on the other hand, could run the woods without restrictions. With those things in mind I called a meeting of all the Cubans.

I told them, "You need to consider what you want to do over the near-term. Some of you could still sign on as a hand on a ship sailing from here. Also, since you've been sharecropping, some of you have enough money to hire passage to another country. Lots of black people have also joined the Seminoles. I don't advise that, though. They'll lose in the end. Lots of them won't survive the war. The United States government will be relentless in moving or killing the Indians and the black people with them. Of course you can also stay on here as you have been doing."

Pablo, one of the more vocal of the Cubans, said, "We've talked about all of our choices and it seems none are very good. If we ship out, whether as a worker or a passenger, we might end up being confined to the ship as slaves, or simply carried someplace and sold. Joining the Indians isn't an option as far as we see it. We have been treated like family here and we all think we're better off here as sharecroppers than anywhere else."

After the Cubans talked among themselves for a while, Pablo

said, "We don't think the Indians will harm your family or you. Four Toes said your place would be bypassed. We think that we will also be safe here."

I said, "Yes, but time has passed since Four Toes said that. Things have changed. Also, the war will continue for a long time. Pa and my brothers now fight in the south with Colonel Warren. I've just returned from there. It's very probable it was Pa's or my rifle ball that wounded Osceola. There're lots of reasons for them to attack us."

Pablo said, "Yes, and lots of reasons for them not to attack you. Your pa has traded with them for years without cheating them. Also, it has been said that you gave Osceola his life when you could have killed him in a fight. He would be dead if anyone but you had held the musket on him. Then there's the fact that you practically gave Four Toes his wife after he offered you four hundred and fifty dollars for her. And you and Running Dog are like brothers. They would no more kill your family than you would kill Running Dog's or Four Toes' family. We've heard all the stories from Four Toes and we told him about you taking us from the slave runners."

"Things change," I said.

Pablo said, "We're not leaving unless you make us leave. I don't think it'll come to fighting but if it comes down to fighting, we'll be fighting on your side with whatever weapons we can find."

All of them were nodding their heads and saying, "Yeah," or "That's right."

I said, "Okay then, but I'm going to talk to some others about the situation. If I get any ideas, I'll talk with you again. Though it's illegal, I'm going to place muskets in your cabins. You're not to have them outside the cabin except in the case of an attack."

I hadn't been home but a few days when the sergeant who had been by Captain Lewis' farm came to our place for the same purpose.

He said, "There's evidence of increased Indian activity. We feel additional attacks on plantations in the area are eminent."

I said, "You'll get no more help from here than you got at Captain Lewis' place. If we're going to defend a farm, it'll be our own."

Though he left shortly after that, his visit served to heighten my concern for our family's safety. I again checked to be sure our family members and the Cubans had proper weapons in their quarters. We also went over our defensive plans in case of attack. Though Florida Indians usually didn't attack at night, we used one strategy not previously used. We staked a dog out at various places around the buildings each night. As they did when they attacked while we were building the initial cabin, they will continue a fight into the night that started in the daytime. But Indians generally didn't start a fight at night. Still, staking out the dogs at night seemed prudent.

In spite of my concerns, we received no visitors until several nights later. On that night one of the dogs announced with his barking that something was wrong. Slipping from the house and making my way in the direction of the barking, which then stopped, I soon heard a muted conversation. Recognizing one of the voices as Pablo's, I crept closer. Though they were speaking Spanish I could understand enough Spanish to follow what they were saying.

Pablo was saying, "We're all here on the place. The young Mister Isaac is also here."

A second voice, which I recognized as Four Toes, said, "Good. All of you need to stay close to the farm for the next couple of days."

Having got close to them, I spoke up then. "Pablo, Four Toes, what's going on?"

Four Toes said, "Nothing that concerns you or yours, Isaac. And I'm glad it doesn't. I would dread to have you sneaking up on me in the dark. You move quieter than anyone I know."

I said, "I have interests and concerns for people beyond the boundaries of this farm. Do you know of Captain Lewis' farm on the St. Johns River?"

He said, "I know of the farm. It was attacked, some time back, unsuccessfully, by a small group of warriors."

I said, "The oldest girl, Louisa, and I are to marry soon. If their farm is attacked, I'll take it as an attack on my family."

Still too far away to see them, or to be seen in the dark, I waited several seconds before he answered.

He said, "It'll not be attacked by anyone I have influence with."

As I moved closer, I said, "Good. It's good to see you again, my friend. Someday we might meet again under better circumstances."

After reaching out to clasp my hand and Pablo's, Four Toes melted into the darkness.

I contemplated whether or not to carry an alarm to the various plantations along the St. Johns. After much consideration it seemed like a futile effort; everyone was already at a heightened state of alarm. My cautioning them that there might be an attack in the next few days would not cause them to increase their readiness. I did, however, leave that night for Captain Lewis' farm. Based on Four Toes' word, I was fairly confident our place would not be attacked. I wasn't as sure about Lewis' place. Four Toes said that those people over whom he had influence would not attack there. Since he was not a major chief, I didn't know how far Four Toes' influence might extend.

After talking with Samuel, Ma, my sisters, and Pablo, I left on horseback that night. Traveling into a quartering wind, I paused frequently to sniff for wood smoke, listen for unusual sounds, or to take heed of the lack of the normal night sounds that might signal the presence of one or more people other than me. I timed my arrival so I would get there in the light of day and not get shot upon arrival.

My presence at Louisa's home provided no benefit beyond my peace of mind and some pleasant time spent with Louisa. No visitors approached their farm, Indian or otherwise, until January 20, my second day there. Then a schooner stopped at the dock. It was carrying soldiers, two of whom were wounded. The occupants of the schooner brought word that the Alachua Seminoles had attacked at the Anderson Plantation and others along the river on January 19. Several plantations were burned. Other owners were abandoning their farms all over the territory. They were then seeking the safer environment of Mandarin, Jacksonville, or some other place with a military presence. Even those safe havens were under occasional attack.

Later, Pa reported that during this same time his company was skirmishing with various groups of Miccosukee, Creek, and black Seminoles. Also in January of 1836, President Jackson named General Winfield Scott as commander of the war in Florida. Seven hundred additional regular soldiers were assigned to his command. Additional effort was also made to close down any smuggling of arms to the Indians along Florida's coast. In early February, General Edmund Gaines sailed on steamboats from New Orleans to Fort Brooke with 1,100 additional regulars and volunteers. They arrived on February 7. Though I was not at Fort Brooke, I remember the day well. What I remember was that it got down to seven degrees at Black Creek that night. The record cold spell killed our fruit trees and lots of other things. There was ice on the water in the slower parts of the creek, and even some snow. Some of our animals died from that record-breaking freeze. Even at that late date in history, less than one out of four homes on the frontier had a fireplace or any other kind of heat in the house. At most homes the cooking was done outdoors over an open fire. Some people died from the cold. It was a date remembered by lots of us.

General Gaines was already in Florida when he learned that General Scott had been chosen to command the war on the

Seminoles. Ignoring the fact he was not then the top general, Gaines left Fort Brooke in mid-February for Fort King. Though Gaines' force was too large to be attacked by the Seminoles, its movement was observed. Word of the unit's size was sent to the Withlacoochee Cove where Alligator, Jumper, and the other Indian chiefs started gathering a large force of their own.

While still two days from Fort King, General Gaines' army came upon the remains of Major Dade's men. They buried the remains in two common graves—one large grave for the enlisted men and a smaller one for the officers. In spite of the work of the scavengers at the Dade massacre, Gaines could tell what had happened to those troops. And, in spite of knowing Scott had already replaced him, Gaines was so angered at what he saw that he decided to pursue and punish the Indians.

At Fort King, Gaines ordered supplies from Fort Drane for a thousand of his men. Then, on February 26, and with nine days' rations, Gaines marched his men to the Withlacoochee. He was certain he could overpower any Indians there and destroy their villages. Pa and my two brothers, who were still in the area with Warren's volunteers, filled me in on what happened until Gaines departed Fort King. Four Toes and various others filled me in on what happened later.

Gaines had seventy-five friendly Indians with him to act as guides and scouts as he marched south. Had he taken Pa, George, or Asa, or any of the men who had previously fought at the Withlacoochee, things might have turned out differently, but he didn't. After two days of hard marching, General Gaines' column reached the river. His Indian guides assured Gaines they had taken him to the ford. The river was forty yards wide at the place and had a steep bank. There was no ford there.

While Gaines was approaching the river, the Seminoles, probably aided by Gaines' Indian guides, had set up an ambush. Though the river was down from its depth of the prior December, it was still deep at the place Gaines was led. Based on

General Clinch's efforts to cross the river in December, the Indian guides had not only led him to a deep spot, they had also left a canoe on the opposite bank from him.

Wanting to be sure the river was fordable and to get the canoe, General Gaines ordered a squad of men to remove their boots and wade across. Other troops came forward to observe. The Seminoles then fired at all those within range. Their first volley killed one and wounded a number of others. After an hour of shooting across the river at each other, General Gaines ordered a withdrawal. Eighteen of Gaines' men were wounded in the encounter but only the one died.

Moving downstream the next day to an open pinewood area where the friendly Indians assured him the crossing really was, Gaines again ordered a squad to wade the river. Again the Seminoles, who had already taken up position on the far side, fired on them. One lieutenant was killed.

Again Gaines withdrew. This time he sent runners to Fort Drane to ask General Clinch for reinforcements. With a thousand of his own soldiers and facing what he thought might be eight hundred Indians and blacks, Gaines ordered a defensive breastwork of logs built. While defending the breastworks, he also assigned some of his men to build a bridge across the river. Though there were few casualties as a result, the Indians moved around and shot at pretty much whomever they pleased for several days.

After seven days, the Indians sent a delegation to talk about a truce. Not accustomed to long campaigns, the Indians had been fighting for three months and were ready to quit and go back to their families. As it happened, Pa and the boys arrived with General Clinch's reinforcements while the negotiations were going on. The fight that occurred when their group saw some Indians resulted in the Seminoles breaking into small groups and leaving for their villages. Though Four Toes said Osceola, Jumper, and Alligator were still willing to negotiate, General Scott, the new commander on the scene, didn't follow up. Scott also didn't chase the Indians and destroy their villages. He was mad because Gaines had undertaken an expedition without his permission and didn't want Gaines to get credit for any good outcome.

March 7, 1836

Frontiersmen all over Florida had been fighting off Indian raids ever since the hostilities heated up. While Congress didn't declare war, they did vote money to fight the Indians. There was more than enough money in the treasury. The government had several million dollars collected from selling government land throughout the United States and in the Florida Territory.

In addition to the regular army troops being used, militia units were being raised in the Florida Territory and in the various states. Georgia and South Carolina militia began arriving in north Florida in late March and early April. Even with their arrival it soon became clear to everyone that this would not be a short war.

Pa, George, and Asa were discharged on March 5, after six months of service with Colonel Warren, and arrived home on March 7. Louisa turned twenty-two years old that same day. Because I was at Louisa's house, I didn't get to talk to Pa and the boys until a couple of days later.

In spite of the fact that we, and several other farmers who had traded with and been friendly with the Indians, were not attacked, I continued to be concerned about the fate of the Cubans should something happen to me and my family. Having inquired with various authorities as to how to assure the Cubans' freedom in the event something should happen to us, I called a family meeting, which included them.

When everyone was assembled, I said, "I've thought long and hard about the situation with our Cuban friends. I've come to the conclusion that the only way to permanently solve the problem is to have them declared legally free persons. In order to do that, we have to verify they were born in the United States. That's why I asked everyone to be at this meeting. Since Susan and I took them from the smugglers and didn't turn them over to the authorities, the problem is mine and I'll do what's necessary. On the chance anyone here is asked about their background, we all need to have a common story. If everyone is willing to stick to a common story about their background, I've made one up and I'll tell you what it is."

After a brief discussion everyone agreed to support my story about the former Cuban slaves being born in Spanish Florida. Having been sold back and forth between Spanish citizens and Indians, they spoke mostly Spanish. Their Spanish owners sold them to the Indians and left when Florida became a United States territory. I then bought them from the Indians. Since the complete Spanish archives were never turned over to the United States government, no one could dispute the story. I could get Running Dog, and others, to verify I had bought them if an inquiry was ever made. After saying that I would pay the expenses for the legal work, I left for Jacksonville to have the paperwork completed and recorded.

Considering the tenuous position most settlers found themselves in because of the Indian conflict, our family had been doing extremely well. Though our trade with most ships' captains had diminished—most of the captains were afraid to navigate Black Creek because they could be shot at from the shoreline—we were still managing to ship our own products. We were just not able to purchase and ship as many other things as we previously had. Upon my return from Jacksonville in April, things took a turn for the worse.

I didn't have a clue anything was different at home until I

rounded the last bend in the creek in my sail canoe and entered the straight run to our docks. Skimming along before a brisk wind, I saw a ship at the docks and what looked like dozens of men at work building a stockade and various other buildings. Since many of them were wearing civilian clothes, it took a few seconds to realize they were militia. The uniforms of the regular soldiers were immediately recognized.

Pa met me as I dropped the sail and glided up to the shore.

I said, "What's going on?"

"They've taken the farm for a military reservation."

"All of it?"

"Not for the fort proper, but yes. All the farm will be under their control."

"Did they give you a paper or anything?"

"No. I asked for one but the colonel said, 'This is United States property. We'll talk about that later.'"

"They can't just take the place."

"They already did. Almost twenty people have come here hunting refuge already. It's going to be a regular fort for sure."

"How about my place?"

"They said they were going to take anything they needed: timber, wood, sheep, cattle, fruit, anything. They didn't place any boundaries on where they would take things."

"They have to give you a paper so you can be reimbursed."

"I haven't found anyone who claims to have the authority."

Pa was not soon to be given a paper. They did let him keep his house and an acre of land. While those things were happening to us, General Scott organized another offensive against the Indians at the Withlacoochee Cove. Then he divided his force— which consisted of 4,800 militia from Florida, Louisiana, Alabama, Georgia, and South Carolina, as well as some regulars—into three armies, which theoretically would then surround and destroy the Indians. After announcing a plan for communication based on firing cannons, the armies moved out.

The attack was a disaster from the beginning. As the three armies left for their respective positions, the Indians attacked individual stragglers, out-riders, and pickets. Those attacks continued throughout the mission. Burdened with cannons, heavy equipment, and other weapons and supplies on wagons, the soldiers were like ducks waddling along with a fox darting in occasionally to get one of them.

Due to their victory over Major Dade's command and the battles they fought to a draw along the Withlacoochee, the Seminoles were very confident. They carried no equipment and supplies beyond their rifles, scalping knives, and a two-day supply of food. They carried only small amounts of ammunition. Their women cooked and brought fresh food and ammunition to the warriors at predetermined places. The Indians could then travel two to three times faster than the soldiers could. They also arrived rested and ready for battle. The Indians provided few opportunities for the slow-moving troops to attack. Almost all battles were fought at places the Seminoles chose and ended at times the Seminoles chose.

Other than building a fort, Scott's center army accomplished nothing besides getting a few men killed and wounded, and eating all their provisions before they returned to Fort Brooke. Scott's left army, which was supposed to close on the Withlacoochee from south of St. Augustine, was attacked while crossing the St. Johns River. When the first hundred men were across, the Indians attacked that group. A number of soldiers were killed and wounded.

Scott's other army had some success. They burned the Indian towns of Okihumphy and Peliklakaha, and a couple of smaller ones. They also managed to engage the Seminoles, but with little success other than causing the Indians to disperse into the swamps. The Seminoles then ambushed a relief column sent to evacuate Fort Alabama to retrieve the sick and wounded left there. That temporarily ended the heavy fighting in Florida.

It also ended General Scott's activities in Florida. On May 1, he was ordered to Alabama to round up some Creeks who were resisting being moved west. Governor Call was then placed in charge of removing the Indians from Florida. Having fought with him during the First Seminole War in 1818, we thought Call would be more effective than his predecessors had been.

Louisa and I were married only days before Call was placed in charge of the Florida offensive. Our mothers were hoping to have the wedding in a church, but the Indian situation didn't allow for that. Our family would probably have been at peace with the Indians except for the army making a military reservation out of our land. While our place had been left alone before the military moved in, after the fort was built it and our adjoining property became a target for sniping and small raids. A couple of our horses were killed while grazing in the area. Given the situation, Louisa and I were married by a local justice of the peace on May 12, 1836.

Since Governor Call would only be in command until General Jessup arrived in the fall, he tried to get a summer campaign going against the Seminoles. In spite of how we felt about Governor Call, many others did not support him. Some career army officers resented him being placed in charge and acted in such a way as to delay his preparation. As a result, Call didn't get his campaign started until September. It's probably just as well that he was delayed. Temperatures stayed pretty much in the high nineties and even reached above a hundred degrees on several days throughout July and August; because of the heat a summer campaign would have most certainly been a miserable failure. His fall campaign wasn't any more effective than previous ones had been. Mostly his men just marched around and got shot at.

General Jessup then organized a winter campaign in November of 1836. Marching his men to the Withlacoochee, he prepared to do battle over that area once more. He did manage to drive the Indians from their villages but could never get them into a standup battle. A standup battle was just not the way Indians fought.

Because we were unhappy about the military taking our land for a fort without a promise of compensation, we didn't volunteer for that campaign. During the same spring and summer we mostly stayed at Black Creek and tried to get in a crop, only to have most of it confiscated by the military commander of the fort that was built on our place. The only member of our family to serve in Call's and Jessup's campaigns was Louisa's brother Henry. Henry seemed to be constantly signed up for one militia unit or another. He volunteered that time from September of 1836 through January of 1837. He was then with Governor Call in the campaign along the Withlacoochee. An excellent marksman and a good scout, Henry saw lots of action in that campaign. Having enlisted to serve through January, Henry was also present at part of General Jessup's winter campaign of 1836–37.

In addition to the fighting in the Withlacoochee River area, Indians across Florida were demoralizing the white population with attacks by small groups of warriors. They were attacking and burning stagecoaches, killing messengers, burning farms, attacking towns, and in general terrorizing the citizens. Though carried out with bands of only fifteen to twenty warriors, attacks along Black Creek, the St. Johns, and even into the edge of Jacksonville were not uncommon. As can be imagined, all trade along Black Creek had come to a halt. Most trade throughout the area was at a standstill.

Jessup then started discussions with the Seminoles about another treaty. After writing some tentative agreements about emigration, he ordered a cease-fire and organized a council meeting with all the chiefs he could contact. In general, the Indians honored the cease-fire order. Wildcat, who had not heard about the cease-fire, led an attack on a military camp at Lake Monroe. Captain Charles Mellon, several soldiers, and some Seminoles were killed there. Additional soldiers and Indians were wounded.

After General Jessup's agreement with the Seminoles along the Withlacoochee River, there was no fighting in that area other than the one attack by Wildcat's group. The fighting also subsided in Mosquito County, along the St. Johns River. There were some small attacks in other places along the St. Johns but no major ones.

The Seminoles and the Americans spent the spring and summer growing and harvesting their crops. This was particularly important to the Seminoles of the Withlacoochee area since Jessup had captured 1,500 of their cattle and they were short on food. Their ammunition was mostly gone, which limited their hunting ability. They had to revert to doing most of their hunting with bows and arrows and using deadfalls and other kinds of traps, thus saving their ammunition. It would have been the perfect time for Jessup to press his advantage.

Growing food seemed important to my family also, right up until the military confiscated most of our crops. In addition to feeding his own troops, the military commander had to feed the civilians who had taken refuge in the fort. There were so many civilians in the fort at the time that they were sleeping four to six people to a room. There were lots of hungry and sick people at the fort. Many died with the fever.

General Jessup then met in council with a number of chiefs to reach an agreement on the total cessation of hostilities. At the council meeting the chiefs agreed to emigrate if the government would buy their animals. General Jessup agreed and wrote up the necessary papers to make that happen. When the War Department approved his agreement, Jessup began a campaign to persuade the Seminoles to emigrate peacefully. Friendly Indians were sent to encourage others to come in and register to be removed. Lots of the Indians came. News of this was welcomed by Jessup and by the War Department. The government soon began to discharge militia volunteers as being unnecessary to the war effort, even before their enlistment was up.

Word of these developments reached us soon after Louisa and I got married. Even as we received word of the breakthrough in the military's relationship with the Seminoles, white people pretending to be slave owners and white planters began raiding south into the reservation to retrieve runaway slaves. Some of them were indiscriminately taking any black people they came across. As a result of this activity the peaceful situation began to deteriorate.

We received word of this and other troubles on June 12, 1837. While riding near the fort to check on our cattle grazing nearby, I noticed my horse's ears point forward. It was a certain signal that something or someone unusual was nearby. Noting the way my horse's gaze was fixed, I swung down on the opposite side of him. After dismounting, I lifted one of the horse's front hooves to conceal the fact I was alert to danger. I also palmed a pistol, which was then concealed between the horse and me. My head bowed as though to look at the horse's hoof, I scanned the underbrush for any unusual sign. Seeing nothing, I lowered the horse's hoof and started to unsheathe my rifle when a voice spoke from a thicket.

"Isaac, it's Four Toes."

Recognizing his voice, I stuck my pistol in my belt and stepped from behind my horse as he stepped into the trail in front of me.

"What brings you here, my friend," I said.

He replied, "I come with a warning and for your advice, or help."

Leading my horse and approaching him, I said, "I'm always ready to help, but what's the warning about?"

He said, "The agreement between General Jessup and the chiefs has been violated by the slave hunters and by my people. Two weeks ago almost a thousand of my people were gathered near Fort Brooke and another location to be moved to the west. We had been waiting there many days for the ships to take us.

Though there were lots of ships anchored offshore, no effort was made to put us on them. Word arrived that slave hunters were coming to take any blacks and people having mixed blood they could find before we were taken aboard. My family and I were among those at Fort Brooke. As you know, my wife is a black Cuban and my children are of mixed blood. Fearing some of our people would be taken, some of us left the fort that day.

"Osceola and a hundred warriors showed up that night and mingled with the Seminoles camped near the fort. Under threat of death, they took Micanopy and several others with them as captives when they left. They also told the others to return to their homes or they would be killed. Everyone left that night. Not one Seminole was at either fort the next morning. The warning for you is that there will be no peace. You should be alert. Though it isn't your doing, it's known that a fort has been built on your property. As to the advice or help, I want you to tell me where Running Dog and his people are so I can join them. My people are tired of fighting."

I asked, "Is your family safe?"

"For now. I left them at our village."

"Are you all right? Do you have supplies?"

"Yes. It's easy to feed one person and to find places for one horse to graze."

"And your family, do they have food?"

"Things are not good, Isaac, but we get by."

"You stay here. Someone near the fort might mistake you for an enemy. I'll be back with a packhorse and food."

"I can't take a gift. I already owe you too much."

"I'm the one that's in debt. I let you overpay me for your wife."

"I paid almost nothing."

"She cost me nothing. I'll be back soon. Stay under cover."

Later, as I was packing the horse's pack with food, Louisa asked, "Are you going someplace?"

"The food's for Four Toes and his family."

"They're here?"

"He's here but his family is south of here. Because the slavers are rounding up all blacks, I'm sending them to join Running Dog's clan."

"Wish them luck."

Returning to Four Toes, I drew a map in the sand, gave him the horse and supplies, and wished him well. I also said, "Some time in the future, a chance will come for you and Running Dog to go west. If I'm able, I'll come for you or send someone."

Clasping my hand, he left.

As General Jessup began to realize his peaceful approach to gathering the Indians for emigration was failing, he turned to more forceful methods. In July he ordered that all captive Indians or blacks failing to cooperate were to be hanged. Worried about the political implications of that policy, he soon rescinded the order. Jessup also concluded that the rules of warfare should be suspended and that deception and deceit should be employed where useful.

Claiming that volunteer soldiers were not suitable for fighting Indians, Jessup also requested additional regular troops. His request was denied and he was ordered to raise volunteer companies again. Jessup then spent the summer months raising troops and resupplying for a fall campaign. He concluded that a summer campaign would be useless because most of his troops were sick with yellow fever that summer.

While yielding to the requirement to raise volunteers, Jessup insisted they be mounted. While this was theoretically an advantage, in reality it was not always so. The Florida forest, swamp, hammock, and scrub palmetto lands did not provide adequate grazing opportunity for a large herd of horses, so food had to be carried for the horses if they were to be in good enough condition to be of use.

Jessup then ordered wagons with watertight bodies, reinforced steamboats for the rivers, rubber-and flat-bottomed boats, and dozens of other items not previously used in any war. Jessup also ordered some of the new Cochran repeating rifles and Colt revolvers. One problem was that there were few of those new weapons available and obtaining ammunition for them was next to impossible even after you had the weapon. Another problem was that the Cochran rifles never worked properly.

While Jessup was preparing for the fall campaign, the Seminoles were also preparing. Powder and shot was being purchased from the Cuban fishing camps along the west coast of Florida. Also, the Seminoles were gathering and storing their crops. Additionally, they were procuring livestock in any way they could. Most of this involved the rustling of livestock owned by white planters.

Many of the Seminoles and escaped slaves were tired of the fighting. Almost out of clothing and living on the barest of diets, many of them were not in physical condition to continue. Their situation was so bad that some of the slaves who had earlier escaped to join the Seminoles began to return to their white owners. Dressed in rags, diseased, and malnourished, they decided that serving as a slave was a better life than they were living. These returning blacks also told stories of being mistreated by the Seminoles. I learned from some Seminole friends that their tales of mistreatment and escape were fabrications intended to return them in good standing with their owners.

When there was a call for mounted volunteers, I did not respond. With Louisa soon to have our first child, I wasn't anxious to be away from home for an extended period of time. I did, however, offer to scout on a temporary basis. Pa, Asa, and Samuel, on the other hand, heeded the call to enlist. They enlisted at Fort Hickman on August 5, 1837, for a six-month period. Pa, then fifty-seven years old but well mounted, was given the dangerous and exhausting job of scouting.

The call for me to act as a scout was not long in coming. Late on the morning of September 5, 1837, a rider arrived from Fort Peyton, which is located south of St. Augustine.

Finding me, he said, "General Hernandez needs you as an interpreter and scout. Four slaves showed up at Fort Peyton yesterday. They claim to know the location of a Seminole camp and have agreed to lead the general to it. The general doesn't trust them and wants you to translate; he also wants you and your Pa to help with the scouting."

I asked, "Where's the general now?"

He said, "He's riding south with five companies. We'll have to hurry if we're to catch them in time. Your Pa and brothers are with them."

"Where're they going?" I asked.

"South of the Tamoka River, near some burned plantations," he replied.

Needing to overtake the general's command, we took two horses each and left immediately. It was two days later when we overtook the general's group.

While the four slaves seemed to be making an effort to guide the regiment to the Indian encampment, they didn't appear to be sure exactly where they were going.

Upon our arrival, the general said, "Isaac, I need several of you to scout the area tomorrow. These people could cause us to stumble around and get ambushed. Other than in an ambush, I think we can hold our own with any warriors the Indians have in this area. However, I'm ever mindful of what happened to Major Dade."

I said, "I'd be happy to help, General. Pa, Asa, Samuel, and I can leave before daylight."

I then got with Pa and my brothers and we decided to split up the area to the front and sides of where we were camped. We then spent the early hours of the evening catching each other up on any news and stories we knew. Later that night it rained hard.

The next morning a heavy fog hung over the area. Because

of the fog, it was almost an hour later than usual before it was light enough to see. We scouts then changed our plans and left riding in pairs, me with Pa and Asa with Samuel. Though the fog was so thick we might ride up to someone before we knew it, it also provided some benefits. First, it would prevent us from being seen from a distance. Secondly, the ground was so damp from the moisture the fog provided, and from the rain the previous night, that our horse's hooves made almost no noise when stepping on leaves and pine straw.

We agreed to speak only in a whisper since our voices would carry further than we could see. Also, I gave Pa one of two rattlesnake rattles I carried. They were something from which the sound wouldn't carry very far, and a sound that would not be investigated if heard; I frequently used them as a means of communication when scouting with other people.

Traveling southeast, we kept our horses at a slow walk. We decided I would watch the ground for sign and Pa would watch and listen intently for any danger that might threaten us. I was, therefore, riding in front so Pa's horse's hooves wouldn't wipe out any sign. Weaving back and forth to cover the area thoroughly, we traveled in this manner for over two hours.

We had just turned left where a trail forked when we heard voices off to our right. There were only a few words spoken but it was enough to cause us to freeze in place. The speaker was moving toward the junction of the trail we had turned left on. Had we turned right, we would have ridden straight into them. From the sound of their voices, they could not have been forty yards away. Motioning to Pa, I swung down and placed my hand on my horse's nose. It was a precaution taken in case there were other horses in the area. A whinny would give our location away. Pa did the same thing. We then checked the powder in the flash-pans of our weapons.

By the time we had finished checking our weapons, the people who had done the talking had passed us by at thirty yards and proceeded up the trail we had come down. Though we had not heard the sound of their movement, we learned where they were when a voice said, "Fresh horse tracks. Two of them."

A second voice said, "They're no concern of ours. We're going where they came from."

The first voice had the accent of a plantation slave from an English-speaking plantation. The second voice had an accent that also placed him as a black person but with a special quality that also identified him as one who had for a long time resided with Muskogee-speaking people.

Hearing nothing more, I motioned Pa to hold my horse and I eased back up the trail to be sure they had moved on and were not, in fact, stalking us. The trail turned out to be empty and their moccasin tracks continued north. The ground was so coated with leaves and straw that it took several minutes of study to determine there were four or five of them.

Returning to Pa, I told him what I had observed, and said, "They're traveling toward our camp. I think one of us should follow them. Such a small group can't attack our camp, but they could shoot a picket or someone out for a walk to relieve himself. Also, one of us ought to backtrack them for a while and see if there's anything of interest where they came from."

Pa said, "I'll follow them."

I led my horse while traveling south on foot. Being cautious, it took two hours to cover a distance that could have otherwise been covered in an hour. Deciding there was little to be gained by backtracking further, I turned and retraced the route just traveled. Alternately walking my horse and then trotting him, I soon arrived at where Pa and I had split up. Dismounting there and leading my horse, I continued at a fast walk. Much to my surprise, the tracks Pa was following led directly into our camp.

As I arrived in camp, Pa said, "It looks like we were following some big fish. There were five of them. They walked right into camp before they realized it. John Philip, one of King Philip's former slaves, is one of them. The general has been talking to him ever since they came in. I told the general you were backtracking them and he wants to talk to you as soon as you get here."

During that time Pa was leading me to the general, who was first being kind to and then threatening John Philip.

Turning to me, the general said, "Walk with me a ways."

Speaking to Pa and a couple of captains, General Hernandez said, "You three come, too."

When we were some distance from John Philip, the general looked at me and asked,

"What did you find?"

I said, "Nothing. I followed their back trail for over three miles. They held a pretty steady course. Finding no other sign, I came back."

After contemplating this new information for almost half a minute, the general said, "The three miles you tracked them and the two miles you traveled before you heard them would tend to indicate they had been coming from the south since well before daylight. There's almost no way they could have known we were here until they walked in on us. Would you agree?"

I said, "We could have been seen yesterday. The person who spotted us could have ridden hard to their camp and alerted them we were here. They could have then left this morning early and walked here. But, what with the heavy thunderstorms yesterday and last night, I don't think that's likely. Why would they come straight here?"

"To set up an ambush," he said. "I think, however, that they were surprised we were here. And, without very much persuasion John Philip has agreed to lead me to King Philip's camp."

"You didn't lean on him some, did you?"

"A little," he said, "but he came around pretty quick. He said he's in love with a slave on one of the plantations and was on his way there. He wants to be left alone to live with her after this is all over."

I said, "Love makes a person do lots of strange things. We could do enough scouting to be sure there's no ambush."

"I'm counting on that," he said. "We're going to move south some and bivouac closer to their camp. I want you to go with John Philip and check out King Philip's camp during the early evening hours if you can find it. Then meet us at the burned-out Anderson Plantation, the former Dun-Lawton place. It still has some good defensive positions and some covered areas."

I looked questioningly at Pa and he answered my unspoken question by saying, "Yes, I know where it is." That was important because I planned to stay and observe the Indian camp while someone came back for the general.

Pa, my brothers, John Philip, and I soon left to scout King Philip's camp. John Philip was in the lead and I was riding second in line. I spoke to him only twice during the first two hours. One time was to have us dismount and walk while our horses rested.

The second time, I said, "John, in case you haven't noticed, my musket is pointed toward your back. If I get the feeling there's something wrong, that there's a trap, I'm going to shoot you. You best be alert and do things right. If anything goes wrong, I don't care whose fault it is, yours or mine, I'm going to shoot you."

Not wanting him to misunderstand, I said it in English and Muskogee.

He only nodded.

Stopping me an hour before dark and pointing, John Philip said, "King Philip camps there."

We then got in some thick cover and rested until dark. Shortly after dark, Pa, John Philip, and I went forward to check out the camp. Approaching from downwind, we easily got within viewing distance of the camp without being discovered. As was typical with Seminole camps, there were no night guards. That was probably the biggest mistake in military tactics the Seminoles made. The only time I've ever known of Indians posting guards at night was when they wanted to hold a herd of cattle in a small location and didn't have a cow-pen. We didn't see or hear any dogs. Having heard the Seminoles were mostly going hungry, it didn't surprise me any. I suspected they had eaten their dogs.

Since Pa knew the location of the Anderson Plantation, I asked him to meet the general and guide him to King Philip's camp. Taking Asa and John Philip with him, Pa left. Samuel and I remained to observe the activities in King Philip's camp. The two of us decided to alternate turns sleeping until the general's regiment arrived. We had three hours sleep each when Pa approached our position that night. The general and two other officers were with Pa. Having circled the camp during one of my shifts on duty, I knew the layout and told them where everything was.

The general asked, "Has there been any activity in the camp tonight?"

I said, "No more than someone occasionally getting up for some relief."

The general asked, "How many are there?"

I said, "Twenty, more or less."

The general then gave orders as to how the attack would be carried out. Leaving forty-five men to guard the horses, he placed thirty-five men on foot on each of three sides of the camp as a blocking force. Hernandez then lined two companies—a hundred mounted men—on the fourth side of the camp. The placement of everyone was finished several hours before daylight. I was on the left flank of the camp with Pa's company. We remained in position until daylight. Having had only three hours of sleep since four o'clock the previous morning, I took advantage of that time to get a few more hours of sleep. I'm sure many of those around me did too.

At first light the general ordered his mounted men to charge the camp. The soldiers fired a few shots. The Seminoles didn't fire a single shot. One Seminole was slightly wounded. Counting the wounded one, we captured nineteen Indians. King Philip, the head chief of the Mosquito County area, was among those captured.

When one of the captured Indians offered to lead the general to another encampment of warriors if he could be set free, the general took two companies of soldiers and captured a band of Uchee Indians. In the fight a lieutenant was killed.

Since Louisa was due to have a baby in November, I didn't go on that trip. I felt the best course was for me to get back to Black Creek. I told the general I was leaving and offered to help again when needed. I don't know why he wanted me anyway. I learned my scouting from Pa, and the general had Pa with him. I guess he thought because Pa was fifty-seven years old that he had slowed a step. It was a mistake people often made. I couldn't think of anyone I would rather have standing behind me than Pa. Also, Pa spoke excellent Muskogee.

September 18, 1837

Arriving back at Fort Heileman, I found Louisa doing well with her pregnancy. Otherwise, the situation at the fort was not good—rations were short, some people were sick, people were sleeping six to eight to a room, and there was constant anticipation of an attack by the Seminoles. Within days of my arrival at the fort, the company Pa and my brothers were serving in returned there.

I had been hearing for some time that all the captured Indians, and those who walked in to surrender, were being sent to Fort Brooke or other forts on the west coast of Florida to be transported to New Orleans and subsequently to the west. Pa, Asa, and Samuel further confirmed this when they returned. It was rumored that hundreds of Indians, perhaps even more than a thousand, had been transported west. I began to think about Running Dog and Four Toes, and that it was time for me to see about making arrangements for them. With that in mind, I sought out General Hernandez to make a proposal.

Finding the general on October 2, I told him of Running Dog's and Four Toes' situation and of the fact that I had told them I would try to arrange for their safe transport once the opportunity presented itself.

The general said, "I'm authorized to hold and transfer all surrendering hostiles. All the prisoners I'm currently holding in this part of the territory are at the old fort at St. Augustine."

I replied, "These aren't hostiles. They're living near the Everglades in south Florida. They mostly stay on an island there. They've been there for over two years."

"Do you know how to contact them?"

"Yes." I said, "I know almost exactly where they are. Some while back the government offered cash incentives for the Indians in west Florida to voluntarily go west. I'm here trying to get those same incentives for Running Dog and his people, and to get the government to make the arrangements for them to move."

"I'm not authorized to offer incentives, only to accept their surrender," he said.

"They can't very well surrender because they haven't been fighting. Who could I talk to about incentives for them and their safe removal?"

He replied, "The military has been charged with removal of the Seminoles by force. Any other arrangement would have to be made through Commissioner Harris."

Thanking the general for his time and information, I then wrote a letter to Commissioner Harris telling him the situation and requesting his assistance.

After being out on a short reconnaissance mission, in early October the company Pa and my brothers were serving in returned to Black Creek again. I heard from them that Wildcat,

King Philip's son, had learned of his father's capture and, with several other chiefs, had gone to St. Augustine to discuss the situation with General Hernandez. Though they were wearing their white feathers and silver headbands, the equivalent of a white flag, Hernandez had them seized and placed them in the fort with his other prisoners. The fort had been converted into a prison.

When General Jessup first heard of Wildcat's capture, the general ordered that he be hanged for the recent kidnappings of Indian leaders near Fort Brooke. The general changed his mind and Wildcat was released when he promised to turn in all the runaway blacks in his tribe and return stolen livestock to the owners. Wildcat soon returned to Fort Peyton under a white flag, but he would not enter the fort. It was fortunate for him because General Jessup had ordered that any Indians entering the fort be taken prisoner. Wildcat then convinced General Hernandez to go to the Indian camp for a meeting. There, Hernandez learned Osceola was in the area and that he would soon be coming in for a conference at that same meeting. General Hernandez then sent orders for five mounted companies to surround and take prisoner all the Indians gathered there after Osceola's arrival. The company Pa was serving with was one of those companies.

On the morning of October 21, 1837, the five companies reached the meeting place and surrounded the Indians. Outnumbered more than three to one, the Seminoles gave up without firing a shot. Most of the St. Johns warriors were captured at that gathering, along with their chiefs. Osceola and his group were also captured. Over a hundred Indians were taken at that meeting. They were then marched to the old fort, Castillo de San Marcos, at St. Augustine, then called Fort Marion, and kept with the other prisoners being held there. It was a sad day when Pa and the boys returned and told me of that dishonorable act. It was not long after that when General Hernandez asked me to scout for a raid he was going to make at Spring Hill. Disgusted with them making prisoners of those who were wearing white feathers, I declined. Without my help General Hernandez captured a large number of Seminoles and slaves on that trip.

November 12, 1837, three days after the general's return with his prisoners, Louisa had our first son. Out of respect and admiration for Andrew Jackson, we decided to name him Andrew. On that same day I received a letter from the commissioner, which authorized the payment for a ship to move Running Dog and his band to Louisiana. Two military officers would be responsible for their safe passage to the new Indian Territory in the west. I was to arrange for a ship, which would be paid for by a draft on a New Orleans bank, and guide them to meet the ship. The price for the ship was not to exceed a thousand dollars. Also, incentive money in the amount of $7000 would be on deposit in the same bank. Five thousand would be paid to Running Dog upon his appearance at the bank. Two thousand would be paid to Four Toes; his band was much smaller than Running Dog's band.

The following day I went to Louisa's mother's house to inquire about any ship stopping there that I might know the captain of. Black Creek was so narrow that ships could be shot at from shore and we were not getting much traffic. We would need someone we could trust for the move. I also gave Pracilla the news about her new grandson, Andrew, and learned from her that a ship's captain I knew was to dock there in the next few days. I also learned that Indians, along with their black slaves, were being shipped almost monthly to the west. Over a thousand were said to have already been shipped from the west coast and 155 more, including Osceola, were being held for shipment at Fort Marion in St. Augustine.

After leaving word for the captain about what I needed, I returned with Louisa's sister, Caroline, to Black Creek. Caroline was to stay with Louisa for a few weeks while Louisa got her strength back.

On November 19 a rider came to get me for a conference with the captain I had left a message for. Leaving the same day, we arrived at Louisa's mother's home on the twentieth. There, I learned the captain would, for a thousand dollars, transport Running Dog's and Four Toes' clans from a harbor I designated on the west coast of Florida to New Orleans. The Indians or the army would have to provide food while they were on board. The captain also knew of an honest riverboat captain who would transport Running Dog up the Mississippi River. The captain calculated, with a stop in Cuba, he could be at the designated place within twenty days. He agreed to wait there for my group for up to seven days from the appointed time.

The distance from Black Creek to Running Dog's camp was over three hundred miles, so I returned to Black Creek and prepared to leave the next day. When I left, the packhorse I was leading carried coffee, corn, jerked beef, salt pork, beans, rice, my bed roll, and extra ammunition. I was armed with my .69 caliber rifle, a single-shot pistol, and a double-barrel shotgun. It wasn't hard to stay under cover as I rode. Away from the occasional plantation or small farm, Florida was mostly covered with thick vegetation in that area.

Staying west of the St. Johns River and avoiding military roads, I planned to stick to the river's general course until reaching a point east of the Ocklawaha River. Most of the Indian ambushes occurred on or close to military roads. Crossing Silver River east of Silver Springs, I would then ride straight down the Florida Territory. By riding a little west of south, and making good time, I hoped to arrive at Running Dog's camp in twelve days.

By the middle of the third morning I had crossed the Silver River west of Silver Springs, which was ten miles past Fort King and the old road from Fort King to the Ocklawaha, and was then approaching the Ocklawaha River. I planned to cross the river south of Fort King and pass through Okahumpka on my way to Running Dog's camp. Given the battles that had been fought and the number of Indians captured in the area, there should be few

Indians around Okahumpka. That was where my plans hit a snag.

While riding on a trail through thick cover, I couldn't see a thing when my horse slowed his pace slightly, raised his head, and neighed. An answering neigh came from less than fifty yards straight ahead of me. The odds were lots better than fifty percent that I didn't want to meet the rider of the other horse. I was traveling on a game trail. Most soldiers would be on their military roads or certainly on trails more passable than the one I was on. Most Indians who were traveling would be avoiding military roads and, thus, be on game trails.

Pulling my horse sharply to the left, I kicked his ribs to try to clear the trail before there was a confrontation. In that, at least, I was successful. That did not negate the fact my horse had given me away. Any Indian could read the sign my horses left and tell there was only one rider leading a loaded packhorse. Trimmed but not shod, my horse's tracks would not tell whether I was an Indian or not. It would make little difference to those I was trying to avoid. If they were Indians, they would want to catch me if I was not an Indian. If they were not Indians, they would want to catch me if I was. In either case, a heavily loaded packhorse was worth checking out. Whoever it was, they would probably be after me. Assuming there were more than one of them, which I couldn't know for sure, I would have to be quick and lucky to avoid being run down.

Doing what I knew worked best for the animals and people I had hunted, as soon as I was clear of the trail, I lit out in a straight line south. Many an animal and person has been killed or captured because of circling. Still, most animals and people will circle when chased. They'll mostly head for an area they know well and circle in that area. Men, when jumped, will mostly backtrack. They're always familiar with the area they just came through and might not know the area ahead. I figured that heading straight south would give me a few minutes head start before they were on my trail. Anyone in pursuit should look for me to circle and go north. If they reacted in that way, I might even gain ten or fifteen minutes.

After running my horses for two hundred yards, I stopped and faced toward where I had been. I could hear running horses and could see flashes of movement between the leaves as riders were coming toward me at seventy-five yards. I had not gained the few minutes I was hoping for. Where I was at the moment the vegetation was a little thinner than it usually was in the area. Lifting my rifle, I squeezed off a round toward a flash in the leaves. I was more expecting to scare them into stopping than to hit anything.

Even as I squeezed off the shot, I was thinking they might be friendly Indians. There were Choctaw, Lower Creek, Shawnee, and other eastern Indians companies fighting with our army. I knew of ten companies containing fifty Choctaws each that were in Florida at the time. I had been on patrols with one of those companies. Knowing I would be just as dead if shot by a friendly Indian as I would if shot by a hostile, I put the thought from my mind.

Thinking there was only one of me, and that I might have fired my only shot, the Indians kept charging toward me. Jerking my shotgun out of the saddle scabbard and shoving my rifle in it, I fired at the closest Indian and he went down. More importantly, the second shot gave the others pause for thought and the others reigned in. Apparently they were no longer sure how many people there were with me or how many guns might face them. The typical person only had one single-barrel gun and, thus, one shot.

Firing the second barrel of the shotgun at a suspected location to keep them thinking, I turned my horse and started south again. While listening intently for any sound that would give me direction, I walked my horses. Since the horses were walking, I also managed to reload both barrels of the shotgun. Thinking that if I was smart I should throw the heavy pack off of my pack-horse and make a run for it, I stepped down from my horse, dumped the pack, and strapped my bedroll behind my saddle. My pursuers would not be hampered by a loaded packhorse. They might also stop to retrieve and inspect the pack. Stepping back in the saddle, I then put my horses into a run, again head-ed south.

I hadn't gone an additional two hundred yards before break-ing out into a small clearing. Before I could take stock of the sit-uation, shots rang out from the far edge of the clearing. Hit in the head with one of the musket-balls, my saddle horse went head over heels, tossing me to the ground. My second horse was jerked head-over-heels by the leather strap he was hitched to the back of my saddle with. The strap broke from the impact, and he scram-bled to his feet and ran off. Even while falling I could see there were four puffs of smoke from those who had fired at me. Knowing about the clearing and thinking I might run south, the leader of my adversaries had sent those four warriors ahead at a run. They had managed to get into position while I stopped to fire at those who were pursuing. I knew right then that these were experienced people and that I was in big trouble.

Apparently thinking I was hit, one of the Indians broke from cover and ran toward me. The other three must have stayed in place to reload their weapons. Bruised, but not seriously hurt, I came to my knees, leveled my shotgun on the charging Indian, and pulled a trigger. It didn't fire. The second barrel failed to fire also. My fall had knocked the powder from the flash-pan. Fumbling for my pistol, which was still in my belt, I shot him in the chest just as he drove his knife into the left arm I threw up to ward him off.

Scrambling behind my dead horse for cover, I then put pow-der in the flash pans of my shotgun and reloaded the revolver. Because it was bleeding quite a bit, I also tied a leather strap over the knife wound. I was thinking only minutes would pass before one of the three remaining Indians circled the clearing and shot me from the flank, or before those behind me arrived on the scene and shot me from the rear.

Taking my bedroll and shotgun in my right hand, and with the pistol tucked in my belt, I dashed to the closest bushes for cover. Though my left arm was of some use, I didn't use it for fear of increasing the blood loss. My movement drew fire from all three of my nearby adversaries.

Not being hit and reaching the bushes, I turned right. The Ocklawaha River was in that direction. Its thick vegetation would be the best place for concealment. My flight was not a mad dash. Placing my feet where they would leave the least sign and being careful not to bend grass, break limbs, or bend bushes in the direction I was going, I moved slowly once under cover. It would take a slow, careful tracker to follow me while I was on foot and trying not to leave a trail.

My only thoughts were of survival. I would be of no use to my friends dead. If I allowed myself to think about helping Running Dog's clan, I probably would be killed. It was clear that those hunting me were experienced and good at what they were doing. It did cross my mind that dropping the pack from the packhorse had probably saved my life. Had they not stopped for the pack, those behind me would have caught me in the clearing.

Since at least two of their friends were wounded or dead, those hunting me would know I was dangerous. There would be no more mad dashes of pursuit. They would hunt me down methodically and systematically so I also had adequate time to be methodical. Stopping, I checked my weapons, including the knife I had pulled from my left arm. The still-bleeding wound was beginning to hurt so I took time to bind it tightly with a sleeve cut from my shirt. It was then late in November, and cold, I was wearing a buckskin coat over my shirt. The stout coat had prevented the stab wound to my arm from being more severe than it was.

Hearing nothing in the way of pursuit, I slung my sleeping roll over my shoulder and proceeded to the river's edge. Had it been summer, in order to lighten the load the sleeping roll would have been abandoned. Because it was late November, the bedroll would be needed during the cold nights.

At the river, I again paused to listen. After most of a minute had passed there was a splash in the marshy area away from the river. I knew my pursuers would not be that careless. It was obvious they had startled a hog or deer and the startled animal had splashed the water while running away from them. I then knew where some of them were.

Without hesitation I stepped into the river. It was fifty yards wide and very deep there. Placing a large, dry limb I had carried into the water for that purpose under my right armpit, I held my shotgun and blanket out of the water with my right hand while treading water and guiding myself with my feet as the current carried me downstream. It occurred to me that I didn't have to be concerned about alligators or moccasins because they aren't active in cold weather. The alligators would have buried themselves in mud and slowed down their breathing to survive the cold spell. Though numbed by the cold water, the pain in my left arm was almost unbearable.

After drifting with the current for over five hundred yards I found a hiding place. A hollowed-out cypress stump stood in the water's edge. It had probably been standing there for hundreds of years. Half in the water and half out, the stump had rotted away on the inside and some on the side toward the river. It was solid on the side toward the bank. Standing twenty feet tall and seven feet in diameter, the hollowed-out stump would make an excellent hiding place. After dragging myself into the hollow of the stump, I was invisible except for someone who might be directly in front of me on the river or on the far bank. Since it was relatively dark in the stump, it was even possible I would not be seen from the far bank. Like an animal, I had gone into a hole. Unlike some animals, I had left no trail.

Sitting on a spot above water, but with my feet in the water, I again checked my equipment. The powder in my powder horn was dry and the shotgun was primed and dry, but the pistol was soaked and could not be fired until it was cleaned and reloaded. My dead saddle horse was lying on my rifle and I had to leave it. With only one useful arm, I probably could not have carried two long-guns anyway. Everything in my possibles bag was wet, including the jerked beef carried there to snack on occasionally. Having lost considerable blood, and feeling weak, I began chewing on some jerky in an attempt to revive myself. Not wanting to make the slightest sound, I didn't try to clean and reload the pistol. Until those hunting me tired of the chase, my best chance was to remain hidden and silent. With the good use of only one hand, and no horse, I wouldn't stand a very good chance in flight or fight.

With my heart rate then back to normal and my situation assessed, I began to think about my mission. There were only a limited number of days left to get Running Dog's clan to the ship. My rifle was gone and I was without a horse and wounded; the situation did not look good. Still, my number-one priority was to stay alive.

My thinking was slowed because of the shock of my wound and the shock of the cold water, but I soon thought to use the limb, previously used as a flotation device, as a brace between the inner walls of the stump to stand on. My feet were growing numb from being in the cold water. Though I had to remain standing, at least I was then out of the water and almost invisible to anyone on the river or on the far riverbank. Also I could use my dry wool blanket for some warmth. Braced against the inner wall of the stump, I had been standing on my limb and shaking from the cold for what seemed like an hour, but had probably only been a few minutes, when I heard voices.

Speaking in Muskogee, the first voice said, "He's gone, vanished without a trace after going in the river. He's probably dead."

A second and more mature voice said, "He's not dead. This one is a seasoned warrior. He might have floated in the water for a long way. I'm beginning to think we should give up looking for him. He's not worth anything to us one way or the other. Also, I'm not sure we want to find him."

The younger voice said, "John Chopka said for us to search down this side of the river until the afternoon's half gone. Then we should return to camp."

The other voice said, "I would just as soon rest until time for us to go back to camp. No one would know. He has nothing we want and he's dangerous. We already have his pack, horses, rifle, and most of his other things."

The first voice said, "Amotto and Heischa might know. They're searching the other side of the river."

Their voices tailed off as they proceeded south. Within minutes I spotted, through a crack in the rotted out area at eye level, movement on the other side of the river. Two Indians were moving southwest on that bank. The sun having moved to the west and the opening being to the east, it was dark in the stump and they couldn't see me. My dark blanket was almost invisible because of the shadows in the stump. I was also protected from their view by the part of the stump that had not rotted.

It seemed that only the four of them were searching downriver. And, the two who were on my side of the river didn't seem to want to find me. Counting the seconds off in order to concentrate on something to help ease the pain, I remained on my uncomfortable perch for another half-hour before easing back out of the stump and into the river. The water almost felt warm by comparison to how cold I had been while perched on the stick. My trembling and shaking subsided after entering the water and moving some.

Climbing out of the river on the same side from which I entered, I took great pains to leave no sign. My arm was hurting and my body was stiff from standing on the perch. I soon discovered that, in addition to being cold, I was almost exhausted. Additionally, everything besides my blanket, shotgun, and the powder in my powder horn was wet. The blanket was a little damp from having been wrapped around my clothes.

Traveling through a thick hammock, I soon found an opening in the canopy where the sun was hitting the ground. After wringing out my clothes the best I could, I laid my clothes out in the patch of sunlight to dry as much as they would. It was the best that could be done at the time. A fire was out of the question. I then rolled up in my blanket and lay on some leaves in the sun for what warmth it gave, and slept.

Awaking a half-hour before dark with my body shaking from the cold, I found my things were still damp. In spite of that, I became warmer after putting on my buckskins. I then cleaned and loaded my pistol and thought about my predicament. Cold, wounded, on foot, and weak from loss of blood, I wasn't sure I could complete my mission. I finally decided I should head for Fort King, Fort Brooke, or one of the various other forts that had been built throughout the area. Going to a fort would place me off schedule at the very best, as they were out of my way. I did have the remainder of Running Dog's money in my possibles bag, however, and could buy a horse and supplies at a fort. That was a positive. Still, if I headed for a fort, it would have to be one that would also take me toward Running Dog's camp. Otherwise, I might be too late getting there to help Running Dog. That ruled out Fort King.

But what of the Indians who were hunting me? Four of them had gone south with instructions to hunt for half the afternoon, then return to camp. Half the afternoon there and half the afternoon back, they must be camped nearby. Considering that they were traveling north when I encountered them, they might be camped south of that point. Perhaps they had been headed north for a raid, or to sharp-shoot at Fort King. The odds seemed good that they were camped south of where we met. That meant they were probably still south of me.

Making up my mind to head for Fort Brooke and to look for a chance to steal a horse along the way, I returned to the game trail on which I met the Indians and started south. Refreshed from sleeping, though still weak from my ordeal, the loss of blood, and the cold, I maintained as fast a pace as was possible along the game trail in order to warm myself. A quarter-moon and the stars gave adequate light for travel. Though weak, I had been walking rapidly for fifteen minutes when the unmistakable smell of wood smoke filled the air. Wetting my finger in my mouth and holding it up to test the wind direction, I then walked toward the source of the smoke while facing the southeasterly breeze.

Within minutes there was a glimmer of light through the leaves. Had the leaves not been thinned by the cold weather, I would have almost been in the camp before seeing the light. As it was, I was still over a hundred yards from the camp when the light from a small fire became visible.

Creeping to within fifty yards, I observed the camp. A hastily constructed pole pen held eight horses. Several other horses were tethered where they could graze. Shifting locations, I also discovered a few horses outside the pen that were not tethered but had their front legs hobbled. They could move about to forage but could not move much more than three hundred yards during the entire night. As near as could be determined there were twenty warriors in the camp. One seemed to be seriously injured, perhaps from my rifle or shotgun that day. As was usual with the Seminoles in a night camp, no guards were posted. All of them were still awake at that time, however.

My first thought was to wait until midnight to steal a horse but then the thought came to me that the staked and hobbled horses' owners might put them in the pen or on a picket line before retiring. Also, by acting immediately, the casual talking around the campfire might cover any small noise created by my efforts. Finding a hobbled pony a hundred yards from the campfire, I cut his hobbles and led him another hundred yards away before tethering him to a tree. Returning to the area in which they were grazing, I did the same with a second horse.

I returned to a place near the camp and watched for most of an hour while trying to think of a plan to get my rifle and pack back. During that time a few of the warriors retired for the night. Failing to come up with anything practical and safe related to getting my pack and rifle back, I decided to release as many horses as I could. Doing so would delay any pursuit. Searching for hobbled or tethered horses, one by one I cut their restraints and led them further away from the camp. Soon, only the horses in the pen were left. Most of the warriors were then under their blankets and retired for the night. Crawling up to the side of the pen away from the camp, I found the pen was made of a single row of poles lashed to trees. Also, my pack was lying on the ground between the pen and the campfire. From its shape, it looked like half of the contents had been removed.

Three hours had passed since I first spotted the campfire; it was then after ten o'clock and most of the Indians had covered themselves with their blankets and were sleeping. Only three still sat around the campfire. Each of those three had a blanket wrapped around him. Since they were not talking, they might also have been dozing. In spite of the fact it was within a couple of yards of two sleeping warriors, I decided to retrieve my pack. Unless one of the Indians decided to step away from the small fire and relieve himself, or one of those who was sleeping woke up, I probably would not be seen. If seen, I would fire both barrels of my shotgun at those who presented the most danger and dart away into the darkness. Since there were already two horses staked out for my getaway, everything should work out. If seen, or not, I would get my pack even if I had to shoot those Indians who first spotted me.

Rubbing dirt on my face and hands to keep them from shining because of the light from the stars and moon, or the glow the small fire provided, I walked around the horse pen to the last point that a tree covered my approach. The pack was fifteen yards from the horse pen and thirty yards from the fire, but only two yards from one sleeping warrior. With a couple of the sleeping warriors and the pack lined up between the fire and me, I used what little cover they provided. My knees and elbows spread to keep low, I wormed my way toward the pack. It took most of two minutes to travel the fifteen yards. After reaching the pack, I started crawling backwards, inching my pack along. Watching the Indians' faces intently, at least the one who was facing toward me across the fire, I looked for any movement that would indicate I had been seen. His head tilted forward, the Indian appeared to be staring at the small campfire or dozing. Since the three Indians who were awake were facing the fire, their eyes would not be adjusted to see out into the darkness. That was to my advantage. Still, had the fire been bigger, I probably could not have gone for the pack without being seen. While crawling, the pain in my left arm from the knife wound was intense. In my dazed state, retrieving the pack had almost become an obsession so I bore the pain. Alternately moving the shotgun and the pack with my right hand, I backed away into the darkness. Four minutes after first touching the pack, I had it behind the tree and was again concealed.

My luck and the luck of some of the Indians was good. I got my pack without any trouble and none of them died that night. Going to the darkest side of the horse pen, I cut the rawhide holding a pole in place and removed it from the fence. If the Seminoles didn't notice the problem within a few minutes, those horses would be gone also. Slinging my shotgun across my shoulders and neck and taking the pack in my right hand—along with a couple of halters, lead ropes, and a blanket for the horse I would be riding—I returned to the tethered horses. My pack was in place on the pony and I was preparing to mount and ride away when shouting erupted from the Indian camp. It was clear they had discovered their horses were gone. They would be most of the next day catching the horses and might never catch them all.

Riding slowly because it was dark after the moon set, I traveled only eight miles over the next three hours. At a place the tree canopy was open enough to allow some sunlight through, there was grass for the horses; there I staked my two horses out and built a small fire. The pack still contained twenty pounds of corn, a cooking pot, some beans, salt pork, and half the rice that had originally been in it. All else had been removed. Most notable among the things that had been removed was my extra powder, wadding, shot, and a change of clothes. I then had only the powder in my powder horn and the wadding and shot in my possibles bag.

After boiling some water and my bandage, I cleaned the knife wound in my arm and replaced the bandage. The process was painful, almost to the point of being unbearable. Putting some beans, salt pork, and water on to boil, I then lay close to the fire and slept. There was no thermometer but it must have been thirty-five degrees. My blanket, though still slightly damp, was comforting when warmed by the fire.

Only a few live coals remained under the pot when I awoke, chilled to the bone. Adding some dry sticks and straw soon created an almost smokeless fire. It was important there be little smoke because day was breaking.

I didn't really expect pursuit. If they did follow, it would be with only a few warriors. It would require some time to gather more than a few horses. Also, they had plundered the pack for things that were of immediate value to them. As far as they knew, I had little of value other than two of their horses. Actually, along with the shooting and fishing supplies in my possibles bag, which was carried all the time, I also had the balance of Running Dog's gold coins, and my powder horn was full. I was not in bad shape as far as being equipped.

The horses having then rested for several hours, I broke camp an hour after daylight and continued south. At a large lake in the early afternoon, I intentionally laid a trail by riding directly across an open, dry prairie. Entering the woods after crossing the prairie, I rode for a hundred yards before finding a place to stake out the horses where they could graze. Returning to the edge of the lake, I then settled in to fish for the afternoon and watch the route used crossing the prairie. If there was pursuit, I needed to know it. If there were not too many of them, I could then go on the offensive.

By mid-afternoon all the fish that would be useful were swimming on a stringer in the edge of the lake. In less than another hour an afternoon thunderstorm developed. Rushing back to the horses, I rode until the storm subsided. My trail was then washed out for miles. There was then little chance the Indians could track me.

It was seven days later when I found Running Dog's camp. During those seven days I didn't see anyone and saw little sign of where anyone had been. Or I should say I almost found Running Dog's camp. Close to where their village should be there was some sign of people—horse tracks, bent bushes, game trails wider than they should be. I had scouted the area for an hour and seemed no closer to figuring out where they were than when the sign was first noticed when, glancing up from scanning the ground for sign, I saw Running Dog approaching in the trail not fifty yards in front of me.

"You always do that," I said. "There's no one else who can get that close to me without me knowing."

"So it's been said around the campfires," he said. "Your reputation as a tracker and warrior has grown over the fifteen years that we've been friends."

"It's a good thing we're brothers," I said, "or else my scalp would be hanging from your lodge pole."

Being kind, he said, "You were careless because you knew it was our village that was close by."

"I've been looking hard enough for it," I said. "I've been down a couple of dead ends. I finally decided the sign was laid on purpose to lead people astray and was about to expand the search area to find out why."

"Yes, it was," he said. "We'll have to cross almost a mile of knee-deep water and tall grass to get to our camp. We live on a large island. You had eliminated just about every other possibility and were getting close to figuring it out. Your reputation as a scout and hunter is well earned. What brings you here at this time?"

"Things are not going well for the Seminoles, Running Dog. Many of them are giving up or they are being captured. All those are being sent west. Some others are dying in the fight. Lots of women and children are in rags and are often hungry. As I said I would, I've made arrangements for your safe passage to the west. Also, I've gained promises of some incentives that'll be paid to you and your people and to Four Toes."

"There have been many promises. Perhaps these will be kept."

"They will. The money's already in a bank in New Orleans. Also, the ship that'll carry you is owned by my wife's family."

"We heard about your wife from Four Toes. Mourning Dove said nothing but she was sad for a while. Later she accepted a husband."

"That's good," I said, as he led the way toward his camp.

We spent six days preparing to leave. Everything that could be carried was packed. Unlike the more combative Seminoles, Running Dog's clan was well stocked with food and clothing. They had spent their time and energy seeing to their well-being instead of fighting and hiding. Every horse and every person was heavily laden as we made the move to meet the ship. This was, in part, because they only had twelve horses, fourteen with my two. They had intentionally maintained a small horse herd to keep from having to feed them.

There was little enough excitement until we met the two army officers the ship's captain had picked up for the trip, a major and a lieutenant. The major became upset when he saw the fully armed band of Indians. I had already cleared it with the captain for them to keep their weapons, unloaded, for the trip. They would need them in the west. The major at first demanded they give up their weapons. After the captain, Running Dog, and I talked with him, and I explained these were not hostiles, he relented.

As my friends were being shuttled to the ship in longboats, I took the opportunity to take Mourning Dove's hand as she stepped into the boat.

As our eyes met, she smiled and said, "Goodbye."

Smiling back, I said, "Thank you."

It was the last time I saw my dear friend.

Riding one horse, I led my other and Running Dog's horses, tied head-to-tail, as I headed back toward Black Creek. Going straight up the west coast of Florida, within four days I arrived at Fort Brooke and sold all the horses but two. Two of those sold were the two I had taken from the Indians the night after the encounter. If they met me, they would not know it was I who had shot up their group. From Fort Brooke I rode inland in order to avoid the bend of the Withlacoochee River. The most militant of the Seminoles still returned frequently to that area. It was a place of continuing battle.

Detouring to avoid contact each time there was any sign of Indians, which was almost never, I arrived at Fort King four days later. After resting my horses for a day at Fort King, I left for Black Creek and home.

By chance alone, the timing of my trip to move Running Dog was such that I avoided the campaign by General Jessup to Lake Okeechobee. Also, being already on the ship, Running Dog didn't get caught up in that fight. He probably would not have become involved anyway because the fight took place on the east side of the lake. Running Dog's clan had been living on the west side.

I found upon returning home that, prior to that campaign, Osceola was allowed to send a runner to offer his people the chance to surrender. The Miccosukee braves and black Seminoles rejected the offer and voted to continue the war. General Jessup learned of this in mid-December. Jessup made the bearer of the news a prisoner. He also arrested Micanopy and his followers, who were then camped near Fort Mellon while discussing a truce agreement. Their capture was clearly in violation of the agreement that had been worked out with Micanopy to attend the discussions.

Actually it was Colonel Zachary Taylor who attacked the Indians near Lake Okeechobee. On December 19, 1837, Taylor left Fort Gardener, on the east coast of Florida, for the Kissimmee River. He had received information that a Seminole force was gathering there.

While proceeding on his mission, Taylor learned where a small band of Indians and black slaves were camped. Using a company of Delaware Indians and a company of Shawnee Indians operating with his command, Taylor captured them. He then assigned a company of Indians to escort the seventy-plus captive Seminoles and their slaves to the coast for shipment west. Taylor then marched his command toward Lake Okeechobee.

Four hundred Indians and black fighters were waiting at Lake Okeechobee to fight Taylor. The Seminoles chose to conduct their part of the battle from a dry hammock. A wide, boggy swamp filled with tall sawgrass had to be crossed to get to the hammock. The swamp was so boggy a horse could not be ridden through it. Men could walk there only with difficulty. On their dry hammock, the Indians carved notches in trees to brace their rifles and cut brush to use for concealment. Also, they cut crisscrossed shooting lanes through the saw grass so they would have open shots as the advancing soldiers neared their positions.

At noon on Christmas Day, Taylor ordered a charge by ele-

ments of his command. The Seminoles had open shots at the soldiers and friendly Indians as they struggled through the muddy
shooting lanes. A hundred and thirty-eight of Taylor's men were
either killed or wounded. According to the Seminole report,
fewer than thirty of their number were killed or wounded. After
three hours, the Indians abandoned the battle. With so many
casualties, Taylor called the campaign off. Though that large battle was a failure, Taylor declared his campaign a success because
he had earlier captured some Indians, their animals, and their
supplies.

As I was involved in, or as word came about, various conflicts, I often thought about the time that we set out to take our
small piece of Florida. We could not have imagined the turmoil
and strife that would occur as the United States moved to establish rule over the whole territory of Florida.

January 1, 1838

On January 1, Osceola and his party—almost two hundred men, women, and children—were delivered to Fort
Moultrie, South Carolina. They were transferred there from the
Old Spanish Fort in St. Augustine, Florida. That group of prisoners included no black people or people of mixed black blood.
It was assumed they would be the cause of trouble, so all people
of black lineage had been separated and sent to Fort Brooke.
Wildcat and several other Indians had escaped from the old fort
where they were all being held prisoner before the transfer.

Also on January 1, we had some trouble with a group of
Seminoles at Black Creek. To say they made a surprise attack on
my farm, which was some distance from the fort on our property, would not be totally accurate because we were always fearful

of an attack. Still, their attack was without warning other than for the barking of a dog. That wasn't much of a warning because a dog was frequently barking at something. I was at the fort when the gunfire erupted. There was a volley of shots as the Seminoles opened the attack at and around our house. A few scattered shots followed the volley.

Hearing the shots, I grabbed my weapons, mounted my already saddled horse at a run, and rode as hard as I could toward the house. By the time I got within three hundred yards of the buildings, all was quiet except for the drum of my horse's hooves and the squeak of saddle leather as he ran. My eyes alert for any movement, I saw no one as I entered the yard and dismounted with my horse still at almost a full run. A double-barrel shotgun held at the ready, I burst through the door to the main house. It was empty. The only sound I heard was the crackle of the cook-fire in the fireplace and the song of a bird outside.

Shouting for Louisa, I rushed through the house and out into the backyard. As I looked about in desperation, one of the Cuban women emerged from one of the outbuildings.

As she ran toward me, she was shouting, "I think everybody might be dead except for Miss Louisa, Juanita, and their babies."

I said, "What do you mean? Where are they?"

Crying, she said, "The Seminoles took them."

I said, "Where? What direction did they go?"

Pointing, she said, "In the woods. There!"

I released her arms that I had been holding as we heard the approaching sound of running horses. It was my brother, George, and some others from the fort.

At that time, one of the Cuban men came from behind the barn. Holding a piece of clothing wrapped around his bleeding and useless left arm, he was in shock. He was babbling about how the Indians were in the house before anyone saw them, about the Indians taking the women and children, and about Rodriguez being dead and scalped. His rambling talk was of little use in terms of gathering information so I turned back to the woman.

"How many were there?" I asked.

"Lots," she said. "Maybe a dozen."

Turning to George, I said, "I'm going after them. You and the others gather some food and bedrolls, and follow."

"We'll go with you now," George said.

"No!" I said. "We might run straight into an ambush. Also, this might be a long chase. We'll need food and bedrolls."

"I'm going with you," George said. "The others can bring supplies."

"Okay," I said. Turning to the others, I added, "We'll leave a well-marked trail. You men supply yourself here and follow us as soon as you can. You also might want to send to the fort to get a company of militia to follow. We'll be outnumbered otherwise."

Taking some biscuits and fried bacon, and leading a spare horse each, which we got from two of the other riders, George and I left. Since the Seminoles had a twenty-minute head start, we held our horses to a steady trot in the hopes of closing the gap. The group we were following was mounted and thus leaving an easy trail to follow. Having two horses each, George and I figured to close on them in an hour or two. We switched horses every twenty minutes so as not to wear them out. The Seminoles didn't have enough mounts to alternate theirs, even with the horses they took from our farm. Also, Louisa and Juanita would be riding two of those.

As we rode, George said, "If we catch them, we're probably in trouble. There's a dozen of them and two of us. Also, they could lay in wait and ambush us."

I said, "I've been thinking about that. They won't try an ambush. They can't know only two of us are following. They'll probably think we'd come with a full company."

George asked, "What's the plan?"

I said, "For right now it's pushing them some and not giving them time to think about the women. I'd like to be close to them before dark. They'll probably make camp by dark or a little after. They can't be much more than a couple of miles ahead of us."

The Seminoles were walking their horses and I began calculating how long it would take us to catch them. Figuring we were traveling at almost twice their speed, I decided we would catch them within the hour. Not having any idea about what to do when we caught them, I slowed our pace to gain time to think. No more than five minutes passed before the trail we were following forked.

George, who was then in the lead, reined in and said, "They've split up. About half have taken each trail. What'll we do now?"

I said, "Let me look at the tracks."

After studying the tracks for a couple of minutes, I said, "At least one of the horses they took from my place took the right hand fork. I'm hoping either Louisa or Juanita is riding him. We'll try the right fork."

George said, "How did you recognize that track."

I said, "When I last trimmed it, I noticed where a rock or something cut his right forefoot."

George said, "I could take the left fork just in case."

"No," I said, "We'll soon know if Louisa took the right fork. We've talked about this sort of thing. She'll leave a broken limb, a small piece of torn cloth on the ground, or some other such sign to show which trail she's on. We'll ride slow and look carefully. If there's no sign within the first three hundred yards, we're on the wrong trail."

It was 150 yards further down the trail that we spotted one of the baby's booties in the trail. Louisa had dropped it. Since it was in a horse's track and none of the horses had stepped on it, I figured she must have been riding close to the back of the line. After recovering the bootie and sending George back to mark the trail for those who were following, I again nudged my horses into a trot. The odds had changed some but, at six or seven to two, they were still not in our favor.

It was a half a mile farther before George, who had run his horses some, caught up.

Fifteen minutes later I thought I had figured out where the band we were following was going and said as much to George.

"They're headed for a shallow creek ford, which is less than a half-hour ahead of us. If I can beat them to the ford, I might be able do something there."

"I'll go, too," George said.

"No. You follow the trail and keep it marked for the others. Also, I could be wrong and we could lose them if we both go. Five minutes from now fire one of your weapons and every five minutes after that. They'll think you're firing a shot to signal others who follow you. That'll also confirm to them that we're behind them; and keep them thinking about pursuit instead of about the women. And, with a shot fired behind them, they would never think we might get in front of them."

Kicking my horses into a gallop, I left the trail and swung to the right far enough to bypass the Seminoles without them hearing or seeing me. I switched horses every five minutes to keep from killing one. Five minutes after splitting off I heard George fire his musket. In eighteen minutes more I came within sight of the ford. If I was right, I was as much as ten minutes ahead of the Indians. After concealing my horses far enough away that they wouldn't whinny as the other animals approached, I quickly looked at the ground near the ford to be sure they had not yet passed there. I then concealed myself twenty-five yards from the ford in thick brush.

Thinking Louisa would be riding near the rear of the column, my plan was to wait on the same side of the creek they would enter from and shoot the Indians behind her after the last of them entered the creek. I would then shout for Louisa to run her horse toward me. If there were no more than three behind her, it might work. I had a rifle, a double-barrel shotgun, and a dueling pistol. Thus, I had four shots without reloading. If there were three behind her, the fourth shot would be for the one leading her horse. There wasn't much room for error. I was praying that she was one of the last riders. If she were close to the front, I would need to be on the other side of the creek.

After checking the priming of my weapons twice, I settled down motionless to wait. Where I was hiding I would not see the Indians until just as each one entered the water and they wouldn't see me at all until the first shot was fired. It being the least accurate of my three weapons as the distance increased, I planned to shoot the pistol first and at the closest Seminole.

Since they were walking their horses I didn't hear them until they were fifty yards from me. I then heard them pass by at twenty yards. I saw the first of them as he walked his horse into the water. The rest followed at close intervals. The horse I was looking for turned out to be the sixth to appear from behind the screen of bushes blocking my view of them and their view of me. A mounted Indian was leading him.

My breath caught in my chest as I saw Louisa and the baby. Blocking them from my thoughts, I forced myself to concentrate on the task at hand. Since there were eight sets of horse's tracks in the bunch we were following, I prepared to shoot the eighth person that appeared, if it wasn't Juanita. The seventh and eighth riders were Indians.

Bracing my pistol over a low branch on the bush I was concealed behind, I squeezed off the round. Though he was momentarily hidden by the puff of smoke from the black powder, I knew exactly where my bullet struck. I was then looking for the seventh rider as the smoke was blown to one side by the wind. One barrel of the shotgun was used on him, thus saving the more difficult shot, the one at the brave leading Louisa's horse, for my rifle. He would also be the closest to her. It wasn't safe to use the shotgun on him.

As I lined up the third shot, I noticed Louisa, with great presence of mind, had leaned forward and jerked the halter from the hand of the Indian leading her horse. He made it easy. Instead of running for the far bank, as he should have, he was trying to regain control of Louisa's horse when I shot him.

Since Louisa then had her horse headed for the bank from which she entered the creek, and the other Indians had reached cover on the far bank of the creek, I concentrated on reloading the discharged barrel of the shotgun. Within twenty seconds I finished reloading it. The baby held in one arm, Louisa had already swung down beside me. Placing the baby on the ground, she busied herself loading the rifle.

Since the four Indians on the other bank stayed under cover and did not try to come back across the creek, I handed the shotgun to Louisa and loaded the pistol. Amazingly, during all that time and commotion Andrew wasn't crying.

Finally Louisa spoke. "Oh, Isaac. I knew you would come."

"George is coming up the trail behind you. He probably started running his horses when he heard the shooting. I guess we got lucky. I was out of my mind over concern for you."

"Thank goodness you didn't act out of your mind. You looked cool and calm."

"That was the only way it would work," I said.

The Indians then started taking shots at where they thought we were. After giving Louisa the shotgun and getting the rifle from her, we both returned their fire. Since we were both behind trees, the Seminoles shooting at us caused no harm. Our shooting so close to him did cause Andrew to begin crying.

At that point, we heard the pounding of George's horse's hooves as he raced toward us. Leaving Louisa to watch the ford I stopped him short of the creek.

Seeing Louisa, George said, "Juanita wasn't with them?"

"No," I said. "She's got to be with the other bunch. There were seven of these. There's still four on the other side of the creek. There wasn't time for but three shots."

"I heard the first three shots, and some others later."

I said, "It's probably too late and they'll never catch them, but we should start our riders after the other bunch."

The Indians had then stopped shooting. Thinking they might cross at a less favorable place and flank us, we caught up a couple of their loose ponies and headed back down the trail. The two ponies behind Louisa had followed her horse back out of the creek. In order to keep the Indians from, perhaps, outdistancing us and ambushing us, we kept our horses at a trot. It was twenty minutes later when we met the riders who were following us, and thirty minutes more before we met a thirty-five-person company of militia from the fort.

We put the militia on the trail of those holding Juanita captive and headed home. Asa and George rode with the militia company. After losing the trail of the Indians in a swamp, the company returned to the fort three days later without making contact.

I tried to get Louisa to move to the fort but she refused. She didn't think the Indians would soon be back at our place. She was right, of course

The battle with the Seminoles for Florida continued. Over the next days and weeks there were continuing raids by small bands of Seminoles in north Florida and a couple of large battles in south Florida. General Jessup then invited some of the chiefs to his camp for talks about peace. The general also made an appeal to the secretary of war to allow the Seminoles to stay in the deep south of Florida. When permission was denied, Jessup ordered that the eight hundred Indians who were camped near him during the peace talks be taken prisoner. Once again the army resorted to trickery and deceit. Those eight hundred would not have been easily captured other than with deception.

Colonel Twiggs, the same Twiggs who finally gave Pa a paper authorizing payment after the war for his land and crops that had been confiscated, and who later tried to help him recover his property by getting the letter enforced, commanded the force that took those Seminoles captive.

February 5, 1838

Having served our six-month enlistment, George, Asa, and I were mustered out of the militia as the company was disbanded. Most of the large battles were then taking place further south. There were, however, still some raids by small parties of Indians occurring in northeast Florida.

My brother, George, soon enlisted in a militia company again. It was through him and Louisa's brothers that I heard a lot about the fighting in the south over the next couple of years.

A series of commanders were in charge of the forces in Florida during that time. Brigadier General Zachary Taylor replaced General Jessup. Taylor was soon placed under another general, Alexander Macomb. Macomb was then authorized to negotiate with the Indians about remaining in south Florida. After meeting with several chiefs at Fort King and coming to an agreement about them staying in south Florida, Macomb then announced an end to hostilities and returned to Washington, leaving Taylor in command.

There were then a few weeks of peace. Unfortunately, some of the chiefs had not been included in the negotiations and they didn't keep the peace. In July of 1839, 250 warriors under the leadership of Billy Bowlegs attacked a group of thirty-plus soldiers and civilians under the command of Colonel William Harvey and killed most of that group. We were back at war. That was when Louisa's brother, Henry, enlisted for the last time.

In August of 1839, Louisa had our second child, Jane. She was named after her aunt. I was then supervising some of the farming. Pa was working as a wheelwright for the military for the large sum of forty-five dollars a month and had been for some time.

After the attack by Billy Bowlegs' group, a party of Seminoles was brought back to Florida from the west to attempt to persuade those still fighting to give up and go west. Their effort persuaded over two hundred Seminoles to give up. They were then sent west.

As more and more Indians were carried west, those still in Florida became so few that they were difficult to find. Indians were then scattered all over Florida. Some of them were even on islands in the Everglades. There were also small bands terrorizing the white population in north and east Florida by murdering the owners of small farms, looting, and plundering. There were also some larger bands still fighting south of Paynes Prairie.

It was also in late 1839 that the government purchased some bloodhounds from Cuba. The dogs had been used for tracking escaped black slaves in Cuba. I was told of the impending arrival of the bloodhounds and told I would no longer be needed for any expeditions to track the Seminoles, which was fine with me and I told them so. I had been called on frequently before then. I had always had some sympathy for the Seminoles' plight and it was with mixed feelings that I hunted them down. Also, there were lots of other things I was good at. I certainly wouldn't miss the work and would get to sleep in my bed more often.

On May 19, 1840, a group of warriors led by Wildcat ambushed a military detachment near Paynes Prairie, killing six and wounding several others. Some raiding parties also killed the passengers and drivers of several coaches and wagons near St. Augustine about that time. Some of these attacks were less than a one-day ride from our place. In retaliation, the newly arrived General Walker Keith Armistead ordered sweeps made through all the swamps and riverbanks. Few Indians were found but several hundred acres of the Seminoles' fields were destroyed. Villages were also burned and livestock was taken.

It wasn't long after the attack by Wildcat's group that I was approached about scouting and tracking again. A colonel sent from Fort King found me at home.

The colonel said, "Isaac, I was sent to get you to scout for the army. We haven't been having much success in finding some of the small bands of Indians."

"What about the bloodhounds General Taylor sent to Cuba for? According to all that was said about them, you should have caught all the Indians by now."

"Haven't you heard? The dogs didn't work out very well."

I had heard but I said, "No. Tell me about it."

"In trials, while using slaves to lay a trail, the dogs did great. But, when they were taken to the swamps to trail Indians, they refused to trail them. It seems they were trained to trail blacks and they just wouldn't trail Indians. It's assumed that because of their diet, or for some other reason, Indians just smell different. Also, there was a general hue and cry by the do-gooders and the press across the country about the inhumanity of using dogs to catch Indians. That project was dropped. They never found a single Indian."

"That's too bad. And after all the money that was spent on the project. A hundred and fifty dollars a dog, it's been said, for the thirty-three dogs, and more for their handlers. There was also at least a thousand dollars spent on shipping them here from Cuba and it must have been a thousand dollars to ship them back. I'd like to have seen one of those dogs. I've never seen a dog worth more than two or three dollars. But then I guess those turned out to not be worth much either."

He said, "No, I guess not. What can I tell the general about you tracking for us?"

Not answering directly, I said, "I understand there's been a move afoot to increase the regular soldiers' salary by two dollars a month and to give them some incentives for staying in for ten years or more."

"That's true," he said. "But they're only making seven dollars a month now, not eight as was talked about. And the long-term incentive is going to be dropped, too. What does that have to do with you? Oh, I see. You're going to negotiate with me about your pay. We only have two rates of pay for the kind of work you do—scout and chief scout. We can pay you as a chief scout."

"No," I said. "You have a third rate, which is for dogs. I've found lots of Indians and your hundred-and-fifty-dollar dogs haven't found any. It would seem that I'm worth more than a dog, maybe even thirty-three dogs. The most I've ever made, while scouting, is a dollar a day. And some of the scouting I've done was only at a soldier's pay, which was then six dollars a month."

The colonel didn't like where the conversation was going and he was getting a little exasperated. Curtly, he said, "What shall I tell the general?"

"As of right now you can tell him you haven't made me a reasonable offer."

"I'm offering you a job as chief of scouts."

"Well then, I guess you can tell him I declined. I'm certainly worth more than a dog and handler. How much did you pay the handlers, anyway?"

"I understand the government refused to pay after the dogs didn't work out."

"I appreciate the offer but I'm doing pretty well now. Also, other than in the deep south, there aren't many Indians causing much trouble right now."

Exasperated, he said, "There have been murders by Indians within a one-day ride of your house."

"Like I said, not many Indians. But, they're close enough and cause enough trouble for me to stay close to home for a while and look after the family. In case of real need, and when he decides I'm as valuable as a dog, tell the general he can send for me."

While a few small groups of Seminoles, and some small groups of Creeks from Alabama and Georgia who had recently drifted down into Florida, still operated in north Florida, most of the bigger battles were then occurring in the southern part of the territory. In early August of 1840, a hundred braves in canoes, under the leadership of Chekika, raided Indian Key. They killed seven people, killed some animals, and stole everything they could carry. They then burned the building.

Wildcat and his followers, as well as the newly arriving Indians, were still making life miserable for those of us in northeast Florida. The road from the town of Picolata to St. Augustine, on which a military escort was provided, was the scene of continuing murders by Wildcat's band. Also, some small bands of Creeks that had moved into the Apalachicola basin were making life miserable for farmers and travelers there.

The 1840 census of Florida showed that only 54,000 people were living in the territory of Florida. Of those, 34,000 were living between the Apalachicola and Suwannee Rivers. It was easy for the Indians to come and go without notice across the millions of acres of the Florida Territory, even in the more populated northern-middle part of the territory.

Upon taking command of the military in Florida, General Armistead tried to bribe two bands of Indians still operating in northeast Florida to move west. He offered Tiger Tail and Halleck Tustenuggee $5,000 each to move their bands. After considering the offer for two weeks, by way of declining they secretly left the area of the fort. I guess they didn't want to say no and then be imprisoned while wearing their white feathers as their friends had been. After the failure of that effort, an officer from Fort King again visited me.

Again finding me at home, he said, "Isaac, General Armistead intends to hunt down the Indians in groups, or one by one. He wants you to help."

"We've talked about this before. Has he decided I'm worth as much as a dog?"

He replied, "The general said to offer you a dollar a day for now. He has also ordered that the mobilization of regulars and militia be stepped up until he has forty-five hundred regulars and two thousand militia in the field. It's his plan to mount such an effort that he'll drive the Indians from this area, kill, or capture them. He's also willing to bribe any who are willing to be bribed."

Breaking in, I said, "You said a dollar a day for now. Go on from there."

"On December eleventh, a company of, possibly, a hundred militia will be signed on at Fort Heileman. You can join that company and draw twenty-four dollars a month as their chief scout and interpreter. You can also continue drawing your dollar a day for tracking and interpreting as long as that company is active."

"And what would my duties be?"

He replied, "For now, you would act as an independent tracker. You can capture or bribe any Indian you find. The purpose is to remove them from Florida. You'll be paid a bonus of ten dollars each for every Indian you turn over to a fort commander, regardless of how you get them. If they come in voluntarily, Armistead will pay two hundred and fifty dollars to each brave, a hundred to each woman, and fifty to each child."

"What about those who force me to shoot them?" I asked.

"The general wants them alive, if possible. He doesn't get much credit for an Indian that was, theoretically, left dead in the swamp," he answered. "There will be no payment for those you have to shoot and leave in the woods."

"It sounds pretty risky to me," I said. "Lots of the Indians I know personally are either dead or have already gone west."

"That's the offer," he said.

Louisa, who had been around the fireplace cooking and had brought us some coffee, said nothing.

Looking at Louisa, I said, "It's not a bad offer."

When she made no response, I said to the officer, "You said ten dollars for every man, woman, and child. I assume that includes black Seminoles as well as all kinds of Indians."

"That's right," he said.

"When would I start and who would I report to?" I asked.

"You would start today and would report to no one until December eleventh. Then you would sign in with Captain Thigpen's company at the fort," he said. "After that, you would be a member of the company but would still work mostly on your own, unless the company was in hot pursuit. Then you would scout and interpret for Thigpen."

"There are two conditions. You'll have to find a room in Fort Heileman for Louisa and the kids without having to take a room from any other civilians. Also, I'll expect to be reimbursed for all my expenses: supplies, ammunition, ferry fees, and anything else."

"Consider it done," he said.

"Where's the last point of contact you had with any Indians?" I asked.

"The general wants the Indians removed from the Withlacoochee area first," he said.

"The army has been trying to clear that area since eighteen-thirty-six," I said. "Our first fight with Osceola was south of Paynes Prairie. The second fight I was in with him was south of the Withlacoochee. I'll work my way up the St. Johns and try to find Wildcat first. He's the one causing all the trouble around here. It'll be a couple of weeks before I make it to the Withlacoochee."

"It's been said that you know the area well and can get the job done," he said.

Standing, we shook hands on the deal. Louisa then asked the officer about the health of his family and wished him well. He soon departed.

Louisa then said, "I would rather you hadn't agreed."

"You could have spoken up,"

"You wanted to go."

"The money's good and you'll be okay."

"You've been tied down to a dull life too long. I think you're missing the hunt. And it's not me I'm concerned about."

"I know. But it's a good offer and something I can do better than most. Pa and I set out to take us a little piece of Florida and I guess we're still working on it. I'll leave in the morning but will be back for three or four days before December eleventh to spend a few days with you and the kids before joining the captain. Don't worry about me. I know how to stay out of trouble."

November 15, 1840

*L*ouisa and the two children were safely in the fort when I rode south toward Fort King. Having a brace of dueling pistols in my belt, I was armed a little more heavily than usual. I also led a packhorse loaded with enough supplies for the horses and me for a week. Another key part of my gear was three large white turkey feathers and a silver headband. Part of my plan was to pick up more supplies at Fort King and to hit the general up for one of those Colt revolvers I had seen some of the officers carrying.

Knowing Wildcat and his band were frequently active on the east side of the St. Johns River, I held a southeast course so as to reach the St. Johns directly across from Picolata. A steamboat landing had been built at Picolata in 1835. There was also a ferry and I could get passage across at that point. Also, Wildcat had murdered lots of people on the Picolata to St. Augustine road but less frequently worked the road west of the river. I planned to get ferried across the river to Picolata, then swing south and work the edge of the river swamp for sign. Wildcat should be on the east side of the river and south of the road from Picolata to St. Augustine. Wearing three white turkey feathers in a silver headband as a white flag, I could ride into his camp and ride out again with my hair still in place, and probably could in most any Indian

255

camp. In spite of the fact the army hadn't honored their white flags or feathers, Indians would honor the feathers. Also, I knew Wildcat personally and could sit down and eat with him. I didn't expect him or his people to agree to move west, and wasn't about to brace his whole clan for a fight, but I didn't think it would hurt anything to let him know I was in the business of offering money to those who would voluntarily go west. Word has a way of spreading among the Indians. If Wildcat knew, lots of them would soon know.

In Picolata, I inquired about any recent Indian sightings. After hearing lots of rumors but with no factual information, I left the next day to look for tracks while traveling south. On my packhorse were five one-gallon jugs of rum purchased in Picolata. While deciding to stock up with personal supplies at Picolata, the rum was the only trade good I carried. As a precaution, I put my silver headband and white feathers on once out of the sight of white people.

Riding slowly and keeping a sharp eye out for sign of people, I traveled little more than twenty miles during the next two days before finding some fresh horse tracks. I found them toward the end of the second day. As near as I could tell, I was somewhere across the river from a community named Palatka. Though I suspected that Seminole ponies had made the tracks, it wasn't for certain whether white Americans or Seminoles left the sign. I decided to follow the tracks until dark but had not ridden for more than an hour when my horse lifted his head slightly and his ears went forward. Raising my left arm, palm forward, and with my reigns in my right hand, which was also close to the butt of a pistol, I continued riding down the trail. They saw me at the same time I spotted them but, since I had my hand up, they thought I had seen them first. It turned out to be Wildcat with a band of nineteen braves.

Speaking as I approached them, I used the Muskogee word for Wildcat, "Coacoochee, I've been searching for you."

Though Wildcat spoke some English, I spoke in Muskogee so the others would know what was said.

"Isaac, you wear the white feathers," he said.

The Indians had never given me a Muskogee name so he said my name in English. Other than that he spoke in Muskogee also.

"I come to talk of peaceful times and things," I said. "You're traveling and I would ride with you to your village and drink some rum."

When he didn't immediately respond, it occurred to me that he might not want to show me where his village was and was thinking the situation over.

I said, "I wear the white feathers and I'm just as honorable as you are. I could not use any information against you that was gained while wearing the white feathers."

Waving for me to follow, he resumed his travel. I fell in behind him. The other braves fell in behind me. It wasn't long after dark that we arrived at Wildcat's permanent camp. Even in the dark it was evident a crop had been planted there the previous spring, and fall and winter gardens were in evidence. It was clear that the village was in pretty good shape.

There appeared to be seventy or eighty members of the clan and a number of small cook-fires were in use. The clan members were scattered about the village but quickly gathered when word spread that a white man had ridden into camp. As my eyes swept the crowd to assess the tone of it and to look for familiar faces, the face of a black woman standing back in the shadows momentarily caught my eye. It was a full minute later that recollection registered with me. Glancing back at her to be sure, I was looking into the eyes of Juanita. Lifting a hand, she placed it over her mouth so I let my eyes drift on to the next person without giving any sign of recognition.

My mind was racing. It appeared that part of Wildcat's band had kidnapped Juanita and Louisa. Had I not moved quickly, Louisa would be living in this village, if she were still alive. Also,

Juanita had signaled for me to remain silent. There were definitely some things I needed to learn from her.

After Wildcat and I arrived at his shelter and were dismounted, I again glanced about to see if I could spot Juanita. The clan members had mostly gone back to their cook-fires and she was not visible.

Wildcat said in English, "After we tend to our horses, sit and eat with me, Isaac. You can also stay in my shelter tonight. Tell me why you came to see me."

As we unsaddled the horses, I said, "I've been hired by the army to talk to you, and to the others, about going west. I've been authorized to offer two hundred and fifty dollars for each brave who comes in, a hundred dollars for each woman and fifty for each child."

"A bribe," he said.

"If you want to call it that," I said.

"General Armistead offered Tiger Tail a bribe of five thousand dollars," he said.

"It was too little and the general is ashamed of his offer," I said. "If all your people came in it would amount to much more than five thousand dollars. It also would for Tiger Tail at this new price."

"I don't understand your numbers completely," he said. "How much for all of my people?"

Wildcat was one of only a few Seminoles who could use numbers, though not very well.

"Counting the old men, how many men do you have?" I asked.

"Do you count the black people?"

"Yes."

"Twenty-six."

"How many women?"

"Thirty-one."

"And children?"

"Fifteen."

After doing some calculations, I said, "The total for all of them would be ten thousand and one hundred dollars. That's more than double the amount the general offered Tiger Tail."

We had cared for our horses and were seating ourselves around the cook-fire before he spoke again. Then it wasn't about the money.

"You looked at the black woman, Juanita. You looked about when we arrived at my shelter, perhaps to see her again."

"I didn't think it showed."

"To others it did not, I think, but I was observing you to see what your reaction would be to all things and people. Do you know her?"

"Yes, I know her."

"How?"

"She was stolen from my house."

"And the white woman that was taken?"

"My wife."

"I heard about it. It was you who killed the three braves at the creek?"

"Yes. Were you on the raid?"

"No. They were Halleck Tustenuggee's warriors. We traded two horses for Juanita and her child."

"I don't know Halleck Tustenuggee personally. Does he know it was my farm his men raided?"

"I don't think so. No one said anything about it. I don't know if he knows of you. Because of Osceola, I've stayed away from your farm."

"Thank you. I appreciate that. I'll not help with any raid on your village."

"Good. Are you interested in the black woman?"

"My wife would be interested in her," I said. "I'd like to ask her if she wants to go back. Where's her son? He would be two years old."

"He sleeps in her shelter. You can talk to the woman tomorrow."

"Does she have a husband here?"

"Nothing permanent," he said.

While we were talking and eating I had uncorked a gallon of rum. Our conversation then turned to other subjects and remembrances as we relaxed. Wildcat was still awake and talking to me as I crawled into my bedroll and went to sleep. As I dozed off, he seemed to be talking to himself. My next-to-last thought was about what a hangover he would have the next morning. My last thought was that the Indians had still not developed the habit of posting a night guard.

I awoke the next morning as the first streaks of light showed in the east. After rolling my bedroll and tying it to my pack, my first order of business was to wash up in the nearby river, something we had neglected the night before. I then found Juanita, who was up and warming food at her cook-fire.

Approaching her, I said, "Wildcat and I talked about you last night. He noticed that we looked at each other and that you covered your mouth. I told him you were stolen from my house. I also told him my wife was taken and, though he already knew it, that I killed three warriors to take her back."

"I heard about the fight at the creek crossing and was afraid for what might happen to you if he found out," she said. "That's why I covered my mouth."

"I'm wearing the white feathers," I said. "Nothing can happen to me here. The situation also presents a problem. Since I found you here while wearing the feathers, I can't steal you back. It's a matter of honor. I told Wildcat I wouldn't use anything I learned here against him."

I then went on to explain to her about my assignment with the army.

Then I said, "Are you happy here or would you like to get away?"

"Oh, I need to get away," she said, "but it's impossible. I don't know where I am or how to get to anywhere else. Also, I couldn't get very far carrying a two-year-old. They would only track me down and bring me back."

"There is a way," I said. "It would be easy for you to escape and carry your child. While washing I saw several canoes concealed at the edge of the river."

"I know about those," she said. "But I don't know anywhere to go. I don't even know where we are or what river this is."

"It's the St. Johns," I said. "My place is downriver from here."

"That's not the name the Indians call it."

"No, it isn't. If you were to take your baby and get in a canoe shortly after everyone is sleeping tonight and paddle downriver, it would take you until sometime late tomorrow to get to Picolata. That's a community on this side of the side of the river, the right side as you're going downriver. There's a steamboat landing and ferry there. You can't miss it. It's less than thirty miles from here. There are soldiers stationed at the town. I'll give you a paper saying you belong to me and that they are to get you to Fort Heileman. You should have no problem at all. There's also a community near here on the far side of the river named Palatka. There are soldiers there also but I'm not sure whether it's upriver or downriver from here. Anyway, you would be better off going to Picolata."

She couldn't believe how simple it was so we talked about it for several more minutes. She spoke pretty good broken English. Since Wildcat, who was nursing a hangover in his shelter, was the only one in camp who spoke fair English, no one knew what we were saying.

When I returned to Wildcat's cook-fire, he was eating and asked me to join him.

He said, "You talked to the woman?"

"Yes," I said. "She wants to return to the farm, but I told her

I couldn't steal her because I found her while wearing the white feathers. I told her I would return and trade for her someday. I don't have much with me that I don't need. What would it take to trade for her?"

"Since she belonged to you before, we would take two horses for her," he said, "and the rest of this jug of rum."

"I'll leave that jug and a full one," I said. "If she's still here, and in good shape when I come back this way, I'll give two good horses for her. Now I'm going to ride upriver and go to Fort King. I'll then talk to Tiger Tail and Halleck Tustenuggee, if I can find them. The offer I made last night is good—ten thousand and one hundred dollars for your whole clan to go west. You can sell your cows, horses, and pigs, and the army will pay all the expenses of moving. The general said you can keep your slaves, all but Juanita, who I'll trade for."

"We'll think about it," he said.

Riding south for a couple of hours, I then turned west and swam my horses across the St. Johns. It's narrow enough for animals to swim at many points south of where I then was. I then traveled along the east bank of the Ocklawaha River to the point where the Silver River enters it. The swamps along those, and other rivers, were where most Indians would be found. I didn't have much of a plan beyond arriving at Fort King and testing the system to see if I would be reimbursed for expenses as promised. The receipts from crossing the St. Johns, the five one-gallon jugs of rum, and my other supplies should be a good test. I wasn't wearing the white feathers but planned to put them on before entering any other villages.

As I traveled, there was some sign of Indians here and there but since it was mostly cold sign I didn't try to follow any of it. It was on the north side of Silver River and before getting to Silver Springs that I encountered some additional Indians. Actually, I saw part of a moccasin track. It was in a wet place where a foot had made an impression. The footprint had muddy water in it.

Since the mud hadn't settled, the track couldn't be more than a few minutes old.

Once I had identified the track, there was adequate sign to follow the person—grass was bent, dead leaves were broken from the weight of the foot, and there was the occasional outline of a moccasin. The hardest part was to decide whether to follow where the track was leading or to follow where it had come from. Sometimes the more interesting place is where the person just left. I decided, however, to follow the person.

Donning the white feathers and leading my horses, I followed at a slow pace. If the person was going someplace, I didn't want to catch up before she arrived there. Medium-long and narrow, it looked like a woman's track. The footprints soon entered a well-beaten path. It was obviously a path made and used by humans. Within minutes after donning my white feathers I walked out into a small clearing that held three shelters and a dozen Indians. Raising my left hand, palm forward, I spoke to them in Muskogee as I approached.

"Wearing the white feathers, I come in peace."

None of them knew me and they didn't seem very reassured about my intentions. The two warriors and two older boys picked up their weapons.

Seeing some freshly caught fish they had been cleaning, I said, "I followed the tracks of a woman to your village, perhaps one who has been fishing or tending the fish traps. I'm alone and came to talk."

Pointing at one of the older boys, I added, "Send him to check my back-trail. The horses leave lots of sign and are easy to backtrack. You'll then know I'm alone."

One of the warriors nodded at the boy and he left. They seemed to relax a little then so I told them I would like to drink some rum and tell them why I was there. Since I had the rum they were more than willing.

We sat and talked for the better part of an hour. I told them why I was there and made them the offer of being paid to go west. I also told of my friends Running Dog and Four Toes. They knew of them. I told them of my friends going west and that they liked it there, though I had no assurance it was true. Most of the clan found something to do close enough to us so they could hear what was said.

I didn't try to fast-talk them into going west. We just discussed the pros and cons. They had lots of questions. Not knowing all the answers, I told them what seemed logical to me. The biggest point in favor of them going was that they wouldn't have to live in fear of the soldiers finding them. This small group had already suffered six deaths from the war. That's why there were only two adult men and so few children in the small clan. I told them, of course, that the soldiers could find them just as easily as I had.

One of them asked, "What about our hogs and chickens?"

They had no cattle or horses.

I said, "You can sell everything at Fort King that you can't carry with you."

There were other such questions. Finally, they said they would discuss it and think about it. Taking that as a cue, I left them sitting around their fire and prepared to start my own fire.

One of the older women then approached me and said, "You'll eat with us."

It wasn't meant as a question.

I said, "If I can contribute to the meal, I would like to."

While they were not starving, they obviously didn't have more than they needed. They were in for a hard winter. The temperature had dropped below freezing on three nights already at Black Creek, which was unusual that far south and at that time of year. I wasn't sure what the date was but knew it was late November. Since I had bought supplies at Picolata and had eaten with Wildcat for a couple of days, I had two weeks' rations in my pack. Knowing Fort King was little more than a half-day ride and

I could stock up there at the army's expense, I contributed all of
it.

The bravest of the women and children got up enough
courage to ask me questions as we ate. They were not questions
about moving so much as about how white people lived.
Although they lived only fifteen miles from Fort King, the
younger children had never seen a white person.

As the day passed there were discussions between different
individuals and small groups. This mostly happened out of my
hearing. I suspected it was about going west but couldn't be sure
of that. I thought about what could be said to encourage them
but came to the conclusion I had said everything there was to say.

Late in the afternoon one of the men asked me to stay the
night with them.

Also, he said, "We're talking about going west but nothing
has been decided."

I said, "I'll be happy to stay the night. If there's anything I
can add to the discussion, ask me. I'm not trying to talk you into
going. It's for you to decide."

He said, "I think everything has been said. There're some
who want to go and others who don't."

I said, "From my end of it, it's not an all-or-nothing decision. Some of you could go and some could stay. You might not
feel that way, however."

I had noticed that one woman, who looked to be about
seven months pregnant, was involved in most of the discussions.
As the men and women gathered to talk soon after our conversation, she was again in the middle of the discussion. At that time
it came to me what she might be talking about. There were stories about some of the Indians smothering their babies in order
not to be found because of the babies crying when soldiers were
near. Even as I thought of that the woman was waving her hands
in the air while she talked. She then placed her hands on her
stomach. Almost certainly my hunch was right. Not wanting to

participate in her distress, I turned and stared at the cook-fire for a time. I retired early to leave them to their deliberations.

It was after we had eaten the next morning and all twelve were gathered around me that their spokesman said, "We are considering going west but there are some that disagree. Tell us about the weather there. It's cold here sometimes but I've been told it's much colder there. We might die from the cold. What's different about that than dying here because of the soldiers?"

I said, "I've never been west but I am told it's cold in the winter. It's probably no colder than north Alabama or north Georgia. Many of your people are from there. If you go, however, I'll see that each of you gets a warm shirt and pair of pants, or a dress, and a blanket each."

I figured I would press the general about those things. If he refused, I would pay for the clothes out of my ten dollars a person. All of those things couldn't total more than thirty or forty dollars for this small group.

Seeing from her facial expressions that the pregnant woman was all for it, I looked at her as I said, "It's okay by me if only one person goes or if everyone goes. The same offer stands in either case. In your case, I'll see that the general counts your unborn child and that you get fifty dollars for the child also. That'll make it a hundred and fifty for you. The fifty dollars and the clothes is all I can probably get out of the general."

Looking around the circle, I added, "I'll see that you get a fair price for your livestock at Fort King, too, or I'll buy them."

Realizing there was nothing else to say, I then started getting my pack ready to go.

After several minutes passed the spokesman came to me and said, "We would like for you to stay another night. Tomorrow morning we'll go with you to Fort King. We agree to be sent west under the conditions you said."

As I pulled the pack back off of my horse, I said, "We should leave by at least mid-morning. That'll get us to Fort King before dark. We can use my horses to help carry your things and I'll walk."

We were a mile and a half from Fort King the next morning when five armed Indians came out of the woods in front of us. I was surprised to see Wildcat was their leader.

He said, "We've been waiting for you, Isaac. You said you were going to Fort King. You've been a long time getting here. Where's Juanita?"

I said, "What do you mean, where's Juanita? She was at your camp when I left."

He said, "She slipped away during the night after you left. She took a canoe so I thought she had gone across the river to join you."

"I haven't seen her since leaving your camp," I said. "I expected you to take good care of her until I returned with two horses. I've been with these people for most of the last three days, getting them ready to go west. There's been no woman with me. You can ask them."

Looking at the group with me, Wildcat said, "Is this true? Have you seen a black woman?"

My little clan's spokesman said, "He has been alone all the time. There was no woman, Wildcat."

I said, "If you get her back in good health, I'll make it three horses. My wife will be concerned about her."

Perplexed, Wildcat led his warriors off toward his main camp.

The general made good on my promises to those twelve Indians. He acted like he didn't like it but he knew as well as I did that my efforts had produced as many people to emigrate that month as his entire force of four thousand regulars and two thousand militia had. They were a real bargain for him. He also paid me for the rum, the ride across the river, and for replenishing my supplies. I also persuaded him to assign me one of the new Colt revolvers.

Leaving the next day, I carried several safe passes in my pack. I was to give them to any Indians I talked to about going west, whether they wanted to go then or not. Credit was to be given me for any Indians who subsequently came in to emigrate bearing one. During the next ten days I located two small villages along the Withlacoochee River and spent a night in each telling them about the offer made by the general for them to go west. I continued to wear the white feathers, of course. Leaving those people with passes with my name on them, I then pointed my horse northeast and went home.

December 11, 1840

Eighty of us were mustered into Captain Thigpen's company on December 11. No one but the captain knew about my other arrangement with the general. He seemed happy enough just to have me along as a scout and tracker. Other than Wildcat, or some of the other Indians the army was after, no one knew the territory as well as I did. There was one handicap in having me as a scout. I couldn't lead a company to Wildcat's home village. I had not made that agreement with any of the other clans because I had found their village without any assistance from anyone.

The general soon had most of the six thousand soldiers under his command searching the swamps and riverbanks of the Florida Territory for Indians and the black people living with them. Since I already knew where a couple of their smaller villages were, and had a good idea where some others were, our company was more productive than most units in rounding up Seminoles. In spite of the fact that the company brought them in,

I was still getting the ten dollars for each of them.

We didn't get into many shooting scrapes with the Indians during those few months. The general preferred that we bribe them rather than taking them by force. Usually what would happen is that we would move the company into position around a small village during the wee hours of the morning. When the first light of the day broke, I would ride into the village wearing my white feathers and tell them they were surrounded by soldiers and give them a chance to surrender. Since there were more women and children in the villages than warriors, they almost always surrendered. If they went peacefully, the general always paid them the bribe money.

As part of a deal that the others in the village would surrender peacefully, we even let a couple of warriors escape one time. Those we let escape didn't belong to the clan we had surrounded. They were just there for the night. Also, each had a wife and children in another place. It seemed only fair to let them go to their families. I gave each of them a pass with my name on it and they promised they would consider bringing their families in. Some of them did, too. I know because, even though I wasn't there at the time they came in, I got ten dollars each for those who showed up at the fort under the protection of a pass with my name on it. We did get into a pitched battle with a couple of small groups of braves. They had a few casualties and we had a few. The survivors who were not captured dispersed and vanished into the swamps. Thinking it wouldn't be very productive, or smart, I didn't try to track down each one of those individuals.

The Indians we gathered were usually Miccosukees or Red Stick Creeks. There were also a few small groups of Lower Creeks, who were then moving into north Florida because of the efforts to move them from Alabama or Georgia to the west. The Florida Territory was far less populated with white people than were the states bordering it so it was natural for them to try to escape to Florida. These new arrivals kept the situation dangerous in north Florida. They raided farms in order to obtain food and supplies.

Some of them were determined to resist being sent west.

The Army made a strong effort to round up Indians throughout the winter. That was always the busiest time of year. The heat and humidity made fight, flight, and pursuit nearly impossible in the summer, especially for the out-of-state units that were not accustomed to the hot, humid weather.

Over a period of time General Armistead came to the conclusion that there were a lot of people in Florida who wanted the Indian War to continue because they were profiting from the war. He then ordered all civilians be removed from the military payroll. Thigpen's company of militia was then mustered out on March 24, 1841. Also, all other militia companies were disbanded in March. I was a civilian again and unemployed until three days later when a colonel arrived at Black Creek from Fort King.

He said, "Isaac, the general wants you on the payroll at a dollar and a half a day and expenses. He'll also continue to pay ten dollars for each Seminole you bring in alive. You've made his record look good with your work to date."

"Is the bribe price still the same?"

"The general doesn't like for it to be called a bribe but, yes, it is the same."

"I'm not anxious to do it but I will under the condition that I work when and where I want to. You won't be billed for any days I'm not working. Also, I might need some help now and then and will put George or Asa on for that purpose. They'll need to get a dollar a day. Additionally, I had to turn my Colt revolver in when mustered out. I want it back and want to keep it as personal property when the job ends."

"Fair enough. I'm authorized to approve those kinds of arrangements."

The colonel also looked Pa up and told him to stay on the payroll as a wheelwright at forty-five dollars a month. A good wheelwright was mighty hard to find.

That night Louisa was especially affectionate and I soon found out why.

She said, "Isaac, I want you to take care and not let any Indians get your hair. We're going to have another baby in early September."

I smiled. "How do you know the date?"

"You were home from December eighth through eleventh."

"I'm glad about the baby and proud of you. It's also good that Juanita is back home. She's very good at dealing with new babies."

Juanita had arrived home without incident four days after she left Wildcat's village.

Wildcat was the Indian the general really wanted me to track down. He was the subject of a visit from the colonel from Fort King in May of 1841.

Locating me, the colonel said, "Isaac, the general really wants Wildcat captured and sent west. He wants you to take on that particular job."

I replied, "I can't do it, Colonel. There are two problems. First, he led me to his village when I was wearing white feathers. I told him then that I wouldn't use the information against him. Second, he and I have a deal. I'm not going to raid his camp and he's not going to raid my farm."

"You knew where his village was all the time?" the Colonel asked.

"I've eaten with him and drunk rum at his cook-fire," I answered. "He might not be there now, however. He's supposed to have moved further south. I could find him in a week or two. I'll talk to him but I'll not bring him in except voluntarily."

"He moved south to someplace around the Kissimmee River," the colonel said. "He came in for a negotiation in March, but returned to the swamps."

"Then I know just about where he is. Do you want me to talk to him?" I asked.

"Yes, we do," he said.

"I'll leave tomorrow, but I'll not promise anything beyond talk," I said.

The three-week trip was a waste of time, at least for the short-term. Wildcat and I talked, drank some rum, and ate. Wildcat even said he was thinking seriously about coming in but there was no immediate result. Also, the subject of Juanita came up. I told him she had made her way back to my farm and that he was out two horses.

I later learned that Wildcat came in during June and surrendered. Over the next three or four months he is supposed to have brought in over three hundred of his people to be moved west. When that information got to me, I sent a letter to Army headquarters requesting payment of $3,000 for the three hundred of them. That would be the right price based on my agreement with the general. A couple of months later I got a letter saying Wildcat's people had come in for other reasons than my visit. There was no warrant enclosed with the letter. I never was able to collect on that bill and wasn't even able to collect the ten dollars for Wildcat who initially came in with one of my passes.

In addition to continually pursuing the Indians in order to send them west, Colonel Worth, who was then in charge in Florida, implemented a policy of settling additional white people in Florida. The area between the Suwannee River and our place was a focal point of this population expansion. Settlements were started at Johns Town, Fort White, Cedar Hammock, Branford, the Natural Bridge, White Springs, and several other places. By the end of 1841 there was a combined population of over four hundred whites and slaves living in that part of the state. That was a part of the territory previously populated only by Indians. To help these settlements get started, the government provided the people food and some other supplies. Also, in addition to those at Fort White, which had been a fort since 1837, soldiers were stationed at the other settlements.

During 1841 almost nine hundred Indians and black people were sent west. Though there were some murders and some fights between small groups of civilians and Indians, during the last nine months of that year the official war was conducted entirely by regular soldiers. During that time I continued to operate on my own. I also scouted sometimes for one small force or another. On September 3, 1841, our third child, Isaac III, was born. Because I knew when the baby was due, I arranged to be home at that time.

In December of 1841, Halleck Tustenuggee, the same chief who had kidnapped Louisa and Juanita, attacked Mandarin. Mandarin is a settlement twenty miles northeast of our Black Creek farm. The band of about twenty warriors killed several residents, occupied the settlement overnight, looted what they wanted, and burned some buildings. Soldiers were soon in pursuit of them. Though they were chased for weeks, none of the Indians were captured. I didn't get the word on that operation until it was too late for me to join in the hunt. Aided by George and Asa, I would have gone after Tustenuggee but the army had already messed up the trail. That's one Indian I had a grudge against but never got a shot at.

By January of 1842, over four thousand Indians and black people had been killed, died, or had been sent west. In February of 1842 alone, Colonel Worth sent over two hundred Indians west. He then recommended the military be reduced and that the remaining three hundred or so Indians in Florida be allowed to remain on a reservation in south Florida. The Secretary of War rejected that request. A serious hunt was then started for individuals and small groups of Indians. A bounty was offered of a hundred dollars for every Indian killed or captured. Not wanting to hunt down people just to kill them, I then ceased tracking for the government except for the occasional small band that caused trouble in northeast Florida.

Within a couple of months Halleck Tustenuggee was found,

along with forty warriors, and the last big battle of the war was fought. Halleck and most of his men broke off the fight and escaped. They did, however, lose most of their provisions.

Within weeks, Colonel Worth enticed Halleck in to negotiate. Taking a page from General Jessup's book, Colonel Worth then sprang a trap and captured over a hundred of Halleck's band under the guise of negotiating.

Though on August 14, 1842, an announcement was made that the war was over, the hunt for Indians continued. There were still several hundred Seminoles left in Florida. Because there were so few, the Indians were almost impossible to find. Taking a couple of my brothers on as helpers, I still managed to bring in a few that caused trouble in north Florida during the fall and winter months. We didn't shoot any that we didn't have to, though. In November, Louisa told me that we were expecting a fourth child.

PART V

The Struggle Continues

April 1, 1843

F ree of the war, Louisa and I set about developing our farm and raising our family. I still did some surveying and some blacksmith work but because a few of the surviving Cubans were still with us, my working at those things did not slow down the work on the farm.

On July 4, 1843, our fourth child, David, was born.

Pa had then started the slow process of trying to reclaim title to our property from the government and trying to get compensation for the farm goods, timber, livestock, and other things that

275

were taken. The government soon grew tired of dealing with Pa and moved the fort to the St. Johns River. When I say moved the fort, I mean they literally moved the fort. Doors and windows were removed from the various buildings. These along with everything that could be moved were carried off in a steamship to rebuild on the St. Johns. Pa was left with nothing besides his house and the dirt, which was stripped of timber, fence rails, and any other thing that was useful to the military. He had bought some additional land in the same area back during the war and at the time had quite a bit of property. I had not been buying land the way Pa had and only had 280 acres.

Though Louisa and I both wanted a large family, it wasn't until March 1, 1845 that our fifth child, Henry, was born. That event occurred two days before the Florida Territory became a state. Because Florida was then a state, and because we were white males twenty-one years of age or over who had served in the militia during the Seminole War, and were citizens of the United States, and residents of Florida, Pa, my brothers, and I got to vote in the elections that same year.

Over the next few years the Seminole Indians pretty much stayed hidden in the Everglades. There were a few problems in north Florida with small bands of Creeks who moved in from Alabama. They were being rounded up and sent west. These Creeks were trying to avoid that. I spent a couple of months hunting some of them, but they were usually caught easily enough. Things then settled down for several years, at least as far as Indian trouble was concerned.

As the years passed, our family continued to grow. In January of 1847, another son, John, was born. In December of 1849, we lost Jacob within days of his birth. In December of 1851, our son William was born. On January 19, 1853, God blessed us with a second daughter, Elizabeth. I guess she was sent to replace David, whom He had taken away on January eighth of that year.

December 25, 1855

Along with our Christmas dinner came word that the Seminoles had gone on the warpath again. They had burned a couple of forts and ambushed a small detachment of soldiers in south Florida. One of my older boys, two nephews on my side of the family, two of Louisa's nephews, and one of her brothers headed off to war. Being a few years too old and a step too slow, I didn't get to go. The stories I heard later were from relatives.

In opening the Third Seminole War, the Indians attacked plantations and houses on the west coast. They also attacked wagon trains and small detachments of soldiers along the Manatee River and around Fort Meade. It turned out that there were over a thousand Indians in south Florida instead of the three hundred that had been estimated.

Billy Bowlegs led the initial attacks. It's been said that Billy Bowlegs was furious about some of his banana trees being cut down by surveyors. To add insult to injury, some of those who cut down the trees then carried off some of Bowlegs' bananas. He attacked that group with forty warriors and killed or wounded most of them.

As well as the fighting in south Florida, small bands of Seminoles attacked all over the length and breadth of the state again. There were not more than fifteen or twenty in any of the Indian bands in north Florida, but they did considerable damage and really kept people scared. For whatever reason, they again stayed away from our place, the farms belonging to my and Louisa's close families, and a few of our neighbors' farms. George said it was probably because of the reputation we had earned from tracking them over the past years.

William, a nephew of mine, told me of one raid in which the

Indians stole eight mules and horses and twelve slaves, and killed everyone on a plantation. The Indians made the mistake of stealing too many things and overloading their animals. They were slow because the animals were overloaded, and left an easy trail to follow; the band of Indians were found and attacked the next morning at dawn. The Indians made a mistake, the same one they had made throughout the First and Second Seminole Wars—they didn't post a guard that night. Most of the band was killed, wounded, or captured. William was wounded, too, though not seriously. He was only out of the fighting for six weeks.

Pa died in 1857. He left provisions in his will, along with the money to make it happen, that all the black people living on his farm and my farm were to be legally set free. I was the administrator of Pa's estate and carried out his wishes. There were some people who didn't like the fact that we had freed those people and we were harassed some. We then left Black Creek—I moved the family to Bradford County.

In order to put additional pressure on the Indians, a reward was offered of $500 per man, $250 per woman, and $100 per child. Some independent militia companies were then formed to hunt Indians for money. If they had offered that kind of money back during the Second Seminole War, we would probably have been wealthy from the number I brought in.

After chasing small bands of Indians for most of a year only to have them vanish into the swamps, Captain Parkhill's company found the last major concentrations of Seminoles in 1857. After some fighting, during which Parkhill was killed, most of the Indians again vanished into the swamp.

I didn't have any relatives with Parkhill but I had a nephew with Colonel George Rogers who, with a regiment of three hundred men and several independent militia companies, conducted the last major drive against the Seminoles. They pursued the Indians in canoes, on foot, and on horseback. In their pursuit, they destroyed huge fields of pumpkins, beans, potatoes, corn, rice, and melons. Also, several small villages were burned, live-stock was taken, and Indians' boats were taken or destroyed.

All the time the Indians were being pursued through the swamps, efforts were under way to negotiate the surrender of Billy Bowlegs. In April of 1858 Bowlegs, along with 120 of his people, accepted a negotiated surrender. Bowlegs got several thousand dollars as part of the deal. Also, each warrior got a thousand dollars and each woman and child got a hundred dollars. The government also bought all of their property that was movable—boats, livestock, and such.

After Bowlegs and his band were shipped out on May 7, on May 8, 1858, a proclamation was issued ending the war. It was estimated that only a hundred Indians were still in Florida then. Over the next few months Bowlegs was hired to negotiate with those Indians still in Florida. They succeeded in getting over seventy more to move. There are still Indians left in the Everglades, but no one knows how many. I suspect there're lots more than thirty, though. Anyway, they haven't been seen for years.

Epilogue

States began seceding from the Union a couple of years after the Indian wars ended. In 1861 Florida became the third state to do so, after South Carolina and Mississippi. Months passed and a bloody civil war started between the North and South. As they had in the Indian wars, my family members answered the call to duty. I'm Henry, the only one of the boys in Isaac Jr. and Louisa's family old enough to enlist who survived the Civil War. After the war I married and raised six boys and four girls.

In 1862 my oldest brother, Andrew, was captured by the Yankees in Kentucky. Many years later we learned that he died from an illness in a Yankee train while on the way to a prisoner exchange at Vicksburg. Another brother of mine, Isaac III, was killed in September 1864 while in the front rank of a charge on Sherman's troops outside Atlanta. He was ill with a high fever and was told not to go but he got in line for that fight anyway.

Two of Uncle George's boys also fought for the Confederacy. One son, also named Isaac, was killed at Petersburg while on picket duty. He was shot in the head. His brother, William, lost an eye from an artillery shell at the battle at St. John's Bluff, near Jacksonville, in 1862. He actually lost the eye because of the flying debris created by the artillery shell. It was the kind of shell that does not explode. William got that shell and took it home with him. A little thing like losing an eye didn't stop William; after a couple of weeks to recover he returned to the fight until the war ended in 1865. William survived the war and raised a family. This is the same William who fought in the Third Seminole War.

Fortunately, Grandpa (Isaac Sr.) died before the Civil War and did not have to know about what happened to his grandchildren. Pa also died before knowing what happened to his children. Ma was not so lucky—she lived until 1878, and had to live with all the gruesome details, which was really hard on her.

Some people thought that we were fighting about slavery. There may have been some who were doing that but, speaking for my brothers and cousins, we were fighting for our family and our country.

There are lots of people who say, "It was a rich man's war and a poor man's fight." I think that about sums it up.

After the war William and I gathered wild cattle across Florida and herded them to various ports. Most of the herds were driven to Punta Rassa and sold there. Uncle George converted a sailboat into a steamboat. He bought some of our cattle for resale. We pretty much got rich gathering wild cattle. In 1889 the United States government made it illegal for individuals to own gold. William and I both had a box of gold under our bed that we got from selling cattle to the Cubans, so we were hit hard by that rule.

Maybe I'll get a chance to tell you about some of our cattle-gathering adventures someday. My friend Ben has already told you some of our Civil War adventures in the book *Confederate Money*.

Author's Note

The stories from which this novel was composed were taken from real historical events. Many of the facts used here were gleaned from military records, census materials, court records, congressional records, property records, and other family sources.

Many of my grandparents and/or their families—Anderson, Barber, Bowen, Clements (Clemmons or Clemons), Douglass (Douglas), Fraser, Green, Grimes, Hunter, Mann, Mattiar, Thompson, Touchstone, and Varnes (Varn)—were all pioneers in the South, and were instrumental in the taking and development of Florida. Some were in the places and involved in the events described in the story. Some of these clans settled in Florida even before Spain ceded it to the United States.

Isaac Varn and his family arrived in the Territory of Florida from Camden County, Georgia, in 1820, two years before Spain ceded Florida to the United States and twenty-five years before Florida became a state. They settled at the forks of Black Creek, now Middleburg, Florida. At the time of Isaac Varn Senior's arrival, Florida was estimated to have fewer than fifteen thousand residents, including Indians and runaway slaves. The Indian and black people—free, runaway, and the Indians' slaves—then outnumbered the white people by more than two to one.

My great great grandparents, David J. Mann and his wife, Loviney Barber, arrived by wagon train at Baker County, Florida, in 1829, about the same time as my grandparents, Frederick Douglass and Bethany Anderson and John Douglass and Lydia

Thompson, arrived in what is now Union County, Florida. Most of the others arrived in Florida about the same time or shortly thereafter. Grandfather David Mann's family, Loviney and the children, were sent to Georgia while David fought the Seminoles during the Second Seminole War. Others moved their families to the nearest town or to military posts while they fought in the war.

Even before the official start of the First Seminole War, and before moving to Florida, Isaac Varn Senior fought the Seminoles under a number of circumstances. A seasoned warrior, Isaac had fought under the command of General Andrew Jackson in the Creek Indian War at Horseshoe Bend, Alabama, and against the British in the War of 1812. According to family oral history (the official roster, except for seven names, was accidentally destroyed), Isaac was with the famous Unit 32 of Camden County. Later, from age fifty-five to age fifty-eight, Isaac Varn Senior also fought in the Second Seminole War. Isaac was frequently accompanied by his sons during that war. Isaac Varn Senior's sons and all of their descendants changed their last name to Varnes. A surveyor and wheelwright, in addition to his other talents, Isaac Sr. worked at those occupations for the military after his enlistments as a soldier and scout during the Second Seminole War. When his talent as a wheelwright was discovered, Isaac was paid forty-five dollars per month. A common soldier received only six dollars per month.

While the Varnes family was involved in a number of battles during the Second Seminole War, their first major battle was fought against two hundred Seminoles under the command of Osceola and three other chiefs north of Micanopy, Florida, close to the southern lip of Paynes Prairie.

In 1838 and 1839, George Varnes was on the Muster Roll of Captain John L. Thigpen's Company of Florida Militia, Eastern District, East Florida, commanded by Colonel David E. Twiggs. After the war Twiggs, then a major general, tried to help Isaac Sr.

get his land back from the United States government and to get reimbursed for the use of his timber, orchards, and other farm products. The government had taken Isaac's land for a military reservation and to build Fort Heileman at what is now Middleburg, Florida. Isaac's timber was cut for military use. His orchard was also used but not maintained by the military.

Before returning Isaac's land, the military sent a steamship up Black Creek to Isaac's place and removed the doors, windows, and other materials from Isaac's buildings. Those things were then moved to a new location to build another fort on the St. Johns River. His fence rails had been used for firewood and his farmland had been neglected to the point that brush and young trees had invaded the fields. Though Isaac finally got some of his land back, he was never reimbursed for the various other losses. The fort itself still was operational on part of Isaac's land when he died in 1857. Even though the United States Senate twice passed a bill to reimburse him, the House never did.

George's oldest son, William Varnes, at age eighteen, served in the Third Seminole Indian War. My great great grandmother Louisa Mattair's six brothers served in one or both of the Second and Third Seminole Wars.

After mostly surviving the Seminole wars, these families took heavy losses during the Civil War. In addition to a massive number of cousins and uncles killed, great grandfather John Anderson and great great grandfather William James Mann were killed while fighting for the Confederacy.

Acknowledgments

Organizations and agencies that were helpful in developing the historical and cultural setting for the novel include the Varnes Association, the Florida State Archives, the National Archives, the Florida Park Service, and the National Park Service.

William Grady Varnes of Palatka, Florida, another of Isaac Junior and Louisa's grandsons, also provided a considerable amount of information about the Varnes (Varn) and Mattair (Mattier) family history. Earl Varnes, a cousin and great great grandson of George Varnes, also provided extensive information about the Varnes family. He also read *Black Creek* as a work in progress. Irwin Strickland also read the work in progress and offered suggestions. Thanks also go to Doyle Varnes, another cousin and another of Isaac Varnes Junior's great great grandsons, and to his wife Ramona for their contributions. Various members of the families mentioned above provided family historical information.

John Davis, an English professor at Piedmont College in Georgia, gave technical assistance with this book and with my previous book, *Confederate Money*. His name was inadvertently omitted from the acknowledgments in that book.

I extend a special thank you to my wife, Jill Varnes, and our youngest daughter, Julia Rae Varnes Strnad, for their encouragement and assistance.

Thanks are also extended to Diane Davis for typing the first draft of the manuscript.

I would also like to recognize the editorial staff at Pineapple Press. They do a great job.

Though I read many other helpful books and documents over the years, those listed below warrant special mention: Canter

Brown Jr., *Florida's Peace River Frontier* (1991); Carl Carmer, Editor, *Florida: The Long Frontier* (1967); Ruby Leach Carson, *Fabulous Florida* (1942); William T. Cash, *The Story of Florida* (1938); Charles H. Coe, *Red Patriots: The Story of the Seminoles* (1968); David R. Colburn and Jane L. Landers, *The African American Heritage of Florida* (1995); James W. Covington, *The Seminoles of Florida* (1993); William R. Ervin, *Let Us Alone* (1983); T. Frederick Davis, *History of Jacksonville, Florida and Vicinity 1513 to 1924* (1925) Facsimile, University of Florida Press; Daniel P. Gold, *History of Duval County* (1929); Mary B. Graff, *Mandarin on the Saint Johns* (1953); W. H. G. Kingston, *In the Wilds of Florida*, (1880); Frank Laumer, *Encounter by the River*, Florida Historical Quarterly, 46 (April 1968), 338; Frank Laumer, Editor, *Amidst a Storm of Bullets* (1998); John K. Mahon, *History of the Second Seminole War 1835–1842* (1985); Sidney Walter Martin, *Florida During the Territorial Days* (1944); Ann Jasberger McFadden, Indexer, *Index of Florida Master Rolls, Seminole Indian Wars* (1998); Edwin C. McReynolds, *The Seminoles* (1957); Clifton Paisley, *The Red Hills of Florida, 1828–1865* (1989); Kenneth W. Porter, *The Black Seminoles* (1996); Charlton W. Tebeau, *A History of Florida* (1971); Brent Richards Weisman, *Unconquered People: Florida's Seminole and Miccosukee Indians (1999);* James Leitch Wright, *Creeks and Seminoles* (1929).

www.ingramcontent.com/pod-product-compliance
Lightning Source LLC
Chambersburg PA
CBHW020350120726
47904CB00002B/528

* 9 7 8 1 5 6 1 6 4 6 8 6 9 *